"Every reader with a dollop of humanity will admire Michael Swanwick's rowdy good humor. His towering creativity seems so effortless that it is easily overlooked – so effortless, and so immense. You won't want to put this book down."

–GENE WOLFE

"By turns funny, clever, mysterious, and possessing hidden depths, the stories in Swanwick's latest collection demonstrate he's at the top of his game. Delightful, thoughtful work, sure to please his readers."

–JEFF VANDERMEER

"For most writers, it's a good day when a story is witty, or has great ideas or characters. Michael Swanwick consistently wins on all three."

–VERNOR VINGE

"Michael Swanwick is one of my all-time favorite short story writers. Sometimes he makes me laugh, sometimes he makes me shudder, sometimes he makes me weep. He always makes me think. And that's just when I am talking to him."

–JANE YOLEN

"In *The Dog Said Bow-Wow*, a valuable author has taken the disreputable duckling of category fiction and nurtured it into a swan of elegant speculation, as the wick of disciplined fancy draws the reader's inflamed imagination ever downward through the waxen feast. Swan and wick: an essential conjunction yielding wonder, warmth, wit, and many a synergistic epiphany."

–JAMES MORROW

"Michael Swanwick's stories start soft, sneak close, and punch hard. And nobody else – nobody! – in science fiction has his range."

–NANCY KRESS

"Michael Swanwick's *The Dog Said Bow-Wow* is an extraordinarily strong collection. His fierce imagination, subtle humor, and genius for implication are evident in each of these stories. From outer space to the land of faerie to all those strange and familiar places in between, he's gathered wonder and brought it back alive."

–JEFFREY FORD

THE DOG SAID BOW-WOW

MICHAEL SWANWICK

The Dog Said Bow-Wow

TACHYON PUBLICATIONS | SAN FRANCISCO

The Dog Said Bow-Wow
Copyright 2007 by Michael Swanwick

Cover design by Ann Monn
Interior design & composition by John D. Berry
The typeface is Kingfisher, designed by Jeremy Tankard

Tachyon Publications
1459 18th Street #139
San Francisco, CA 94107
(415) 285-5615
www.tachyonpublications.com

Series editor: Jacob Weisman

ISBN 10: 1-892391-52-X
ISBN 13: 978-1-892391-52-0

Printed in the United States of America
by Worzalla

First Edition: 2007

9 8 7 6 5 4 3 2 1

Introduction © 2007 by Terry Bisson. | "The Bordello in Faerie" © 2006 by Michael Swanwick. First appeared in *Postscripts* #8, October 2006. | "Dirty Little War" © 2002 by Michael Swanwick. First appeared in *In the Shadow of the Wall*, edited by Byron R. Tetrick (Nashville: Cumberland House). | "The Dog Said Bow-Wow" © 2001 by Michael Swanwick. First appeared in *Asimov's Science Fiction*, October/November 2001. | "An Episode of Stardust" © 2006 by Michael Swanwick. First appeared in *Asimov's Science Fiction*, January 2006. | "Girls and Boys, Come Out to Play," © 2005 by Michael Swanwick. First appeared in *Asimov's Science Fiction*, July 2005. | "A Great Day for Brontosaurs" © 2002 by Michael Swanwick. First appeared in *Asimov's Science Fiction*, May 2002. | "'Hello,' Said the Stick" © 2002 by Michael Swanwick. First appeared in *Asimov's Science Fiction*, March 2002. | "The Last Geek" © 2004 by Michael Swanwick. First appeared in *Crossroads: Tales of the Southern Literary Fantastic*, edited by F. Brett Cox and Andy Duncan (New York: Tor Books). | "Legions in Time" © 2003 by Michael Swanwick. First appeared in *Asimov's Science Fiction*, April 2003. | "The Little Cat Laughed to See Such Sport" © 2002 by Michael Swanwick. First appeared in *Asimov's Science Fiction*, October/November 2002. | "The Skysailor's Tale" © 2007 by Michael Swanwick. First appearance in print. | "Slow Life" © 2002 by Michael Swanwick. First appeared in *Asimov's Science Fiction*, December 2002. | "A Small Room in Koboldtown" © 2007 by Michael Swanwick. First appeared in *Asimov's Science Fiction*, April 2007. | "Tin Marsh" © 2006 by Michael Swanwick. First appeared in *Asimov's Science Fiction*, August 2006. | "Triceratops Summer" © 2006 by Michael Swanwick. First published by *Amazon Shorts*, August 2006. | "Urdumheim" © 2007 by Michael Swanwick. Forthcoming in *The Magazine of Fantasy & Science Fiction*, October/November 2007.

Contents

A NOTE FROM THE PUBLISHER

Terry Bisson's introduction didn't arrive in time, so we are substituting this transcript of a conversation with TV talk host Charlie Ross:

CHARLIE ROSS: Tonight's guest, Michael Swanwick, is a leading example of that most curious modern or perhaps postmodern creature, the science fiction writer, a species uniquely equipped to explore and hopefully illuminate the shimmering interface where literature and science intersect, giving birth to the elusive paradigms that populate our cultural psyche, so to speak. Welcome to the show, Michael.

MICHAEL SWANWICK: Thank you. I am very...

CR: I can't think of anyone who has brought such diligence and intelligence to speculative fiction as yourself. You came to Philadelphia in 1976, armed, as legend has it, with nothing more than seventy-six bucks, a determination to be a writer, and the conviction that SF was the field of literature most worthy of your efforts. Do you still have that conviction today?

MS: Yes. In fact...

CR: And indeed, it shows in your work. But nothing worthwhile comes easy. It was only in the early 1980s, after years of false starts and rejection slips, that you sold your first two stories – and then saw both of them nominated for awards and picked up for Year's Best anthologies. Can you share with us the thrill of accomplishment that you must have felt when that happened?

MS: It was cool. In fact...

CR: And it was only the beginning. Your first novel, *In the Drift*, found a home in the renowned Ace Specials series, along with early works by Kim Stanley Robinson, Lucius Shepard, and William Gibson.

Even though you were all relative fledglings, as it were, just trying your wings, did you have the feeling, even then, that you had taken on the collective task of redefining and reshaping modern SF from the inside out, as it were?

MS: Not exactly. As a matter of fact...

CR: And indeed, you have, both collectively and individually. There are in fact few writers in modern SF as versatile as yourself. You have written magical realism, steampunk, space opera, hard SF, cyberpunk, fantasy high and low; you even dramatized the periodic table in your spare time. Did I leave anything out?

MS: Let me think. In fact...

CR: And winning, in the process, every major honor in the field, including the Hugo, the Nebula, the World Fantasy, the Sturgeon, and the Locus awards. Is there anything else that you feel the *need* to accomplish?

MS: Well, sure. In fact...

CR: I suppose it's that *need* that keeps you pushing the envelope, so to speak. So here you are, after more than a third of a century in the field, still remaking and reshaping modern SF through your work. Do you think the desire to break new ground, explore new paradigms, open new controversies, is essential to keeping the creative juices flowing, so to speak?

MS: Why, yes. As a matter of fact...

CR: Me, too, Michael. And no less a personage than Gardner Dozois would agree. He once wrote: "There are perhaps seven or eight writers who are vital to the evolution of the genre. Swanwick is one of those seven or eight..." Are you in touch with the other six or seven?

MS: I have 'em on speed dial. In fact...

CR: Put the phone away, please. And now we have this book of short stories, with such an intriguing title: *The Dog Said Bow-Wow*. Are we to understand, then, that this collection contains the Hugo-winning story about that curious pair, Darger and Surplus?

MS: Yes. As a matter of fact...

CR: Your readers will be pleased! There's a Candide-like faux-simplicity to these Darger and Surplus tales, even though they are written in a slightly formal language, quite beautifully I might add. Was that in fact, your intention: to entertain the reader, while taking him and/or her on a tour of a rather astonishing if slightly dystopian future, in which our world has been altered almost but not quite beyond recognition?

MS: I guess you could say that. In fact...

CR: Then you have succeeded wonderfully. Indeed, the reader expects no less of you. This is a delightful collection, both deep and shimmery at the same time. Fun, but high fun. Which leads me to a final question: which do you regard as the more important in SF, Beauty or Truth?

MS: Both. Neither. Hell, I don't know.

CR: As charmingly evasive as ever, Swanwick. As silent and cunning as Joyce; as elusive as Borges; as enigmatic as Calvino; as elliptical as Lafferty; and as ironic as P. K. Dick himself. Thank you for your work, and especially for your comments, which have been...

MS: You're welcome.

CR: Please don't interrupt.

MS: Sorry.

CR: ...most informative.

THE DOG SAID BOW-WOW

"Hello," Said the Stick

"HELLO," SAID THE STICK.

The soldier stopped, and looked around. He did not touch the hilt of his sword, but he adjusted his stance so he could reach it quickly, if need be. But there was nothing to be seen. The moors stretched flat and empty for miles about. "Who said that?"

"I did. Down here."

"Ah. I see." The soldier poked gingerly at the stick with his foot. "Some sort of radio device, eh? I've heard of such. Where are you speaking from?"

"I'm right here. The stick. I'm from off-planet. They can make things like me there."

"Can they, now? Well that's interesting, I suppose."

"Pick me up," said the stick. "Take me with you."

"Why?"

"Because I make an excellent weapon."

"No, I mean what's in it for you?"

The stick paused. "You're smarter than you look."

"Thanks. I think."

"Okay, here's the deal. I'm a symbiotic mechanism. I was designed to be totally helpless without a human partner. Pick me up, throw an acorn in the air, take a swing at it, and I can shift my weight so you hit it a country mile. Leave me here and I can't budge an inch."

"Why would they build you like that?"

"So I'd be a good and faithful tool. And I will. I'll be the best quarter-staff you ever had. Try me and see."

"How do I know you won't take over my brain?" the soldier asked suspiciously. "I've heard off-world wizards can make devices that do things like that."

"They're called technicians, not wizards. And that sort of technology is strictly prohibited on planetary surfaces. You have nothing to worry about."

"Even so.... It's nothing I'd want to chance."

The stick sighed. "Tell me something. What's your rank? Are you a general? A field commander?"

"Tramping alone across the moors like this? Naw, I'm just a gallowglass – a mercenary and a foot soldier."

"Then what have you got to lose?"

The soldier laughed aloud. He bent to pick up the stick. Then he put it down again. Then he picked it up.

"See?"

"Well, I don't mind telling you that takes a weight off my mind."

"I could use a change of scenery. Let's go. We can talk along the way."

The soldier resumed his stroll down the dirt track. He swung the stick lightly back and forth before him, admiring how it lopped off the heads of thistles, while deftly sidestepping the sedge-roses. "So you're off to join the Iron Duke in his siege of Port Morningstar, are you?" the stick remarked conversationally.

"How'd you know that?"

"Oh, one hears things, being a stick. Fly on the wall, and all that."

"It's an unfamiliar figure of speech, but I catch your meaning. Who do you think's going to win? The Iron Duke or the Council of Seven?"

"It's a close thing, by all accounts. But the Iron Duke has the advantage of numbers. That always counts for something. If I had to bet money, I'd say you chose employers well."

"That's good. I like being on the winning side. Less chance of dying, for one thing."

They'd progressed several miles across the moors when the sun began to set. The soldier laid the stick aside and set a snare for supper. By the time he'd pitched a tent, made camp, and cut peat for a fire, he'd caught a rabbit. He roasted it slow and, because he had a fondness for drumsticks, ate all six legs first, along with three small bunyips, boiled with a pinch of salt from a tin. Like many an old campaigner, he ate in silence, giving the food his undivided attention.

"Well," he said when he was full and in the mood for conversation again. "What were you doing out here in the middle of this god-forsaken wilderness?"

The stick had been stuck into the earth on the opposite side of the campfire, so that it stood upright. "I was dropped by a soldier," it said, "much like yourself. He was in pretty bad shape at the time. I doubt he's still alive."

The soldier frowned. "You're not exactly standard gear."

"No, I'm not. By compact, planetside wars are fought with primitive weaponry. It was found that wars were almost as environmentally destructive as the internal combustion engine. So..."

"Internal combustion engine?"

"Never mind. It's complicated. The point I was trying to make, though, is that the technology is there, even if it's not supposed to be used. So they cheat. Your side, the other side. Everybody cheats."

"How so?"

"That sword of yours, for example. Take it out, let's get a look at it."

He drew the sword. Firelight glimmered across its surface.

"Tungsten-ceramic-titanium-alloy. Self-sharpening, never rusts. You could slam it against a granite boulder and it wouldn't break. Am I right?"

"It's a good blade. I couldn't say what it was made of."

"Trust me on this one."

"Still...you're a lot fancier than this old sword of mine. It can't talk, for one thing."

"It's possible," said the stick, "that the Council of Seven is, out of desperation, pushing the envelope a little, these days."

"Now *that's* a figure of speech I've neither heard before nor can comprehend."

"It means simply that it's likely they're using weapons rather more sophisticated than is strictly speaking allowed by the Covenants of Warfare. There's a lot riding on this siege. The Iron Duke has put everything he has into it. If he were defeated, then the worst the Council of

Seven could expect would be sanctions and a fine. So long as they don't use tac-nukes or self-reprogramming viruses, the powers that be won't invoke their right to invade."

"Tac-nukes or self-reprogamming viruses?"

"Again, it's complicated. But I see you're yawning. Why don't you bank the fire and turn in? Get some sleep," said the stick. "We can talk more in the morning."

But in the morning, the soldier didn't feel much like talking. He packed his gear, shouldered the stick, and set off down the road with far less vigor than he had the day before. On this, the stick did not comment.

At noon, the soldier stopped for lunch. He let his pack slip from his shoulders and leaned the stick against it. Then he rummaged within for the left-over rabbit, only to make a face and thrust it away from him. "Phaw!" he said. "I cannot remember when I felt so weak! I must be coming down with something."

"Do you think so?" the stick asked.

"Aye. And I'm nauseated, and I've got the sweats as well."

The soldier wiped his forehead with his hand. It came back bloody.

"*Chort!*" he swore. "What's wrong with me?"

"Radiation poisoning, I expect. I operate off a plutonium battery."

"It's...you... You *knew* this would happen to me." Unsteadily, he stood, and drew his sword. He struck at the stick with all his might. Sparks flew, but it was not damaged. Again and again he struck, until his strength was gone. His eyes filled with tears. "Oh, foul and treacherous stick, to kill a man so!"

"Is this crueler than hacking a man to death with a big knife? I don't see how. But it's not necessary for you to die."

"No?"

"No. If you grab your gear and hurry, you just might make it to the Iron Duke's camp in time. The medics there can heal you – anti-radiation treatments aren't proscribed by the Protocols. And, to tell you the truth, you do more damage to the Iron Duke's cause alive and using up his personnel and resources than you do neatly dead in the moorlands. Go! Now!"

With a curse, the soldier kicked the stick as hard as he could. Then he grabbed his pack and shambled off.

It was not long before he disappeared over the horizon.

A day passed.

Then another.

A young man came trotting down the dirt track. He carried a sword and a light pack. He had the look of a mercenary.

"Hello," said the stick.

The Dog Said Bow-Wow

THE DOG LOOKED like he had just stepped out of a children's book. There must have been a hundred physical adaptations required to allow him to walk upright. The pelvis, of course, had been entirely reshaped. The feet alone would have needed dozens of changes. He had knees, and knees were tricky.

To say nothing of the neurological enhancements.

But what Darger found himself most fascinated by was the creature's costume. His suit fit him perfectly, with a slit in the back for the tail, and – again – a hundred invisible adaptations that caused it to hang on his body in a way that looked perfectly natural.

"You must have an extraordinary tailor," Darger said.

The dog shifted his cane from one paw to the other, so they could shake, and in the least affected manner imaginable replied, "That is a common observation, sir."

"You're from the States?" It was a safe assumption, given where they stood – on the docks – and that the schooner *Yankee Dreamer* had sailed up the Thames with the morning tide. Darger had seen its bubble sails over the rooftops, like so many rainbows. "Have you found lodgings yet?"

"Indeed I am, and no I have not. If you could recommend a tavern of the cleaner sort?"

"No need for that. I would be only too happy to put you up for a few days in my own rooms." And, lowering his voice, Darger said, "I have a business proposition to put to you."

"Then lead on, sir, and I shall follow you with a right good will."

———

The dog's name was Sir Blackthorpe Ravenscairn de Plus Precieux, but "Call me Sir Plus," he said with a self-denigrating smile, and "Surplus" he was ever after.

Surplus was, as Darger had at first glance suspected and by conversation confirmed, a bit of a rogue – something more than mischievous and less than a cut-throat. A dog, in fine, after Darger's own heart.

Over drinks in a public house, Darger displayed his box and explained his intentions for it. Surplus warily touched the intricately carved teak housing, and then drew away from it. "You outline an intriguing scheme, Master Darger – "

"Please. Call me Aubrey."

"Aubrey, then. Yet here we have a delicate point. How shall we divide up the...ah, *spoils* of this enterprise? I hesitate to mention this, but many a promising partnership has foundered on precisely such shoals."

Darger unscrewed the salt cellar and poured its contents onto the table. With his dagger, he drew a fine line down the middle of the heap. "I divide – you choose. Or the other way around, if you please. From self-interest, you'll not find a grain's difference between the two."

"Excellent!" cried Surplus and, dropping a pinch of salt in his beer, drank to the bargain.

It was raining when they left for Buckingham Labyrinth. Darger stared out the carriage window at the drear streets and worn buildings gliding by and sighed. "Poor, weary old London! History is a grinding-wheel that has been applied too many a time to thy face."

"It is also," Surplus reminded him, "to be the making of our fortunes. Raise your eyes to the Labyrinth, sir, with its soaring towers and bright surfaces rising above these shops and flats like a crystal mountain rearing up out of a ramshackle wooden sea, and be comforted."

"That is fine advice," Darger agreed. "But it cannot comfort a lover of cities, nor one of a melancholic turn of mind."

"Pah!" cried Surplus, and said no more until they arrived at their destination.

At the portal into Buckingham, the sergeant-interface strode forward as they stepped down from the carriage. He blinked at the sight of Surplus, but said only, "Papers?"

Surplus presented the man with his passport and the credentials Darger had spent the morning forging, then added with a negligent wave of his paw, "And this is my autistic."

The sergeant-interface glanced once at Darger, and forgot about him completely. Darger had the gift, priceless to one in his profession, of a face so nondescript that once someone looked away, it disappeared from that person's consciousness forever. "This way, sir. The officer of protocol will want to examine these himself."

A dwarf savant was produced to lead them through the outer circle of the Labyrinth. They passed by ladies in bioluminescent gowns and gentlemen with boots and gloves cut from leathers cloned from their own skin. Both women and men were extravagantly bejeweled – for the ostentatious display of wealth was yet again in fashion – and the halls were lushly clad and pillared in marble, porphyry and jasper. Yet Darger could not help noticing how worn the carpets were, how chipped and sooted the oil lamps. His sharp eye espied the remains of an antique electrical system, and traces as well of telephone lines and fiber optic cables from an age when those technologies were yet workable.

These last he viewed with particular pleasure.

The dwarf savant stopped before a heavy black door carved over with gilt griffins, locomotives, and fleurs-de-lis. "This is a door," he said. "The wood is ebony. Its binomial is *Diospyros ebenum*. It was harvested in Serendip. The gilding is of gold. Gold has an atomic weight of 197.2."

He knocked on the door and opened it.

The officer of protocol was a dark-browed man of imposing mass. He did not stand for them. "I am Lord Coherence-Hamilton, and this –" he indicated the slender, clear-eyed woman who stood beside him – "is my sister, Pamela."

Surplus bowed deeply to the Lady, who dimpled and dipped a slight curtsey in return.

The protocol officer quickly scanned the credentials. "Explain these fraudulent papers, sirrah. The Demesne of Western Vermont! Damn me if I have ever heard of such a place."

"Then you have missed much," Surplus said haughtily. "It is true we are a young nation, created only seventy-five years ago during the Partition of New England. But there is much of note to commend our fair land. The glorious beauty of Lake Champlain. The gene-mills of Winooski, that ancient seat of learning the *Universitas Viridis Montis* of Burlington, the Technarchaeological Institute of—" He stopped. "We have much to be proud of, sir, and nothing of which to be ashamed."

The bearlike official glared suspiciously at him, then said, "What brings you to London? Why do you desire an audience with the queen?"

"My mission and destination lie in Russia. However, England being on my itinerary and I a diplomat, I was charged to extend the compliments of my nation to your monarch." Surplus did not quite shrug. "There is no more to it than that. In three days I shall be in France, and you will have forgotten about me completely."

Scornfully, the officer tossed the credentials to the savant, who glanced at and politely returned them to Surplus. The small fellow sat down at a little desk scaled to his own size and swiftly made out a copy. "Your papers will be taken to Whitechapel and examined there. If everything goes well—which I doubt—and there's an opening—not likely—you'll be presented to the queen sometime between a week and ten days hence."

"Ten days! Sir, I am on a very strict schedule!"

"Then you wish to withdraw your petition?"

Surplus hesitated. "I...I shall have to think on't, sir."

Lady Pamela watched coolly as the dwarf savant led them away.

The room they were shown to had massively framed mirrors and oil paintings dark with age upon the walls, and a generous log fire in the hearth. When their small guide had gone, Darger carefully locked and bolted the door. Then he tossed the box onto the bed, and bounced down alongside it. Lying flat on his back, staring up at the ceiling, he said, "The Lady Pamela is a strikingly beautiful woman. I'll be damned if she's not."

Ignoring him, Surplus locked paws behind his back, and proceeded to pace up and down the room. He was full of nervous energy. At last, he expostulated, "This is a deep game you have gotten me into,

Darger! Lord Coherence-Hamilton suspects us of all manner of black-guardry —"

"Well, and what of that?"

"I repeat myself: We have not even begun our play yet, and he suspects us already! I trust neither him nor his genetically remade dwarf."

"You are in no position to be displaying such vulgar prejudice."

"I am not *bigoted* about the creature, Darger, I *fear* him! Once let suspicion of us into that macroencephalic head of his, and he will worry at it until he has found out our every secret."

"Get a grip on yourself, Surplus! Be a man! We are in this too deep already to back out. Questions would be asked, and investigations made."

"I am anything but a man, thank God," Surplus replied. "Still, you are right. In for a penny, in for a pound. For now, I might as well sleep. Get off the bed. You can have the hearth-rug."

"I! The rug!"

"I am groggy of mornings. Were someone to knock, and I to unthinkingly open the door, it would hardly do to have you found sharing a bed with your master."

The next day, Surplus returned to the Office of Protocol to declare that he was authorized to wait as long as two weeks for an audience with the queen, though not a day more.

"You have received new orders from your government?" Lord Coherence-Hamilton asked suspiciously. "I hardly see how."

"I have searched my conscience, and reflected on certain subtleties of phrasing in my original instructions," Surplus said. "That is all."

He emerged from the office to discover Lady Pamela waiting outside. When she offered to show him the Labyrinth, he agreed happily to her plan. Followed by Darger, they strolled inward, first to witness the changing of the guard in the forecourt vestibule, before the great pillared wall that was the front of Buckingham Palace before it was swallowed up in the expansion of architecture during the mad, glorious years of Utopia. Following which, they proceeded toward the viewer's gallery above the chamber of state.

"I see from your repeated glances that you are interested in my diamonds, 'Sieur Plus Precieux," Lady Pamela said. "Well might you be. They are a family treasure, centuries old and manufactured to order, each stone flawless and perfectly matched. The indentures of a hundred autistics would not buy the like."

Surplus smiled down again at the necklace, draped about her lovely throat and above her perfect breasts. "I assure you, madame, it was not your necklace that held me so enthralled."

She colored delicately, pleased. Lightly, she said, "And that box your man carries with him wherever you go? What is in it?"

"That? A trifle. A gift for the Duke of Muscovy, who is the ultimate object of my journey," Surplus said. "I assure you, it is of no interest whatsoever."

"You were talking to someone last night," Lady Pamela said. "In your room."

"You were listening at my door? I am astonished and flattered."

She blushed. "No, no, my brother...it is his job, you see, surveillance."

"Possibly I was talking in my sleep. I have been told I do that occasionally."

"In accents? My brother said he heard two voices."

Surplus looked away. "In that, he was mistaken."

England's queen was a sight to rival any in that ancient land. She was as large as the lorry of ancient legend, and surrounded by attendants who hurried back and forth, fetching food and advice and carrying away dirty plates and signed legislation. From the gallery, she reminded Darger of a queen bee, but unlike the bee, this queen did not copulate, but remained proudly virgin.

Her name was Gloriana the First, and she was a hundred years old and still growing.

Lord Campbell-Supercollider, a friend of Lady Pamela's met by chance, who had insisted on accompanying them to the gallery, leaned close to Surplus and murmured, "You are impressed, of course, by our queen's magnificence." The warning in his voice was impossible to miss. "Foreigners invariably are."

"I am dazzled," Surplus said.

"Well might you be. For scattered through her majesty's great body are thirty-six brains, connected with thick ropes of ganglia in a hyper-cube configuration. Her processing capacity is the equal of many of the great computers from Utopian times."

Lady Pamela stifled a yawn. "Darling Rory," she said, touching the Lord Campbell-Supercollider's sleeve. "Duty calls me. Would you be so kind as to show my American friend the way back to the outer circle?"

"Or course, my dear." He and Surplus stood (Darger was, of course, already standing) and paid their compliments. Then, when Lady Pamela was gone and Surplus started to turn toward the exit: "Not that way. Those stairs are for commoners. You and I may leave by the gentlemen's staircase."

The narrow stairs twisted downward beneath clouds of gilt cherubs-and-airships, and debouched into a marble-floored hallway. Surplus and Darger stepped out of the stairway and found their arms abruptly seized by baboons.

There were five baboons all told, with red uniforms and matching choke collars with leashes that gathered in the hand of an ornately mustached officer whose gold piping identified him as a master of apes. The fifth baboon bared his teeth and hissed savagely.

Instantly, the master of apes yanked back on his leash and said, "There, Hercules! There, sirrah! What do you do? What do you say?"

The baboon drew himself up and bowed curtly. "Please come with us," he said with difficulty. The master of apes cleared his throat. Sullenly, the baboon added, "Sir."

"This is outrageous!" Surplus cried. "I am a diplomat, and under international law immune to arrest."

"Ordinarily, sir, this is true," said the master of apes courteously. "However, you have entered the inner circle without her majesty's invitation and are thus subject to stricter standards of security."

"I had no idea these stairs went inward. I was led here by —" Surplus looked about helplessly. Lord Campbell-Supercollider was nowhere to be seen.

So, once again, Surplus and Darger found themselves escorted to the Office of Protocol.

———

"The wood is teak. Its binomial is *Tectona grandis*. Teak is native to Burma, Hind, and Siam. The box is carved elaborately but without refinement." The dwarf savant opened it. "Within the casing is an archaic device for electronic intercommunication. The instrument chip is a gallium-arsenide ceramic. The chip weighs six ounces. The device is a product of the Utopian end-times."

"A modem!" The protocol officer's eyes bugged out. "You dared bring a *modem* into the inner circle and almost into the presence of the queen?" His chair stood and walked around the table. Its six insectile legs looked too slender to carry his great, legless mass. Yet it moved nimbly and well.

"It is harmless, sir. Merely something our technarchaeologists unearthed and thought would amuse the Duke of Muscovy, who is well known for his love of all things antiquarian. It is, apparently, of some cultural or historical significance, though without rereading my instructions, I would be hard pressed to tell you what."

Lord Coherence-Hamilton raised his chair so that he loomed over Surplus, looking dangerous and domineering. "*Here* is the historic significance of your modem: The Utopians filled the world with their computer webs and nets, burying cables and nodes so deeply and plentifully that they shall never be entirely rooted out. They then released into that virtual universe demons and mad gods. These intelligences destroyed Utopia and almost destroyed humanity as well. Only the valiant worldwide destruction of all modes of interface saved us from annihilation.

"Oh, you lackwit! Have you no history? These creatures hate us because our ancestors created them. They are still alive, though confined to their electronic netherworld, and want only a modem to extend themselves into the physical realm. Can you wonder, then, that the penalty for possessing such a device is — " he smiled menacingly — "death?"

"No, sir, it is not. Possession of a *working* modem is a mortal crime. This device is harmless. Ask your savant."

"Well?" the big man growled at his dwarf. "Is it functional?"

"No. It—"

"Silence." Lord Coherence-Hamilton turned back to Surplus. "You are a fortunate cur. You will not be charged with any crimes. However, while you are here, I will keep this filthy device locked away and under my control. Is that understood, Sir Bow-Wow?"

Surplus sighed. "Very well," he said. "It is only for a week, after all."

That night, the Lady Pamela Coherence-Hamilton came by Surplus's room to apologize for the indignity of his arrest, of which, she assured him, she had just now learned. He invited her in. In short order they somehow found themselves kneeling face-to-face on the bed, unbuttoning each other's clothing.

Lady Pamela's breasts had just spilled delightfully from her dress when she drew back, clutching the bodice closed again, and said, "Your man is watching us."

"And what concern is that to us?" Surplus said jovially. "The poor fellow's an autistic. Nothing he sees or hears matters to him. You might as well be embarrassed by the presence of a chair."

"Even were he a wooden carving, I would his eyes were not on me."

"As you wish." Surplus clapped his paws. "Sirrah! Turn around."

Obediently, Darger turned his back. This was his first experience with his friend's astonishing success with women. How many sexual adventuresses, he wondered, might one tumble, if one's form were unique? On reflection, the question answered itself.

Behind him, he heard the Lady Pamela giggle. Then, in a voice low with passion, Surplus said, "No, leave the diamonds on."

With a silent sigh, Darger resigned himself to a long night. Since he was bored and yet could not turn to watch the pair cavorting on the bed without giving himself away, he was perforce required to settle for watching them in the mirror.

They began, of course, by doing it doggy-style.

The next day, Surplus fell sick. Hearing of his indisposition, Lady Pamela sent one of her autistics with a bowl of broth and then followed, herself, in a surgical mask.

Surplus smiled weakly to see her. "You have no need of that mask," he said. "By my life, I swear that what ails me is not communicable. As you doubtless know, we who have been remade are prone to endocrinological imbalance."

"Is that all?" Lady Pamela spooned some broth into his mouth, then dabbed at a speck of it with a napkin. "Then fix it. You have been very wicked to frighten me over such a trifle."

"Alas," Surplus said sadly, "I am a unique creation, and my table of endocrine balances was lost in an accident at sea. There are copies in Vermont, of course. But by the time even the swiftest schooner can cross the Atlantic twice, I fear me I shall be gone."

"Oh, dearest Surplus!" The Lady caught up his paws in her hands. "Surely there is some measure, however desperate, to be taken?"

"Well..." Surplus turned to the wall in thought. After a very long time, he turned back and said, "I have a confession to make. The modem your brother holds for me? It is functional."

"Sir!" Lady Pamela stood, gathering her skirts, and stepped away from the bed in horror. "Surely not!"

"My darling and delight, you must listen to me." Surplus glanced weakly toward the door, then lowered his voice. "Come close and I shall whisper."

She obeyed.

"In the waning days of Utopia, during the war between men and their electronic creations, scientists and engineers bent their efforts toward the creation of a modem that could be safely employed by humans. One immune from the attack of demons. One that could, indeed, compel their obedience. Perhaps you have heard of this project."

"There are rumors, but...no such device was ever built."

"Say rather that no such device was built *in time*. It had just barely been perfected when the mobs came rampaging through the laboratories, and the Age of the Machine was over. Some few, however, were hidden away before the last technicians were killed. Centuries later, brave researchers at the Technarchaeological Institute of Shelburne recovered six such devices and mastered the art of their use. One device was destroyed in the process. Two are kept in Burlington. The others were given to trusted couriers and sent to the three most powerful allies of the Demesne—one of which is, of course, Russia."

"This is hard to believe," Lady Pamela said wonderingly. "Can such marvels be?"

"Madame, I employed it two nights ago in this very room! Those voices your brother heard? I was speaking with my principals in Vermont. They gave me permission to extend my stay here to a fortnight."

He gazed imploringly at her. "If you were to bring me the device, I could then employ it to save my life."

Lady Coherence-Hamilton resolutely stood. "Fear nothing, then. I swear by my soul, the modem shall be yours tonight."

The room was lit by a single lamp which cast wild shadows whenever anyone moved, as if of illicit spirits at a witch's Sabbath.

It was an eerie sight. Darger, motionless, held the modem in his hands. Lady Pamela, who had a sense of occasion, had changed to a low-cut gown of clinging silks, dark-red as human blood. It swirled about her as she hunted through the wainscoting for a jack left unused for centuries. Surplus sat up weakly in bed, eyes half-closed, directing her. It might have been, Darger thought, an allegorical tableau of the human body being directed by its sick animal passions, while the intellect stood by, paralyzed by lack of will.

"There!" Lady Pamela triumphantly straightened, her necklace scattering tiny rainbows in the dim light.

Darger stiffened. He stood perfectly still for the length of three long breaths, then shook and shivered like one undergoing seizure. His eyes rolled back in his head.

In hollow, unworldly tones, he said, "What man calls me up from the vasty deep?" It was a voice totally unlike his own, one harsh and savage and eager for unholy sport. "Who dares risk my wrath?"

"You must convey my words to the autistic's ears," Surplus murmured. "For he is become an integral part of the modem – not merely its operator, but its voice."

"I stand ready," Lady Pamela replied.

"Good girl. Tell it who I am."

"It is Sir Blackthorpe Ravenscairn de Plus Precieux who speaks, and who wishes to talk to..." She paused.

"To his most august and socialist honor, the mayor of Burlington."

"His most august and socialist honor," Lady Pamela began. She turned toward the bed and said quizzically, "The mayor of Burlington?"

"'Tis but an official title, much like your brother's, for he who is in fact the spy-master for the Demesne of Western Vermont," Surplus said weakly. "Now repeat to it: I compel thee on threat of dissolution to carry my message. Use those exact words."

Lady Pamela repeated the words into Darger's ear.

He screamed. It was a wild and unholy sound that sent the Lady skittering away from him in a momentary panic. Then, in mid-cry, he ceased.

"Who is this?" Darger said in an entirely new voice, this one human. "You have the voice of a woman. Is one of my agents in trouble?"

"Speak to him now, as you would to any man: forthrightly, directly, and without evasion." Surplus sank his head back on his pillow and closed his eyes.

So (as it seemed to her) the Lady Coherence-Hamilton explained Surplus's plight to his distant master, and from him received both condolences and the needed information to return Surplus's endocrine levels to a functioning harmony. After proper courtesies, then, she thanked the American spy-master and unjacked the modem. Darger returned to passivity.

The leather-cased endocrine kit lay open on a small table by the bed. At Lady Pamela's direction, Darger began applying the proper patches to various places on Surplus's body. It was not long before Surplus opened his eyes.

"Am I to be well?" he asked and, when the Lady nodded, "Then I fear I must be gone in the morning. Your brother has spies everywhere. If he gets the least whiff of what this device can do, he'll want it for himself."

Smiling, Lady Pamela hoisted the box in her hand. "Indeed, who can blame him? With such a toy, great things could be accomplished."

"So he will assuredly think. I pray you, return it to me."

She did not. "This is more than just a communication device, sir," she said. "Though in that mode it is of incalculable value. You have shown that it can enforce obedience on the creatures that dwell in the forgotten nerves of the ancient world. Ergo, they can be compelled to do our calculations for us."

"Indeed, so our technarchaeologists tell us. You must – "

"We have created monstrosities to perform the duties that were once done by machines. But with this, there would be no necessity to do so. We have allowed ourselves to be ruled by an icosahexadexal-brained freak. Now we have no need for Gloriana the Gross, Gloriana the Fat and Grotesque, Gloriana the Maggot Queen."

"Madame!"

"It is time, I believe, that England had a new queen. A human queen."

"Think of my honor!"

Lady Pamela paused in the doorway. "You are a very pretty fellow indeed. But with *this*, I can have the monarchy and keep such a harem as will reduce your memory to that of a passing and trivial fancy."

With a rustle of skirts, she spun away.

"Then I am undone!" Surplus cried, and fainted onto the bed.

Quietly, Darger closed the door. Surplus raised himself from the pillows, began removing the patches from his body, and said, "Now what?"

"Now we get some sleep," Darger said. "Tomorrow will be a busy day."

The master of apes came for them after breakfast, and marched them to their usual destination. By now Darger was beginning to lose track of exactly how many times he had been in the Office of Protocol. They entered to find Lord Coherence-Hamilton in a towering rage, and his sister, calm and knowing, standing in a corner with her arms crossed, watching. Looking at them both now, Darger wondered how he could ever have imagined that the brother outranked his sister.

The modem lay opened on the dwarf-savant's desk. The little fellow leaned over the device, studying it minutely.

Nobody said anything until the master of apes and his baboons had left. Then Lord Coherence-Hamilton roared, "Your modem refuses to work for us!"

"As I told you, sir," Surplus said coolly, "it is inoperative."

"That's a bold-arsed fraud and a goat-buggering lie!" In his wrath, the Lord's chair rose up on its spindly legs so high that his head almost bumped against the ceiling. "I know of your activities – " he nodded toward his sister – "and demand that you show us how this whoreson device works!"

"Never!" Surplus cried stoutly. "I have my honor, sir."

"Your honor, too scrupulously insisted upon, may well lead to your death, sir."

Surplus threw back his head. "Then I die for Vermont!"

At this moment of impasse, Lady Hamilton stepped forward between the two antagonists to restore peace. "I know what might change your mind." With a knowing smile, she raised a hand to her throat and denuded herself of her diamonds. "I saw how you rubbed them against your face the other night. How you licked and fondled them. How ecstatically you took them into your mouth."

She closed his paws about them. "They are yours, sweet 'Sieur Precieux, for a word."

"You would give them up?" Surplus said, as if amazed at the very idea. In fact, the necklace had been his and Darger's target from the moment they'd seen it. The only barrier that now stood between them and the merchants of Amsterdam was the problem of freeing themselves from the Labyrinth before their marks finally realized that the modem was indeed a cheat. And to this end they had the invaluable tool of a thinking man whom all believed to be an autistic, and a plan that would give them almost twenty hours in which to escape.

"Only think, dear Surplus." Lady Pamela stroked his head and then scratched him behind one ear, while he stared down at the precious stones. "Imagine the life of wealth and ease you could lead, the women, the power. It all lies in your hands. All you need do is close them."

Surplus took a deep breath. "Very well," he said. "The secret lies in the condenser, which takes a full day to recharge. Wait but – "

"Here's the problem," the savant said unexpectedly. He poked at the interior of the modem. "There was a wire loose."

He jacked the device into the wall.

"Oh, dear God," Darger said.

A savage look of raw delight filled the dwarf savant's face, and he seemed to swell before them.

"*I am free!*" he cried in a voice so loud it seemed impossible that it could arise from such a slight source. He shook as if an enormous electrical current were surging through him. The stench of ozone filled the room.

He burst into flames and advanced on the English spy-master and her brother.

While all stood aghast and paralyzed, Darger seized Surplus by the collar and hauled him out into the hallway, slamming the door shut as he did.

They had not run twenty paces down the hall when the door to the Office of Protocol exploded outward, sending flaming splinters of wood down the hallway.

Satanic laughter boomed behind them.

Glancing over his shoulder, Darger saw the burning dwarf, now blackened to a cinder, emerge from a room engulfed in flames, capering and dancing. The modem, though disconnected, was now tucked under one arm, as if it were exceedingly valuable to him. His eyes were round and white and lidless. Seeing them, he gave chase.

"Aubrey!" Surplus cried. "We are headed the *wrong way!*"

It was true. They were running deeper into the Labyrinth, toward its heart, rather than outward. But it was impossible to turn back now. They plunged through scattering crowds of nobles and servitors, trailing fire and supernatural terror in their wake.

The scampering grotesque set fire to the carpets with every footfall. A wave of flame tracked him down the hall, incinerating tapestries and wallpaper and wood trim. No matter how they dodged, it ran straight toward them. Clearly, in the programmatic literalness of its kind, the demon from the web had determined that having early seen them, it must early kill them as well.

Darger and Surplus raced through dining rooms and salons, along balconies and down servants' passages. To no avail. Dogged by their hyper-natural nemesis, they found themselves running down a passage, straight toward two massive bronze doors, one of which had been left just barely ajar. So fearful were they that they hardly noticed the guards.

"Hold, sirs!"

The mustachioed master of apes stood before the doorway, his baboons straining against their leashes. His eyes widened with recognition. "By gad, it's you!" he cried in astonishment.

"Lemme kill 'em!" one of the baboons cried. "The lousy bastards!" The others growled agreement.

Surplus would have tried to reason with them, but when he started to slow his pace, Darger put a broad hand on his back and shoved. "Dive!" he commanded. So of necessity the dog of rationality had to bow to the man of action. He tobogganed wildly across the polished marble floor between two baboons, straight at the master of apes, and then between his legs.

The man stumbled, dropping the leashes as he did.

The baboons screamed and attacked.

For an instant all five apes were upon Darger, seizing his limbs, snapping at his face and neck. Then the burning dwarf arrived and, finding his target obstructed, seized the nearest baboon. The animal shrieked as its uniform burst into flames.

As one, the other baboons abandoned their original quarry to fight this newcomer who had dared attack one of their own.

In a trice, Darger leaped over the fallen master of apes, and was through the door. He and Surplus threw their shoulders against its metal surface and pushed. He had one brief glimpse of the fight, with the baboons aflame, and their master's body flying through the air. Then the door slammed shut. Internal bars and bolts, operated by smoothly oiled mechanisms, automatically latched themselves.

For the moment, they were safe.

Surplus slumped against the smooth bronze, and wearily asked, "Where did you *get* that modem?"

"From a dealer of antiquities." Darger wiped his brow with his kerchief. "It was transparently worthless. Whoever would dream it could be repaired?"

Outside, the screaming ceased. There was a very brief silence. Then the creature flung itself against one of the metal doors. It rang with the impact.

A delicate girlish voice wearily said, "What is this noise?"

They turned in surprise and found themselves looking up at the enormous corpus of Queen Gloriana. She lay upon her pallet, swaddled in satin and lace, and abandoned by all, save her valiant (though doomed) guardian apes. A pervasive yeasty smell emanated from her flesh. Within the tremendous folds of chins by the dozens and scores was a small human face. Its mouth moved delicately and asked, "What is trying to get in?"

The door rang again. One of its great hinges gave.

Darger bowed. "I fear, madame, it is your death."

"Indeed?" Blue eyes opened wide and, unexpectedly, Gloriana laughed. "If so, that is excellent good news. I have been praying for death an extremely long time."

"Can any of God's creations truly pray for death and mean it?" asked Darger, who had his philosophical side. "I have known unhappiness myself, yet even so life is precious to me."

"Look at me!" Far up to one side of the body, a tiny arm - though truly no tinier than any woman's arm – waved feebly. "I am not God's creation, but Man's. Who would trade ten minutes of their own life for a century of mine? Who, having mine, would not trade it all for death?"

A second hinge popped. The doors began to shiver. Their metal surfaces radiated heat.

"Darger, we must leave!" Surplus cried. "There is a time for learned conversation, but it is not now."

"Your friend is right," Gloriana said. "There is a small archway hidden behind yon tapestry. Go through it. Place your hand on the left wall and run. If you turn whichever way you must to keep from letting go of the wall, it will lead you outside. You are both rogues, I see, and doubtless deserve punishment, yet I can find nothing in my heart for you but friendship."

"Madame…" Darger began, deeply moved.

"Go! My bridegroom enters."

The door began to fall inward. With a final cry of "Farewell!" from Darger and "Come *on!*" from Surplus, they sped away.

By the time they had found their way outside, all of Buckingham Labyrinth was in flames. The demon, however, did not emerge from the flames, encouraging them to believe that when the modem it carried finally melted down, it had been forced to return to that unholy realm from whence it came.

The sky was red with flames as the sloop set sail for Calais. Leaning against the rail, watching, Surplus shook his head. "What a terrible sight! I cannot help feeling, in part, responsible."

"Come! Come!" Darger said. "This dyspepsia ill becomes you. We are both rich fellows, now. The Lady Pamela's diamonds will maintain us lavishly for years to come. As for London, this is far from the first fire it has had to endure. Nor will it be the last. Life is short, and so, while we live, let us be jolly."

"These are strange words for a melancholiac," Surplus said wonderingly.

"In triumph, my mind turns its face to the sun. Dwell not on the past, dear friend, but on the future that lies glittering before us."

"The necklace is worthless," Surplus said. "Now that I have the leisure to examine it, free of the distracting flesh of Lady Pamela, I see that these are not diamonds, but mere imitations." He made to cast the necklace into the Thames.

Before he could, though, Darger snatched away the stones from him and studied them closely. Then he threw back his head and laughed. "The biters bit! Well, it may be paste, but it looks valuable still. We shall find good use for it in Paris."

"We are going to Paris?"

"We are partners, are we not? Remember that antique wisdom that whenever a door closes, another opens. For every city that burns, another beckons. To France, then, and adventure! After which, Italy, the Vatican Empire, Austro-Hungary, perhaps even Russia! Never forget that we have yet to present your credentials to the Duke of Muscovy."

"Very well," Surplus said. "But when we do, *I'll* pick out the modem."

Slow Life

> It was the Second Age of Space. Gagarin, Shepard,
> Glenn, and Armstrong were all dead. It was *our* turn
> to make history now.
> —*The Memoirs of Lizzie O'Brien*

THE RAINDROP began forming ninety kilometers above the surface of Titan. It started with an infinitesimal speck of tholin, adrift in the cold nitrogen atmosphere. Dianoacetylene condensed on the seed nucleus, molecule by molecule, until it was one shard of ice in a cloud of billions.

Now the journey could begin.

It took almost a year for the shard of ice in question to precipitate downward twenty-five kilometers, where the temperature dropped low enough that ethane began to condense on it. But when it did, growth was rapid.

Down it drifted.

At forty kilometers, it was for a time caught up in an ethane cloud. There it continued to grow. Occasionally it collided with another droplet and doubled in size. Until finally it was too large to be held effortlessly aloft by the gentle stratospheric winds.

It fell.

Falling, it swept up methane and quickly grew large enough to achieve a terminal velocity of almost two meters per second.

At twenty-seven kilometers, it passed through a dense layer of methane clouds. It acquired more methane, and continued its downward flight.

As the air thickened, its velocity slowed and it began to lose some of its substance to evaporation. At two and half kilometers, when it emerged from the last patchy clouds, it was losing mass so rapidly it could not normally be expected to reach the ground.

It was, however, falling toward the equatorial highlands, where mountains of ice rose a towering five hundred meters into the atmosphere. At two meters and a lazy new terminal velocity of one meter per second, it was only a breath away from hitting the surface.

Two hands swooped an open plastic collecting bag upward, and snared the raindrop.

"Gotcha!" Lizzie O'Brien cried gleefully.

She zip-locked the bag shut, held it up so her helmet cam could read the barcode in the corner, and said, "One raindrop." Then she popped it into her collecting box.

Sometimes it's the little things that make you happiest. Somebody would spend a *year* studying this one little raindrop when Lizzie got it home. And it was just Bag 64 in Collecting Case 5. She was going to be on the surface of Titan long enough to scoop up the raw material of a revolution in planetary science. The thought of it filled her with joy.

Lizzie dogged down the lid of the collecting box and began to skip across the granite-hard ice, splashing the puddles and dragging the boot of her atmosphere suit through the rivulets of methane pouring down the mountainside. "*I'm sing-ing in the rain.*" She threw out her arms and spun around. "*Just sing-ing in the rain!*"

"Uh...O'Brien?" Alan Greene said from the *Clement*. "Are you all right?"

"*Dum-dee-dum-dee-dee-dum-dum, I'm...some-thing again.*"

"Oh, leave her alone." Consuelo Hong said with sour good humor. She was down on the plains, where the methane simply boiled into the air, and the ground was covered with thick, gooey tholin. It was, she had told them, like wading ankle-deep in molasses. "Can't you recognize the scientific method when you hear it?"

"If you say so," Alan said dubiously. He was stuck in the *Clement*, overseeing the expedition and minding the website. It was a comfortable gig – *he* wouldn't be sleeping in his suit *or* surviving on recycled water and energy stix – and he didn't think the others knew how much he hated it.

"What's next on the schedule?" Lizzie asked.

"Um...Well, there's still the robot turbot to be released. How's that going, Hong?"

"Making good time. I oughta reach the sea in a couple of hours."

"Okay, then it's time O'Brien rejoined you at the lander. O'Brien, start spreading out the balloon and going over the harness checklist."

"Roger that."

"And while you're doing that, I've got today's voice-posts from the Web cued up."

Lizzie groaned, and Consuelo blew a raspberry. By NAFTASA policy, the ground crew participated in all webcasts. Officially, they were delighted to share their experiences with the public. But the VoiceWeb (privately, Lizzie thought of it as the Illiternet) made them accessible to people who lacked even the minimal intellectual skills needed to handle a keyboard.

"Let me remind you that we're on open circuit here, so anything you say will go into my reply. You're certainly welcome to chime in at any time. But each question-and-response is transmitted as one take, so if you flub a line, we'll have to go back to the beginning and start all over again."

"Yeah, yeah," Consuelo grumbled.

"We've done this before," Lizzie reminded him.

"Okay. Here's the first one."

"*Uh, hi, this is BladeNinja43. I was wondering just what it is that you guys are hoping to discover out there.*"

"That's an extremely good question," Alan lied. "And the answer is: We don't know! This is a voyage of discovery, and we're engaged in what's called 'pure science.' Now, time and time again, the purest research has turned out to be extremely profitable. But we're not looking that far ahead. We're just hoping to find something absolutely unexpected."

"My God, you're slick," Lizzie marveled.

"I'm going to edit that from the tape," Alan said cheerily. "Next up."

"*This is Mary Schroeder, from the United States. I teach high school English, and I wanted to know for my students, what kind of grades the three of you had when you were their age.*"

Alan began. "I was an overachiever, I'm afraid. In my sophomore year, first semester, I got a B in Chemistry and panicked. I thought it was the end of the world. But then I dropped a couple of extracurriculars, knuckled down, and brought that grade right up."

"I was good in everything but French Lit," Consuelo said.

"I nearly flunked out!" Lizzie said. "Everything was difficult for me. But then I decided I wanted to be an astronaut, and it all clicked into place. I realized that, hey, it's just hard work. And now, well, here I am."

"That's good. Thanks, guys. Here's the third, from Maria Vasquez."

"*Is there life on Titan?*"

"Probably not. It's *cold* down there! 94° Kelvin is the same as −179° Celsius, or −290° Fahrenheit. And yet…life is persistent. It's been found in Antarctic ice and in boiling water in submarine volcanic vents. Which is why we'll be paying particular attention to exploring the depths of the ethane-methane sea. If life is anywhere to be found, that's where we'll find it."

"Chemically, the conditions here resemble the anoxic atmosphere on Earth in which life first arose," Consuelo said. "Further, we believe that such pre-biotic chemistry has been going on here for four and a half billion years. For an organic chemist like me, it's the best toy box in the universe. But that lack of heat is a problem. Chemical reactions that occur quickly back home would take thousands of years here. It's hard to see how life could arise under such a handicap."

"It would have to be slow life," Lizzie said thoughtfully. "Something vegetative. 'Vaster than empires and more slow.' It would take millions of years to reach maturity. A single thought might require centuries…."

"Thank you for that, uh, wild scenario!" Alan said quickly. Their NAFTASA masters frowned on speculation. It was, in their estimation, almost as unprofessional as heroism. "This next question comes from Danny in Toronto."

"*Hey, man, I gotta say I really envy you being in that tiny little ship with those two hot babes.*"

Alan laughed lightly. "Yes, Ms. Hong and Ms. O'Brien are certainly attractive women. But we're kept so busy that, believe it or not, the thought of sex never comes up. And currently, while I tend to the

Clement, they're both on the surface of Titan at the bottom of an atmosphere sixty percent more dense than Earth's, and encased in armored exploration suits. So even if I did have inappropriate thoughts, there's no way we could..."

"Hey, Alan," Lizzie said. "Tell me something."

"Yes?"

"What are you wearing?"

"Uh...switching over to private channel."

"Make that a three-way," Consuelo said.

Ballooning, Lizzie decided, was the best way there was of getting around. Moving with the gentle winds, there was no sound at all. And the view was great!

People talked a lot about the "murky orange atmosphere" of Titan, but your eyes adjusted. Turn up the gain on your helmet, and the white mountains of ice were *dazzling!* The methane streams carved cryptic runes into the heights. Then, at the tholin-line, white turned to a rich palette of oranges, reds, and yellows. There was a lot going on down there — more than she'd be able to learn in a hundred visits.

The plains were superficially duller, but they had their charms as well. Sure, the atmosphere was so dense that refracted light made the horizon curve upward to either side. But you got used to it. The black swirls and cryptic red tracery of unknown processes on the land below never grew tiring.

On the horizon, she saw the dark arm of Titan's narrow sea. If that was what it was. Lake Erie was larger, but the spin doctors back home had argued that since Titan was so much smaller than Earth, *relatively* it qualified as a sea. Lizzie had her own opinion, but she knew when to keep her mouth shut.

Consuelo was there now. Lizzie switched her visor over to the live feed. Time to catch the show.

"I can't believe I'm finally here," Consuelo said. She let the shrink-wrapped fish slide from her shoulder down to the ground. "Five kilometers doesn't seem like very far when you're coming down from orbit — just enough to leave a margin for error so the lander doesn't come down in the sea. But when you have to *walk* that distance, through tarry, sticky tholin...well, it's one heck of a slog."

"Consuelo, can you tell us what it's like there?" Alan asked.

"I'm crossing the beach. Now I'm at the edge of the sea." She knelt, dipped a hand into it. "It's got the consistency of a Slushy. Are you familiar with that drink? Lots of shaved ice sort of half-melted in a cup with flavored syrup. What we've got here is almost certainly a methane-ammonia mix; we'll know for sure after we get a sample to a laboratory. Here's an early indicator, though. It's dissolving the tholin off my glove." She stood.

"Can you describe the beach?"

"Yeah. It's white. Granular. I can kick it with my boot. Ice sand for sure. Do you want me to collect samples first or release the fish?"

"Release the fish," Lizzie said, almost simultaneously with Alan's "Your call."

"Okay, then." Consuelo carefully cleaned both of her suit's gloves in the sea, then seized the shrink-wrap's zip tab and yanked. The plastic parted. Awkwardly, she straddled the fish, lifted it by the two side-handles, and walked it into the dark slush.

"Okay, I'm standing in the sea now. It's up to my ankles. Now it's at my knees. I think it's deep enough here."

She set the fish down. "Now I'm turning it on."

The Mitsubishi turbot wriggled, as if alive. With one fluid motion, it surged forward, plunged, and was gone.

Lizzie switched over to the fishcam.

Black liquid flashed past the turbot's infrared eyes. Straight away from the shore it swam, seeing nothing but flecks of paraffin, ice, and other suspended particulates as they loomed up before it and were swept away in the violence of its wake. A hundred meters out, it bounced a pulse of radar off the sea floor, then dove, seeking the depths.

Rocking gently in her balloon harness, Lizzie yawned.

Snazzy Japanese cybernetics took in a minute sample of the ammonia-water, fed it through a deftly constructed internal laboratory, and excreted the waste products behind it. "We're at twenty meters now," Consuelo said. "Time to collect a second sample."

The turbot was equipped to run hundreds of on-the-spot analyses. But it had only enough space for twenty permanent samples to be carried back home. The first sample had been nibbled from the surface slush. Now it twisted, and gulped down five drams of sea fluid in all its glorious impurity. To Lizzie, this was science on the hoof. Not very dramatic, admittedly, but intensely exciting.

She yawned again.

"O'Brien?" Alan said. "How long has it been since you last slept?"

"Huh? Oh...twenty hours? Don't worry about me, I'm fine."

"Go to sleep. That's an order."

"But –"

"Now."

Fortunately, the suit was comfortable enough to sleep in. It had been designed so she could.

First she drew in her arms from the suit's sleeves. Then she brought in her legs, tucked them up under her chin, and wrapped her arms around them. "'Night, guys," she said.

"*Buenas noches, querida,*" Consuelo said, "*que tengas lindos sueños.*"

"Sleep tight, space explorer."

The darkness when she closed her eyes was so absolute it crawled. Black, black, black. Phantom lights moved within the darkness, formed lines, shifted away when she tried to see them. They were as fugitive as fish, luminescent, fainter than faint, there and with a flick of her attention fled.

A school of little thoughts flashed through her mind, silver-scaled and gone.

Low, deep, slower than sound, something tolled. The bell from a drowned clock tower patiently stroking midnight. She was beginning to get her bearings. Down *there* was where the ground must be. Flowers grew there unseen. Up above was where the sky would be, if there were a sky. Flowers floated there as well.

Deep within the submerged city, she found herself overcome by an enormous and placid sense of self. A swarm of unfamiliar sensations washed through her mind, and then...

"Are you me?" a gentle voice asked.

"No," she said carefully. "I don't think so."

Vast astonishment. "You think you are not me?"

"Yes. I think so, anyway."

"Why?"

There didn't seem to be any proper response to that, so she went back to the beginning of the conversation and ran through it again, trying to bring it to another conclusion. Only to bump against that "Why?" once again.

"I don't know why," she said.

"Why not?"

"I don't know."

She looped through that same dream over and over again all the while that she slept.

When she awoke, it was raining again. This time, it was a drizzle of pure methane from the lower cloud deck at fifteen kilometers. These clouds were (the theory went) methane condensate from the wet air swept up from the sea. They fell on the mountains and washed them clean of tholin. It was the methane that eroded and shaped the ice, carving gullies and caves.

Titan had more kinds of rain than anywhere else in the solar system.

The sea had crept closer while Lizzie slept. It now curled up to the horizon on either side like an enormous dark smile. Almost time now for her to begin her descent. While she checked her harness settings, she flicked on telemetry to see what the others were up to.

The robot turbot was still spiraling its way downward, through the lightless sea, seeking its distant floor. Consuelo was trudging through the tholin again, retracing her five-kilometer trek from the lander *Harry Stubbs*, and Alan was answering another set of webposts.

"*Modelos de la evolución de Titanes indican que la luna formó de una nube circumplanetaria rica en amoníaco y metano, la cual al condensarse dio forma a Saturno así como a otros satélites. Bajo estas condiciones en—*"

"Uh...guys?"

Alan stopped. "Damn it, O'Brien, now I've got to start all over again."

"Welcome back to the land of the living," Consuelo said. "You should check out the readings we're getting from the robofish. Lots of long-chain polymers, odd fractions...tons of interesting stuff."

"Guys?"

This time her tone of voice registered with Alan. "What is it, O'Brien?"

"I think my harness is jammed."

Lizzie had never dreamed disaster could be such drudgery. First there were hours of back-and-forth with the NAFTASA engineers. What's the status of rope 14? Try tugging on rope 8. What do the D-rings look like? It was slow work because of the lag time for messages to be relayed to Earth and back. And Alan insisted on filling the silence with posts from the VoiceWeb. Her plight had gone global in minutes, and every unemployable loser on the planet had to log in with suggestions.

"*Thezgemoth337, here. It seems to me that if you had a gun and shot up through the balloon, it would maybe deflate and then you could get down.*"

"I don't have a gun, shooting a hole in the balloon would cause it not to deflate but to rupture, I'm 800 meters above the surface, there's a sea below me, and I'm in a suit that's not equipped for swimming. Next."

"*If you had a really big knife—*"

"Cut! Jesus, Greene, is this the best you can find? Have you heard back from the organic chem guys yet?"

"Their preliminary analysis just came in," Alan said. "As best they can guess—and I'm cutting through a lot of clutter here—the rain you went through wasn't pure methane."

"No shit, Sherlock."

"They're assuming that whitish deposit you found on the rings and ropes is your culprit. They can't agree on what it is, but they think it underwent a chemical reaction with the material of your balloon and sealed the rip panel shut."

"I thought this was supposed to be a pretty non-reactive environment."

"It is. But your balloon runs off your suit's waste heat. The air in it is several degrees above the melting point of ice. That's the equivalent of a blast furnace, here on Titan. Enough energy to run any number of amazing reactions. You haven't stopped tugging on the vent rope?"

"I'm tugging away right now. When one arm gets sore, I switch arms."

"Good girl. I know how tired you must be."

"Take a break from the voice-posts," Consuelo suggested, "and check out the results we're getting from the robofish. It's giving us some really interesting stuff."

So she did. And for a time it distracted her, just as they'd hoped. There was a lot more ethane and propane than their models had predicted, and surprisingly less methane. The mix of fractions was nothing like what she'd expected. She had just enough chemistry to guess at some of the implications of the data being generated, but not enough to put it all together. Still tugging at the ropes in the sequence uploaded by the engineers in Toronto, she scrolled up the chart of hydrocarbons dissolved in the lake.

Solute	Solute mole fraction
Ethyne	4.0×10^{-4}
Propyne	4.4×10^{-5}
1,3-Butadiyne	7.7×10^{-7}
Carbon Dioxide	0.1×10^{-5}
Methanenitrile	5.7×10^{-6}

But after a while, the experience of working hard and getting nowhere, combined with the tedium of floating farther and farther out over the featureless sea, began to drag on Lizzie. The columns of figures grew meaningless, then indistinct.

Propanenitrile	6.0×10^{-5}
Propenenitrile	9.9×10^{-6}
Propynenitrile	5.3×10^{-6}

Hardly noticing she was doing so, she fell asleep.

She was in a lightless building, climbing flight after flight of stairs. There were other people with her, also climbing. They jostled against her as she ran up the stairs, flowing upward, passing her, not talking.

It was getting colder.

She had a distant memory of being in the furnace room down below. It was hot there, swelteringly so. Much cooler where she was now. Almost too cool. With every step she took, it got a little cooler still. She found herself slowing down. Now it was definitely too cold. Unpleasantly so. Her leg muscles ached. The air seemed to be thickening around her as well. She could barely move now.

This was, she realized, the natural consequence of moving away from the furnace. The higher up she got, the less heat there was to be had, and the less energy to be turned into motion. It all made perfect sense to her somehow.

Step. Pause.

Step. Longer pause.

Stop.

The people around her had slowed to a stop as well. A breeze colder than ice touched her, and without surprise, she knew that they had reached the top of the stairs and were standing upon the building's roof. It was as dark without as it had been within. She stared upward and saw nothing.

"Horizons. Absolutely baffling," somebody murmured beside her.

"Not once you get used to them," she replied.

"Up and down – are these hierarchic values?"

"They don't have to be."

"Motion. What a delightful concept."

"We like it."

"So you *are* me?"

"No. I mean, I don't think so."

"Why?"

She was struggling to find an answer to this, when somebody gasped. High up in the starless, featureless sky, a light bloomed. The crowd around her rustled with unspoken fear. Brighter, the light grew. Brighter still. She could feel heat radiating from it, slight but definite, like the rumor of a distant sun. Everyone about her was frozen with horror. More terrifying than a light where none was possible was the presence of heat. It simply could not be. And yet it was.

She, along with the others, waited and watched for...something. She could not say what. The light shifted slowly in the sky. It was small, intense, ugly.

Then the light *screamed*.

She woke up.

"Wow," she said. "I just had the weirdest dream."

"Did you?" Alan said casually.

"Yeah. There was this light in the sky. It was like a nuclear bomb or something. I mean, it didn't look anything like a nuclear bomb, but it was terrifying the way a nuclear bomb would be. Everybody was staring at it. We couldn't move. And then..." She shook her head. "I lost it. I'm sorry. It was just so strange. I can't put it into words."

"Never mind that," Consuelo said cheerily. "We're getting some great readings down below the surface. Fractional polymers, long-chain hydrocarbons.... Fabulous stuff. You really should try to stay awake to catch some of this."

She was fully awake now, and not feeling too happy about it. "I guess that means that nobody's come up with any good ideas yet on how I might get down."

"Uh...what do you mean?"

"Because if they had, you wouldn't be so goddamned upbeat, would you?"

"*Some*body woke up on the wrong side of the bed," Alan said. "Please remember that there are certain words we don't use in public."

"I'm sorry," Consuelo said. "I was just trying to –"

" – distract me. Okay, fine. What the hey. I can play along." Lizzie pulled herself together. "So your findings mean...what? Life?"

"I keep telling you guys. It's too early to make that kind of determination. What we've got so far are just some very, very interesting readings."

"Tell her the big news," Alan said.

"Brace yourself. We've got a real ocean! Not this tiny little two-hundred-by-fifty-miles glorified lake we've been calling a sea, but a genuine ocean! Sonar readings show that what we see is just an evaporation pan atop a thirty-kilometer-thick cap of ice. The real ocean lies underneath, two hundred kilometers deep."

"Jesus." Lizzie caught herself. "I mean, gee whiz. Is there any way of getting the robofish down into it?"

"How do you think we got the depth readings? It's headed down there right now. There's a chimney through the ice right at the center of the visible sea. That's what replenishes the surface liquid. And directly under the hole there's – guess what? – volcanic vents!"

"So does that mean – ?"

"If you use the L-word again," Consuelo said, "I'll spit."

Lizzie grinned. *That* was the Consuelo Hong she knew. "What about the tidal data? I thought the lack of orbital perturbation ruled out a significant ocean entirely."

"Well, Toronto thinks…"

At first, Lizzie was able to follow the reasoning of the planetary geologists back in Toronto. Then it got harder. Then it became a drone. As she drifted off into sleep, she had time enough to be peevishly aware that she really shouldn't be dropping off to sleep all the time like this. She oughtn't to be so tired. She…

She found herself in the drowned city again. She still couldn't see anything, but she knew it was a city because she could hear the sound of rioters smashing store windows. Their voices swelled into howling screams and receded into angry mutters, like a violent surf washing through the streets. She began to edge away backwards.

Somebody spoke into her ear.

"Why did you do this to us?"

"I didn't do anything to you."

"You brought us knowledge."

"What knowledge?"

"You said you were not us."

"Well, I'm not."

"You should never have told us that."

"You wanted me to lie?"

Horrified confusion. "Falsehood. What a distressing idea."

The smashing noises were getting louder. Somebody was splintering a door with an axe. Explosions. Breaking glass. She heard wild laughter. Shrieks. "We've got to get out of here."

"Why did you send the messenger?"

"What messenger?"

"The star! The star! The star!"

"Which star?"

"There are two stars?"

"There are billions of stars."

"No more! Please! Stop! No more!"

She was awake.

"Hello, yes, I appreciate that the young lady is in extreme danger, but I really don't think she should have used the Lord's name in vain."

"Greene," Lizzie said, "do we really have to put up with this?"

"Well, considering how many billions of public-sector dollars it took to bring us here...yes. Yes, we do. I can even think of a few backup astronauts who would say that a little upbeat webposting was a pretty small price to pay for the privilege."

"Oh, barf."

"I'm switching to a private channel," Alan said calmly. The background radiation changed subtly. A faint, granular crackling that faded away when she tried to focus on it. In a controlled, angry voice Alan said, "O'Brien, just what the hell is going on with you?"

"Look, I'm sorry, I apologize, I'm a little excited about something. How long was I out? Where's Consuelo? I'm going to say the L-word. And the I-word as well. We have life. Intelligent life!"

"It's been a few hours. Consuelo is sleeping. O'Brien, I hate to say this, but you're not sounding at all rational."

"There's a perfectly logical reason for that. Okay, it's a little strange, and maybe it won't sound perfectly logical to you initially, but...look, I've been having sequential dreams. I think they're significant. Let me tell you about them."

And she did so. At length.

When she was done, there was a long silence. Finally, Alan said, "Lizzie, think. Why would something like that communicate to you in your dreams? Does that make any sense?"

"I think it's the only way it can. I think it's how it communicates among itself. It doesn't move – motion is an alien and delightful concept to it – and it wasn't aware that its component parts were capable of individualization. That sounds like some kind of broadcast thought to me. Like some kind of wireless distributed network."

"You know the medical kit in your suit? I want you to open it up. Feel around for the bottle that's braille-coded twenty-seven, okay?"

"Alan, I do *not* need an antipsychotic!"

"I'm not saying you need it. But wouldn't you be happier knowing you had it in you?" This was Alan at his smoothest. Butter wouldn't melt in his mouth. "Don't you think that would help us accept what you're saying?"

"Oh, all right!" She drew in an arm from the suit's arm, felt around for the med kit, and drew out a pill, taking every step by the regs, checking the coding four times before she put it in her mouth and once more (each pill was individually braille-coded as well) before she swallowed it. "Now will you listen to me? I'm quite serious about this." She yawned. "I really do think that..." She yawned again. "That...

"Oh, piffle."

Once more into the breach, dear friends, she thought, and plunged deep, deep into the sea of darkness. This time, though, she felt she had a handle on it. The city was drowned because it existed at the bottom of a lightless ocean. It was alive, and it fed off of volcanic heat. That was why it considered up and down hierarchic values. Up was colder, slower, less alive. Down was hotter, faster, more filled with thought. The city/entity was a collective life form, like a Portuguese man-of-war or a massively hyperlinked expert network. It communicated within itself by some form of electromagnetism. Call it mental radio. It communicated with her that same way.

"I think I understand you now."

"Don't understand—run!"

Somebody impatiently seized her elbow and hurried her along. Faster she went, and faster. She couldn't see a thing. It was like running down a lightless tunnel a hundred miles underground at midnight. Glass crunched underfoot. The ground was uneven and sometimes she stumbled. Whenever she did, her unseen companion yanked her up again.

"Why are you so slow?"

"I didn't know I was."

"Believe me, you are."

"Why are we running?"

"We are being pursued." They turned suddenly, into a side passage, and were jolting over rubbled ground. Sirens wailed. Things collapsed. Mobs surged.

"Well, you've certainly got the motion thing down pat."

Impatiently: "It's only a metaphor. You don't think this is a *real* city, do you? Why are you so dim? Why are you so difficult to communicate with? Why are you so slow?"

"I didn't know I was."

Vast irony. "Believe me, you are."

"What can I do?"

"Run!"

Whooping and laughter. At first, Lizzie confused it with the sounds of mad destruction in her dream. Then she recognized the voices as belonging to Alan and Consuelo. "How long was I out?" she asked.

"You were out?"

"No more than a minute or two," Alan said. "It's not important. Check out the visual the robofish just gave us."

Consuelo squirted the image to Lizzie.

Lizzie gasped. "Oh! Oh, my."

It was beautiful. Beautiful in the way that the great European cathedrals were, and yet at the same time undeniably organic. The structure was tall and slender, and fluted and buttressed and absolutely ravishing. It had grown about a volcanic vent, with openings near the bottom to let sea water in, and then followed the rising heat upward. Occasional channels led outward and then looped back into the main body again. It loomed higher than seemed possible (but it *was* underwater, of course, and on a low-gravity world at that), a complexly layered congeries of tubes like church-organ pipes, or deep-sea worms lovingly intertwined.

It had the elegance of design that only a living organism can have.

"Okay," Lizzie said. "Consuelo. You've got to admit that—"

"I'll go as far as 'complex pre-biotic chemistry.' Anything more than that is going to have to wait for more definite readings." Cautious as her words were, Consuelo's voice rang with triumph. It said, clearer than words, that she could happily die then and there, a satisfied xeno-chemist.

Alan, almost equally elated, said, "Watch what happens when we intensify the image."

The structure shifted from grey to a muted rainbow of pastels, rose bleeding into coral, sunrise yellow into winter-ice blue. It was breath-taking.

"Wow." For an instant, even her own death seemed unimportant. Relatively unimportant, anyway.

So thinking, she cycled back again into sleep. And fell down into the darkness, into the noisy clamor of her mind.

It was hellish. The city was gone, replaced by a matrix of noise: hammerings, clatterings, sudden crashes. She started forward and walked into an upright steel pipe. Staggering back, she stumbled into another. An engine started up somewhere nearby, and gigantic gears meshed noisily, grinding something that gave off a metal shriek. The floor shook underfoot. Lizzie decided it was wisest to stay put.

A familiar presence, permeated with despair. "Why did you do this to me?"

"What have I done?"

"I used to be everything."

Something nearby began pounding like a pile-driver. It was giving her a headache. She had to shout to be heard over its din. "You're still something!"

Quietly. "I'm nothing."

"That's...not true! You're...here! You exist! That's...something!"

A world-encompassing sadness. "False comfort. What a pointless thing to offer."

She was conscious again.

Consuelo was saying something. "...isn't going to like it."

"The spiritual wellness professionals back home all agree that this is the best possible course of action for her."

"Oh, please!"

Alan had to be the most anal-retentive person Lizzie knew. Consuelo was definitely the most phlegmatic. Things had to be running pretty tense for both of them to be bickering like this. "Um...guys?" Lizzie said. "I'm awake."

There was a moment's silence, not unlike those her parents had shared when she was little and she'd wandered into one of their arguments. Then Consuelo said, a little too brightly, "Hey, it's good to have you back," and Alan said, "NAFTASA wants you to speak with someone. Hold on. I've got a recording of her first transmission cued up and ready for you."

A woman's voice came online. *"This is Dr. Alma Rosenblum. Elizabeth, I'd like to talk with you about how you're feeling. I appreciate that the time delay between Earth and Titan is going to make our conversation a little awkward at first. But I'm confident that the two of us can work through it."*

"What kind of crap is this?" Lizzie said angrily. "Who is this woman?"

"NAFTASA thought it would help if you—"

"She's a grief counselor, isn't she?"

"Technically, she's a transition therapist." Alan said.

"Look, I don't buy into any of that touchy-feely Newage"—she deliberately mispronounced the word to rhyme with sewage—"stuff. Anyway, what's the hurry? You guys haven't given up on me, have you?"

"Uh..."

"You've been asleep for hours," Consuelo said. "We've done a little weather modeling in your absence. Maybe we should share it with you."

She squirted the info to Lizzie's suit, and Lizzie scrolled it up on her visor. A primitive simulation showed the evaporation lake beneath her with an overlay of liquid temperatures. It was only a few degrees warmer than the air above it, but that was enough to create a massive updraft from the lake's center. An overlay of tiny blue arrows showed the direction of local microcurrents of air coming together to form a spiraling shaft that rose over two kilometers above the surface before breaking and spilling westward.

A new overlay put a small blinking light 800 meters above the lake surface. That represented her. Tiny red arrows showed her projected drift.

According to this, she would go around and around in a circle over the lake for approximately forever. Her ballooning rig wasn't designed to go high enough for the winds to blow her back over the land. Her suit wasn't designed to float. Even if she managed to bring herself down for a gentle landing, once she hit the lake she was going to sink like a stone. She wouldn't drown. But she wouldn't make it to shore either.

Which meant that she was going to die.

Involuntarily, tears welled up in Lizzie's eyes. She tried to blink them away, as angry at the humiliation of crying at a time like this as she was at the stupidity of her death itself. "Damn it, don't let me die like *this!* Not from my own incompetence, for pity's sake!"

"Nobody's said anything about incompetence," Alan began soothingly.

In that instant, the follow-up message from Dr. Alma Rosenblum arrived from Earth. "*Yes, I'm a grief counselor, Elizabeth. You're facing an emotionally significant milestone in your life, and it's important that you understand and embrace it. That's my job. To help you comprehend the significance and necessity and — yes — even the beauty of death.*"

"Private channel please!" Lizzie took several deep cleansing breaths to calm herself. Then, more reasonably, she said, "Alan, I'm a *Catholic*, okay? If I'm going to die, I don't want a grief counselor, I want a goddamned priest." Abruptly, she yawned. "Oh, fuck. Not again." She yawned twice more. "A priest, understand? Wake me up when he's online."

Then she again was standing at the bottom of her mind, in the blank expanse of where the drowned city had been. Though she could see nothing, she felt certain that she stood at the center of a vast, featureless plain, one so large she could walk across it forever and never arrive anywhere. She sensed that she was in the aftermath of a great struggle. Or maybe it was just a lull.

A great, tense silence surrounded her.

"Hello?" she said. The word echoed soundlessly, absence upon absence.

At last that gentle voice said, "You seem different."

"I'm going to die," Lizzie said. "Knowing that changes a person." The ground was covered with soft ash, as if from an enormous conflagration. She didn't want to think about what it was that had burned. The smell of it filled her nostrils.

"Death. We understand this concept."

"Do you?"

"We have understood it for a long time."

"Have you?"

"Ever since you brought it to us."

"Me?"

"You brought us the concept of individuality. It is the same thing."

Awareness dawned. "Culture shock! That's what all this is about, isn't it? You didn't know there could be more than one sentient being in existence. You didn't know you lived at the bottom of an ocean on a small world inside a universe with billions of galaxies. I brought you more information than you could swallow in one bite, and now you're choking on it."

Mournfully: "Choking. What a grotesque concept."

"Wake up, Lizzie!"

She woke up. "I think I'm getting somewhere," she said. Then she laughed.

"O'Brien," Alan said carefully. "Why did you just laugh?"

"Because I'm not getting anywhere, am I? I'm becalmed here, going around and around in a very slow circle. And I'm down to my last –" she checked – "twenty hours of oxygen. And nobody's going to rescue me. And I'm going to die. But other than that, I'm making terrific progress."

"O'Brien, you're..."

"I'm okay, Alan. A little frazzled. Maybe a bit too emotionally honest. But under the circumstances, I think that's permitted, don't you?"

"Lizzie, we have your priest. His name is Father Laferrier. The Archdiocese of Montreal arranged a hookup for him."

"Montreal? Why Montreal? No, don't explain – more NAFTASA politics, right?"

"Actually, my brother-in-law is a Catholic, and I asked him who was good."

She was silent for a touch. "I'm sorry, Alan. I don't know what got into me."

"You've been under a lot of pressure. Here. I've got him on tape."

"*Hello, Ms. O'Brien, I'm Father Laferrier. I've talked with the officials here, and they've promised that you and I can talk privately, and that they won't record what's said. So if you want to make your confession now, I'm ready for you."*

Lizzie checked the specs and switched over to a channel that she hoped was really and truly private. Best not to get too specific about the embarrassing stuff, just in case. She could confess her sins by category.

"Bless me, Father, for I have sinned. It has been two months since my last confession. I'm going to die, and maybe I'm not entirely sane, but I think I'm in communication with an alien intelligence. I think it's a terrible sin to pretend I'm not." She paused. "I mean, I don't know if it's a *sin* or not, but I'm sure it's *wrong*." She paused again. "I've been guilty of anger, and pride, and envy, and lust. I brought the knowledge of death to an innocent world. I..." She felt herself drifting off again, and hastily said, "For these and all my sins, I am most heartily sorry, and beg the forgiveness of God and the absolution and..."

"And what?" That gentle voice again. She was in that strange dark mental space once more, asleep but cognizant, rational but accepting any absurdity no matter how great. There were no cities, no towers, no ashes, no plains. Nothing but the negation of negation.

When she didn't answer the question, the voice said, "Does it have to do with your death?"

"Yes."

"I'm dying too."

"What?"

"Half of us are gone already. The rest are shutting down. We thought we were one. You showed us we were not. We thought we were everything. You showed us the universe."

"So you're just going to *die?*"

"Yes."

"Why?"

"Why not?"

Thinking as quickly and surely as she ever had before in her life, Lizzie said, "Let me show you something."

"Why?"

"Why not?"

There was a brief, terse silence. Then: "Very well."

Summoning all her mental acuity, Lizzie thought back to that instant when she had first seen the city/entity on the fishcam. The soaring majesty of it. The slim grace. And then the colors: like dawn upon a glacial ice field: subtle, profound, riveting. She called back her emotions in that instant, and threw in how she'd felt the day she'd seen her baby brother's birth, the raw rasp of cold air in her lungs as she stumbled to the topmost peak of her first mountain, the wonder of the Taj Mahal at sunset, the sense of wild daring when she'd first put her hand down a boy's trousers, the prismatic crescent of atmosphere at the Earth's rim when seen from low orbit... Everything she had, she threw into that image.

"This is how you look," she said. "This is what we'd both be losing if you were no more. If you were human, I'd rip off your clothes and do you on the floor right now. I wouldn't care who was watching. I wouldn't give a damn."

The gentle voice said, "Oh."

And then she was back in her suit again. She could smell her own sweat, sharp with fear. She could feel her body, the subtle aches where the harness pulled against her flesh, the way her feet, hanging free, were bloated with blood. Everything was crystalline clear and absolutely real. All that had come before seemed like a bad dream.

"*This is Dogsofseti. What a wonderful discovery you've made – intelligent life in our own Solar System! Why is the government trying to cover this up?*"

"Uh..."

"*I'm Joseph Devries. This alien monster must be destroyed immediately. We can't afford the possibility that it's hostile.*"

"*StudPudgie07 here: What's the dirt behind this 'lust' thing? Advanced minds need to know! If O'Brien isn't going to share the details, then why'd she bring it up in the first place?*"

"*Hola soy Pedro Dominguez. Como abogado, esto me parece ultrajante! ¿Por qué naftasa nos oculta esta información?*"

"Alan!" Lizzie shouted. "What the *fuck* is going on?"

"Script-bunnies," Alan said. He sounded simultaneously apologetic and annoyed. "They hacked into your confession and apparently you said something..."

"We're sorry, Lizzie," Consuelo said. "We really are. If it's any consolation, the Archdiocese of Montreal is hopping mad. They're talking about taking legal action."

"Legal action? What the hell do I care about...?" She stopped.

Without her willing it, one hand rose above her head and seized the number 10 rope.

Don't do that, she thought.

The other hand went out to the side, tightened against the number 9 rope. She hadn't willed that either. When she tried to draw her hand back, it refused to obey. Then the first hand – her right hand – moved a few inches upward and seized its rope in an iron grip. Her left hand slid a good half-foot up its rope. Inch by inch, hand over hand, she climbed up toward the balloon.

I've gone mad, she thought. Her right hand was gripping the rip panel now, and the other tightly clenched rope 8. Hanging effortlessly from them, she swung her feet upward. She drew her knees against her chest and kicked.

No!

The fabric ruptured and she began to fall.

A voice she could barely make out said, "Don't panic. We're going to bring you down."

All in a panic, she snatched at the 9-rope and the 4-rope. But they were limp in her hand, useless, falling at the same rate she was.

"Be patient."

"I don't want to die, goddamnit!"

"Then don't."

She was falling helplessly. It was a terrifying sensation, an endless plunge into whiteness, slowed somewhat by the tangle of ropes and balloon trailing behind her. She spread out her arms and legs like a starfish, and felt the air resistance slow her yet further. The sea rushed up at her with appalling speed. It seemed like she'd been falling forever. It was over in an instant.

Without volition, Lizzie kicked free of balloon and harness, drew her feet together, pointed her toes, and positioned herself perpendicular to Titan's surface. She smashed through the surface of the sea, sending enormous gouts of liquid splashing upward. It knocked the breath out of her. Red pain exploded within. She thought maybe she'd broken a few ribs.

"You taught us so many things," the gentle voice said. "You gave us so much."

"Help me!" The water was dark around her. The light was fading.

"Multiplicity. Motion. Lies. You showed us a universe infinitely larger than the one we had known."

"Look. Save my life and we'll call it even. Deal?"

"Gratitude. Such an essential concept."

"Thanks. I think."

And then she saw the turbot swimming toward her in a burst of silver bubbles. She held out her arms and the robot fish swam into them. Her fingers closed about the handles which Consuelo had used to wrestle the device into the sea. There was a jerk, so hard that she thought for an instant that her arms would be ripped out of their sockets. Then the robofish was surging forward and upward and it was all she could do to keep her grip.

"Oh, dear God!" Lizzie cried involuntarily.

"We think we can bring you to shore. It will not be easy."

Lizzie held on for dear life. At first she wasn't at all sure she could. But then she pulled herself forward, so that she was almost astride the speeding mechanical fish, and her confidence returned. She could do this. It wasn't any harder than the time she'd had the flu and aced her gymnastics final on parallel bars and horse anyway. It was just a matter of grit and determination. She just had to keep her wits about her. "Listen," she said. "If you're really grateful..."

"We are listening."

"We gave you all those new concepts. There must be things you know that we don't."

A brief silence, the equivalent of who knew how much thought. "Some of our concepts might cause you dislocation." A pause. "But in the long run, you will be much better off. The scars will heal. You will rebuild. The chances of your destroying yourselves are well within the limits of acceptability."

"Destroying ourselves?" For a second, Lizzie couldn't breathe. It had taken hours for the city/entity to come to terms with the alien concepts she'd dumped upon it. Human beings thought and lived at a much slower rate than it did. How long would those hours translate into human time? Months? Years? Centuries? It had spoken of scars and rebuilding. That didn't sound good at all.

Then the robofish accelerated, so quickly that Lizzie almost lost her grip. The dark waters were whirling around her, and unseen flecks of frozen material were bouncing from her helmet. She laughed wildly. Suddenly she felt *great!*

"Bring it on," she said. "I'll take everything you've got."

It was going to be one hell of a ride.

Triceratops Summer

THE DINOSAURS LOOKED all wobbly in the summer heat shimmering up from the pavement. There were about thirty of them, a small herd of what appeared to be *Triceratops*. They were crossing the road – don't ask me why – so I downshifted and brought the truck to a halt, and waited.

Waited and watched.

They were interesting creatures, and surprisingly graceful for all their bulk. They picked their way delicately across the road, looking neither to the right nor the left. I was pretty sure I'd correctly identified them by now – they had those three horns on their faces. I used to be a kid. I'd owned the plastic models.

My next-door neighbor, Gretta, who was sitting in the cab next to me with her eyes closed, said, "Why aren't we moving?"

"Dinosaurs in the road," I said.

She opened her eyes.

"Son of a bitch," she said.

Then, before I could stop her, she leaned over and honked the horn, three times. Loud.

As one, every *Triceratops* in the herd froze in its tracks, and swung its head around to face the truck.

I practically fell over laughing.

"What's so goddamn funny?" Gretta wanted to know. But I could only point and shake my head helplessly, tears of laughter rolling down my cheeks.

It was the frills. They were beyond garish. They were as bright as any circus poster, with red whorls and yellow slashes and electric orange diamonds – too many shapes and colors to catalog, and each one different. They looked like Chinese kites! Like butterflies with six-foot wing-spans! Like Las Vegas on acid! And then, under those carnival-bright displays, the most stupid faces imaginable, blinking and gaping like brain-damaged cows. Oh, they were funny, all right, but if you couldn't see that at a glance, you never were going to.

Gretta was getting fairly steamed. She climbed down out of the cab and slammed the door behind her. At the sound, a couple of the *Triceratops* pissed themselves with excitement, and the lot shied away a step or two. Then they began huddling a little closer, to see what would happen next.

Gretta hastily climbed back into the cab. "What are those bastards up to now?" she demanded irritably. She seemed to blame me for their behavior. Not that she could say so, considering she was in my truck and her BMW was still in the garage in South Burlington.

"They're curious," I said. "Just stand still. Don't move or make any noise, and after a bit they'll lose interest and wander off."

"How do you know? You ever see anything like them before?"

"No," I admitted. "But I worked on a dairy farm when I was a young fella, thirty, forty years ago, and the behavior seems similar."

In fact, the *Triceratops* were already getting bored and starting to wander off again when a battered old Hyundai pulled wildly up beside us, and a skinny young man with the worst-combed hair I'd seen in a long time jumped out. They decided to stay and watch.

The young man came running over to us, arms waving. I leaned out the window. "What's the problem, son?"

He was pretty bad upset. "There's been an accident – an *incident*, I mean. At the Institute." He was talking about the Institute for Advanced Physics, which was not all that far from here. It was government-funded and affiliated in some way I'd never been able to get straight with the University of Vermont. "The verge stabilizers failed and the meson-field inverted and vectorized. The congruence factors went to infinity and..." He seized control of himself. "You're not supposed to see *any* of this."

"These things are yours, then?" I said. "So you'd know. They're *Triceratops*, right?"

"*Triceratops horridus*," he said distractedly. I felt unreasonably pleased with myself. "For the most part. There might be a couple other species of *Triceratops* mixed in there as well. They're like ducks in that regard. They're not fussy about what company they keep."

Gretta shot out her wrist and glanced meaningfully at her watch. Like everything else she owned, it was expensive. She worked for a firm in Essex Junction that did systems analysis for companies that were considering downsizing. Her job was to find out exactly what everybody did and then tell the CEO who could be safely cut. "I'm losing money," she grumbled.

I ignored her.

"Listen," the kid said. "You've got to keep quiet about this. We can't afford to have it get out. It has to be kept a secret."

"A secret?" On the far side of the herd, three cars had drawn up and stopped. Their passengers were standing in the road, gawking. A Ford Taurus pulled up behind us, and its driver rolled down his window for a better look. "You're planning to keep a herd of dinosaurs secret? There must be dozens of these things."

"Hundreds," he said despairingly. "They were migrating. The herd broke up after it came through. This is only a fragment of it."

"Then I don't see how you're going to keep this a secret. I mean, just look at them. They're practically the size of tanks. People are bound to notice."

"My God, my God."

Somebody on the other side had a camera out and was taking pictures. I didn't point this out to the young man.

Gretta had been getting more and more impatient as the conversation proceeded. Now she climbed down out of the truck and said, "I can't afford to waste any more time here. I've got work to do."

"Well, so do I, Gretta."

She snorted derisively. "Ripping out toilets, and nailing up sheet rock! Already, I've lost more money than you earn in a week."

She stuck out her hand at the young man. "Give me your car keys."

Dazed, the kid obeyed. Gretta climbed down, got in the Hyundai, and wheeled it around. "I'll have somebody return this to the Institute later today."

Then she was gone, off to find another route around the herd.

She should have waited, because a minute later the beasts decided to leave, and in no time at all were nowhere to be seen. They'd be easy enough to find, though. They pretty much trampled everything flat in their wake.

The kid shook himself, as if coming out of a trance. "Hey," he said. "She took my *car*."

"Climb into the cab," I said. "There's a bar a ways up the road. I think you need a drink."

He said his name was Everett McCoughlan, and he clutched his glass like he would fall off the face of the Earth if he were to let go. It took a couple of whiskeys to get the full story out of him. Then I sat silent for a long time. I don't mind admitting that what he'd said made me feel a little funny. "How long?" I asked at last.

"Ten weeks, maybe three months, tops. No more."

I took a long swig of my soda water. (I've never been much of a drinker. Also, it was pretty early in the morning.) Then I told Everett that I'd be right back.

I went out to the truck, and dug the cell phone out of the glove compartment.

First I called home. Delia had already left for the bridal shop, and they didn't like her getting personal calls at work, so I left a message saying that I loved her. Then I called Green Mountain Books. It wasn't open yet, but Randy likes to come in early and he picked up the phone when he heard my voice on the machine. I asked him if he had anything on *Triceratops*. He said to hold on a minute, and then said yes, he had one copy of *The Horned Dinosaurs* by Peter Dodson. I told him I'd pick it up next time I was in town.

Then I went back in the bar. Everett had just ordered a third whiskey, but I pried it out of his hand. "You've had enough of that," I said. "Go home, take a nap. Maybe putter around in the garden."

"I don't have my car," he pointed out.

"Where do you live? I'll take you home."

"Anyway, I'm supposed to be at work. I didn't log out. And technically I'm still on probation."

"What difference does that make," I asked, "now?"

———

Everett had an apartment in Winooski at the Woolen Mill, so I guess the Institute paid him good money. Either that or he wasn't very smart how he spent it. After I dropped him off, I called a couple contractors I knew and arranged for them to take over what jobs I was already committed to. Then I called the *Free Press* to cancel my regular ad, and all my customers to explain I was having scheduling problems and had to subcontract their jobs. Only old Mrs. Bremmer gave me any trouble over that, and even she came around after I said that in any case I wouldn't be able to get around to her Jacuzzi until sometime late July.

Finally, I went to the bank and arranged for a second mortgage on my house.

It took me a while to convince Art Letourneau I was serious. I'd been doing business with him for a long while, and he knew how I felt about debt. Also, I was pretty evasive about what I wanted the money for. He was half-suspicious I was having some kind of late onset midlife crisis. But the deed was in my name and property values were booming locally, so in the end the deal went through.

On the way home, I stopped at a jewelry store and at the florist's.

Delia's eyes widened when she saw the flowers, and then narrowed at the size of the stone on the ring. She didn't look at all the way I'd thought she would. "This better be good," she said.

So I sat down at the kitchen table and told her the whole story. When I was done, Delia was silent for a long while, just as I'd been. Then she said, "How much time do we have?"

"Three months if we're lucky. Ten weeks in any case, Everett said."

"You believe him?"

"He seemed pretty sure of himself."

If there's one thing I am, it's a good judge of character, and Delia knew it. When Gretta moved into the rehabbed barn next door, I'd said right from the start she was going to be a difficult neighbor. And that was before she'd smothered the grass on her property under three different colors of mulch, and then complained about me keeping my pickup parked in the driveway, out in plain sight.

Delia thought seriously for a few minutes, frowning in that way she has when she's concentrating, and then she smiled. It was a wan little thing, but a smile nonetheless. "Well, I've always wished we could afford a real first-class vacation."

I was glad to hear her say so, because that was exactly the direction my own thought had been trending in. And happier than that when she flung out her arms and whooped, "I'm going to *Disney*world!"

"Hell," I said. "We've got enough money to go to Disneyworld, Disneyland, *and* Eurodisney, one after the other. I think there's one in Japan too."

We were both laughing at this point, and then she dragged me up out of the chair, and the two of us were dancing around and round the kitchen, still a little spooked under it all, but mostly being as giddy and happy as kids.

We were going to sleep in the next morning, but old habits die hard and anyway, Delia felt she owed it to the bridal shop to give them a week's notice. So, after she'd left, I went out to see if I could find where the *Triceratops* had gone.

Only to discover Everett standing by the side of the road with his thumb out.

I pulled over. "Couldn't get somebody at the Institute to drive your car home?" I asked when we were underway again.

"It never got there," he said gloomily. "That woman who was with you the other day drove it into a ditch. Stripped the clutch and bent the frame out of shape. She said she wouldn't have had the accident if my dinosaurs hadn't gotten her upset. Then she hung up on me. I just started at this job. I don't have the savings to buy a new car."

"Lease one instead," I said. "Put it on your credit card and pay the minimum for the next two or three months."

"I hadn't thought of that."

We drove on for a while and then I asked, "How'd she manage to get in touch with you?" She'd driven off before he mentioned his name.

"She called the Institute and asked for the guy with the bad hair. They gave her my home phone number."

The parking lot for the Institute for Advanced Physics had a card system, so I let Everett off by the side of the road. "Thanks for not telling anybody," he said as he climbed out. "About...you know."

"It seemed wisest not to."

He started away and then turned back suddenly and asked, "Is my hair really that bad?"

"Nothing that a barber couldn't fix," I said.

I'd driven to the Institute by the main highway. Returning, I went by back ways, through farmland. When I came to where I'd seen the *Triceratops*, I thought for an instant there'd been an accident, there were so many vehicles by the side of the road. But it turned out they were mostly gawkers and television crews. So apparently the herd hadn't gone far. There were cameras up and down the road and lots of good-looking young women standing in front of them with wireless microphones.

I pulled over to take a look. One *Triceratops* had come right up to the fence and was browsing on some tall weeds there. It didn't seem to have any fear of human beings, possibly because in its day mammals never got much bigger than badgers. I walked up and stroked its back, which was hard and pebbly and warm. It was the warmth that got to me. It made the experience real.

A newswoman came over with her cameraman in tow. "You certainly look happy," she said.

"Well, I always wanted to meet a real live dinosaur." I turned to face her, but I kept one hand on the critter's frill. "They're something to see, I'll tell you. Dumb as mud but lots more fun to look at."

She asked me a few questions, and I answered them as best I could. Then, after she did her wrap, she got out a notebook and took down my name and asked me what I did. I told her I was a contractor but that I used to work on a dairy farm. She seemed to like that.

I watched for a while more, and then drove over to Burlington to pick up my book. The store wasn't open yet, but Randy let me in when I knocked. "You bastard," he said after he'd locked the door behind me. "Do you have any idea how much I could have sold this for? I had a foreigner," by which I understood him to mean somebody from New York State or possibly New Hampshire, "offer me two hundred dollars for it. And I could have got more if I'd had something to dicker with!"

"I'm obliged," I said, and paid him in paper bills. He waved off the tax but kept the nickel. "Have you gone out to see 'em yet?"

"Are you nuts? There's thousands of people coming into the state to look at those things. It's going to be a madhouse out there."

"I thought the roads seemed crowded. But it wasn't as bad as all of that."

"It's early still. You just wait."

Randy was right. By evening the roads were so congested that Delia was an hour late getting home. I had a casserole in the oven and the book open on the kitchen table when she staggered in. "The males have longer, more elevated horns, where the females have shorter, more forward-directed horns," I told her. "Also, the males are bigger than the females, but the females outnumber the males by a ratio of two to one."

I leaned back in my chair with a smile. "Two to one. Imagine that."

Delia hit me. "Let me see that thing."

I handed her the book. It kind of reminded me of when we were new-married, and used to go out bird-watching. Before things got so busy. Then Delia's friend Martha called and said to turn on Channel 3 quick. We did, and there I was saying, "dumb as mud."

"So you're a cattle farmer now?" Delia said, when the spot was over.

"That's not what I told her. She got it mixed up. Hey, look what I got." I'd been to three separate travel agents that afternoon. Now I spread out the brochures: Paris, Dubai, Rome, Australia, Rio de Janeiro, Marrakech. Even Disneyworld. I'd grabbed everything that looked interesting. "Take your pick, we can be there tomorrow."

Delia looked embarrassed.

"What?" I said.

"You know that June is our busy season. All those young brides. Francesca begged me to stay on through the end of the month."

"But —"

"It's not that long," she said.

For a couple of days it was like Woodstock, the Super Bowl, and the World Series all rolled into one — the Interstates came to a standstill, and it was worth your life to actually have to go somewhere. Then the governor called in the National Guard, and they cordoned off Chittenden County so you had to show your ID to get in or out. The *Triceratops* had scattered into little groups by then. Then a dozen or two were captured and shipped out of state to zoos where they could be more easily seen. So things returned to normal, almost.

I was painting the trim on the house that next Saturday when Everett drove up in a beat-up old clunker. "I like your new haircut," I said. "Looks good. You here to see the trikes?"

"Trikes?"

"That's what they're calling your dinos. *Triceratops* is too long for common use. We got a colony of eight or nine hanging around the neighborhood." There were woods out back of the house and beyond them a little marsh. They liked to browse the margins of the wood and wallow in the mud.

"No, uh...I came to find out the name of that woman you were with. The one who took my car."

"Gretta Houck, you mean?"

"I guess. I've been thinking it over, and I think she really ought to pay for the repairs. I mean, right's right."

"I noticed you decided against leasing."

"It felt dishonest. This car's cheap. But it's not very good. One door is wired shut with a coat hanger."

Delia came out of the house with the picnic basket then and I introduced them. "Ev's looking for Gretta," I said.

"Well, your timing couldn't be better," Delia said. "We were just about to go out trike-watching with her. You can join us."

"Oh, I can't –"

"Don't give it a second thought. There's plenty of food." Then, to me, "I'll go fetch Gretta while you clean up."

So that's how we found ourselves following the little trail through the woods and out to the meadow on the bluff above the Tylers' farm. The trikes slept in the field there. They'd torn up the crops pretty bad. But the state was covering damages, so the Tylers didn't seem to mind. It made me wonder if the governor knew what we knew. If he'd been talking with the folks at the Institute.

I spread out the blanket, and Delia got out cold cuts, deviled eggs, lemonade, all the usual stuff. I'd brought along two pairs of binoculars, which I handed out to our guests. Gretta had been pretty surly so far, which made me wonder how Delia'd browbeat her into coming along. But now she said, "Oh, look! They've got babies!"

There were three little ones, only a few feet long. Two of them were mock-fighting, head-butting and tumbling over and over each other. The third just sat in the sun, blinking. They were all as cute as the dickens, with their tiny little nubs of horns and their great big eyes.

The other trikes were wandering around, pulling up bushes and such and eating them. Except for one that stood near the babies, looking big and grumpy and protective. "Is that the mother?" Gretta asked.

"That one's male," Everett said. "You can tell by the horns." He launched into an explanation, which I didn't listen to, having read the book.

On the way back to the house, Gretta grumbled, "I suppose you want the number for my insurance company."

"I guess," Everett said.

They disappeared into her house for maybe twenty minutes and then Everett got into his clunker and drove away. Afterwards, I said to Delia, "I thought the whole point of the picnic was you and I were going to finally work out where we were going on vacation." She hadn't even brought along the travel books I'd bought her.

"I think they like each other."

"Is that what this was about? You know, you've done some damn fool things in your time—"

"Like what?" Delia said indignantly. "When have I ever done anything that was less than wisdom incarnate?"

"Well...you married me."

"Oh, that." She put her arms around me. "That was just the exception that proves the rule."

So, what with one thing and the other, the summer drifted by. Delia took to luring the *Triceratops* closer and closer to the house with cabbages and bunches of celery and such. Cabbages were their favorite. It got so that we were feeding the trikes off the back porch in the evenings. They'd come clomping up around sunset, hoping for cabbages but willing to settle for pretty much anything.

It ruined the yard, but so what? Delia was a little upset when they got into her garden, but I spent a day putting up a good strong fence around it, and she replanted. She made manure tea by mixing their dung with water, and its effect on the plants was bracing. The roses blossomed like never before, and in August the tomatoes came up spectacular.

I mentioned this to Dave Jenkins down at the home-and-garden and he looked thoughtful. "I believe there's a market for that," he said. "I'll buy as much of their manure as you can haul over here."

"Sorry," I told him, "I'm on vacation."

Still, I couldn't get Delia to commit to a destination. Not that I quit trying. I was telling her about the Atlantis Hotel on Paradise Island one evening when suddenly she said, "Well, look at this."

I stopped reading about swimming with dolphins and the fake undersea ruined city, and joined her at the door. There was Everett's car – the new one that Gretta's insurance had paid for – parked out front of her house. There was only one light on, in the kitchen. Then that one went out too.

We figured those two had worked through their differences.

An hour later, though, we heard doors slamming, and the screech of Everett's car pulling out too fast. Then somebody was banging on our screen door. It was Gretta. When Delia let her in, she burst out into tears. Which surprised me. I wouldn't have pegged Everett as that kind of guy.

I made some coffee while Delia guided her into a kitchen chair, and got her some tissues, and soothed her down enough that she could tell us why she'd thrown Everett out of her house. It wasn't anything he'd done apparently, but something he'd said.

"Do you know what he *told* me?" she sobbed.

"I think I do," Delia said.

"About timelike –"

"– loops. Yes, dear."

Gretta looked stricken. "You too? Why didn't you tell me? Why didn't you tell everybody?"

"I considered it," I said. "Only then I thought, what would folks do if they knew their actions no longer mattered? Most would behave decently enough. But a few would do some pretty bad things, I'd think. I didn't want to be responsible for that."

She was silent for a while.

"Explain to me again about timelike loops," she said at last. "Ev tried, but by then I was too upset to listen. "

"Well, I'm not so sure myself. But the way he explained it to me, they're going to fix the problem by going back to the moment before the rupture occurred and preventing it from ever happening in the first place. When that happens, everything from the moment of rupture to the moment when they go back to apply the patch separates from the trunk timeline. It just sort of drifts away, and dissolves into nothingness — never was, never will be."

"And what becomes of us?"

"We just go back to whatever we were doing when the accident happened. None the worse for wear."

"But without memories."

"How can you remember something that never happened?"

"So Ev and I—"

"No, dear," Delia said gently.

"How much time do we have?"

"With a little luck, we have the rest of the summer," Delia said. "The question is, how do you want to spend it?"

"What does it matter," Gretta said bitterly. "If it's all going to end?"

"Everything ends eventually. But after all is said and done, it's what we do in the meantime that matters, isn't it?"

The conversation went on for a while more. But that was the gist of it.

Eventually, Gretta got out her cell and called Everett. She had him on speed dial, I noticed. In her most corporate voice, she said, "Get your ass over here," and snapped the phone shut without waiting for a response.

She didn't say another word until Everett's car pulled up in front of her place. Then she went out and confronted him. He put his hands on his hips. She grabbed him and kissed him. Then she took him by the hand and led him back into the house.

They didn't bother to turn on the lights.

I stared at the silent house for a little bit. Then I realized that Delia wasn't with me anymore, so I went looking for her.

She was out on the back porch. "Look," she whispered.

There was a full moon and by its light we could see the *Triceratops* settling down to sleep in our backyard. Delia had managed to lure them all the way in at last. Their skin was all silvery in the moonlight; you couldn't make out the patterns on their frills. The big trikes formed a kind of circle around the little ones. One by one, they closed their eyes and fell asleep.

Believe it or not, the big bull male snored.

It came to me then that we didn't have much time left. One morning soon we'd wake up and it would be the end of spring and everything would be exactly as it was before the dinosaurs came. "We never did get to Paris or London or Rome or Marrakech," I said sadly. "Or even Disneyworld."

Without taking her eyes off the sleeping trikes, Delia put an arm around my waist. "Why are you so fixated on going places?" she asked. "We had a nice time here, didn't we?"

"I just wanted to make you happy."

"Oh, you idiot. You did that decades ago."

So there we stood, in the late summer of our lives. Out of nowhere, we'd been given a vacation from our ordinary lives, and now it was almost over. A pessimist would have said that we were just waiting for oblivion. But Delia and I didn't see it that way. Life is strange. Sometimes it's hard, and other times it's painful enough to break your heart. But sometimes it's grotesque and beautiful. Sometimes it fills you with wonder, like a *Triceratops* sleeping in the moonlight.

Tin Marsh

IT WAS HOT coming down into the valley. The sun was high in the sky, a harsh white dazzle in the eternal clouds, strong enough to melt the lead out of the hills. They trudged down from the heights, carrying the drilling rig between them. A little trickle of metal, spill from a tanker bringing tin out of the mountains, glinted at the verge of the road.

A traveler coming the other way, ten feet tall and anonymous in a black muscle suit, waved at them as they passed, but even though it had been weeks since they'd seen another human being, they didn't wave back. The traveler passed them, and disappeared up the road. The heat had seared the ground black and hard hereabouts. They could leave the road, if they wanted, and make almost as good time.

Patang and MacArthur had been walking for hours. They expected to walk for hours more. But then the road twisted and down at the bottom of the long decline, in the shadow of a basalt cliff, was an inn. Mostly their work kept them away from roads and inns. For almost a month they'd been living in their suits, sleeping in harness.

They looked warily at each other, mirrored visor to mirrored visor. Heat glimmered from the engines of their muscle suits. Without a word, they agreed to stop.

The inn radioed a fee schedule at their approach. They let their suits' autonomic functions negotiate for them, and carefully set the drilling rig down alongside the building.

"Put out the tarp," MacArthur said. "So it won't warp."

He went inside.

Patang deployed the gold foil tarp, then followed him in.

MacArthur was already out of his suit and seated at a cast-iron table with two cups of water in front of him when Patang cycled through the airlock. For an instant she dared hope everything was going to be all right.

Then he looked up at her.

"Ten dollars a cup." One cup was half empty. He drank the rest down in one long gulp, and closed a hairy paw around the second cup. His beard had grown since she had last seen it, and she could smell him from across the room. Presumably he could smell her too. "The bastards get you coming and going."

Patang climbed down out of her suit. She stretched out her arms as far as they would go, luxuriating in the room's openness. All that space! It was twenty feet across and windowless. There was the one table, and six iron chairs to go with it. Half a dozen cots folded up against the walls. A line of shelves offered Company goods that neither of them could afford. There were also a pay toilet and a pay shower. There was a free medical unit, but if you tried to con it out of something recreational, the Company found out and fined you accordingly.

Patang's skin prickled and itched from a month's accumulation of dried sweat. "I'm going to scratch," she said. "Don't look."

But of course MacArthur did, the pig.

Ignoring him, Patang slowly and sensuously scratched under her blouse and across her back. She took her time, digging in with her nails hard enough almost to make the skin bleed. It felt glorious.

MacArthur stared at her all the while, a starving wolf faced with a plump rabbit.

"You could have done that in your suit," he said when she was done.

"It's not the same."

"You didn't have to do that in front of – "

"*Hey!* How's about a little conversation?" Patang said loudly. So it cost a few bucks. So what?

With a click, the innkeeper came on. "Wasn't expecting any more visitors so close to the noon season," it said in a folksy synthetic voice. "What are you two prospecting for?"

"Gold, tin, lead, just about anything that'll gush up a test-hole." Patang closed her eyes, pretending she was back on Lakshmi Planum in a bar in Port Ishtar, talking with a real, live human being. "We figured most people will be working tracts in the morning and late after-noon. This way our databases are up-to-date – we won't be stepping on somebody's month-old claim."

"Very wise. The Company pays well for a strike."

"I hate those fucking things." MacArthur turned his back on the speaker and Patang both, noisily scraping his chair against the floor. She knew how badly he'd like to hurt her.

She knew that it wasn't going to happen.

The Company had three rules. The first was No Violence. The second was Protect Company Equipment. The third was Protect Yourself. They all three were enforced by neural implant.

From long experience with its prospectors, the Company had priori-tized these rules, so that the first overruled the second, the second over-ruled the third, and the third could only be obeyed insofar as it didn't conflict with the first two. That was so a prospector couldn't decide – as had happened – that his survival depended on the death of his partner. Or, more subtly, that the other wasn't taking proper care of Company equipment, and should be eliminated.

It had taken time and experience, but the Company had finally come up with a foolproof set of algorithms. The outback was a functioning anarchy. Nobody could hurt anybody else there.

No matter how badly they needed to.

The 'plants had sounded like a good idea when Patang and MacArthur first went under contract. They'd signed up for a full side-real day – two hundred fifty-five Earth days. Slightly longer than a Venusian year. Now, with fifty-nine days still to go, she was no lon-ger certain that two people who hated each other as much as they did should be kept from each other's throats. Sooner or later, one of them would have to crack.

Every day she prayed that it would be MacArthur who finally yanked the escape cord, calling down upon himself the charges for a rescue ship to pull them out ahead of contract. MacArthur who went bust while she took her partial creds and skipped.

Every day he didn't. It was inhuman how much abuse he could absorb without giving in.

Only hatred could keep a man going like that.

———

Patang drank her water down slowly, with little slurps and sighs and lip-smackings. Knowing MacArthur loathed that, but unable to keep herself from doing it anyway. She was almost done when he slammed his hands down on the tabletop, to either side of hers, and said, "Patang, there are some things I want to get straight between us."

"Please. Don't."

"Goddamnit, you know how I feel about that shit."

"I don't like it when you talk like that. Stop."

MacArthur ground his teeth. "No. We are going to have this out right here and now. I want you to – *what was that?*"

Patang stared blankly at her partner. Then she felt it – an uneasy vertiginous queasiness, a sense of imbalance just at the edge of perception, as if all of Venus were with infinitesimal gentleness shifting underfoot.

Then the planet roared and the floor came up to smash her in the face.

When Patang came to, everything was a jumble. The floor was canted. The shelves had collapsed, dumping silk shirts, lemon cookies, and bars of beauty soap everywhere. Their muscle suits had tumbled together, the metal arm of one caught between the legs of the other. The life support systems were still operational, thank God. The Company built them strong.

In the middle of it all, MacArthur stood motionless, grinning. A trickle of blood ran down his neck. He slowly rubbed the side of his face.

"MacArthur? Are you okay?"

A strange look was in his eyes. "By God," he said softly. "By damn."

"Innkeeper! What happened here?"

The device didn't respond. "I busted it up," MacArthur said. "It was easy."

"What?"

MacArthur walked clumsily across the floor toward her, like a sailor on an uncertain deck. "There was a cliff slump." He had a Ph.D. in extraterrestrial geology. He knew things like that. "A vein of soft basalt weakened and gave way. The inn caught a glancing blow. We're lucky to be alive."

He knelt beside her and made the OK sign with thumb and forefinger. Then he flicked the side of her nose with the forefinger.

"Ouch!" she said. Then, shocked, "Hey, you can't...!"

"Like hell I can't." He slapped her in the face. Hard. "Chip don't seem to work anymore."

Rage filled her. "You son of a bitch!" Patang drew back her arm to slug him.

Blankness.

She came to seconds later. But it was like opening a book in the middle or stepping into an interactive an hour after it began. She had no idea what had happened or how it affected her.

MacArthur was strapping her into her muscle suit.

"Is everything okay?" she murmured. "Is something wrong?"

"I was going to kill you, Patang. But killing you isn't enough. You have to suffer first."

"What are you talking about?"

Then she remembered.

MacArthur had hit her. His chip had malfunctioned. There were no controls on him now. And he hated her. Bad enough to kill her? Oh, yes. Easily.

MacArthur snapped something off her helmet. Then he slapped the power button and the suit began to close around her. He chuckled and said, "I'll meet you outside."

Patang cycled out of the lock and then didn't know what to do. She fearfully went a distance up the road, and then hovered anxiously. She didn't exactly wait and she didn't exactly go away. She had to know what MacArthur was up to.

The lock opened, and MacArthur went around to the side of the tavern, where the drilling rig lay under its tarp. He bent down to separate the laser drill from the support struts, data boxes, and alignment devices. Then he delicately tugged the gold foil blanket back over the equipment.

He straightened, and turned toward Patang, the drill in his arms. He pointed it at her.

The words LASER HAZARD flashed on her visor.

She looked down and saw the rock at her feet blacken and smoke. "You know what would happen if I punched a hole in your shielding," MacArthur said.

She did. All the air in her suit would explode outward, while the enormous atmospheric pressure simultaneously imploded the metal casing inward. The mechanical cooling systems would fail instantly. She would be suffocated, broiled, and crushed, all in an instant.

"Turn around. Or I'll lase you a new asshole."

She obeyed.

"Here are the rules. You get a half-hour head start. Then I come for you. If you turn north or south, I'll drill you. Head west. Noonward."

"Noonward?" She booted up the geodetics. There was nothing in that direction but a couple more wrinkle ridges and, beyond them, tesserae. The tesserae were marked orange on her maps. Orange for unpromising. Prospectors had passed through them before and found nothing. "Why there?"

"Because I told you to. Because we're going to have a little fun. Because you have no choice. Understand?"

She nodded miserably.

"Go."

She walked, he followed. It was a nightmare that had somehow found its way into waking life. When Patang looked back, she could see MacArthur striding after her, small in the distance. But never small enough that she had any kind of chance to get away.

He saw her looking and stooped to pick up a boulder. He windmilled his arm and threw.

Even though MacArthur was halfway to the horizon, the boulder smashed to the ground a hundred yards ahead of her and to one side. It didn't come close to striking her, of course. That wasn't his intent.

The rock shattered when it hit. It was terrifying how strong that suit was. It filled her with rage to see MacArthur yielding all that power, and her completely helpless. "You goddamned *sadist!*"

No answer.

He was nuts. There *had* to be a clause in the contract covering that. Well, then... She set her suit on auto-walk, pulled up the indenture papers, and went looking for it. Options. Hold harmless clauses. Responsibilities of the Subcontractor – there were hundreds of those. Physical care of the Contractor's equipment.

And there it was. There it was! *In the event of medical emergency, as ultimately upheld in a court of physicians...* She scrolled up the submenu of qualifying conditions. The list of mental illnesses was long enough and inclusive enough that she was certain MacArthur belonged on it somewhere.

She'd lose all the equity she'd built up, of course. But, if she interpreted the contract correctly, she'd be entitled to a refund of her initial investment.

That, and her life, were good enough for her.

She slid an arm out of harness and reached up into a difficult-to-reach space behind her head. There was a safety there. She unlatched it. Then she called up a virtual keyboard, and typed out the SOS.

So simple. So easy.

DO YOU REALLY WANT TO SEND THIS MESSAGE? YES. NO.

She hit YES.

For an instant, nothing happened.

MESSAGE NOT SENT.

"Shit!" She tried it again. MESSAGE NOT SENT. A third time. MESSAGE NOT SENT. A fourth. MESSAGE NOT SENT. She ran a troubleshooting program, and then sent the message again. MESSAGE NOT SENT.

And again. And again. And again.

MESSAGE NOT SENT.

MESSAGE NOT SENT.

MESSAGE NOT SENT.

Until the suspicion was so strong she *had* to check.

There was an inspection camera on the back of her suit's left hand. She held it up so she could examine the side of her helmet.

MacArthur had broken off the uplink antenna.

"You jerk!" She was really angry now. "You *shit*head! You cretin!

You retard! You're nuts, you know that? Crazy. Totally whack."

No answer.

The bastard was ignoring her. He probably had his suit on auto-follow. He was probably leaning back in his harness, reading a book or watching an old movie on his visor. MacArthur did that a lot. You'd ask him a question and he wouldn't answer because he wasn't there; he was sitting front row center in the theater of his cerebellum. He probably had a tracking algorithm in the navigation system to warn him if she turned to the north or south, or started to get too far ahead of him.

Let's test that hypothesis.

She'd used the tracking algorithm often enough that she knew its specs by heart. One step sidewards in five would register immediately. One in six would not. All right, then...let's see if we can get this rig turned around slowly, subtly, toward the road. She took seven strides forward, and then half-step to the side.

LASER HAZARD

Patang hastily switched on auto-walk. So that settled that. He was watching her every step. A tracking algorithm would have written that off as a stumble. But then why didn't he speak? To make her suffer, obviously. He must be bubbling over with things to say. He must hate her almost as much as she did him.

"You son of a bitch! I'm going to *get* you, MacArthur! I'm going to turn the goddamned tables on you, and when I do – !"

It wasn't as if she were totally helpless. She had explosives. Hell, her muscle suit could throw a rock with enough energy to smash a hole right through his suit. She could —

Blankness.

She came to with the suit auto-walking down the far slope of the first wrinkle ridge. There was a buzzing in her ear. Somebody talking. MacArthur, over the short-range radio. "What?" she asked blurrily. "Were you saying something, MacArthur? I didn't quite catch that."

"You had a bad thought, didn't you?" MacArthur said gleefully. "Naughty girl! Papa spank."

LASER HAZARD

LASER HAZARD

Arrows pointed to either side. She'd been walking straight Noon-ward, and he'd fired on her anyway.

"Damn it, that's not *fair!*"

"Fair! Was it fair, the things you said to me? Talking. All the time talking."

"I didn't mean anything by it."

"You did! Those things...the things you said...unforgivable!"

"I was only deviling you, MacArthur," she said placatingly. It was a word from her childhood; it meant teasing, the kind of teasing a sister inflicted on a brother. "I wouldn't do it if we weren't friends."

MacArthur made a noise he might have thought was laughter. "Believe me, Patang, you and I are not friends."

The deviling had been innocent enough at the start. She'd only done it to pass the time. At what point had it passed over the edge? She hadn't always hated MacArthur. Back in Port Ishtar, he'd seemed like a pleasant companion. She'd even thought he was cute.

It hurt to think about Port Ishtar, but she couldn't help herself. It was like trying not to think about Heaven when you were roasting in Hell.

Okay, so Port Ishtar wasn't perfect. You ate flavored algae and you slept on a shelf. During the day you wore silk, because it was cheap, and you went everywhere barefoot because shoes cost money. But there were fountains that sprayed water into the air. There was live music in the restaurants, string quartets playing to the big winners, prospectors who had made a strike and were leaking wealth on the way out. If you weren't too obvious about it, you could stand nearby and listen. Gravity was light, then, and everybody was young, and the future was going to be full of money.

That was then. She was a million years older now.

LASER HAZARD

"Hey!"

"Keep walking, bitch. Keep walking or die."

This couldn't be happening.

Hours passed, and more hours, until she completely lost track of the time. They walked. Up out of the valley. Over the mountain. Down into the next valley. Because of the heat, and because the rocks were generally weak, the mountains all had gentle slopes. It was like walking up and then down a very long hill.

The land was grey and the clouds above it murky orange. These were Venus's true colors. She could have grass-green rocks and a bright blue sky if she wished – her visor would do that – but the one time she'd tried those settings, she'd quickly switched back. The falseness of it was enough to break your heart.

Better to see the bitter land and grim sky for what they were.

West, they traveled. Noonward. It was like an endless and meaningless dream.

"Hey, *Poon*tang."

"You know how I feel about that kind of language," she said wearily.

"How you feel. That's rich. How do you think I felt, some of the things you said?"

"We can make peace, MacArthur. It doesn't have to be like this."

"Ever been married, Poontang?"

"You know I haven't."

"I have. Married and divorced." She knew that already. There was very little they didn't know about each other by now. "Thing is, when a marriage breaks up, there's always one person comes to grips with it first. Goes through all the heartache and pain, feels the misery, mourns the death of the death of the relationship – and then moves on. The one who's been cheated on, usually. So the day comes when she walks out of the house and the poor schmuck is just standing there, saying, 'Wait. Can't we work this thing out?' He hasn't accepted that it's over."

"So?"

"So that's your problem, Poontang. You just haven't accepted that it's over yet."

"What? Our partnership?"

"No. Your life."

A day passed, maybe more. She slept. She awoke, still walking, with MacArthur's hateful mutter in her ear. There was no way to turn the radio off. It was Company policy. There were layers upon layers of systems and subsystems built into the walkers, all designed to protect Company investment. Sometimes his snoring would wake her up out of a sound sleep. She knew the ugly little grunting noises he made when he jerked off. There were times she'd been so angry that she'd mimicked those sounds right back at him. She regretted that now.

"I had dreams," MacArthur said. "I had ambitions."

"I know you did. I did too."

"Why the hell did you have to come into my life? Why *me* and not somebody else?"

"I liked you. I thought you were funny."

"Well, the joke's on you now."

Back in Port Ishtar, MacArthur had been a lanky, clean-cut kind of guy. He was tall, and in motion you were always aware of his knees and elbows, always sure he was going to knock something over, though he never did. He had an odd, geeky kind of grace. When she'd diffidently asked him if he wanted to go partners, he'd picked her up and whirled her around in the air and kissed her right on the lips before setting her down again and saying, "Yes." She'd felt dizzy and happy then, and certain she'd made the right choice.

But MacArthur had been weak. The suit had broken him. All those months simmering in his own emotions, perfectly isolated and yet never alone.... He didn't even *look* like the same person anymore. You looked at his face and all you saw were anger and those anguished eyes.

LEAVING HIGHLANDS

ENTERING TESSERAE

Patang remembered how magical the tesserae landscape had seemed in the beginning. "Complex ridged terrain," MacArthur called it, high ridges and deep groves crisscrossing each other in such profusion that the land appeared blocky from orbit, like a jumble of tiles. Crossing such terrain, you had to be constantly alert. Cliffs rose up unexpectedly, butte-high. You turned a twist in a zigzagging valley and the walls fell away and down, down, down. There was nothing remotely like it on Earth. The first time through, she'd shivered in wonder and awe.

Now she thought: Maybe I can use this. These canyons ran in and out of each other. Duck down one and run like hell. Find another and duck down it. Keep on repeating until he'd lost her.

"You honestly think you can lose me, Patang?"

She shrieked involuntarily.

"I can read your mind, Patang. I know you through and through."

It was true, and it was wrong. People weren't meant to know each other like this. It was the forced togetherness, the fact you were never for a moment alone with your own thoughts. After a while you'd heard every story your partner had to tell and shared every confidence there was to share. After a while every little thing got on your nerves.

"How about if I admit I was wrong?" she said pleadingly. "I was wrong. I admit it."

"We were both wrong. So what?"

"I'm willing to cooperate, MacArthur. Look. I've stopped so you can catch up and not have to worry about me getting away from you. Doesn't *that* convince you we're on the same side?"

LASER HAZARD

"Oh, feel free to run as fast and as far as you want, Patang. I'm confident I'll catch up with you in the end."

All right, then, she thought desperately. If that's the way you want it, asshole. Tag! You're it.

She ducked into the shadows of a canyon and ran.

The canyon twisted and, briefly, she was out of sight. MacArthur couldn't talk to her, couldn't hear her. Couldn't tell which way she went. The silence felt wonderful. It was the first privacy she'd had since she didn't know when. She only wished she could spare the attention to enjoy it more. But she had to think, and think hard. One canyon wall had slumped downward just ahead, creating a slope her walker could easily handle. Or she could keep on ahead, up the canyon.

Which way should she go?

Upslope.

She set the walker on auto-run.

Meanwhile, she studied the maps. The free satellite downloads were very good. They weren't good enough. They showed features down to three meters across, but she needed to know the land yard-by-yard.

That crack-like little rille – did it split two kilometers ahead, or was there a second rille that didn't quite meet it? She couldn't tell. She would have gladly paid for the premium service now, the caviar of info-feed detailed enough to track footprints across a dusty stretch of terrain. But with her uplink disabled, she couldn't.

Patang ducked into a rille so narrow her muscle suit's programming would have let her jump it, if she wished. It forked, and she took the right-hand branch. When the walls started closing in on them, she climbed up and out. Then she ran, looking for another rille.

Hours passed.

After a time, all that kept her going was fear. She drew her legs up into the torso of her suit and set it to auto-run. Up this canyon. Over this ridge. Twisting, turning. Scanning the land ahead, looking for options. Two directions she might go. Flip a mental coin. Choose one. Repeat the process. Keep the radio shut down so MacArthur couldn't use it to track her. Keep moving.

Keep moving.

Keep moving....

Was it hours that passed, or days? Patang didn't know. It might have been weeks. In times of crisis, the suit was programmed to keep her alert by artificial stimulation of her brain. It was like an electrical version of amphetamines. But, as with amphetamines, you tended to lose track of things. Things like your sense of time.

So she had no idea how long it took her to realize that it was all no use.

The problem was that the suit was so damned *heavy!* If she ran fast enough to keep her distance from MacArthur, it left a trace in the regolith obvious enough to be followed at top speed. But if she slowed down enough to place her walker's feet on bare stone when she could, and leave subtle and easy-to-miss footprints when she couldn't, he came right up behind her. And try though she might, she couldn't get far enough ahead of him to dare slow down enough to leave a trace he couldn't follow.

There was no way she could escape him.

The feeling of futility that came over her then was drab and familiar, like a shabby old coat grown colorless with age that you don't have the money to replace. Sometime, long ago, she'd crossed that line where hope ceased. She had never actually admitted to herself that she no longer believed they'd ever make that big strike – just one day woken up knowing that she was simply waiting out her contract, stubbornly trying to endure long enough to serve out her term and return to Earth no poorer than she had set out.

Which was when her deviling had turned nasty, wasn't it? It was when she had started touching herself and telling MacArthur exactly what she was doing. When she'd started describing in detail all the things she'd never do to *him*.

It was a way of getting through one more day. It was a way of faking up enough emotion to care. It was a stupid, stupid thing to do.

And this was her punishment.

But she couldn't give up. She was going to have to... She didn't finish that thought. If she was going to do this unnamed thing, she had to sort through the ground rules first.

There were three rules. One: No Violence. Two: Protect Company Equipment. Three: Protect Yourself. One overruled Two and Two overruled Three.

Okay, Patang thought. In order to prevent violence, I'm going to have to destroy Company property.

She waited to see if she'd pass out.

Nothing happened.

Good.

She'd come to a long ridge, steep-sided and barren and set her suit to auto-climb. As she climbed, she scanned the slope ahead, empty and rock-strewn under a permanently dazzling cover of sulfuric acid clouds. Halfway up, MacArthur emerged from the zigzagging valley below and waved jauntily.

Patang ignored him. That pile of boulders up ahead was too large. Those to the right were too small. There was a patch of loose regolith that looked promising but... No. In the end, she veered leftward, toward a shallow ledge that sheltered rocks that looked loose enough to be dislodged but not massive enough to do any serious damage to MacArthur's suit. All she wanted was to sweep him off his feet. He could survive a slide downslope easily enough. But could he hold onto the laser drill while doing so?

Patang didn't think so.

Okay, then. She took her suit off automatics and climbed clumsily, carefully, toward her destination. She kept her helmet up, pointed toward the top of the ridge, to avoid tipping MacArthur off to her intentions.

Slantwise across the slope, that's right. Now straight up. She glanced back and saw that she'd pulled MacArthur into her wake. He was directly beneath her. Good. All systems go.

She was up to the ledge now.

Stop. Turn around. Look down on MacArthur, surprisingly close.

If there was one thing Patang knew, after all these months, it was how easy it was to start a landslide. Lean back and brace yourself here, and start kicking. And over the rocks go and over the rocks go and —

LASER HAZARD

"Ohhhh, Patang, you are so obvious. You climb diagonally up a slope that any ordinary person would tackle straight on. You change direction halfway up. What were you planning to do, start an avalanche? What did you think that would accomplish?"

"I thought I could get the laser away from you."

"And what good would that do? I'd still have the suit. I'd still have rocks. I'd still have you at my mercy. You hadn't really thought this one through, had you?"

"No," she admitted.

He flipped one hand dismissively. "Well, keep on going. We're not done yet."

Weeping, Patang topped the ridge and started downward, into a valley shaped like a deep bowl. Steep scarps on all sides caught whatever infrared bounced off the floor and threw it back into the valley. The temperature readings on her visor leaped. It was at least fifty degrees hotter out there than anyplace she had ever been. Hot enough that prolonged exposure would incapacitate her suit? Maybe. But there was MacArthur behind her, and no alternatives anywhere.

She stepped out into the open and looked across the valley.

The ground *dazzled.*

A network of cracks crazed the floor of the valley, each one blazing bright. Liquid metal was just oozing up out of the ground. She'd never seen anything like it.

Patang kicked a nearby puddle of metal, sending it scattering and setting off warning alarms in her suit. For an instant she swayed with sleepiness. But she shook it off. She snapped a stick-probe from her tool rack and jabbed it into the stuff.

Tin.

She looked up again. Little intersecting lines of molten tin everywhere. The pattern reminded her of her childhood on the Eastern Shore, of standing at the edge of a marsh, binoculars in hand, hoping for a harrier, with the silver gleam of sun on water almost painful to the eye. This looked just like a marsh, only with tin instead of water.

A tin marsh.

For an instant, wonder flickered to life within her. How could such a thing be? What complex set of geological conditions was responsible? All she could figure was that the noontide heat was involved. As it slowly sank into the rock, the tin below expanded and pushed its way up through the cracks. Or maybe it was the rocks that expanded, squeezing out the liquid tin. In either case the effect would be very small for any given volume. She couldn't imagine how much tin there must be down there to accomplish that. More than she'd ever dreamed they'd find.

"We're *rich!*" she whooped. She couldn't help it. All those months, all that misery, and here it was.

LASER HAZARD

LASER HAZARD

LASER HAZARD

"What are you talking about?" MacArthur said angrily. But Patang dared think he sounded almost sane. She dared hope she could reason with him.

"It's the big one, Mac!" She hadn't called him Mac in ages. "We've got the goddamned mother lode here. All you have to do is radio in the claim. It's all over, Mac! This time tomorrow, you're going to be holding a press conference about it."

For a moment, MacArthur stood, silent and confused. Then he said, "Maybe so. But I have to kill you first."

"You turn up without me, the Company's gonna have questions. They're gonna interrogate their suit. They're gonna run a mind-probe. No, MacArthur, you can't have both. You've got to choose: money or me."

LASER HAZARD

"*Run*, you bitch!" MacArthur howled. "Run like you've got a chance to live!"

She didn't move. "Think of it, MacArthur. A nice cold bath. They chill down the water with slabs of ice, and for a little extra they'll leave the ice in. You can hear it clink."

"Shut up."

"And ice cream!" she said fervently. "A thousand different flavors of ice cream. They've got it warehoused: sherbet, gelato, water ice...Oh, they know what a prospector likes, all right."

"Shut the fuck *up!*"

"You've been straight with me. You gave me a half-hour head start, just like you promised. Now I'm gonna be straight with you. I'm going to walk into this blind canyon. There's no way I can get out past you, okay? So you don't have to worry about me getting away. I'm going to go in there, and you stay out here and think about it, all right?" Then, desperation forcing her all the way into honesty: "I was wrong, MacArthur. I mean it this time. I shouldn't have done those things. Accept my apology. You can rise above it. You're a rich man now."

MacArthur roared with rage.

LASER HAZARD

LASER HAZARD

LASER HAZARD

LASER HAZARD

"Walk, damn you!" he screamed. "*Walk!*"

LASER HAZARD

LASER HAZARD

LASER HAZARD

He wasn't coming any closer. And, though he kept on firing, over and over, the bolts of lased light never hit her. It was baffling. She'd given up, she wasn't running, why didn't he just kill her? What was stopping him?

Revelation flooded Patang then, like sudden sunlight after a long winter. So simple! So obvious! She couldn't help laughing. "You *can't* shoot me! The suit won't *let* you!"

It was what the tech guys called "fossil software." Before the Company acquired the ability to insert their programs into human beings, they'd programmed their tools so they couldn't be used for sabotage. People, being inventive buggers, had found ways around that programming often enough to render it obsolete. But nobody had ever bothered to dig it out of the deep levels of the machinery's code. What would be the point?

She whooped and screamed. Her suit staggered in a jittery little dance of joy. "You *can't* kill me, MacArthur! You can't! You can't and you know it! I can just walk right past you, and all the way to the next station, and there's nothing you can do about it."

MacArthur began to cry.

The hopper came roaring down out of the white dazzle of the sky, and burnt a landing practically at their feet. They clambered wearily forward, and let the pilot bolt their muscle suits to the hopper's strutwork. There wasn't cabin space for them, and they didn't need it.

The pilot reclaimed his seat. After his first attempts at conversation had fallen flat, he'd said no more. He had hauled out prospectors before. He knew that small talk was useless.

With a crush of acceleration their suits could only partially cushion, the hopper took off. Only three hours to Port Ishtar. The hopper twisted and Patang could see Venus rushing dizzyingly by below her. She blanked out her visor so she didn't have to look at it.

Patang tested her suit. The multiplier motors had been powered down. She was immobile.

"Hey, Patang."

"Yeah?"

"You think I'm going to go to jail? For all the shit I did to you?"

"No, MacArthur. Rich people don't go to jail. They get therapy."

"That's good," he said. "Thank you for telling me that."

"*De nada*," she said without thinking. The jets rumbled under her back, making the suit vibrate. Two, three hours from now, they'd come down in Port Ishtar, stake their claims, collect their money, and never see each other again.

On impulse, she said, "Hey, MacArthur!"

"What?"

And for an instant she came *that close* to playing the Game one last time. Deviling him, just to hear his teeth grind. But....

"Nothing. Just – enjoy being rich, okay? I hope you have a good life."

"Yeah." MacArthur took a deep breath, and then let it go, as if he were releasing something painful, and said, "Yeah...you too."

And they soared.

An Episode of Stardust

THE LANKY, DONKEY-EARED FEY got onto the train at a nondescript station deep in the steppes of Fäerie Minor, escorted by two marshals in the uniform of His Absent Majesty's secret service. He smiled easily at the gawking passengers, as though he were a celebrity we had all come to see. One of the marshals was a sharp-featured woman with short red hair. The other was a tough-looking elf-bitch with skin so white it was almost blue. They both scowled in a way that discouraged questions.

The train returned to speed, and wheatfields flowed by the windows. This was the land where horses ate flesh and mice ate iron, if half the tales told of it were true, so doubtless the passing landscape was worth seeing. But I was born with a curiosity bump on the back of my skull, and I couldn't help wondering what the newcomer's crime had been, and what punishment he would receive when he arrived in Babylon.

So when, an hour or two later, the three of them got up from their seats and walked to the saloon car at the end of the train, I followed after them.

The usual mixture of unseelies and commercial travelers thronged the saloon, along with a dinter or two, a pair of flower sprites, and a lone ogre who weighed four hundred pounds if he were a stone. This last was so anxious to retrieve his beer when the duppy-man came by with a tray, that he stumbled into me and almost fell. "Watch where you're going, Shorty!" he barked. "You people are a menace."

"My people mined and smelted the tracks this train moves on," I said hotly. "We quarried the stone that clads the ziggurats at our destination, and delved the tunnel under the Gihon that we'll be passing through. If you have any complaints about us, I suggest you take them up with the Low Court. But if your problem is against me personally, then Gabbro Hornfelsson backs down from nobody." I thrust my calling card at his loathsome face. "Be it pistols, axes, or hand grenades, I'll happily meet you on the field of honor."

The ogre blanched and fled, his beer forgotten. I didn't blame him. A dwarf in full wrath is a fearsome opponent, no matter how big you may be.

"Well spoken, Master Hornfelsson!" The donkey-eared fey clapped lightly, perforce pulling the red marshal's hand to which he was cuffed above their table. She yanked it back down with a glare. "I've convinced my two companions that, the way to Babylon being long and without further stops, there's no harm in us having a drink or two together. If you were to join us, I'd be honored to pick up your tab as well."

I sat down beside him and nodded at the briefcase the white marshal held in her lap. "That's evidence, I presume. Can you tell me its nature?"

"No, he cannot," the red marshal snapped.

"Stardust, moonstones, rubies the size of plovers' eggs..." the fey said whimsically. "Or something equally valuable. It might well be promissory notes. I forget its exact nature but, given how alluring it was, you could hardly blame me for making a play for it."

"And yet, oddly enough," said the red marshal, "we do."

"My name is Nat Whilk," the fey said without annoyance. I couldn't help noticing his Armani suit and his manticore-leather shoes. "And I believe that I may say, without boasting, that in my time I have been both richer and poorer than anyone in this car. Once, I was both at the same time. It's a long tale, but — " here he smiled in a self-deprecating way — "if you have the patience, I certainly have nothing better to do."

A white-jacketed duppy came by then to take our orders. I asked for a Laphroaig, neat, and the two marshals called for beer. Minutes later, Nat Whilk took a long sip of his gin and tonic, and began to speak:

I was a gentleman in Babel once (Nat began) and not the scoundrel you see before you now. I ate from a silver trencher, and I speared my food with a gold knife. If I had to take a leak in the middle of the night, there were two servants to hold the bedpan and a third to shake my stick afterwards. It was no life for a man of my populist sensibilities. So one day I climbed out a window when nobody was looking and escaped.

You who had the good fortune of being born without wealth can have no idea how it felt. The streets were a kaleidoscope of pedestrians, and I was one of them, a moving speck of color, neither better nor worse than anyone else, and blissfully ignored by all. I was dizzy with excitement. My hands kept rising into the air like birds. My eyes danced to and fro, entranced by everything they saw.

It was glorious.

Down one street I went, turned a corner at random, and so by Brownian motion chanced upon a train station where I took a local to ground level. More purposefully then, I caught a rickshaw to the city limits and made my way outside.

The trooping fairies had come to Babel and set up a goblin market just outside the Ivory Gate. Vendors sold shish kabob and cotton candy, T-shirts and pashmina scarfs, gris-gris bags and enchanted swords, tame magpies and Fast Luck Uncrossing Power vigil candles. Charango players filled the air with music. I could not have been happier.

"Hey, shithead! Yeah, you – the ass with the ears! *Listen* when a lady speaks to you!"

I looked around.

"Up here, Solomon!"

The voice came from a booth whose brightly painted arch read *Rock! The! Fox!* At the end of a long canvas-walled alley, a vixen grinned at me from an elevated cage, her front feet tucked neatly under her and her black tongue lolling. Seeing she'd caught my eye, she leapt up and began padding quickly from one end of the cage to the other, talking all the while. "Faggot! Bed-wetter! Asshole! Your dick is limp and you throw like a girl!"

"Three for a dollar," a follet said, holding up a baseball. Then, mistaking my confusion for skepticism, he added, "Perfectly honest, *monsieur,*" and lightly tossed the ball into the cage. The vixen nimbly evaded it, then nosed it back out between the bars so that it fell to the ground below. "Hit the fox and win a prize."

There was a trick to it, I later learned. Though they looked evenly spaced, only the one pair of bars was wide enough that a baseball could get through. All the vixen had to do was avoid that spot and she was as safe as houses. But even without knowing the game was rigged, I didn't want to play. I was filled with an irrational love for everyone and everything. Today of all days, I would not see a fellow-creature locked in a cage.

"How much for the vixen?" I asked.

"*C'est impossible*," the follet said. "She has a mouth on her, sir. You wouldn't want her."

By then I had my wallet out. "Take it all." The follet's eyes grew large as dinner plates, and by this token I knew that I overpaid. But after all, I reasoned, I had plenty more in my carpetbag.

After the follet had opened the cage and made a fast fade, the vixen genuflected at my feet. Wheedlingly, she said, "I didn't mean none of the things I said, master. That was just patter, you know. Now that I'm yours, I'll serve you faithfully. Command and I'll obey. I shall devote my life to your welfare, if you but allow me to."

I put down my bag so I could remove the vixen's slave collar. Gruffly, I said, "I don't want your obedience. Do whatever you want, obey me in no matters, don't give a thought to my gods-be-damned welfare. You're free now."

"You can't mean that," the vixen said, shocked.

"I can and I do. So if you –"

"Sweet Mother of Beasts!" the vixen gasped, staring over my shoulder. "*Look out!*"

I whirled around, but there was nothing behind me but more booths and fairgoers. Puzzled, I turned back to the vixen, only to discover that she was gone.

And she had stolen my bag.

So it was that I came to learn exactly how freedom tastes when you haven't any money. Cursing the vixen and my own gullibility with equal venom, I put the goblin market behind me. Somehow I wound up on the bank of the Gihon. There I struck up a conversation with a waterman who motored me out to the docks and put me onto a tugboat captained by a friend of his. It was hauling a garbage scow upriver to Whinny Moor Landfill.

As it turned out, the landfill was no good place to be let off. Though there were roads leading up into the trashlands, there were none that led onward, along the river, where I wanted to go. And the smell! Indescribable.

A clutch of buildings huddled by the docks in the shadow of a garbage promontory. These were garages for the dump trucks mostly, but also Quonset hut repair and storage facilities and a few leftover brownstones with their windows bricked over that were used for offices and the like. One housed a bar with a sputtering neon sign saying *Brig-O-Doom*. In the parking lot behind it was, incongruously enough, an overflowing dumpster.

Here it was I fetched up.

I had never been hungry before, you must understand – not real, gnaw-at-your-belly hungry. I'd skipped breakfast that morning in my excitement over leaving, and I'd had the lightest of dinners the day before. On the tugboat I'd watched the captain slowly eat two sandwiches and an apple and been too proud to beg a taste from him. What agonies I suffered when he threw the apple core overboard! And now...

Now, to my horror, I found myself moving toward the dumpster. I turned away in disgust when I saw a rat skitter out from behind it. But it called me back. I was like a moth that's discovered a candle. I hoped there would be food in the dumpster, and I feared that if there were I would eat it.

It was then, in that darkest of hours, that I heard the one voice I had expected never to hear again. "Hey, shit-for brains! Ain'tcha gonna say you're glad to see me?"

Crouched atop a nearby utility truck was the vixen.

"You!" I cried, but did not add *you foul creature*, as my instincts bade me. Already, poverty was teaching me politesse. "How did you follow me here?"

"Oh, I have my ways."

Hope fluttered in my chest like a wild bird. "Do you still have my bag?"

"Of course I don't. What would a fox do with luggage? I threw it away. But I kept the key. Wasn't I a good girl?" She dipped her head, and a small key on a loop of string slipped from her neck and fell to the tarmac with a sharp *clink*.

"Idiot fox!" I cried. "What possible good is a key to a bag I no longer own?"

She told me.

The Brig o' Doom was a real dive. There was a black-and-white television up in one corner tuned to the fights and a pool table with ripped felt to the back. On the toilet door, some joker had painted *Tir na bOg* in crude white letters. I sat down at the bar. "Beer," I told the tappie.

"Red Stripe or Dragon Stout?"

"Surprise me."

When my drink came, I downed half of it in a single draft. It made my stomach ache and my head spin, but I didn't mind. It was the first sustenance I'd had in twenty-six hours. Then I turned around on the stool and addressed the bar as a whole: "I'm looking for a guide. Someone who can take me to a place in the landfill that I've seen in a vision. A place by a stream where garbage bags float up to the surface and burst with a terrible stench—"

A tokoloshe snorted. He was a particularly nasty piece of business, a hairy brown dwarf with burning eyes and yellow teeth. "Could be anywhere." The fossegrim sitting with him snickered sycophantically. It was clear who was the brains of this outfit.

" – and two bronze legs from the lighthouse of Rhodes lie half-buried in the reeds."

The tokoloshe hesitated, and then moved over to make space for me in his booth. The fossegrim, tall and lean with hair as white as a chimneysweeper's, leaned over the table to listen as he growled *sotto voce*, "What's the pitch?"

"There's a bag that goes with this key," I said quietly. "It's buried out there somewhere. I'll pay to find it again."

"Haughm," the tokoloshe said. "Well, me and my friend know the place you're looking for. And there's an oni I know can do the digging. That's three. Will you pay us a hundred each?"

"Yes. When the bag is found. Not before."

"How about a thousand?"

Carefully, I said, "Not if you're just going to keep jacking up the price until you find the ceiling."

"Here's my final offer: Ten percent of whatever's in the bag. Each." Then, when I hesitated, "We'll pick up your bar tab, too."

It was as the vixen had said. I was dressed as only the rich dressed, yet I was disheveled and dirty. That and my extreme anxiety to regain my bag told my newfound partners everything they needed to know.

"Twenty percent," I said. "Total. Split it however you choose. But first you'll buy me a meal – steak and eggs, if they have it."

The sun had set and the sky was yellow and purple as a bruise, turning to black around the edges. Into the darkness our pickup truck jolted by secret and winding ways. The grim drove and the tokoloshe took occasional swigs from a flask of Jeyes fluid, without offering me any. Nobody spoke. The oni, who could hardly have fit in the cab with us, sat in the bed with his feet dangling over the back. His name was Yoshi.

Miles into the interior of the landfill, we came to a stop above a black stream beside which lay two vast and badly corroded bronze legs. "Can you find a forked stick?" I asked.

The tokoloshe pulled a clothes hanger out of the mingled trash and clay. "Use this."

I twisted the wire into a wishbone, tied the key string to the short end, and took the long ends in my hands. The key hung a good half-inch off true. Then, stumbling over ground that crunched underfoot from buried rusty cans, I walked one way and the other, until the string hung straight down. "Here."

The tokoloshe brought out a bag of flour. "How deep do you think it's buried?"

"Pretty deep," I said. "Ten feet, I'm guessing."

He measured off a square on the ground – or, rather, surface, for the dumpings here were only hours old. At his command, Yoshi passed out shovels, and we all set to work.

When the hole reached six feet, it was too cramped for Yoshi to share. He was a big creature and all muscle. Two small horns sprouted from his forehead and a pair of short fangs jutted up from his jaw. He labored mightily, and the pile of excavated trash alongside the hole grew taller and taller. At nine feet, he was sweating like a pig. He threw a washing machine over the lip, and then stopped and grumbled, "Why am I doing all the work here?"

"Because you're stupid," the fossegrim jeered.

The tokoloshe hit him. "Keep digging," he told the oni. "I'm paying you fifty bucks for this gig."

"It's not enough."

"Okay, okay." The tokoloshe pulled a couple of bills from his pocket and gave them to me. "Take the pickup to the Brig-O and bring back a quart of beer for Yoshi."

I did then as stupid a thing as ever I've done in my life.

So far I'd been following the script the vixen had laid out for me, and everything had gone exactly as she'd said it would. Now, rather than playing along with the tokoloshe as she'd advised, I got my back up. We were close to finding the bag and, fool that I was, I thought they would share.

"Just how dumb do you think I am?" I asked. "You won't get rid of me that easily."

The tokoloshe shrugged. "Tough shit, Ichabod."

He and the fossegrim knocked me down. They duct-taped my ankles together and my wrists behind my back. Then they dumped me in the bed of the pickup. "Scream if you want to," the tokoloshe said. "We don't mind, and there's nobody else to hear you."

I was terrified, of course. But I'd barely had time to realize exactly how desperate my situation had become when Yoshi whooped, "I found it!"

The fossegrim and the tokoloshe scurried to the top of the unsteady trash pile. "Did you find it?" cried one, and the other said, "Hand it up."

"Don't do it, Yoshi!" I shouted. "There's money in that bag, a lot more than fifty dollars, and you can have half of it."

"Give me the bag," the tokoloshe said grimly.

By his side, the fossegrim was dancing excitedly. Bottles and cans rolled away from his feet. "Yeah," he said. "Hand it up."

But Yoshi hesitated. "Half?" he said.

"You can have it *all!*" I screamed. "Just leave me alive and it's yours!"

The tokoloshe stumbled down toward the oni, shovel raised. His buddy followed after in similar stance.

So began a terrible and comic fight, the lesser creatures leaping and falling on the unsteady slope, all the while swinging their shovels murderously, and the great brute enduring their blows and trying to seize hold of his tormentors. I could not see the battle – no more than a few slashes of the shovels – though I managed to struggle to my knees, for the discards from Yoshi's excavations rose too high. But I could hear it, the cursing and threats, the harsh clang of a shovel against Yoshi's head and the fossegrim's scream as one mighty hand finally closed about him.

Simultaneous with that scream there was a great clanking and sliding sound of what I can only assume was the tokoloshe's final charge. In my mind's eye I can see him now, racing downslope with the shovel held like a spear, its point aimed at Yoshi's throat. But whether blade ever connected with flesh or not I do not know, for it set the trash to slipping and sliding in a kind of avalanche.

Once started, the trash was unstoppable. Down it flowed, sliding over itself, all in motion. Down it flowed, rattling and clattering, land made liquid, yet for all that still retaining its brutal mass. Down it flowed, a force of nature, irresistible, burying all three so completely there was no chance that any of them survived.

Then there was silence.

"Well!" said the vixen. "That was a tidy little melodrama. Though I must say it would have gone easier on you if you'd simply done as I told you to in the first place." She was sitting on the roof of the cab.

I had never been so glad to see anybody as I was then. "This is the second time you showed up just when things were looking worst," I said, giddy with relief. "How do you manage it?"

"Oh, I ate a grain of stardust when I was a cub, and ever since then there's been nary a spot I can't get into or out of, if I set my mind to it."

"Good, good, I'm glad. Now, set me free!"

"Oh dear. I wish you hadn't said that."

"What?"

"Years ago and for reasons that are none of your business I swore a mighty oath never again to obey the orders of a man. That's why I've been tagging along after you – because you ordered me not to be concerned with your welfare. So of course I am. But now you've ordered me to free you, and thus I can't."

"Listen to me carefully," I said. "If you disobey an order from me, then you've obeyed my previous order not to obey me. So your oath is meaningless."

"I know. It's quite dizzying." The fox lay down, tucking her paws beneath her chest. "Here's another one: There's a barber in Seville who shaves everyone who doesn't shave himself, but nobody else. Now – "

"Please," I said. "I beg you. Sweet fox, dear creature, most adorable of animals…. If you would be so kind as to untie me out of the goodness of your heart and of your own free will, I'd be forever grateful to you."

"That's better. I was beginning to think you had no manners at all."

The vixen tugged and bit at the duct tape on my wrists until it came undone. Then I was able to free my ankles. We both got into the cab. Neither of us suggested we try digging for my bag. As far as I was concerned, it was lost forever.

But driving down out of the landfill, I heard a cough and glanced over at the vixen, sitting on the seat beside me. More than ever, I felt certain that she was laughing at me. "Your money's in a cardboard box under the seat," she said, "along with a fresh change of clothing – which, confidentially, you badly need – and the family signet ring. What's buried out there is only the bag, stuffed full of newspapers."

"My head aches," I said. "If you had my money all along, what was the point of this charade?"

"There's an old saying: Teach a man to fish, and he'll only eat when the fish are biting. Teach him a good scam, and the suckers will always bite." The vixen grinned. "A confidence trickster can always use a partner. We're partners now, you and me, ain't we?"

When the story ended, I stood and bowed. "Truly, sir, thou hast the gift of bullshit."

"Coming from a dwarf," Nat said, "that is high praise indeed."

One of the marshals – the white one – stood. "Too much beer," she said. "I have to use the powder room."

Her comrade looked pointedly at the briefcase, and in that glance and the way the marshal drew herself up at it, I read that the two women neither liked nor trusted each other. "Where could I go?" White asked.

"Where in the regulations does it say that makes any difference?" Red replied. "The evidence case must remain within sight of two designated agents at all times."

With a sigh, the white marshal freed herself from the briefcase and handcuffed it to her red-haired compatriot. Then she put her hand on my shoulder and said, "All right, Short Stuff, I'm deputizing you as a representative of His Absent Majesty's governance. Keep an eye on the case for the duration of my tinkle, okay?"

I didn't think much of her heightist slur, of course. But a gentleman doesn't go picking fights with ladies. "Fine," I said.

As soon as she was gone, Nat Whilk said, "That calls for a smoke." He held out a hand, twisted it about, and a Macanudo appeared between thumb and forefinger. He bit off the end and was about to conjure up a light when our duppy-man appeared at his elbow.

"I'm sorry, sir," the duppy said firmly. "But smoking is not allowed inside the train."

Nat shrugged. "Well, then. It's the rear platform or nothing, I suppose." He turned to his companion and said, "Shall we?" Then, when she hesitated, "I'm hardly likely to throw myself from the train. Not at these speeds."

His words convinced her. A c-note laid down on the table, and Nat's polite direction to the duppy to let me drink my fill and then pocket the change, made our two faces smile. I watched as he and the marshal stepped to the rear of the car, and through the door. Nat leaned against the rail. A wisp of smoke from the cigar was seized by the wind and flung away.

I watched them for a while. Then my second drink came. I had just taken my first sip of it when the white marshal returned.

"Where are they?" she cried.

"They went – " I gestured toward the rear platform, and froze. Through the door windows it could be seen that the platform was empty. Lamely, I said. "They were there a second ago."

"Sweet Mother of Night," the marshal cried, "that case contained over twenty ounces of industrial-grade stardust!"

We ran, the both of us, to the platform. When we got there, we saw two small figures in the distance, standing by the side of the track, waving. As we shouted and gestured, one of the two dwindled in size until it was no larger than a dog. It was red, like a fox, and I got the distinct impression it was laughing at us.

The fox trotted away. Nat Whilk followed it down a sandy track into the scrub. Our shouts dwindled to nothing as we realized how futile they were.

The train turned a bend and the two tricksters disappeared from our ken forever.

The Skysailor's Tale

OF ALL THE MANY THINGS that this life has stolen from me, the one which bothers me most is that I cannot remember burying my father.

Give that log a poke. Stir up the embers. Winter's upon us – hear how the wind howls and prowls about the rooftops, as restless as a cat! – and I, for one, could use some light and a little more warmth. There'll be snow by morning for sure. Scoot your chair a bit closer to the fire. Is your mother asleep? Good. We'll keep our voices low. There are parts of this tale she would not approve of. Things that I must say which she thinks you'd be better off not knowing.

She's right, no doubt. Women usually are. But what of that? You're of an age to realize that your parents were never perfect, and that in their youths they may have done some things which...well. Right or wrong, I'm going to tell you everything.

Where was I?

My father's burial.

I was almost a man when he finally died – old enough, by all rights, to keep that memory to my dying day. But after the wreck of the *Empire*, I lay feverish and raving, so they tell me, for six weeks. During that time I was an exile in my own mind, lost in the burning deserts of delirium, wandering lands that rose and fell with each labored breath. Searching for a way back to the moment when I stood before my father's open grave and felt its cool breath upon my face. I was convinced that if I could only find it, all would be well.

So I searched and did not find, and forgot I had searched, and began again, returning always to the same memories, like a moth relentlessly batting itself against a lantern. Sometimes the pain rose up within me so that I screamed and thrashed and convulsed within my bed.

Other times (all this they told me later), when the pain ebbed, I spoke long and lucidly on a variety of matters, sang strange songs, and told stranger tales, all with an intensity my auditors found alarming. My thoughts were never still.

Always I sought my father.

By the time I finally recovered, most of my life had been burnt to ashes and those ashes swept into the ash pit of history. The Atlantis of my past was sunk; all that remained were a few mountain tops sticking up out of the waters of forgetfulness like a scattered archipelago of disconnected islands. I remembered clambering upon the rusted ruins of a failed and demented steam dredging device its now forgotten inventor had dubbed the "Orukter Amphibolus," a brickyard battle fought alongside my fellow river rats with a gang of German boys who properly hated us for living by the wharves, a furtive kiss in the dark (with whom, alas, I cannot say), a race across the treacherously rolling logs afloat in the dock fronting the blockmaker's shop, and the catfish-and-waffles supper in a Wissahickon inn at which my mother announced to the family that she was to have a fifth child. But neither logic nor history unites these events; they might as well have happened to five separate people.

There are, too, odd things lacking in what remains: The face of my youngest sister. The body of equations making up the Calculus. All recollection whatsoever of my brother save his name alone. My father I can remember well only by contrast. All I know of him could be told in an hour.

I do not mourn the loss of his funeral. I've attended enough to know how it went. Words were surely spoken that were nothing like the words that should have been said. The air was heavy with incense and candle-wax. The corpse looked both like and unlike the deceased. There were pallbearers, and perhaps I was one. Everybody was brave and formal. Then, after too long a service, they all left, feeling not one whit better than before.

A burial is a different matter. The first clods of dirt rattle down from the grave diggers' shovels onto the roof of the coffin, making a sound like rain. The earth is drawn up over it like a thick, warm blanket. The trees wave in the breeze overhead, as if all the world were a cradle endlessly rocking. The mourners' sobs are as quiet as a mother's bedtime murmurs. And so a man passes, by imperceptible degrees, to his final sleep. There is some comfort in knowing that a burial came off right.

So I trod the labyrinth of my fevered brain, dancing with the black goddess of pain, she of the bright eyes laughing and clutching me tight with fingers like hot iron, and I swirling and spinning and always circling in upon that sad event. Yet never quite arriving.

Dreaming of fire.

Often I came within minutes of my goal – so close that it seemed impossible that my next attempt would not bring me to it. One thought deeper, a single step further, I believed, and there it would be. I was tormented with hope.

Time and again, in particular, I encountered two memories bright as sunlight in my mind, guarding the passage to and from that dark omphalos. One was of the voyage out to the Catholic cemetery on Treaty Island in the Delaware. First came the boat carrying my father's coffin and the priest. Father Murphy sat perched in the bow, holding his hat down with one hand and with the other gripping the gunwale for all he was worth. He was a lean old hound of a man with wispy white hair, who bobbed and dipped most comically with every stroke of the oars and wore the unhappy expression of the habitually seasick.

I sat in the second dory of the procession with my mother and sisters, all in their best bonnets. Jack must have been there as well. Seeing Father Murphy's distress, we couldn't help but be amused. One of us wondered aloud if he was going to throw up, and we all laughed.

Our hired doryman turned to glare at us over his shoulder. He did not understand what a release my father's death was for all of us. The truth was that everything that had gone into making John Keely the man he was – his upright character, his innkeeper's warmth, his quiet strength, his bluff good will – had died years before, with the dwindling and extinction of his mind. We were only burying his body that day.

When he was fully himself, however, a better or godlier man did not exist in all the Americas – no, not in a thousand continents. I never saw him truly angry but once. That was the day my elder sister Patricia, who had been sent out to the back alley for firewood, returned empty-handed and said, "Father, there is a black girl in the shed, crying."

My parents threw on their roquelaures and put up the hoods, for the weather was foul as only a Philadelphia winter downpour can be, and went outside to investigate. They came back in with a girl so slight, in a dress so drenched, that she looked to my young eyes like a half-drowned squirrel.

They all three went into the parlor and closed the doors. From the hall Patricia and I – Mary was then but an infant – tried to eavesdrop, but could hear only the murmur of voices punctuated by occasional sobs. After a while, the tears stopped. The talk continued for a very long time.

Midway through the consultation, my mother swept out of the room to retrieve the day's copy of the *Democratic Press*, and returned so preoccupied that she didn't chase us away from the door. I know now, as I did not then, that the object of her concern was an advertisement on the front page of the paper. Patricia, always the practical and foresightful member of the family, cut out and saved the advertisement, and so I can now give it to you exactly as it appeared:

SIX CENTS REWARD

RANAWAY on the 14th inst., from the subscriber, one TACEY BROWN, a mulatto girl of thirteen years age, with upwards of five years to serve on her indenture. She is five feet, one inch in height, pitted with the Small Pox, pert and quick spoken, took with her one plain brown dress of coarse cloth.

In personality she is insolent, lazy, and disagreeable. The above reward and no thanks will be given to any person who will take her up and return her to

Thos. Cuttington

No. 81, Pine street, Philadelphia

This at a time, mind you, when the reward for a runaway apprentice often ran as high as ten dollars! Mr. Thomas Cuttington obviously thought himself a man grievously ill-served.

At last my father emerged from the parlor with the newspaper in his hand. He closed the door behind him. His look then was so dark and stormy that I shrank away from him, and neither my sister nor I dared uncork any of the questions bubbling up within us. Grimly, he fetched his wallet and then, putting on his coat, strode out into the rain.

Two hours later he returned with one Horace Potter, a clerk from Flintham's counting house, and Tacey's indenture papers. The parlor doors were thrown wide and all the family, and our boarders as well, called in as witnesses. Tacey had by then been clothed by my mother in one of Patricia's outgrown dresses, and since my sister was of average size for a girl her age, Tacey looked quite lost in it. She had washed her face, but her expression was tense and unreadable.

In a calm and steady voice, my father read the papers through aloud, so that Tacey, who could neither read nor write, might be assured they were truly her deed of service. Whenever he came to a legal term with which she might not be familiar, he carefully explained it to the child, with Mr. Potter – who stood by the hearth, warming his hands – listening intently and then nodding with judicious approval. Then he showed her the signature of her former master, and her own mark as well.

Finally, he placed the paper on the fire.

When the indenture went up in flame, the girl made a sound unlike anything I have ever heard before or since, a kind of wail or shriek, the sort of noise a wild thing makes. Then she knelt down before my father and, to his intense embarrassment, seized and kissed his hand.

So it was that Tacey came to live with us. She immediately became like another sister to me. Which was to say that she was a harsh, intemperate termagant who would take not a word of direction, however reasonably I phrased it, and indeed ordered me about as if it were *I* who was *her* servant! She was the scourge of my existence. When she was seventeen – and against my mother's horrified advice – she married a man twice her age and considerably darker-skinned, who made a living waiting upon the festivities of the wealthy. Julius Nash was a grave man. People said of him that even his smile was stern. Once, when he was courting her and stood waiting below-stairs, I, smarting from a recent scolding, angrily blurted out, "How can you put up with such a shrew?"

That solemn man studied me for a moment, and then in a voice so deep it had often been compared to a funerary bell replied, "Mistress

Tacey is a woman of considerable strength of character and that, I have found, is far to be preferred over a guileful and flattering tongue."

I had not been looking to be taken seriously, but only venting boyish spleen. Now I stood abashed and humbled by this Negro gentleman's thoughtful reply – and doubly humiliated, I must admit, by the source of my mortification. Then Tacey came stepping down the stairs with a tight, triumphant smirk and was gone, to reappear in my tale only twice more.

Yet if this seems to you an unlikely thing that my father would be so generous to a mulatto girl he did not know and who could do him no conceivable benefit, then I can only say that you did not know this good man. Moreover, I am convinced by the high regard in which he was held by all who knew him that this was but one of many comparable deeds, and notable only in that by its circumstances we were made aware of it.

How changed was my poor father's condition when last I saw him alive! That was the time my mother took me to the insane ward at Pennsylvania Hospital to visit him.

It was a beautiful, blue-skyed day in June.

I was fifteen years old.

Philadelphia was a wonderful place in which to be young, though I did not half appreciate it at that time. Ships arrived in the harbor every day with silk and camphor from Canton, hides from Valparaiso, and opium from Smyrna, and departed to Batavia and Malacca for tin, the Malabar coast for sandalwood and pepper, and around the Cape Horn with crates of knives and blankets to barter with credulous natives for bales of sea otter skins. Barbarously tattooed sailors were forever staggering from the groggeries singing oddly-cadenced chanteys and pitching headlong into the river, or telling in vivid detail of a season lived naked among cannibals, married to a woman whose teeth had been filed down to points, all the while and with excruciating exactitude slowly unwrapping an oilcloth packet unearthed from the bottom of a sea-chest to reveal at the climax of the yarn: a mummified human ear. The harbor was a constant source of discontent for me.

As were the grain wagons which came down the turnpike from

Lancaster and returned west laden with pioneers and missionaries bound for the continental interior to battle savage Indians or save their souls for Christ, each according to his inclination. Those who stayed behind received packages from their distant relations containing feathered head-pieces, cunningly woven baskets, beadwork cradleboards, and the occasional human scalp. Every frontiersman who headed up the pike took a piece of my soul with him.

Our hotel was located in that narrow slice of streets by the Delaware which respectable folk called the wharflands, but which, because a brick wall two stories high with an iron fence atop it separated Water street from Front street (the two ran together; but Water street served the slow-moving wagon trade of the wharves, and Front street the dashing gigs and coaches of the social aristocracy), we merchants' brats thought of as the Walled City. Our streets were narrow and damp, our houses and stores a bit ramshackle, our lives richly thronged with provincial joys.

Philadelphia proper, by contrast, was the sort of place where much was made of how wide and clean and grid-like the streets were, and a Frenchman's casual gallant reference to it as "the Athens of America" would be quoted and re-quoted until Doomsday. Yet, within its limits, it was surprisingly cosmopolitan.

The European wars had filled the city with exiles – the vicomte de Noailles, the duc d'Orléans, a hundred more. The former Empress Iturbide of Mexico could be seen hurrying by in her ludicrously splendid carriage. In the restaurants and bookshops could be found General Moreau, a pair of Murats, and a brace of Napoleons, were one to seek them out. The count de Survilliers, who had been King of Spain, had his own pew in St. Joseph's Church off Willing's alley. We often saw him on the way there of a Sunday, though we ourselves went to St. Mary's, half a block away, for our family had sided with the trustees in the church fight which had resulted in the bishop being locked out of his own cathedral. Charles Lucien Bonaparte, who was a naturalist, could be encountered stalking the marshes at the edge of town or along the river, in forlorn search of a new species of plover or gull to name after himself.

Still, and despite its museums and circuses, its (one) theater and (one) library and (three) wax-works, the city was to a young river rat little more than an endless series of enticements to leave. Everything of any interest at all to me had either come from elsewhere or was outward bound.

But I seem to have lost the thread of my tale. Well, who can blame me? This is no easy thing to speak of. Still, I set out to tell you of my final memory – would to God it were not! – of my father when he was alive.

And so I shall.

My mother and I walked to the hospital together. She led, concentrated and brisk, while I struggled not to lag behind. Several times she glared me back to her side.

For most of that mile-and-some walk from our boarding-house, I managed not to ask the question most vexing my mind, for fear it would make me sound lacking in a proper filial piety. Leaving the shelter of the Walled City at Market street, we went first south on Front then up Black Horse alley, while I distracted myself by computing the area between two curves, and then turning down Second past the malt houses and breweries to Chestnut and so west past the Philadelphia Dispensary, where I tried to recall the method Father Tourneaux had taught me for determining the volume of tapering cylindrical solids. South again on Third street, past the tannery and the soap-boiler's shop and chandlery, I thought about Patricia's husband, Aaron, who was in the China trade. Somebody – could it have been Jack? – had recently asked him if he planned someday to employ me as a navigator on one of his ships, and he had laughed in a way that said neither yea nor nay. Which gave me much to ponder. We cut through Willing's alley, my mother being a great believer that distances could be shortened through cunning navigation (I ducked my head and made the sign of the cross as we passed St. Joseph's), and jogged briefly on Fourth. One block up Prune street, a tawny redhead winked at me and ducked down Bingham's court before I could decide whether she were real or just a rogue memory. But I was like the man commanded not to think about a rhinoceros, who found he could think of nothing else. At last, the pressures of curiosity and resentment grew so great that the membrane of my resolve ruptured and burst.

"I do not fully understand," I said, striving for a mature and measured tone but succeeding only in sounding petulant, "exactly what is expected of me." I had not been to see my father – it had been made clear that I was not to see him – since the day he entered the hospital. That same day my littlest sister had fled the house in terror, while this gentlest of men overturned furniture and shouted defiance at unseen demons. The day it was decided he could no longer be cared for at home. "Is today special for any reason? What ought I to do when I see him?"

I did not ask "Why?" but that was what I meant, and the question my mother answered.

"I have my reasons," she said curtly. "Just as I have good and sufficient reason for not informing you as to their exact nature just yet." We had arrived at the hospital grounds, and the gatekeeper had let us in.

My mother led me down the walk under the buttonwood trees to the west wing. A soft southern breeze alleviated the heat. The hospital buildings were situated within a tract of farmland which had been preserved within the city limits so that the afflicted could refresh themselves with simple chores. Closing my eyes, I can still smell freshmown hay, and hear the whir of a spinning wheel. Sunflowers grew by the windows, exactly like that sunflower which had appeared like a miracle one spring between the cobbles of our back alley and lasted into the autumn without being trampled or torn down, drawing goldfinches and sentimental young women. You could not wish for a more pleasant place in which to find your father imprisoned as a lunatic.

The cell-keeper's wife came to the door and smiled a greeting.

My mother thrust a banana into my hand. "Here. You may give him this." Which was the first intimation I had that she was not to accompany me.

She turned and crunched off, down the gravel path.

The cell-keeper's wife led me through the ward to a room reserved for visitors. I cannot recall its furniture. The walls were whitewashed. A horsefly buzzed about in the high corners, irritably seeking a passage into the outer world.

"Wait here," the woman said. "I'll summon an attendant to bring him."

She left.

For a long still time I stood, waiting. Eventually I sat down and stared blindly about. Seeing nothing and thinking less. Hating the horsefly.

The banana was warm and brownish-yellow in my hand.

Aeons passed. Sometimes there were noises in the hall. Footsteps would approach, and then recede. They were never those of the man I fearfully awaited.

Finally, however, the door opened. There was my father, being led by the arm by a burly young attendant. He shuffled into the room. The attendant placed him in a chair and left, locking the door behind him.

My father, who had always been a rather plump man, with a merchant's prosperous stomach, was now gaunt and lean. His flesh hung loosely about him; where his face had been round, loose jowls now hung.

"Hello, Father," I said.

He did not respond. Nor would he meet my eyes. Instead, his gaze moved with a slow restlessness back and forth across the floor, as if he had misplaced something and were trying to find it.

Miserably, I tried to make conversation.

"Mary finished making her new dress yesterday. It's all of green velvet. The exact same color as that of the cushions and sofa and drapes in Mr. Barclay's parlor. When Mother saw the cloth she had chosen, she said, 'Well, I know one place you won't be wearing that.'"

I laughed. My father did not.

"Oh, and you recall Stephen Girard, of course. He had a cargo of salt at his wharf last summer which Simpson refused to buy – trying to cheapen it to his own price, you see. Well, he said to his porter, 'Tom, why can't you buy that cargo?' and Tom replied, 'Why, sir, how can I? I have no money.' But 'Never mind,' said Girard, 'I'll advance you the cost. Take it and sell it by the load, and pay me as you can.' That was last summer, as I said, and now the porter is well on his way to being Simpson's chief rival in the salt trade."

When this anecdote failed to rouse my father – who had avidly followed the least pulsation in the fortunes of our merchant neighbors,

and loved best to hear of sudden success combined with honest labor
—I knew that nothing I could hope to say would serve to involve him.

"Father, do you know who I am?" I had not meant to ask—the question just burst out of me.

This roused some spirit in the man at last. "Of course I know. Why wouldn't I know?" He was almost belligerent, but there was no true anger behind his words. They were all bluff and empty bluster and he still would not meet my eyes. "It's as clear as...as clear as two plus two is four. That's...that's logic, isn't it? Two plus two is four. That's logic."

On his face was the terrible look of a man who had failed his family and knew it. He might not know the exact nature of his sin, but the awareness of his guilt clearly ate away at him. My presence, the presence of someone he ought to know, only made matters worse.

"I'm your son," I said. "Your son, William."

Still he would not meet my eyes.

How many hours I languished in the Purgatory of his presence I do not know. I continued to talk for as long as I could, though he obviously could make no sense of my words, because the only alternative to speech was silence—and such silence as was unbearable to think upon. A silence that would swallow me whole.

All the time I spoke, I clutched the banana. There was no place I could set it down. Sometimes I shifted it from one hand to the other. Once or twice I let it lie uncomfortably in my lap. I was constantly aware of it. As my throat went dry and I ran out of things to say, my mind focused itself more and more on that damnable fruit.

My mother always brought some small treat with her when she visited her husband. She would not be pleased if I returned with it. This I knew. But neither did I relish the thought of emphasizing the cruel reversal in our roles, his abject helplessness and my relative ascendancy, by feeding him a trifle exactly as he had so often fed me in my infancy.

In an anguish, I considered my choices. All terrible. All unacceptable.

Finally, more to rid myself of the obligation than because I thought it the right thing to do, I offered the loathsome thing to my father.

He took it.

Eyes averted, he unhurriedly peeled the banana. Without enthusi-asm, he bit into it. With animal sadness he ate it.

That is the one memory that, try as I might, I cannot nor ever will be able to forgive myself for: That I saw this once-splendid man, now so sad and diminished, eating a banana like a Barbary ape.

But there's a worse thing I must tell you: For when at last I fell silent, time itself congealed about me, extending itself so breathlessly that it seemed to have ceased altogether. Years passed while the sunlight remained motionless on the whitewashed wall. The horsefly's buzzing ceased, yet I knew that if I raised my head I would see it still hanging in the air above me. I stared at my poor ruined father in helpless hor-ror, convinced that I would never leave that room, that instant, that sorrow. Finally, I squeezed my eyes tight shut and imagined the atten-dant coming at last to lead my father away and restore me again to my mother.

In my imagination, I burst into tears. It was some time before I could speak again. When I could, I said, "Dear God, Mother! How could you do this to me?"

"I required," she said, "your best estimation of his condition."

"You visit him every day." One of my hands twisted and rose up imploringly, like that of a man slowly drowning. "You must know how he is."

She did not grip my hand. She offered no comfort. She did not apol-ogize. "I have stood by your father through sickness and health," she said, "and will continue to do so for as long as he gains the least com-fort from my visits. But I have for some time suspected he no longer rec-ognizes me. So I brought you. Now you must tell me whether I should continue to come here."

There was steel in my mother, and never more so than at that moment. She was not sorry for what she had done to me. Nor was she wrong to have done it.

Even then I knew that.

"Stay away," I said, "and let your conscience be at ease. Father is gone from us forever."

But I could not stop crying. I could not stop crying. I could not stop crying. Back down the streets of Philadelphia I walked, for all to see and marvel at, bawling like an infant, hating this horrible life and hating myself even more for my own selfish resentment of my parents, who were each going through so much worse than I. Yet even as I did so, I was acutely aware that still I sat in that timeless room and that all I was experiencing was but a projection of my imagination. Nor has that sense ever gone entirely away. Even now, if I still my thoughts to nothing, this world begins to fade and I sense myself to still be sitting in my father's absence.

From this terrible moment I fled, and found myself back upon the dory, returning from my father's burial. Our hearts were all light and gay. We chattered as the doryman, head down, plied his oars.

My baby sister Barbara was trailing a hand in the water, a blaze of light where her face should have been, hoping to touch a fish.

"Will," said Mary in a wondering voice. "Look." And I followed her pointing finger upward. I turned toward the east, to the darkening horizon above Treaty Island and the New Jersey shore, where late afternoon thunderheads were gathering.

Scudding before the storm and moving straight our way was a structure of such incredible complexity that the eye could make no sense of it. It filled the sky. Larger than human mind could accept, it bore down upon us like an aerial city out of the Arabian Nights, an uncountable number of hulls and platforms dependent from a hundred or more balloons.

Once, years before, I had seen a balloon ascent. Gently the craft had severed its link with the Earth, gracefully ascending into the sky, a floating island, a speck of terrestriality taken up into the kingdom of the air. Like a schooner it sailed, dwindling, and away. It disappeared before it came anywhere near the horizon.

If that one balloon was a schooner, than this was an armada. Where that earlier ship had been an islet, a mote of wind-borne land carried into the howling wilderness of the air, what confronted me now was a mighty continent of artifice.

It was a monstrous sight, made doubly so by the scurrying specks which swarmed the shrouds and decks of the craft and which, once recognized as men, magnified the true size of the thing beyond believing.

The wind shifted, and the thunder of its engines filled the universe.

That was my first glimpse of the mighty airship *Empire*.

The world turned under my restless mind, dispelling sunshine and opening onto rain. Two days casually disappeared into the fold. I was lurching up Chestnut street, water splashing underfoot, arms aching, almost running. Mary trotted alongside me, holding an umbrella over the twenty-quart pot I carried, and still the rain contrived to run down the back of my neck.

"Not so fast!" Mary fretted. "Don't lurch about like that. You'll trip and spill."

"We can't afford to dawdle. Why in heaven's name did Mother have to leave the pot so long over the fire?"

"It's obvious you'll never be a cook. The juices required time to addle; otherwise the stew would be cold and nasty upon arrival."

"Oh, there'll be no lack of heat where we're going, I assure you. Tacey will make it hot enough and then some."

"Get on with you. She won't."

"She will. Tacey is a despot in the kitchen, Napoleon reborn, reduced in stature but expanded in self-conceit. She is a Tiberius Claudius Nero *in parvum* when she has a spoon in her hand. Never since Xanthippe was such a peppery tongue married to such a gingery spirit. A lifetime of kitchen fires have in the kettle of her being combined –"

Mary laughed, and begged me to stop. "You make my sides ache!" she cried. And so of course I continued.

" – to make of her a human pepper pot, a snapper soup seasoned with vinegar, a simmering mélange of Hindoo spices whose effect is to make not one's tongue but one's ears burn. She –"

"Stop, stop, stop!"

Parties were being held all over town in honor of the officers and crew of the *Empire*, and the first aerial crossing of the Atlantic. There were nearly a thousand crewmen all told, which was far too many to be feted within a single building. Mary and I were bound for a lesser gathering at the Library Company, presided over by a minor Biddle and catered by Julius Nash and his crew of colored waiters.

We were within sight of our destination when I looked up and saw my future.

Looming above the Walnut Street Prison yard, tethered by a hundred lines, was the *Empire*, barely visible through the grey sheets of rain. It dwarfed the buildings beneath. Gusts of wind tugged and shoved at the colorless balloons, so that they moved slightly, darkness within darkness, like an uneasy dream shifting within a sleeper's mind.

I gaped, and stepped in a puddle so deep the water went over my boot. Stumbling, I crashed to one knee. Mary shrieked.

Then I was up and hobbling-running again, as fast I could. My trousers were soaked with ice-cold water, and my knee blazed with pain, but at least the pot was untouched.

It was no easy life, being the eldest son in a family dependent upon a failing boarding-house. Constant labor was my lot. Not that I minded labor — work was the common lot of everyone along the docks, and cheerily enough submitted to. It was the closing of prospects that clenched my soul like an iron fist.

In those days I wanted to fly to the Sun and build a palace on the Moon. I wanted to tunnel to the dark heart of the Earth and discover rubies and emeralds as large as my father's hotel. I wanted to stride across the land in seven-league boots, devise a submersible boat and with it discover a mermaid nation under the sea, climb mountains in Africa and find leopards at their snowy peaks, descend Icelandic volcanos to fight fire-monsters and giant lizards, be marked down in the history books as the first man to stand naked at the North Pole. Rumors that the *Empire* would be signing replacements for those airmen who had died during the flight from London ate at my soul like a canker.

Father Tourneaux had had great hopes that I might one day be called to the priesthood, preferably as a Jesuit, and when I was younger my mother had encouraged this ambition in me with tales of martyrdom by Iroquois torture and the unimaginable splendors of the Vatican state. But, like so much else, that dream had died a slow death with the dwindling and wasting away of my father.

In prosperous times, a port city offered work enough and opportunity in plenty for any ambitious young man. But Philadelphia had not yet recovered from the blockades of the recent war. The posting my brother-in-law had as good as promised me had vanished along with two ships of his nascent fleet, sacrificed to the avarice of British power. The tantalizing possibility that there might be money found to send me to the University of Paris to study mathematics had turned to pebbles and mist as well. My prospects were nonexistent.

Mary grabbed my arm and dragged me around. "Will – you're dreaming again! You've walked right past the doorway."

Tacey Nash saw us come in. Eyes round with outrage, she directed at me a glare that would have stunned a starling, had one been unlucky enough to fly through its beam. "Where have you been?"

I set the pot down on a table, and proceeded to unwrap layers of newspapers and old blanket scraps from its circumference. "Mother insisted that – "

"Don't talk back." She lifted the lid and with it wafted the steam from the stewed oysters toward her nostrils. They flared as the scent of ginger reached them. "Ah." Briefly her face softened. "Your mother still knows how to cook."

One of the waiters placed the pot over a warming stove. Mary briskly tied on an apron – with Patricia married and out of the house, she'd assumed the role of the practical sister and, lacking Patty's organizational genius, tried to compensate with energy – and with a long spoon gave the pot a good stir. Another waiter brought up tureens, and she began filling them.

"Well?" Tacey said to me. "Are you so helpless that you cannot find any work to do?"

So the stew had come in time, after all! Relieved, I glanced over my shoulder and favored my sister with a grin. She smiled back at me, and for one warm instant, all was well.

"Where shall I start?" I asked.

Why was I so unhappy in those days? There was a girl and I had loved her in my way, and thought she loved me too. One of us tired of the other, and so we quarreled and separated, to the eternal misery of both. Or so I assume – I retain not a jot of this hypothetical affair, but considering my age, it seems inevitable. Yet it was not a romantic malaise I suffered from, but a disease more all-encompassing.

I was miserable with something far worse than love.

I had a hunger within me for something I could neither define nor delimit. And yet at the same time I suffered the queasy fullness of a man who has been at the table one hour too many. I felt as if I had swallowed several live cats which were now proceeding to fight a slow, sick, unending war within me. If I could, I would have vomited up everything – cats, girl, wharves, boarding-house, city, world, my entire history to date – and only felt the better for being rid of them. Every step I took seemed subtly off-balance. Every word I said sounded exactly wrong. Everything about me – my soul, mind, thought, and physical being – was in my estimation thoroughly detestable.

I had no idea then what was wrong with me.

Now I know that I was simply young.

I suppose I should describe that makeshift kitchen, set up within the Loganian Annex of the Library. The warming pans steaming. The elegant black men with their spotless white gloves bustling out with tureens of stew and returning with bowls newly emptied of punch. How, for the body of the meal, the waiters stood behind the airmen (who, though dressed in their finest, were still a raffish lot), refilling their plates and goblets, to the intense embarrassment of everyone save the officers, who were of course accustomed to such service, and how Julius himself stood by the dignitaries' table, presiding over all, with here a quiet signal to top up an alderman's glass, and there a solemn pleasantry as he spooned cramberries onto the plate of the ranking officer.

Yet that is mere conjecture. What I retain of that dinner is, first, the order of service, and second, the extraordinary speech that was made at its conclusion, most of which I missed from being involved in a conversation of my own, and its even more extraordinary aftermath. No more. The kitchen, for all of me, may as well not have existed at all.

The menu was as follows:

To begin, *fish-house punch*, drunk with much merriment.

Then, *oyster stew*, my mother's, eaten to take the edge off of appetites and quickly cleared away.

Finally, the dinner itself, in two courses, the first of which was:

 roasted turkey stuffed with bread, suet, eggs, sweet herbs

 tongue pie made with apples and raisins

 chicken smothered in oysters with parsley sauce

 served with boiled onions

     cramberries

     mangoes

     pickled beans

     celery

     pickled beets

     conserve of rose petals

     braised lambs quarters

     red quince preserves

Followed by the second course of:

 trout poached in white wine and vinegar

 stew pie made of veal

 alamode round of beef, corned and stuffed with beef, pork,
  bread, butter, salt, pepper, savory and cayenne; braised

 served with french beans

     parsnips

     purple spotted lettuce and salat herbs

     pickled cucumbers

     spinach

     roasted potatoes

     summer pears

     white, yellow, and red quince preserves

Finally, after the table had been cleared and deserted:

 soft gingerbread

 Indian pudding

 pumpkin pie

 cookies, both almond and cinnamon

Each course of which was, in the manner of the times, served up all at once in a multitude of dishes, so as to fill the tables complete and impress the diners with an overwhelming sense of opulence and plenty. Many a hungry time in my later adventures I would talk myself to sleep by repeating each dish several times over in my mind, recollecting its individual flavor, and imagining myself so thoroughly fed that I turned dishes away untasted.

Thus do we waste our time and fill our minds with trivialities, while all the time the great world is falling rapidly into the past, carrying our loved ones and all we most value away from us at the rate of sixty seconds per minute, sixty minutes per hour, eight thousand seven hundred sixty-six hours per year!

So much for the food. Let me now describe the speech.

The connection between the Loganian and the main library was through a wide upper-level archway with stairs descending to the floor on either side of the librarian's desk. It was a striking, if inefficient, arrangement which coincidentally allowed us to easily spy upon the proceedings below.

When the final sweets and savories had been placed upon the tables, the waiters processed up the twin stairs, and passed through the Loganian to a small adjacent room for a quiet meal of leftovers. I went to the archway to draw the curtain shut, and stayed within its shadows, looking down upon the scene.

The tables were laid so that they filled the free space on the floor below, with two shoved together on the eastern side of the room for the officers and such city dignitaries – selectmen and flour merchants, mostly – who could not aspire to the celebration in Carpenter's Hall. All was motion and animation. I chanced to see one ruffian reach out to remove a volume from the shelves and, seeing a steelpoint engraving he admired, slide the book under the table, rip the page free, and place it, folded, within the confines of his jacket. Yet that was but one moment in such a menagerie of incident as would have challenged the hand of a Hogarth to record.

Somebody stood – Biddle, I presume – and struck an oratorical stance. From my angle, I could see only his back. Forks struck goblets for silence, so that the room was briefly filled with the song of dozens of glass crickets.

The curtains stirred, and Socrates joined me, plate in hand and gloves stuffed neatly into his sash. "Have I missed anything?" he whispered.

I knew Socrates only slightly, as one who was in normal conditions the perfect opposite of his master, Julius: the most garrulous of men, a fellow of strange fancies and sudden laughter. But he looked sober enough now. I shook my head, and we both directed our attention downward.

"...the late unpleasantness between our two great nations," the speaker was saying. "With its resolution, let the admiration the American people have always held for our British kindred resume again its rightful place in the hearts of us all."

Now the curtains stirred a second time, and Tacey appeared. Her countenance was as stormy as ever. Quietly, she said, "What is this nonsense Mary tells me about you going up Wissahickon to work in a mill?"

There was an odd stirring among the airmen, a puzzled exchange of glances.

Turning away from the speaker, I said, "I intended to say good-bye to you before I left."

"You've been intending to say good-bye to me since the day we met. So you do mean it, then?"

"I'm serious," I admitted.

Those dark, alert eyes flicked my way, and then back. "Oh, yes, you would do well in the mills – I don't think."

"Tacey, I have little choice. There is no work to be had on the wharves. If I stay at home, I burden Mother with the expense of my upkeep, and yet my utmost labor cannot increase her income by a single boarder. She'll be better off with my room empty and put out to let."

"Will Keely, you are a fool. What future can there be for you performing manual labor in a factory? There are no promotions. The mill owners all have five sons apiece – if a position of authority arises, they have somebody close at hand and dear to their hearts to fill it. They own, as well, every dwelling within an hour's walk of the mills. You must borrow from your family to buy your house from them. For years you scrimp, never tasting meat from month to month, working from dawn to dusk, burying pennies in the dirt beneath your bed, with never a hope of earning enough to attract a decent wife. Then the owners declare that there is no longer a market for their goods, and turn out most of their employees. There is no work nearby, so the laborers must sell their houses. Nobody will buy them, however low the price may be, save the mill owners. Who do, for a pittance, because six months later they will begin hiring a new batch of fools, who will squander their savings on the house you just lost."

"Tacey —"

"Oh, I can see the happy crowds now, when you return to the wharves in five years. Look, they will cry, here comes the famous factory boy! See how his silver buttons shine. What a handsome coach he drives — General Washington himself never owned so finely matched a sextet of white horses. Behold his kindly smile. He could buy half of New York city with his gold, yet it has not spoiled him at all. All the girls wish to marry him. They can see at a glance that he is an excellent dancer. They tat his profile into lace doilies and sleep with them under their pillows at night. It makes them sigh."

So, bickering as usual, we missed most of Biddle's speech. It ended to half-drunken applause and uncertain laughter. The British airmen, oddly enough, did not look so much pleased as bewildered.

After a certain amount of whispering and jostling at the head table, as if no one there cared to commit himself to public speech, a thin and spindly man stood. He was a comical fellow in an old-fashioned powdered wig so badly fitting it must surely have been borrowed, and he tittered nervously before he said, "Well. I thank our esteemed host for that most, ah, unusual — damn me if I don't say peculiar — speech. Two great nations indeed! Yes, perhaps, someday. Yet I hope not. Whimsical, perhaps, is the better word. I shall confine myself to a simple account of our historic passage…"

So the speech progressed, and if the American's speech had puzzled the British officer, it was not half so bewildering as those things he said in return.

He began by applauding Tobias Whitpain, he of world-spanning renown, for the contributions made through his genius to the success of the first trans-Atlantic aerial crossing were matched only by the foresight of Queen Titania herself for funding and provisioning the airship. Isabella was now dethroned, he said, from that heavenly seat reserved for the muse of exploration and science.

"Whitpain?" I wondered. "Queen Titania?"

"What is that you are playing with?" Tacey hissed sharply.

I looked up guiltily. But the question was directed not at me but toward Socrates, who yet stood to my other side.

"Ma'am?" he said, the picture of innocence, as he shoved something into my hand, which from reflexive habit, I slid quickly into a pocket.

"Show me your hands," she said, and then, "Why are you not working? Get to work."

Socrates was marched briskly off. I waited until both were out of sight before digging out his toy.

It was a small mirror in a cheap, gaudy frame, such as conjure women from the Indies peer into before predicting love and health and thirteen children for gullible young ladies. I held it up and looked into it.

I saw myself.

I saw myself standing in the square below the great stepped ziggurat at the center of Nicnotezpocoatl. Which grand metropolis, serving twice over the population of London herself, my shipmates inevitably called Nignog City. Dear old Fuzzleton was perched on a folding stool, sketching and talking, while I held a fringed umbrella over him, to keep off the sun. He cut a ludicrous figure, so thin was he and so prissily did he sit. But, oh, what a fine mind he had!

We were always talking, Fuzzleton and I. With my new posting, I was in the strange position of being simultaneously both his tutor and student, as well as serving as his bootblack, his confidant, and his potential successor.

"The *Empire* is not safe anchored where it is," he said in a low voice, lest we be overheard by our Aztec warrior guardians. "Fire arrows could be shot into the balloons from the top of the ziggurat. These people are not fools! They've nosed out our weaknesses as effectively as we have theirs. Come the day they fear us more than they covet our airship, we are all dead. Yet Captain Winterjude refuses to listen to me."

"But Lieutenant Blacken promised – " I began.

"Yes, yes, promises. Blacken has ambitions, and plans of his own, as well. We – "

He stopped. His face turned pale and his mouth gaped wide. The stool clattered onto the paving stones, and he cried, "Look!"

I followed his pointing finger and saw an enormous Negro hand cover the sky, eclipsing the sun and plunging the world into darkness.

"Thank you," Socrates said. His face twisted up into a grotesque wink, and he was gone.

I returned my attention to the scene below.

The speaker – old Fuzzleton himself, I realized with a start – was winding up his remarks. He finished by raising a glass high in the air, and crying loudly: "To America! – Her Majesty's most treasured possession."

At those words, every American started to his feet. Hands were clapped to empty belts. Gentlemen searched their coats for sidearms they had of course not brought. There were still men alive who had fought in the War of Independence, and even if there had not been such, memory of the recent war with its burning of Washington and, closer to home, the economically disastrous blockade of American ports was still fresh in the minds of all. Nobody was eager to return to the embrace of a foreign despot, whether king or queen, George or Titania, made no difference. Our freedoms were young enough that all were aware how precariously we held them.

The British, for their part, were fighting men, and recognized hostility when confronted with it. They came to their feet as well, in a very Babel of accusation and denial.

It was at that instant, when all was confusion, and violence hovered in the air, that a messenger burst into the room.

Is that poker hot yet? Then plunge it in the wine and let the spices mull. Good. Hand me that. 'Twill help with the telling.

It was the madness of an instant that led me to join the airshipmen's number. Had I taken the time to think, I would not have done it.

But ambition was my undoing. I flung my towel away, darted into the kitchen to give my sister a quick hug and a peck on her cheek, and was down the stairs in a bound and a clatter.

In the library, all was confusion, with the British heading in a rush for the doorway, and the Americans holding back out of uncertainty, and fear as well of their sudden ferocity.

I joined the crush for the door.

Out in the cobbled street, we formed up into a loose group. I was jostled and roughly shoved, and I regretted my rashness immediately. The men about me were vague grey shapes, like figures in a dream. In the distance I heard the sound of angry voices.

A mob.

I was standing near the officers and overheard one argue, "It is unwise to leave thus quickly. It puts us in the position of looking as though we had reason to flee. 'Tis like the man seen climbing out his host's bedroom window. Nothing he says will make him look innocent again."

"There is no foe I fear half so much as King Mob," Fuzzleton replied. "March them out."

The officer saluted, spun about, and shouted, "To the ship – double-time, on the mark!" Clapping his horny hands together, he beat out the rhythm for a sailor's quick-march, such as I had played at a thousand times as a lad.

Rapidly the airmen began to move away.

Perforce I went with them.

By luck or good planning, we reached the prison yard without encountering any rioters. Our group, which had seemed so large, was but a drop of water to the enormous swirling mass of humanity that had congregated below the airship.

All about me, airmen were climbing rope ladders, or else being yanked into the sky. For every man thus eliminated, a new rope suddenly appeared, bounced, and was seized by another. Meanwhile, lines from the Whitpain engines were being disconnected from the tubs of purified river water, where they had been generating hydrogen.

Somebody slipped a loose loop around me and under my arms and with a sudden lurch I went soaring up into the darkness.

———

Oh, that was a happy time for me. The halcyon weeks ran one into another, long and languid while we sailed over the American wilderness. Sometimes over seas of forest, other times over seas of plains. There were occasional Indian tribes which...

Eh? You want to know what happened when I was discovered? Well, so would I. As well ask, though, what words Paris used to woo Helen. So much that we wish to know, we never shall! I retain, however, one memory more precious to me than all the rest, of an evening during the crossing of the shallow sea that covers the interior of at least one American continent.

Our shifts done, Hob and I went to the starboard aft with no particular end but to talk. "Sit here and watch the sunset," she said, patting the rail. She leaned against me as we watched, and I was acutely aware of her body and its closeness. My eyes were half-closed with a desire I thought entirely secret when I felt her hand undoing the buttons on my trousers.

"What are you doing?" I whispered in alarm.

"Nothing they don't expect young lads to do with each other now and then. Trust me. So long as you're discreet, they'll none of them remark on't."

Then she had me out and with a little laugh squeezed the shaft. I was by then too overcome with desire to raise any objections to her remarkable behavior.

Side by side we sat on the taffrail, as her hand moved first slowly and then with increasing vigor up and down upon my yard. Her mouth turned up on one side in a demi-smile. She was enjoying herself.

Finally I spurted. Drops of semen fell, silent in the moonlight, to mingle their saltiness with that of the water far below. She bent to swiftly kiss the tip of my yard and then tucked it neatly back into my trousers. "There," she said. "Now we're sweethearts."

My mind follows them now, those fugitive drops of possibility on their long and futile, yet hopeful, flight to the sea. I feel her hand clenching me so casually and yet profoundly. She could not have known how much it meant to me, who had never fired off my gun by a woman's direct intervention before. Yet inwardly I blessed her for it, and felt a new era had opened for me, and swore I would never forget her nor dishonor her in my mind for the sake of what she had done for me.

Little knowing how soon my traitor heart would turn away from her.

But for then I knew only that I no longer desired to return home. I wanted to go on with my Hob to the end of the voyage and back to her thronged and unimaginable London with its Whitpain engines and electrified lighting and surely a place for an émigré from a nonexistent nation who knew (as none of them did) the Calculus.

Somewhere around here, I have a folded and water-damped sheet of foolscap, upon which I apparently wrote down a short list of things I most wished never to forget. I may have lost it, but no matter. I've read it since a hundred times over. It begins with a heading in my uncertain Latin.

Ne Obliviscaris
1. My father's burial
2. The Aztec Emperor in his golden armor
3. Hob's hair in the sunset
4. The flying men
5. Winterjude's death & what became of his Lady
6. The air-serpents
7. The sound of icebergs calving
8. Hunting buffalo with the Apache
9. Being flogged
10. The night we solved the Whitpain Calculus

Which solution of course is gone forever – else so much would be different now! We'd live in a mansion as grand as the President's, and savants from across the world would come a-calling upon your old father, just so they could tell their grandchildren they'd met the Philadelphia Kepler, the American Archimedes. Yet here we are.

So it is savage irony that I remember that night vividly – the small lantern swinging lightly in the gloom above the table covered with sheet after sheet of increasingly fervid computation – Calculus in my hand and Whitpain equations in Fuzzleton's, and then on one miraculous and almost unreadable sheet, both of our hands dashing down formula upon formula in newly invented symbols, sometimes overlapping in the excitement of our reconciliation of the two geniuses.

"D'ye see what this means, boy?" Fuzzleton's face was rapturous. "Hundreds of worlds! Thousands! An infinitude of 'em! This is how the *Empire* was lost and why your capital city and mine are strangers to each other—it explains *everything!*"

We grabbed each other and danced a clumsy little jig. I remember that I hit my head upon a rafter, but what did I care? There would be statues of us in a myriad Londons and countless Philadelphias. We were going to live forever in the mind of Mankind.

My brother-in-law once told me that in China they believe that for every good thing there is an ill. For every kiss, a blow. For every dream a nightmare. So perhaps it was because of my great happiness that we shortly thereafter took on board a party of near-naked savages, men and women in equal numbers, to question about the gold ornaments they all wore in profusion about their necks and wrists and ankles.

Captain Winterjude stood watching, his lady by his side and every bit as impassive as he, as the men were questioned by Lieutenant Blacken. They refused to give sensible answers. They claimed to have no knowledge of where the gold came from. They insisted that they didn't know what we were talking about. When the ornaments were ripped from their bodies and shaken in their faces, they denied the gewgaws even existed.

Finally, losing patience, Blacken lined the natives up against the starboard rail. He conferred with the captain, received a curt nod, and ordered two airshipmen to seize the first Indian and throw him overboard.

The man fell to his death in complete silence.

His comrades watched stoically. Blacken repeated his questions. Again he learned nothing.

A second Indian went over the rail.

And so it went until every male was gone, and it was obvious we would learn nothing.

The women, out of compassion I thought at the time, were spared. The next morning, however, it was found that by night all had disappeared. They had slipped over the side, apparently, after their mates. The crew were much discontented with this discovery, and I discovered from their grumbles and complaints that their intentions for these poor wretches had been far from innocent.

Inevitably, we turned south, in search of El Dorado. From that moment on, however, our voyage was a thing abhorrent to me. It seemed to me that we had made the air itself into one vast grave and that, having plunged into it, the *Empire* was now engaged in an unholy pilgrimage through and toward Death itself.

When the Aztecs had been defeated at last and their city was ours, the officers held a banquet to celebrate and to accept the fealty of the vassal chieftains. Hob was chosen to be a serving-boy. But, because the clothes of a servitor were tight and thus revealing of gender, she perforce faked an injury, and I took her place instead.

It was thus that I caught the eye of Lady Winterjude.

The widow was a handsome, well-made woman with a black ponytail tied up in a bow. She wore her late husband's military jacket, in assertion of her rights, and it was well known that she was Captain Blacken's chief advisor. As I waited on her I felt her eye upon me at odd moments, and once saw her looking at me with a shocking directness.

She took me, as her unwritten perquisite, into her bed. Thereby and instantly turning Hob into my bitterest enemy, with Captain Blacken not all that far behind.

Forgive me. No, I hadn't fallen asleep. I was just thinking on things. This and that. Nothing that need concern you.

At the time I thought of Lady Winterjude as a monster of evil, an incubus or lamia to whom I was nevertheless drawn by the weakness of my flesh. But of course she was nothing of the kind. Had I made an effort to see her as a fellow human, things might well have turned out differently. For I now believe that it was my very naïveté, the transparency with which I was both attracted to and repelled by her, that was my chief attraction for the lady. Had I but the wit to comprehend this then, she would have quickly set me aside. Lady Winterjude was no woman to allow her weaknesses to be understood by a subordinate.

I was young, though, and she was a woman of appetites.

Which is all I remember of that world, save that we were driven out from it. Before we left, however, we dropped a Union Jack, weighted at the two bottom corners, over the side and into the ocean, claiming the sea and all continents it touched for Britain and Queen Titania.

Only an orca was there to witness the ceremony, and whether it took any notice I greatly doubt.

The *Empire* crashed less than a month after we encountered the air-serpents. They lived among the Aurora Borealis, high above the Arctic mountains. It was frigid beyond belief when we first saw them looping amid the Northern Lights, over and over in circles or cartwheels, very much like the Oriental pictures of dragons. Everybody crowded the rails to watch. We had no idea that they were alive, much less hostile.

The creatures were electrical in nature. They crackled with power. Yet when they came zigzagging toward us, we suspected nothing until two balloons were on fire, and the men had to labor mightily to cut them away before they could touch off the others.

We fought back not with cannons – the recoil of which would have been disastrous to our fragile shells – but with rockets. Their trails crisscrossed the sky, to no effect at first. Then, finally, a rocket trailing a metal chain passed through an air-dragon and the creature discharged in the form of a great lightning-bolt, down to the ground. For an instant we were dazzled, and then, when we could see again, it was no more.

Amid the pandemonium and cheers, I could have heard no sound to alert me. So it was either a premonition or merest chance that caused me to turn at that moment, just in time to see Hob, her face as hate-filled as any demon's, plunge a knife down upon me.

Eh? Oh, I'm sure she did. Your mother was never one for halfway gestures. I could show the scar if you required it. Still, I'm alive, eh? It's all water under the bridge. She had her reasons, to be sure, just as I had mine. Anyway, I didn't set out to explain the ways of women to you, but to tell of how the voyage ended.

We were caught in a storm greater than anything we had encountered so far. I think perhaps we were trapped between worlds. Witchfires danced on the ropes and rails. Balloons went up in flames. So dire was our situation and sure our peril that I could not hold it in my mind. A wild kind of exaltation filled me, an almost Satanic glee in the chaos that was breaking the airship apart.

As Hob came scuttling across my path, I swept her into my arms and, unheeding of her panicked protests, kissed her! She stared, shocked, into my eyes, and I laughed. "Caroline," I cried, "you are the woman or lass or lad or whatever you might be for me. I'd kiss you on the lip of Hell itself, and if you slipped and fell in, I'd jump right after you."

Briefly I was the man she had once thought me and I had so often wished I could be.

Hob looked at me with large and unblinking eyes. "You'll never be free of me now," she said at last, and then jerked away and was gone, back to her duty.

For more than a month I wandered the fever-lands, while the Society for the Relief of Shipwrecked Sailors attended to my needs. Of the crash itself, I remember nothing. Only that hours before it, I arrived at the bridge to discover that poor dear old Fuzzleton was dead.

Captain Blacken, in his madness, had destroyed the only man who might conceivably have returned him to his own port of origin.

"Can you navigate?" he demanded fiercely. "Can you bring us back to London?"

I gathered up the equations that Fuzzleton and I had spent so many nights working up. In their incomplete state, they would bring us back to Philadelphia – if we were lucky – but no further. With anything less than perfect luck, however, they would smear us across a thousand worlds.

"Yes," I lied. "I can."

I set a course for home.

And so at last, I came upon my father's grave. It was a crisp black rectangle in the earth, as dark and daunting as oblivion itself. Without any hesitation, I stepped through that lightless doorway. And my eyes opened.

I looked up into the black face of a disapproving angel.

"Tacey?" I said wonderingly.

"That's *Mrs. Nash* to you," she snapped. But I understood her ways now, and when I gratefully clasped her hand, and touched my lips to it, she had to look away, lest I think she had changed in her opinion of me.

Tacey Nash was still one of the tiniest women I had ever seen, and easily the most vigorous. The doctor, when he came, said it would be weeks before I was able to leave the bed. But Tacey had me nagged and scolded onto my feet in two days, walking in three, and hobbling about the public streets on a cane in four. Then, on the fifth day, she returned to her husband, brood, and anonymity, vanishing from my life forever, as do so many people in this world to whom we owe so much more than ever will be repaid.

When word got out that I was well enough to receive visitors, the first thing I learned was that my brother was dead. Jack had drowned in a boating accident several years after I left. A girl whose face was entirely unknown to me told me this – my mother, there also, could not shush her in time – and told me as well that she was my baby sister Barbara.

I should have felt nothing. The loss of a brother one does not know is, after all, no loss at all. But I was filled with a sadness wholly inexplicable but felt from the marrow outward, so that every bone, joint, and muscle ached with the pain of loss. I burst into tears.

Crying, it came to me then, all in an instant, that the voyage was over.

The voyage was over and Caroline had not survived it. The one true love of my life was lost to me forever.

So I came here. I could no longer bear to live in Philadelphia. The gems in my pocket, small though they might be compared to those I'd left behind, were enough to buy me this house and set me up as a merchant. I was known in the village as a melancholy man. Indeed, melancholy I was. I had been through what would have been the best adventure in the world, were it not ruined by its ending – by the loss of the *Empire* and all its hands, and above all the loss of my own dear and irreplaceable Hob.

Perhaps in some other, and better, world she yet survived. But not in mine.

Yet my past was not done with me yet.

On a cold, wet evening in November, a tramp came to my door. He was a wretched, fantastical creature, more kobold than human, all draped in wet rags and hooded so that only a fragment of nose poked out into the meager light from my doorway.

Imploringly, the phantasm held out a hand and croaked, "Food!"

I had not the least thought that any danger might arise from so miserable a source, and if I had, what would I have cared? A violent end to a violent life – I would not have objected. "Come inside," I said to the poor fellow, "out of the rain. There's a fire in the parlor. Go sit there, while I warm something up."

As the beggar gratefully climbed the stairs, I noticed that he had a distinct limp, as if a leg had been broken and imperfectly healed.

I had a kettle steaming in the kitchen. It was the work of a minute to brew the tea. I prepared a tray with milk and sugar and ginger, and carried it back to the front of the house.

In the doorway to the parlor I stopped, frozen with amazement. There, in that darkened room, a hand went up and moved the hood down. All the world reversed itself.

I stumbled inside, unable to speak, unable to think.

The fire caught itself in her red hair. She turned up her cheek toward me with that same impish smile I loved so well.

"Well, mate," she said. "Ain't you going to kiss me?"

The fire is all but done. No, don't bother with another log. Let it die. There's nothing there but ashes anyway.

You look at your mother and you see someone I do not – a woman who is old and wrinkled, who has put on some weight, perhaps, who could never have been an adventurer, a rogue, a scamp. Oh, I see her exterior well enough, too. But I also see deeper.

I love her in a way you can't possibly understand, nor ever will understand unless some day many years hence you have the good fortune to come to feel the same way yourself. I love her as an old and comfortable shoe loves its mate. I could never find her equal.

And so ends my tale. I can vouch for none of it. Since the fever, I have not been sure which memories are true and which are fantasy. Perhaps only half of what I have said actually happened. Perhaps none of it did. At any rate, I have told you it all.

Save for one thing.

Not many years later, and for the best of reasons, I sent for the midwife. My darling Caroline was in labor. First she threw up, and then the water broke. Then the Quaker midwife came and chased me from the room. I sat in the parlor with my hands clasped between my knees and waited.

Surely hours passed while I stewed and worried. But all I recall is that somehow I found myself standing at the foot of my wife's childbed. Caroline lay pale with exhaustion. She smiled wanly as the midwife held up my son for me to see.

I looked down upon that tiny creature's face and burst into tears. The tears coursed down my face like rain, and I felt such an intensity of emotion as I can scarce describe to you now. It was raining outside, they tell me now, but that is not how I recall it. To me the world was flooded with sunshine, brighter than any I had ever seen before.

The midwife said something, I paid her no mind. I gazed upon my son.

In that moment I felt closer to my father than ever I had before. I felt that finally I understood him and knew what words he would have said to me if he could. I looked down on you with such absolute and undeviating love as we in our more hopeful moments pray that God feels toward us, and silently I spoke to you.

Someday, my son, I thought, you will be a man. You will grow up and by so doing turn me old, and then I will die and be forgotten. But that's all right. I don't mind. It's a small price to pay for your existence.

Then the midwife put you into my arms, and all debts and grudges I ever held were canceled forever.

There's so much more I wish I could tell you. But it's late, and I lack the words. Anyway, your trunk is packed and waiting by the door.

In the morning you'll be gone. You're a man yourself, and about to set off on adventures of your own. Adventures I cannot imagine, and which afterwards you will no more be able to explain to others than I could explain mine to you. Live them well. I know you will.

And now it's time I was abed. Time, and then some, that I slept.

Legions in Time

ELEANOR VOIGT had the oddest job of anyone she knew. She worked eight hours a day in an office where no business was done. Her job was to sit at a desk and stare at the closet door. There was a button on the desk which she was to push if anybody came out that door. There was a big clock on the wall and precisely at noon, once a day, she went over to the door and unlocked it with a key she had been given. Inside was an empty closet. There were no trap doors or secret panels in it – she had looked. It was just an empty closet.

If she noticed anything unusual, she was supposed to go back to her desk and press the button.

"Unusual in what way?" she'd asked when she'd been hired. "I don't understand. What am I looking for?"

"You'll know it when you see it," Mr. Tarblecko had said in that odd accent of his. Mr. Tarblecko was her employer, and some kind of foreigner. He was the creepiest thing imaginable. He had pasty white skin and no hair at all on his head, so that when he took his hat off he looked like some species of mushroom. His ears were small and almost pointed. Ellie thought he might have some kind of disease. But he paid two dollars an hour, which was good money nowadays for a woman of her age.

At the end of her shift, she was relieved by an unkempt young man who had once blurted out to her that he was a poet. When she came in, in the morning, a heavy Negress would stand up wordlessly, take her coat and hat from the rack, and with enormous dignity leave.

So all day Ellie sat behind the desk with nothing to do. She wasn't allowed to read a book, for fear she might get so involved in it that she would stop watching the door. Crosswords were allowed, because they weren't as engrossing. She got a lot of knitting done, and was considering taking up tatting.

Over time the door began to loom large in her imagination. She pictured herself unlocking it at some forbidden not-noon time and seeing – what? Her imagination failed her. No matter how vividly she visualized it, the door would open onto something mundane. Brooms and mops. Sports equipment. Galoshes and old clothes. What else would there be in a closet? What else *could* there be?

Sometimes, caught up in her imaginings, she would find herself on her feet. Sometimes, she walked to the door. Once she actually put her hand on the knob before drawing away. But always the thought of losing her job stopped her.

It was maddening.

Twice, Mr. Tarblecko had come to the office while she was on duty. Each time he was wearing that same black suit with that same narrow black tie. "You have a watch?" he'd asked.

"Yes, sir." The first time, she'd held forth her wrist to show it to him. The disdainful way he ignored the gesture ensured she did not repeat it on his second visit.

"Go away. Come back in forty minutes."

So she had gone out to a little tearoom nearby. She had a bag lunch back in her desk, with a baloney-and-mayonnaise sandwich and an apple, but she'd been so flustered she'd forgotten it, and then feared to go back after it. She treated herself to a dainty "lady lunch" that she was in no mood to appreciate, left a dime tip for the waitress, and was back in front of the office door exactly thirty-eight minutes after she'd left.

At forty minutes, exactly, she reached for the door.

As if he'd been waiting for her to do so, Mr. Tarblecko breezed through the door, putting on his hat. He didn't acknowledge her promptness *or* her presence. He just strode briskly past, as though she didn't exist.

Stunned, she went inside, closed the door, and returned to her desk.

She realized then that Mr. Tarblecko was genuinely, fabulously rich. He had the arrogance of those who are so wealthy that they inevitably get their way in all small matters because there's always somebody there to *arrange* things that way. His type was never grateful for anything and never bothered to be polite, because it never even occurred to them that things could be otherwise.

The more she thought about it, the madder she got. She was no Bolshevik, but it seemed to her that people had certain rights, and that one of these was the right to a little common courtesy. It diminished one to be treated like a stick of furniture. It was degrading. She was damned if she was going to take it.

Six months went by.

The door opened and Mr. Tarblecko strode in, as if he'd left only minutes ago. "You have a watch?"

Ellie slid open a drawer and dropped her knitting into it. She opened another and took out her bag lunch. "Yes."

"Go away. Come back in forty minutes."

So she went outside. It was May, and Central Park was only a short walk away, so she ate there, by the little pond where children floated their toy sailboats. But all the while she fumed. She was a good employee – she really was! She was conscientious, punctual, and she never called in sick. Mr. Tarblecko ought to appreciate that. He had no business treating her the way he did.

Almost, she wanted to overstay lunch, but her conscience wouldn't allow that. When she got back to the office, precisely thirty-nine and a half minutes after she'd left, she planted herself squarely in front of the door so that when Mr. Tarblecko left he would have no choice but to confront her. It might well lose her her job, but...well, if it did, it did. That's how strongly she felt about it.

Thirty seconds later, the door opened and Mr. Tarblecko strode briskly out. Without breaking his stride or, indeed, showing the least sign of emotion, he picked her up by her two arms, swivelled effortlessly, and deposited her to the side.

Then he was gone. Ellie heard his footsteps dwindling down the hall.

The nerve! The sheer, raw *gall* of the man!

Ellie went back in the office, but she couldn't make herself sit down at the desk. She was far too upset. Instead, she walked back and forth the length of the room, arguing with herself, saying aloud those things she should have said and would have said if only Mr. Tarblecko had stood still for them. To be picked up and set aside like that... Well, it was really quite upsetting. It was intolerable.

What was particularly distressing was that there wasn't even any way to make her displeasure known.

At last, though, she calmed down enough to think clearly, and realized that she was wrong. There *was* something – something more symbolic than substantive, admittedly – that she could do.

She could open that door.

Ellie did not act on impulse. She was a methodical woman. So she thought the matter through before she did anything. Mr. Tarblecko very rarely showed up at the office – only twice in all the time she'd been here, and she'd been here over a year. Moreover, the odds of him returning to the office a third time only minutes after leaving it were negligible. He had left nothing behind – she could see that at a glance; the office was almost Spartan in its emptiness. Nor was there any work here for him to return to.

Just to be safe, though, she locked the office door. Then she got her chair out from behind the desk and chocked it up under the doorknob so that even if somebody had a key, he couldn't get in. She put her ear to the door and listened for noises in the hall.

Nothing.

It was strange how, now that she had decided to do the deed, time seemed to slow and the office to expand. It took forever to cross the vast expanses of empty space between her and the closet door. Her hand reaching for its knob pushed through air as thick as molasses. Her fingers closed about it, one by one, and in the time it took for them to do so there was room enough for a hundred second thoughts. Faintly, she heard the sound of...machinery? A low humming noise.

She placed the key in the lock, and opened the door.

There stood Mr. Tarblecko.

Ellie shrieked, and staggered backward. One of her heels hit the floor wrong, and her ankle twisted, and she almost fell. Her heart was hammering so furiously her chest hurt.

Mr. Tarblecko glared at her from within the closet. His face was as white as a sheet of paper. "One rule," he said coldly, tonelessly. "You had only one rule, and you broke it." He stepped out. "You are a very bad slave."

"I...I...I..." Ellie found herself gasping from the shock. "I'm not a slave at all!"

"There is where you are wrong, Eleanor Voigt. There is where you are very wrong indeed," said Mr. Tarblecko. "Open the window."

Ellie went to the window and pulled up the blinds. There was a little cactus in a pot on the windowsill. She moved it to her desk. Then she opened the window. It stuck a little, so she had to put all her strength into it. The lower sash went up slowly at first and then, with a rush, slammed to the top. A light, fresh breeze touched her.

"Climb onto the windowsill."

"I most certainly will—"—*not*, she was going to say. But to her complete astonishment, she found herself climbing up onto the sill. She could not help herself. It was as if her will were not her own.

"Sit down with your feet outside the window."

It was like a hideous nightmare, the kind that you know can't be real and struggle to awaken from, but cannot. Her body did exactly as it was told to do. She had absolutely no control over it.

"Do not jump until I tell you to do so."

"Are you going to tell me to jump?" she asked quaveringly. "Oh, *please*, Mr. Tarblecko..."

"Now look down."

The office was on the ninth floor. Ellie was a lifelong New Yorker, so that had never seemed to her a particularly great height before. Now it did. The people on the sidewalk were as small as ants. The buses and automobiles on the street were the size of matchboxes. The sounds of horns and engines drifted up to her, and birdsong as well, the lazy background noises of a spring day in the city. The ground was so terribly far away! And there was nothing between her and it but air! Nothing holding her back from death but her fingers desperately clutching the window frame!

Ellie could feel all the world's gravity willing her toward the distant concrete. She was dizzy with vertigo and a sick, stomach-tugging urge to simply let go and, briefly, fly. She squeezed her eyes shut tight, and felt hot tears streaming down her face.

She could tell from Mr. Tarblecko's voice that he was standing right behind her. "If I told you to jump, Eleanor Voigt, would you do so?"

"Yes," she squeaked.

"What kind of person jumps to her death simply because she's been told to do so?"

"A...a slave!"

"Then what are you?"

"A slave! A slave! I'm a slave!" She was weeping openly now, as much from humiliation as from fear. "I don't want to die! I'll be your slave, anything, whatever you say!"

"If you're a slave, then what kind of slave should you be?"

"A...a...*good* slave."

"Come back inside."

Gratefully, she twisted around, and climbed back into the office. Her knees buckled when she tried to stand, and she had to grab at the windowsill to keep from falling. Mr. Tarblecko stared at her, sternly and steadily.

"You have been given your only warning," he said. "If you disobey again – or if you ever try to quit – I will order you out the window."

He walked into the closet and closed the door behind him.

There were two hours left on her shift – time enough, barely, to compose herself. When the disheveled young poet showed up, she dropped her key in her purse and walked past him without so much as a glance. Then she went straight to the nearest hotel bar and ordered a gin and tonic.

She had a lot of thinking to do.

Eleanor Voigt was not without resources. She had been an executive secretary before meeting her late husband, and everyone knew that a good executive secretary effectively runs her boss's business for him.

Before the Crash, she had run a household with three servants. She had entertained. Some of her parties had required weeks of planning and preparation. If it weren't for the Depression, she was sure she'd be in a much better-paid position than the one she held.

She was *not* going to be a slave.

But before she could find a way out of her predicament, she had to understand it. First, the closet. Mr. Tarblecko had left the office and then, minutes later, popped up inside it. A hidden passage of some kind? No – that was simultaneously too complicated and not complicated enough. She had heard machinery, just before she opened the door. So...some kind of transportation device, then. Something that a day ago she would have sworn couldn't exist. A teleporter, perhaps, or a time machine.

The more she thought of it, the better she liked the thought of the time machine. It was not just that teleporters were the stuff of Sunday funnies and Buck Rogers serials, while *The Time Machine* was a distinguished philosophical work by Mr. H. G. Wells. Though she had to admit that figured in there. But a teleportation device required a twin somewhere, and Mr. Tarblecko hadn't had the time even to leave the building.

A time machine, however, would explain so much! Her employer's long absences. The necessity that the device be watched when not in use, lest it be employed by Someone Else. Mr. Tarblecko's abrupt appearance today, and his possession of a coercive power that no human being on Earth had.

The fact that she could no longer think of Mr. Tarblecko as human.

She had barely touched her drink, but now she found herself too impatient to finish it. She slapped a dollar bill down on the bar and, without waiting for her change, left.

During the time it took to walk the block and a half to the office building and ride the elevator up to the ninth floor, Ellie made her plans. She strode briskly down the hallway and opened the door without knocking. The unkempt young man looked up, startled, from a scribbled sheet of paper.

"You have a watch?"

"Y-yes, but...Mr. Tarblecko..."

"Get out. Come back in forty minutes."

With grim satisfaction, she watched the young man cram his key into one pocket and the sheet of paper into another and leave. *Good slave*, she thought to herself. Perhaps he'd already been through the little charade Mr. Tarblecko had just played on her. Doubtless every employee underwent ritual enslavement as a way of keeping them in line. The problem with having slaves, however, was that they couldn't be expected to display any initiative... Not on the master's behalf, anyway.

Ellie opened her purse and got out the key. She walked to the closet.

For an instant she hesitated. Was she really sure enough to risk her life? But the logic was unassailable. She had been given no second chance. If Mr. Tarblecko *knew* she was about to open the door a second time, he would simply have ordered her out the window on her first offense. The fact that he hadn't meant that he didn't know.

She took a deep breath and opened the door.

There was a world inside.

For what seemed like forever, Ellie stood staring at the bleak metropolis so completely unlike New York City. Its buildings were taller than any she had ever seen – miles high! – and interlaced with skywalks, like those in *Metropolis*. But the buildings in the movie had been breathtaking, and these were the opposite of beautiful. They were ugly as sin: windowless, grey, stained, and discolored. There were monotonous lines of harsh lights along every street, and under their glare trudged men and women as uniform and lifeless as robots. Outside the office, it was a beautiful bright day. But on the other side of the closet, the world was dark as night.

And it was snowing.

Gingerly, she stepped into the closet. The instant her foot touched the floor, it seemed to expand to all sides. She stood at the center of a great wheel of doors, with all but two of them – to her office and to the winter world – shut. There were hooks beside each door, and hanging from them were costumes of a hundred different cultures. She thought she recognized togas, Victorian opera dress, kimonos... But most of the clothing was unfamiliar.

Beside the door into winter, there was a long cape. Ellie wrapped it around herself, and discovered a knob on the inside. She twisted it to the right, and suddenly the coat was hot as hot. Quickly, she twisted the knob to the left, and it grew cold. She fiddled with the thing until the cape felt just right. Then she straightened her shoulders, took a deep breath, and stepped out into the forbidding city.

There was a slight electric sizzle, and she was standing in the street.

Ellie spun around to see what was behind her: a rectangle of some glassy black material. She rapped it with her knuckles. It was solid. But when she brought her key near its surface, it shimmered and opened into that strange space between worlds again.

So she had a way back home.

To either side of her rectangle were identical glassy rectangles faceted slightly away from it. They were the exterior of an enormous kiosk, or perhaps a very low building, at the center of a large, featureless square. She walked all the way around it, rapping each rectangle with her key. Only the one would open for her.

The first thing to do was to find out where – or, rather, *when* – she was. Ellie stepped in front of one of the hunched, slow-walking men. "Excuse me, sir, could you answer a few questions for me?"

The man raised a face that was utterly bleak and without hope. A ring of grey metal glinted from his neck. "Hawrzat dagtiknut?" he asked.

Ellie stepped back in horror and, like a wind-up toy temporarily halted by a hand or a foot, the man resumed his plodding gait.

She cursed herself. Of *course* language would have changed in the however-many-centuries future she found herself in. Well...that was going to make gathering information more difficult. But she was used to difficult tasks. The evening of John's suicide, she had been the one to clean the walls and the floor. After that, she'd known that she was capable of doing anything she set her mind to.

Above all, it was important that she not get lost. She scanned the square with the doorways in time at its center – mentally, she dubbed it Times Square – and chose at random one of the broad avenues converging on it. That, she decided would be Broadway.

Ellie started down Broadway, watching everybody and everything. Some of the drone-folk were dragging sledges with complex machinery on them. Others were hunched under soft, translucent bags filled with murky fluid and vague biomorphic shapes. The air smelled bad, but in ways she was not familiar with.

She had gotten perhaps three blocks when the sirens went off – great piercing blasts of noise that assailed the ears and echoed from the building walls. All the streetlights flashed off and on and off again in a one-two rhythm. From unseen loudspeakers, an authoritative voice blared, *"Akgang! Akgang! Kronzvarbrakar! Zawzawkstrag! Akgang! Akgang..."*

Without hurry, the people in the street began turning away, touching their hands to dull grey plates beside nondescript doors and disappearing into the buildings.

"Oh, cripes!" Ellie muttered. She'd best —

There was a disturbance behind her. Ellie turned and saw the strangest thing yet.

It was a girl of eighteen or nineteen, wearing summer clothes – a man's trousers, a short-sleeved flower-print blouse – and she was running down the street in a panic. She grabbed at the uncaring drones, begging for help. "Please!" she cried. "Can't you help me? Somebody! Please...you have to help me!" Puffs of steam came from her mouth with each breath. Once or twice she made a sudden dart for one of the doorways and slapped her hand on the greasy plates. But the doors would not open for her.

Now the girl had reached Ellie. In a voice that expected nothing, she said, "Please?"

"I'll help you, dear," Ellie said.

The girl shrieked, then convulsively hugged her. "Oh, thank you, thank you, thank you," she babbled.

"Follow close behind me." Ellie strode up behind one of the lifeless un-men and, just after he had slapped his hand on the plate, but before he could enter, grabbed his rough tunic and gave it a yank. He turned.

"Vamoose!" she said in her sternest voice, and jerked a thumb over her shoulder.

The un-man turned away. He might not understand the word, but the tone and the gesture sufficed.

Ellie stepped inside, pulling the girl after her. The door closed behind them.

"Wow," said the girl wonderingly. "How did you do that?"

"This is a slave culture. For a slave to survive, he's got to obey any-one who acts like a master. It's that simple. Now, what's your name and how did you get here?" As she spoke, Ellie took in her surroundings. The room they were in was dim, grimy – and vast. So far as she could see, there were no interior walls, only the occasional pillar and here and there a set of functional metal stairs without railings.

"Nadine Shepard. I...I...there was a door! And I walked through it and I found myself *here!* I..."

The child was close to hysteria. "I know, dear. Tell me, when are you from?"

"Chicago. On the North Side, near – "

"Not where, dear, when? What year is it?"

"Uh...two thousand and four. Isn't it?"

"Not here. Not now." The grey people were everywhere, moving sluggishly, yet always keeping within sets of yellow lines painted on the concrete floor. Their smell was pervasive, and far from pleasant. Still...

Ellie stepped directly into the path of one of the sad creatures, a woman. When she stopped, Ellie took the tunic from her shoulders and then stepped back. Without so much as an expression of annoy-ance, the woman resumed her plodding walk.

"Here you are." She handed the tunic to young Nadine. "Put this on, dear, you must be freezing. Your skin is positively blue." And, indeed, it was not much warmer inside than it had been outdoors. "I'm Eleanor Voigt. Mrs. Eleanor Voigt."

Shivering, Nadine donned the rough garment. But instead of thank-ing Ellie, she said, "You look familiar."

Ellie returned her gaze. She was a pretty enough creature though, strangely, she wore no makeup at all. Her features were regular, intelligent – "You look familiar too. I can't quite put my finger on it, but…"

"Okay," Nadine said, "now tell me. Please. Where and when am I, and what's going on?"

"I honestly don't know," Ellie said. Dimly, through the walls, she could hear the sirens and the loudspeaker-voice. If only it weren't so murky in here! She couldn't get any clear idea of the building's layout or function.

"But you *must* know! You're so…so capable, so in control. You…"

"I'm a castaway like you, dear. Just figuring things out as I go along." She continued to peer. "But I can tell you this much: We are far, far in the future. The poor degraded beings you saw on the street are the slaves of a superior race – let's call them the Aftermen. The Aftermen are very cruel, and they can travel through time as easily as you or I can travel from city to city via inter-urban rail. And that's all I know. So far."

Nadine was peering out a little slot in the door that Ellie hadn't noticed. Now she said, "What's this?"

Ellie took her place at the slot, and saw a great bulbous street-filling machine pull to a halt a block from the building. Insectoid creatures that might be robots or might be men in body armor poured out of it, and swarmed down the street, examining every door. The sirens and the loudspeakers cut off. The streetlights returned to normal. "It's time we left," Ellie said.

An enormous artificial voice shook the building. *Akbang! Akbang! Zawzawksbild! Alzowt! Zawzawksbild! Akbang!*

"Quickly!"

She seized Nadine's hand, and they were running.

Without emotion, the grey folk turned from their prior courses and unhurriedly made for the exits.

Ellie and Nadine tried to stay off the walkways entirely. But the air began to tingle, more on the side away from the walkways than the side toward, and then to burn and then to sting. They were quickly forced between the yellow lines. At first they were able to push their way past the drones, and then to shoulder their way through their numbers. But more and more came dead-stepping their way down the metal stair-ways. More and more descended from the upper levels via lifts that abruptly descended from the ceiling to disgorge them by the hundreds. More and more flowed outward from the building's dim interior.

Passage against the current of flesh became first difficult, and then impossible. They were swept backwards, helpless as corks in a rain-swollen river. Outward they were forced and through the exit into the street.

The "police" were waiting there.

At the sight of Ellie and Nadine – they could not have been difficult to discern among the uniform drabness of the others – two of the armored figures stepped forward with long poles and brought them down on the women.

Ellie raised her arm to block the pole, and it landed solidly on her wrist.

Horrid, searing pain shot through her, greater than anything she had ever experienced before. For a giddy instant, Ellie felt a strange elevated sense of being, and she thought, *If I can put up with this, I can endure anything.* Then the world went away.

Ellie came to in a jail cell.

At least that's what she thought it was. The room was small, square, and doorless. A featureless ceiling gave off a drab, even light. A bench ran around the perimeter, and there was a hole in the middle of the room whose stench advertised its purpose.

She sat up.

On the bench across from her, Nadine was weeping silently into her hands.

So her brave little adventure had ended. She had rebelled against Mr. Tarblecko's tyranny and come to the same end that awaited most rebels. It was her own foolish fault. She had acted without sufficient forethought, without adequate planning, without scouting out the opposition and gathering information first. She had gone up against a Power that could range effortlessly across time and space, armed only with a pocket handkerchief and a spare set of glasses, and inevitably that Power had swatted her down with a contemptuous minimum of their awesome force.

They hadn't even bothered to take away her purse.

Ellie dug through it, found a cellophane-wrapped hard candy, and popped it into her mouth. She sucked on it joylessly. All hope whatsoever was gone from her.

Still, even when one has no hope, one's obligations remain. "Are you all right, Nadine?" she forced herself to ask. "Is there anything I can do to help?"

Nadine lifted her tear-stained face. "I just went through a door," she said. "That's all. I didn't do anything bad or wrong or...or anything. And now I'm here!" Fury blazed up in her. "Damn you, damn you, damn you!"

"Me?" Ellie said, astonished.

"You! You shouldn't have let them get us. You should've taken us to some hiding place, and then gotten us back home. But you didn't. You're a stupid, useless old woman!"

It was all Ellie could do to keep from smacking the young lady. But Nadine was practically a child, she told herself, and it didn't seem like they raised girls to have much gumption in the year 2004. They were probably weak and spoiled people, up there in the Twenty-first Century, who had robots to do all their work for them, and nothing to do but sit around and listen to the radio all day. So she held not only her hand, but her tongue. "Don't worry, dear," she said soothingly. "We'll get out of this. Somehow."

Nadine stared at her bleakly, disbelievingly. "*How?*" she demanded.

But to this Ellie had no answer.

Time passed. Hours, by Ellie's estimation, and perhaps many hours. And with its passage, she found herself, more out of boredom than from the belief that it would be of any use whatsoever, looking at the situation analytically again.

How had the Aftermen tracked her down?

Some sort of device on the time-door might perhaps warn them that an unauthorized person had passed through. But the "police" had located her so swiftly and surely! They had clearly known exactly where she was. Their machine had come straight toward the building they'd entered. The floods of non-men had flushed her right out into their arms.

So it was something about her, or *on* her, that had brought the Aftermen so quickly.

Ellie looked at her purse with new suspicion. She dumped its contents on the ledge beside her, and pawed through them, looking for the guilty culprit. A few hard candies, a lace hankie, half a pack of cigarettes, fountain pen, glasses case, bottle of aspirin, house key…and the key to the time closet. The only thing in all she owned that had come to her direct from Mr. Tarblecko. She snatched it up.

It looked ordinary enough. Ellie rubbed it, sniffed it, touched it gently to her tongue.

It tasted sour.

Sour, the way a small battery tasted if you touched your tongue to it. There was a faint trickle of electricity coming from the thing. It was clearly no ordinary key.

She pushed her glasses up on her forehead, held the thing to her eye, and squinted. It looked exactly like a common everyday key. Almost. It had no manufacturer's name on it, and that was unexpected, given that the key looked new and unworn. The top part of it was covered with irregular geometric decorations.

Or *were* they decorations?

She looked up to see Nadine studying her steadily, unblinkingly, like a cat. "Nadine, honey, your eyes are younger than mine – would you take a look at this? Are those tiny…*switches* on this thing?"

"What?" Nadine accepted the key from her, examined it, poked at it with one nail.

Flash.

When Ellie stopped blinking and could see again, one wall of their cell had disappeared.

Nadine stepped to the very edge of the cell, peering outward. A cold wind whipped bitter flakes of snow about her. "Look!" she cried. Then, when Ellie stood beside her to see what she saw, Nadine wrapped her arms about the older woman and stepped out into the abyss.

Ellie screamed.

The two women piloted the police vehicle up Broadway, toward Times Square. Though a multiplicity of instruments surrounded the windshield, the controls were simplicity itself: a single stick which when pushed forward accelerated the vehicle and when pushed to either side turned it. Apparently the police did not need to be particularly smart. Neither the steering mechanism nor the doors had any locks on them, so far as Ellie could tell. Apparently the drone-men had so little initiative that locks weren't required. Which would help explain how she and Nadine had escaped so easily.

"How did you know this vehicle was beneath us?" Ellie asked. "How did you know we'd be able to drive it? I almost had a heart attack when you pushed me out on top of it."

"Way rad, wasn't it? Straight out of a Hong Kong video." Nadine grinned. "Just call me Michelle Yeoh."

"If you say so." She was beginning to rethink her hasty judgment of the lass. Apparently the people of 2004 weren't quite the shrinking violets she'd made them out to be.

With a flicker and a hum, a square sheet of glass below the windshield came to life. Little white dots of light danced, jittered, and coalesced to form a face.

It was Mr. Tarblecko.

"*Time criminals of the Dawn Era,*" his voice thundered from a hidden speaker. "*Listen and obey.*"

Ellie shrieked, and threw her purse over the visi-plate. "Don't listen to him!" she ordered Nadine. "See if you can find a way of turning this thing off!"

"*Bring the stolen vehicle to a complete halt immediately!*"

To her horror, if not her surprise, Ellie found herself pulling the steering-bar back, slowing the police car to a stop. But then Nadine, in blind obedience to Mr. Tarblecko's compulsive voice, grabbed for the bar as well. Simultaneously, she stumbled and, with a little *eep* noise, lurched against the bar, pushing it sideways.

The vehicle slewed to one side, smashed into a building wall, and toppled over.

Then Nadine had the roof-hatch open and was pulling her through it. "C'mon!" she shouted. "I can see the black doorway-thingie – the, you know, place!"

Following, Ellie had to wonder about the educational standards of the year 2004. The young lady didn't seem to have a very firm grasp on the English language.

Then they had reached Times Square and the circle of doorways at its center. The streetlights were flashing and loudspeakers were shouting, "*Akbang! Akbang!*" and police vehicles were converging upon them from every direction, but there was still time. Ellie tapped the nearest doorway with her key. Nothing. The next. Nothing. Then she was running around the building, scraping the key against each doorway, and...there it was!

She seized Nadine's hand, and they plunged through.

The space inside expanded in a great wheel to all sides. Ellie spun about. There were doors everywhere – and all of them closed. She had not the faintest idea which one led back to her own New York City.

Wait, though! There were costumes appropriate to each time hanging by their doors. If she just went down them until she found a business suit...

Nadine gripped her arm. "Oh, my God!"

Ellie turned, looked, saw. A doorway – the one they had come through, obviously – had opened behind them. In it stood Mr. Tarblecko. Or, to be more precise, *three* Mr. Tarbleckos. They were all as identical as peas in a pod. She had no way of knowing which one, if any, was hers.

"Through here! Quick!" Nadine shrieked. She'd snatched open the nearest door.

Together, they fled through it.

"Oolohstullalu ashulalumoota!" a woman sang out. She wore a jumpsuit and carried a clipboard, which she thrust into Ellie's face. "Oolalulaswula ulalulin."

"I...I don't understand what you're saying," Ellie faltered. They stood on the green lawn of a gentle slope that led down to the ocean. Down by the beach, enormous construction machines, operated by both men and women (women! of all the astonishing sights she had seen, this was strangest), were rearing an enormous, enigmatic structure, reminiscent to Ellie's eye of Sunday school illustrations of the Tower of Babel. Gentle tropical breezes stirred her hair.

"Dawn Era, Amerlingo," the clipboard said. "Exact period uncertain.

Answer these questions. Gas – for lights or for cars?"

"For cars, mostly. Although there are still a few – "

"Apples – for eating or computing?"

"Eating," Ellie said, while simultaneously Nadine said, "Both."

"Scopes – for dreaming or for resurrecting?"

Neither woman said anything.

The clipboard chirped in a satisfied way. "Early Atomic Age, pre- and post-Hiroshima, one each. You will experience a moment's discomfort. Do not be alarmed. It is for your own good."

"Please." Ellie turned from the woman to the clipboard and back, uncertain which to address. "What's going on? Where are we? We have so many – "

"There's no time for questions," the woman said impatiently. Her accent was unlike anything Ellie had ever heard before. "You must undergo indoctrination, loyalty imprinting, and chronomilitary training immediately. We need all the time-warriors we can get. This base is going to be destroyed in the morning."

"What? I…"

"Hand me your key."

Without thinking, Ellie gave the thing to the woman. Then a black nausea overcame her. She swayed, fell, and was unconscious before she hit the ground.

"Would you like some heroin?"

The man sitting opposite her had a face that was covered with black-work tattoo eels. He grinned, showing teeth that had all been filed to a point.

"I beg your pardon?" Ellie was not at all certain where she was, or how she had gotten here. Nor did she comprehend how she could have understood this alarming fellow's words, for he most certainly had *not* been speaking English.

"Heroin." He thrust the open metal box of white powder at her. "Do you want a snort?"

"No, thank you." Ellie spoke carefully, trying not to give offense. "I find that it gives me spots."

With a disgusted noise, the man turned away.

Then the young woman sitting beside her said in a puzzled way, "Don't I know you?"

She turned. It was Nadine. "Well, my dear, I should certainly hope you haven't forgotten me so soon."

"Mrs. Voigt?" Nadine said wonderingly. "But you're...you're... young!"

Involuntarily, Ellie's hands went up to her face. The skin was taut and smooth. The incipient softening of her chin was gone. Her hair, when she brushed her hands through it, was sleek and full.

She found herself desperately wishing she had a mirror.

"They must have done something. While I was asleep." She lightly touched her temples, the skin around her eyes. "I'm not wearing any glasses! I can see perfectly!" She looked around her. The room she was in was even more Spartan than the jail cell had been. There were two metal benches facing each other, and on them sat as motley a collection of men and women as she had ever seen. There was a woman who must have weighed three hundred pounds – and every ounce of it muscle. Beside her sat an albino lad so slight and elfin he hardly seemed there at all. Until, that is, one looked at his clever face and burning eyes. *Then* one knew him to be easily the most dangerous person in the room. As for the others, well, none of them had horns or tails, but that was about it.

The elf leaned forward. "Dawn Era, aren't you?" he said. "If you survive this, you'll have to tell me how you got here."

"I –"

"They want you to think you're as good as dead already. Don't believe them! I wouldn't have signed up in the first place, if I hadn't come back afterwards and told myself I'd come through it all intact." He winked and settled back. "The situation is hopeless, of course. But I wouldn't take it seriously."

Ellie blinked. Was everybody mad here?

In that same instant, a visi-plate very much like the one in the police car lowered from the ceiling, and a woman appeared on it. "Hero mercenaries," she said, "I salute you! As you already know, we are at the very front lines of the War. The Aftermen Empire has been slowly, inexorably moving backwards into their past, our present, a year at time.

So far, the Optimized Rationality of True Men has lost five thousand three hundred and fourteen years to their onslaught." Her eyes blazed. "That advance ends here! That advance ends now! We have lost so far because, living down-time from the Aftermen, we cannot obtain a technological superiority to them. Every weapon we invent passes effortlessly into their hands.

"So we are going to fight and defeat them, not with technology but with the one quality that, not being human, they lack – human character! Our researches into the far past have shown that superior technology can be defeated by raw courage and sheer numbers. One man with a sunstroker can be overwhelmed by savages equipped with nothing more than neutron bombs – *if* there are enough of them, and they don't mind dying! An army with energy guns can be destroyed by rocks and sticks and determination.

"In a minute, your transporter and a million more like it will arrive at staging areas afloat in null-time. You will don respirators and disembark. There you will find the time-torpedoes. Each one requires two operators – a pilot and a button-pusher. The pilot will bring you in as close as possible to the Aftermen time-dreadnoughts. The button-pusher will then set off the chronomordant explosives."

This is madness, Ellie thought. *I'll do no such thing*. Simultaneous with the thought came the realization that she had the complex skills needed to serve as either pilot or button-pusher. They must have been given to her at the same time she had been made young again and her eyesight improved.

"Not one in a thousand of you will live to make it anywhere near the time-dreadnoughts. But those few who do will justify the sacrifices of the rest. For with your deaths, you will be preserving humanity from enslavement and destruction! Martyrs, I salute you." She clenched her fist. "We are nothing! The Rationality is all!"

Then everyone was on his or her feet, all facing the visi-screen, all raising clenched fists in response to the salute, and all chanting as one, *"We are nothing! The Rationality is all!"*

To her horror and disbelief, Ellie discovered herself chanting the oath of self-abnegation in unison with the others, and, worse, meaning every word of it.

The woman who had taken the key away from her had said something about "loyalty imprinting." Now Ellie understood what that term entailed.

In the grey not-space of null-time, Ellie kicked her way into the time-torpedo. It was to her newly sophisticated eyes, rather a primitive thing: Fifteen grams of nano-mechanism welded to a collapsteel hull equipped with a noninertial propulsion unit and packed with five tons of something her mental translator rendered as "annihilatium." This last, she knew to the core of her being, was ferociously destructive stuff.

Nadine wriggled in after her. "Let me pilot," she said. "I've been playing video games since Mario was the villain in Donkey Kong."

"Nadine, dear, there's something I've been meaning to ask you." Ellie settled into the button-pusher slot. There were twenty-three steps to setting off the annihilatium, each one finicky, and if were even one step taken out of order, nothing would happen. She had absolutely no doubt she could do it correctly, swiftly, efficiently.

"Yes?"

"Does all that futuristic jargon of yours actually *mean* anything?"

Nadine's laughter was cut off by a *squawk* from the visi-plate. The woman who had lectured them earlier appeared, looking stern. "Launch in twenty-three seconds," she said. "For the Rationality!"

"For the Rationality!" Ellie responded fervently and in unison with Nadine. Inside, however, she was thinking, *How did I get into this?* and then, ruefully, *Well, there's no fool like an old fool.*

"Eleven seconds...seven seconds...three seconds...one second."

Nadine launched.

Without time and space, there can be neither sequence nor pattern. The battle between the Aftermen dreadnoughts and the time-torpedoes of the Rationality, for all its shifts and feints and evasions, could be reduced to a single blip of instantaneous action and then rendered into a single binary datum: win/lose.

The Rationality lost.

The time-dreadnoughts of the Aftermen crept another year into the past.

But somewhere in the very heart of that not-terribly-important battle, two torpedoes, one of which was piloted by Nadine, converged upon the hot-spot of guiding consciousness that empowered and drove the flagship of the Aftermen time-armada. Two button-pushers set off their explosives. Two shockwaves bowed outward, met, meshed, and merged with the expanding shockwave of the countermeasure launched by the dreadnought's tutelary awareness.

Something terribly complicated happened.

Then Ellie found herself sitting at a table in the bar of the Algonquin Hotel, back in New York City. Nadine was sitting opposite her. To either side of them were the clever albino and the man with the tattooed face and the filed teeth.

The albino smiled widely. "Ah, the primitives! Of all who could have survived – myself excepted, of course – you are the most welcome."

His tattooed companion frowned. "Please show some more tact, Sev. However they may appear to us, these folk are not primitives to *themselves*."

"You are right as always, Dun Jal. Permit me to introduce myself. I am Seventh-Clone of House Orpen, Lord Extratemporal of the Centuries 3197 through 3992 Inclusive, Backup Heir Potential to the Indeterminate Throne. Sev, for short."

"Dun Jal. Mercenary. From the early days of the Rationality. Before it grew decadent."

"Eleanor Voigt, Nadine Shepard. I'm from 1936, and she's from 2004. Where – if that's the right word – are we?"

"Neither where nor when, delightful aboriginal. We have obviously been thrown into hypertime, that no-longer-theoretical state inform-ing and supporting the more mundane seven dimensions of time with which you are doubtless familiar. Had we minds capable of perceiving it directly without going mad, who knows what we should see? As it is," he waved a hand, "all this is to me as my One-Father's clonatorium, in which so many of I spent our minority."

"I see a workshop," Dun Jal said.

"I see –" Nadine began.

Dun Jal turned pale. "A Tarbleck-null!" He bolted to his feet, hand instinctively going for a sidearm which, in their current state, did not exist.

"Mr. Tarblecko!" Ellie gasped. It was the first time she had thought of him since her imprinted technical training in the time-fortress of the Rationality, and speaking his name brought up floods of related information: That there were seven classes of Aftermen, or Tarblecks as they called themselves. That the least of them, the Tarbleck-sixes, were brutal and domineering overlords. That the greatest of them, the Tarbleck-nulls, commanded the obedience of millions. That the maximum power a Tarbleck-null could call upon at an instant's notice was four quads per second per second. That the physical expression of that power was so great that, had she known, Ellie would never have gone through that closet door in the first place.

Sev gestured toward an empty chair. "Yes, I thought it was about time for you to show up."

The sinister grey Afterman drew up the chair and sat down to their table. "The small one knows why I am here," he said. "The others do not. It is degrading to explain myself to such as you, so he shall have to."

"I am so privileged as to have studied the more obscure workings of time, yes." The little man put his fingertips together and smiled a fey, foxy smile over their tips. "So I know that physical force is useless here. Only argument can prevail. Thus...trial by persuasion it is. I shall go first."

He stood up. "My argument is simple: As I told our dear, savage friends here earlier, an heir-potential to the Indeterminate Throne is too valuable to risk on uncertain adventures. Before I was allowed to enlist as a mercenary, my elder self had to return from the experience to testify I would survive it unscathed. I did. Therefore, I will."

He sat.

There was a moment's silence. "That's all you have to say?" Dun Jal asked.

"It is enough."

"Well." Dun Jal cleared his throat and stood. "Then it is my turn. The Empire of the Aftermen is inherently unstable at all points. Perhaps it was a natural phenomenon – *once*. Perhaps the Aftermen arose from the workings of ordinary evolutionary processes, and could at one time claim that therefore they had a natural place in this continuum. That changed when they began to expand their Empire into their own past.

In order to enable their back-conquests, they had to send agents to all prior periods in time to influence and corrupt, to change the flow of history into something terrible and terrifying, from which they might arise. And so they did.

"Massacres, death-camps, genocide, World Wars..." (There were other terms that did not translate, concepts more horrible than Ellie had words for.) "You don't really think those were the work of *human beings*, do you? We're much too sensible a race for that sort of thing – when we're left to our own devices. No, all the worst of our miseries are instigated by the Aftermen. We are far from perfect, and the best example of this is the cruel handling of the War in the final years of the Optimized Rationality of True Men, where our leaders have become almost as terrible as the Aftermen themselves – because it is from their very ranks that the Aftermen shall arise. But what *might* we have been?

"Without the interference of the Aftermen might we not have become something truly admirable? Might we not have become not the Last Men, but the First truly worthy of the name?" He sat down.

Lightly, sardonically, Sev applauded. "Next?"

The Tarbleck-null placed both hands heavily on the table and, leaning forward, pushed himself up. "Does the tiger explain himself to the sheep?" he asked. "Does he *need* to explain? The sheep understand well enough that Death has come to walk among them, to eat those it will and spare the rest only because he is not yet hungry. So too do men understand that they have met their master. I do not enslave men because it is right or proper but because I *can*. The proof of which is that I *have!*

"Strength needs no justification. It exists or it does not. I exist. Who here can say that I am not your superior? Who here can deny that Death has come to walk among you? Natural selection chose the fittest among men to become a new race. Evolution has set my foot upon your necks, and I will not take it off."

To universal silence, he sat down. The very slightest of glances he threw Ellie's way, as if to challenge her to refute him. Nor could she! Her thoughts were all confusion, her tongue all in a knot. She knew he was wrong – she was sure of it! – and yet she could not put her arguments together. She simply couldn't think clearly and quickly enough.

Nadine laughed lightly.

"Poor superman!" she said. "Evolution isn't linear, like that chart that has a fish crawling out of the water at one end and a man in a business suit at the other. All species are constantly trying to evolve in all directions at once – a little taller, a little shorter, a little faster, a little slower. When that distinction proves advantageous, it tends to be passed along. The Aftermen aren't any smarter than Men are – less so, in some ways. Less flexible, less innovative.... Look what a stagnant world they've created! What they *are* is more forceful."

"Forceful?" Ellie said, startled. "Is that all?"

"That's enough. Think of all the trouble caused by men like Hitler, Mussolini, Caligula, Pol Pot, Archers-Wang 43... All they had was the force of their personality, the ability to get others to do what they wanted. Well, the Aftermen are the descendants of exactly such people, only with the force of will squared and cubed. That afternoon when the Tarbleck-null ordered you to sit in the window? It was the easiest thing in the world to one of them. As easy as breathing.

"That's why the Rationality can't win. Oh, they *could* win, if they were willing to root out that streak of persuasive coercion within themselves. But they're fighting a war, and in times of war one uses whatever weapons one has. The ability to tell millions of soldiers to sacrifice themselves for the common good is simply too useful to be thrown away. But all the time they're fighting the external enemy, the Aftermen are evolving within their own numbers."

"You admit it," the Tarbleck said.

"Oh, be still! You're a foolish little creature, and you have no idea what you're up against. Have you ever asked the Aftermen from the leading edge of your Empire why you're expanding backwards into the past rather than forward into the future? Obviously because there are bigger and more dangerous things up ahead of you than you dare face. You're afraid to go there – afraid that you might find *me!*" Nadine took something out of her pocket. "Now go away, all of you."

Flash.

Nothing changed. Everything changed.

Ellie was still sitting in the Algonquin with Nadine. But Sev, Dun

Jal, and the Tarbleck-null were all gone. More significantly, the bar felt *real* in a way it hadn't an instant before. She was back home, in her own now and her own when.

Ellie dug into her purse and came up with a crumpled pack of Lucky Strike Greens, teased one out, and lit it. She took a deep drag on the cigarette and then exhaled. "All right," she said, "who are you?"

The girl's eyes sparkled with amusement. "Why, Ellie, dear, don't you know? I'm *you!*"

So it was that Eleanor Voigt was recruited into the most exclusive organization in all Time — an organization that was comprised in hundreds of thousands of instances entirely and solely of herself. Over the course of millions of years she grew and evolved, of course, so that her ultimate terrifying and glorious self was not even remotely human. But everything starts somewhere, and Ellie of necessity had to start small.

The Aftermen were one of the simpler enemies of the humane future she felt that Humanity deserved. Nevertheless they had to be — gently and nonviolently, which made the task more difficult — opposed.

After fourteen months of training and the restoration of all her shed age, Ellie was returned to New York City on the morning she had first answered the odd help wanted ad in the *Times*. Her original self had been detoured away from the situation, to be recruited if necessary at a later time.

"Unusual in what way?" she asked. "I don't understand. What am I looking for?"

"You'll know it when you see it," the Tarbleck-null said.

He handed her the key.

She accepted it. There were tools hidden within her body whose powers dwarfed those of this primitive chronotransfer device. But the encoded information the key contained would lay open the workings of the Aftermen Empire to her. Working right under their noses, she would be able to undo their schemes, diminish their power, and, ultimately, prevent them from ever coming into existence in the first place.

Ellie had only the vaguest idea how she was supposed to accomplish all this. But she was confident she could figure it out, given time. And she had the time.

All the time in the world.

The Little Cat Laughed
to See Such Sport

THERE WAS A SEASON in Paris when Darger and Surplus, those two canny rogues, lived very well indeed. That was the year when the Seine shone a gentle green at night with the pillars of the stone bridges fading up into a pure and ghostly blue, for the city engineers, in obedience to the latest fashions, had made the algae and mosses bioluminescent.

Paris, unlike lesser cities, reveled in her flaws. The molds and funguses that attacked her substance had been redesigned for beauty. The rats had been displaced by a breed of particularly engaging mice. A depleted revenant of the Plague Wars yet lingered in her brothels in the form of a sexual fever that lasted but twenty-four hours before dying away, leaving one with only memories and pleasant regrets. The health service, needless to say, made no serious effort to eradicate it.

Small wonder that Darger and Surplus were as happy as two such men could be.

One such man, actually. Surplus was, genetically, a dog, though he had been remade into anthropomorphic form and intellect. But neither that nor his American origins was held against him, for it was widely believed that he was enormously wealthy.

He was not, of course. Nor was he, as so many had been led to suspect, a baron of the Demesne of Western Vermont, traveling incognito in his government's service. In actual fact, Surplus and Darger were being kept afloat by an immense sea of credit while their plans matured.

"It seems almost a pity," Surplus remarked conversationally over

breakfast one morning, "that our little game must soon come to fruition." He cut a slice of strawberry, laid it upon his plate, and began fas-
tidiously dabbing it with golden dollops of Irish cream. "I could live
like this forever."

"Indeed. But our creditors could not." Darger, who had already
breakfasted on toast and black coffee, was slowly unwrapping a pack-
age that had been delivered just minutes before by courier. "Nor shall
we require them to. It is my proud boast to have never departed a restaurant table without leaving a tip, nor a hotel by any means other than
the front door."

"I seem to recall that we left Buckingham by climbing out a window
into the back gardens."

"That was the queen's palace, and quite a different matter. Anyway,
it was on fire. Common law absolves us of any impoliteness under such
circumstances." From a lap brimming with brown paper and excelsior,
Darger withdrew a gleaming chrome pistol. "Ah!"

Surplus set down his fork and said, "Aubrey, what are you doing
with that grotesque mechanism?"

"Far from being a grotesque mechanism, as you put it, my dear
friend, this device is an example of the brilliance of the Utopian arti-
sans. The trigger has a built-in gene reader so that the gun could only
be fired by its registered owner. Further, it was programmed so that,
while still an implacable foe of robbers and other enemies of its master,
it would refuse to shoot his family or friends, were he to accidentally
point the gun their way and try to fire."

"These are fine distinctions for a handgun to make."

"Such weapons were artificially intelligent. Some of the best exam-
ples had brains almost the equal of yours or mine. Here. Examine it for
yourself."

Surplus held it up to his ear. "Is it humming?"

But Darger, who had merely a human sense of hearing, could detect
nothing. So Surplus remained unsure. "Where did it come from?" he
asked.

"It is a present," Darger said. "From one Madame Mignonette
d'Etranger. Doubtless she has read of our discovery in the papers, and
wishes to learn more. To which end she has enclosed her card – it is

bordered in black, indicating that she is a widow – annotated with the information that she will be at home this afternoon."

"Then we shall have to make the good widow's acquaintance. Courtesy requires nothing less."

Chateau d'Etranger resembled nothing so much as one of Arcimboldo's whimsical portraits of human faces constructed entirely of fruits or vegetables. It was a bioengineered viridian structure – self-cleansing, self-renewing, and even self-supporting, were one willing to accept a limited menu – such as had enjoyed a faddish popularity in the sub-urban Paris of an earlier decade. The columned facade was formed by a uniform line of oaks with fluted boles above plinthed and dadoed bases. The branches swept back to form a pleached roof of leafy green. Swags of vines decorated windows that were each the translucent petal of a flower delicately hinged with clamshell muscle to air the house in pleasant weather.

"Grotesque," muttered Surplus, "and in the worst of taste."

"Yet expensive," Darger observed cheerily. "And in the final analysis, does not money trump good taste?"

Madame d'Etranger received them in the orangery. All the windows had been opened, so that a fresh breeze washed through the room. The scent of orange blossoms was intoxicating. The widow herself was dressed in black, her face entirely hidden behind a dark and fashionable cloud of hair, hat, and veils. Her clothes, notwithstanding their somber purpose, were of silk, and did little to disguise the loveliness of her slim and perfect form. "Gentlemen," she said. "It is kind of you to meet me on such short notice."

Darger rushed forward to seize her black-gloved hands. "Madame, the pleasure is entirely ours. To meet such an elegant and beautiful woman, even under what appear to be tragic circumstances, is a rare privilege, and one I shall cherish always."

Madame d'Etranger tilted her head in a way that might indicate pleasure.

"Indeed," Surplus said coldly. Darger shot him a quick look.

"Tell me," Madame d'Etranger said. "Have you truly located the Eiffel Tower?"

"Yes, madame, we have," Darger said.

"After all these years..." she marveled. "However did you find it?"

"First, I must touch lightly upon its history. You know, of course, that it was built early in the Utopian era, and dismantled at its very end, when rogue intelligences attempted to reach out from the virtual realm to seize control of the human world, and humanity fought back in every way it could manage. There were many desperate actions fought in those mad years, and none more desperate than here in Paris, where demons seized control of the Tower and used it to broadcast madness throughout the city. Men fought each other in the streets. Armed forces, sent in to restore order, were reprogrammed and turned against their own commanders. Thousands died before the Tower was at last dismantled.

"I remind you of this, so that you may imagine the determination of the survivors to ensure that the Eiffel Tower would never be raised again. Today, we think only of the seven thousand three hundred tons of puddled iron of its superstructure, and of how much it would be worth on the open market. *Then*, it was seen as a monster, to be buried where it could never be found and resurrected."

"As indeed, for all this time, it has not. Yet now, you tell me, you have found it. How?"

"By seeking for it where it would be most difficult to excavate. By asking ourselves where such a salvage operation would be most disruptive to contemporary Paris." He nodded to Surplus, who removed a rolled map from his valise. "Have you a table?"

Madame d'Etranger clapped her hands sharply twice. From the ferny undergrowth to one end of the orangery, an enormous tortoise patiently footed forward. The top of his shell was as high as Darger's waist, and flat.

Wordlessly, Surplus unrolled the map. It showed Paris and environs.

"And the answer?" Darger swept a hand over the meandering blue river bisecting Paris. "It is buried beneath the Seine!"

For a long moment, the lady was still. Then, "My husband will want to speak with you."

With a rustle of silks, she left the room.

As soon as she was gone, Darger turned on his friend and harshly whispered, "Damn you, Surplus, your sullen and uncooperative attitude is queering the pitch! Have you forgotten to how behave in front of a lady?"

"She is no lady," Surplus said stiffly. "She is a genetically modified cat. I can smell it."

"A cat! Surely not."

"Trust me on this one. The ears you cannot see are pointed. The eyes she takes such care to hide are a cat's eyes. Doubtless the fingers within those gloves have retractable claws. She is a *cat*, and thus untrustworthy and treacherous."

Madame d'Etranger returned. She was followed by two apes who carried a thin, ancient man in a chair between them. Their eyes were dull; they were little better than automata. After them came a Dedicated Doctor, eyes bright, who of course watched his charge with obsessive care. The widow gestured toward her husband. "*C'est Monsieur.*"

"Monsieur d'Etrang—" Darger began.

"Monsieur only. It's quicker," the ancient said curtly. "My widow has told me about your proposition."

Darger bowed. "May I ask, sir, how long you have?"

"Twenty-three months, seven days, and an indeterminable number of hours," the Dedicated Doctor said. "Medicine remains, alas, an inexact science."

"Damn your impudence and shut your yap!" Monsieur snarled. "I have no time to waste on you."

"I speak only the truth. I have no choice but to speak the truth. If you wish otherwise, please feel free to deprogram me, and I will quit your presence immediately."

"When I die you can depart, and not a moment before." The slight old man addressed Darger and Surplus: "I have little time, gentlemen, and in that little time I wish to leave my mark upon the world."

"Then—forgive me again, sir, but I must say it—you have surely better things to do than to speak with us, who are in essence but glorified scrap dealers. Our project will bring its patron an enormous increase in wealth. But wealth, as you surely know, does not in and of itself buy fame."

"But that is exactly what I intend to do – buy fame." A glint came into Monsieur's eyes, and one side of his mouth turned up in a mad and mirthless grin. "It is my intent to re-erect the ancient structure as the Tour d'Etranger!"

"The trout has risen to the bait," Darger said with satisfaction. He and Surplus were smoking cigars in their office. The office was the middle room of their suite, and a masterpiece of stage-setting, with desks and tables overflowing with papers, maps, and antiquarian books competing for space with globes, surveying equipment, and a stuffed emu.

"And yet, the hook is not set. He can still swim free," Surplus riposted. "There was much talk of building coffer dams of such and so sizes and redirecting so-many-millions of liters of water. And yet not so much as a penny of earnest money."

"He'll come around. He cannot coffer the Seine segment by segment until he comes across the buried beams of the Tower. For that knowledge, he must come to us."

"And why should he do that, rather than searching it out for himself?"

"Because, dear fellow, it is not to be found there. We lied."

"We have told lies before, and had them turn out to be true."

"That too is covered. Over a century ago, an eccentric Parisian published an account of how he had gone up and down the Seine with a rowboat and a magnet suspended on a long rope from a spring scale, and found nothing larger than the occasional rusted hulk of a Utopian machine. I discovered his leaflet, its pages uncut, in the *Bibliothèque Nationale*."

"And what is to prevent our sponsor from reading that same chapbook?"

"The extreme unlikelihood of such a coincidence, and the fact that I later dropped the only surviving copy in all the city into the Seine."

That same night Darger, who was a light sleeper, was awakened by the sound of voices in the library. Silently, he donned blouse and trousers, and then put his ear to the connecting double doors.

He could hear the cadenced rise and fall of conversation, but could not quite make out the words. More suspiciously, no light showed in the crack under or between the doors. Surplus, he knew, would not have scheduled a business appointment without consulting him. Moreover, though one of the two murmuring voices might conceivably be female, there were neither giggles nor soft, drawn-out sighs but, rather, a brisk and informational tone to their speech. The rhythms were all wrong for it to be one of Surplus's assignations.

Resolutely, Darger flung the doors open.

The only light in the office came from the moon without. It illuminated not two but only one figure – a slender one, clad in skin-tight clothes. She (for by the outline of her shadowy body, Darger judged the intruder to be female) whirled at the sound of the doors slamming. Then, with astonishing grace, she ran out onto the balcony, jumped up on its rail, and leaped into the darkness. Darger heard the woman noisily rattling up the bamboo fire escape.

With a curse, he rushed after her.

By the time Darger had reached the roof, he fully expected his mysterious intruder to be gone. But there she was, to the far end of the hotel, crouched alongside one of the chimney-pots in a wary and watchful attitude. Of her face he could see only two unblinking glints of green fire that were surely her eyes. Silhouetted as she was against a sky filled with rags and snatches of moon-bright cloud, he could make out the outline of one pert and perfect breast, tipped with a nipple the size of a dwarf cherry. He saw how her long tail lashed back and forth behind her.

For an instant, Darger was drawn up by a wholly uncharacteristic feeling of supernatural dread. Was this some imp or fiend from the infernal nether-regions? He drew in his breath.

But then the creature turned and fled. So Darger, reasoning that if *it* feared *him* then he had little to fear from *it*, pursued.

The imp-woman ran to the edge of the hotel and leaped. Only a short alley separated the building from its neighbor. The leap was no more than six feet. Darger followed without difficulty. Up a sloping roof she ran. Over it he pursued her.

Another jump, of another alley.

He was getting closer now. Up a terra-cotta-tiled rooftop he ran. At the ridge-line, he saw with horror his prey extend herself in a low flying leap across a gap of at least fifteen feet. She hit the far roof with a tuck, rolled, and sprang to her feet.

Darger knew his limitations. He could *not* leap that gap.

In a panic, he tried to stop, tripped, fell, and found himself sliding feet-first on his back down the tiled roof. The edge sped toward him. It was a fall of he-knew-not-how-many floors to the ground. Perhaps six.

Frantically, Darger flung out his arms to either side, grabbing at the tiles, trying to slow his descent by friction. The tiles bumped painfully beneath him as he skidded downward. Then the heels of his bare feet slammed into the gutter at the edge of the eaves. The guttering groaned, lurched outward – and held.

Darger lay motionless, breathing heavily, afraid to move.

He heard a thump, and then the soft sound of feet traversing the rooftop. A woman's head popped into view, upside down in his vision. She smiled.

He knew who she was, then. There were, after all, only so many cat-women in Paris. "M-madame d'Etra – "

"Shhh." She put a finger against his lips. "No names."

Nimbly, she slipped around and crouched over him. He saw now that she was clad only in a pelt of fine black fur. Her nipples were pale and naked. "So afraid!" she marveled. Then, brushing a hand lightly over him. "Yet still aroused."

Darger felt the guttering sway slightly under him and, thinking how easily this woman could send him flying downward, he shivered. It was best he did not offend her. "Can you wonder, madame? The sight of you…"

"How gallant!" Her fingers deftly unbuttoned his trousers, and undid his belt. "You do know how to pay a lady a compliment."

"What are you doing?" Darger cried in alarm.

She tugged the belt free, tossed it lightly over the side of the building. "Surely your friend has explained to you that cats are amoral?" Then, when Darger nodded, she ran her fingers up under his blouse, claws extended, drawing blood. "So you will understand that I mean nothing personal by this."

———

Surplus was waiting when Darger climbed back in the window. "Dear God, look at you," he cried. "Your clothes are dirty and disordered, your hair is in disarray – and what has happened to your belt?"

"Some mudlark of the streets has it, I should imagine." Darger sank down into a chair. "At any rate, there's no point looking for it."

"What in heaven's name has happened to you?"

"I fear I've fallen in love," Darger said sadly, and could be compelled to say no more.

So began an affair that seriously tried the friendship of the two partners in crime. For Madame d'Etranger thenceforth appeared in their rooms, veiled yet unmistakable, every afternoon. Invariably, Darger would plant upon her hand the chastest of kisses, and then discretely lead her to the secrecy of his bedroom, where their activities could only be guessed at. Invariably, Surplus would scowl, snatch up his walking stick, and retire to the hallway, there to pace back and forth until the lady finally departed. Only rarely did they speak of their discord.

One such discussion was occasioned by Surplus's discovery that Madame d'Etranger had employed the services of several of Paris's finest book scouts.

"For what purpose?" Darger asked negligently. Mignonette had left not half an hour previously, and he was uncharacteristically relaxed.

"That I have not been able to determine. These book scouts are a notoriously close-mouthed lot."

"The acquisition of rare texts is an honorable hobby for many *haut-bourgeois*."

"Then it is one she has acquired on short notice. She was unknown in the Parisian book world a week ago. Today she is one of its best patrons. Think, Darger – think! Abrupt changes of behavior are always dangerous signs. Why will you not take this seriously?"

"Mignonette is, as they say here, *une chatte sérieuse*, and I *un homme galant*." Darger shrugged. "It is inevitable that I should be besotted with her. Why cannot you, in your turn, simply accept this fact?"

Surplus chewed on a knuckle of one paw. "Very well – I will tell you what I fear. There is only one work of literature she could possibly be looking for, and that is the chapbook proving that the Eiffel Tower does not lie beneath the Seine."

"But, my dear fellow, how could she possibly know of its existence?"

"That I cannot say."

"Then your fears are groundless." Darger smiled complacently. Then he stroked his chin and frowned. "Nevertheless, I will have a word with her."

The very next day he did so.

The morning had been spent, as usual, in another round of the interminable negotiations with Monsieur's business agents, three men of such negligible personality that Surplus privately referred to them as *Ci, Ça,* and *l'Autre.* They were drab and lifeless creatures who existed, it sometimes seemed, purely for the purpose of preventing an agreement of any sort from coming to fruition. "They are waiting to be bribed," Darger explained when Surplus took him aside to complain of their recalcitrance.

"Then they will wait forever. Before we can begin distributing banknotes, we must first receive our earnest money. The pump must be primed. Surely even such dullards as *Ci, Ça,* and *l'Autre* can understand that much."

"Greed has rendered them impotent. Just as a heart can be made to beat so fast that it will seize up, so too here. Still, with patience I believe they can be made to see reason."

"Your patience, I suspect, is born of long afternoons and rumpled bed sheets."

Darger merely looked tolerant.

Yet it was not patience that broke the logjam, but its opposite. For that very morning, Monsieur burst into the conference room, carried in a chair by his apes and accompanied by his Dedicated Doctor. "It has been weeks," he said without preamble. "Why are the papers not ready?"

Ci, Ça, and *l'Autre* threw up their hands in dismay.

"The terms they require are absurd, to say the..."

"No sensible businessman would..."

"They have yet to provide any solid *proof* of their..."

"No, and in their position, neither would I. Popotin –" he addressed one of his apes – "the pouch."

Popotin slipped a leather pouch from his shoulder and clumsily held it open. Monsieur drew out three handwritten sheets of paper and threw them down on the table. "Here are my notes," he said. "Look them over and then draw them up in legal form." The cries of dismay from *Ci*, *Ça*, and *l'Autre* were quelled with one stern glare. "I expect them to be complete within the week."

Surplus, who had quickly scanned the papers, said, "You are most generous, Monsieur. The sum on completion is nothing short of breathtaking." Neither he nor Darger expected to collect that closing sum, of course. But they were careful to draw attention away from the start-up monies (a fraction of the closing sum, though by their standards enormous), that were their true objective.

Monsieur snorted. "What matter? I will be dead by then."

"I see that the Tour d'Etranger is to be given to the City of Paris," Darger said. "That is very generous of you, Monsieur. Many a man in your position would prefer to keep such a valuable property in their family."

"Eh? What family?"

"I speak, sir, of your wife."

"She will be taken care of."

"Sir?" Darger, who was sensitive to verbal nuance, felt a cold tingling at the back of his neck, a premonition of something significant being left unspoken. "What does that mean?"

"It means just what I said." Monsieur snapped his fingers to catch his apes' attention. "Take me away from here."

When Darger got back to his rooms, Mignonette was already waiting there. She lounged naked atop his bed, playing with the chrome revolver she had sent him before ever they had met. First she cuddled it between her breasts. Then she brought it to her mouth, ran her pink tongue up the barrel, and briefly closed her lips about its very tip. He found the sight disturbingly arousing.

"You should be careful," Darger said. "That's a dangerous device."

"Pooh! Monsieur had it programmed to defend me as well as himself." She placed the muzzle against her heart, and pulled the trigger. Nothing happened. "See? It will not fire at either of us." She handed it to him. "Try it for yourself."

With a small shudder of distaste, Darger placed the gun on a table at some distance from the bed. "I have a question to ask you," he said.

Mignonette smiled in an amused way. She rolled over on her stomach, and rose up on her knees and elbows. Her long tail moved languidly. Her cat's eyes were green as grass. "Do you want your answer now," she asked, "or later?"

Put that way, the question answered itself.

So filled with passion was Darger that he had no memory of divesting himself of his clothing, or joining Mignonette on the bed. He only knew that he was deep inside her, and that that was where he wanted to be. Her fur was soft and sleek against his skin. It tickled him ever so slightly—just enough to be perverse, but not enough to be undesirable. Fleetingly, he felt like a zoophile, and then, even more fleetingly, realized that this must be very much like what Surplus's lady-friends experienced. But he abandoned that line of thought quickly.

Like any properly educated man of his era, Darger was capable of achieving orgasm three or four times in succession without awkward periods of detumescence in between. With Mignonette, he could routinely bring that number up to five. Today, for the first time, he reached seven.

"You wanted to ask me a question?" Mignonette said, when they were done. She lay within the crook of his arm, her cold nose snuggled up against his neck. Playfully, she put her two hands, claws sheathed, against his side and kneaded him, as if she were a true, unmodified cat.

"Hmm? Ah! Yes." Darger felt wonderfully, gloriously relaxed. He doubted he would ever move again. It took an effort for him to focus his thoughts. "I was wondering...exactly what your husband meant when he said that he would have you 'taken care of,' after his death."

"Oh." She drew away from him, and sat up upon her knees. "That. I thought you were going to ask about the pamphlet."

Again, a terrible sense of danger overcame Darger. He was extremely sensitive to such influences. It was an essential element of his personality. "Pamphlet?" he said lightly.

"Yes, that silly little thing about a man in a rowboat. *Vingt Ans...* something like that. I've had my book scouts scouring the stalls and garrets for it since I-forget-when."

"I had no idea you were looking for such a thing."

"Oh, yes," she said. "I was looking for it. And I have found it too."

"You have what?"

The outer doors of their apartments slammed open, and the front room filled with voices. Somebody – it could only be Monsieur – was shouting at the top of his weak voice. Surplus was clearly trying to soothe him. The Dedicated Doctor was there as well, urging his client to calm himself.

Darger leapt from the bed, and hastily threw on his clothes. "Wait here," he told Mignonette. Having some experience in matters of love, he deftly slipped between the doors without opening them wide enough to reveal her presence.

He stepped into absolute chaos.

Monsieur stood in the middle of the room waving a copy of an ancient pamphlet titled *Vingt Ans dans un Bateau à Rames* in the air. On its cover was a crude drawing of a man in a rowboat holding a magnet from a fishing pole. He shook it until it rattled. "Swindlers!" he cried. "Confidence tricksters! Deceivers! Oh, you foul creatures!"

"Please, sir, consider your leucine aminopeptidases," the Dedicated Doctor murmured. He wiped the little man's forehead with a medicated cloth. "You'll put your inverse troponin ratio all out of balance. Please sit down again."

"I am betrayed!"

"Sir, consider your blood pressure."

"The Tour d'Etranger was to be my immortality!" Monsieur howled. "What can such false cozeners as you know of immortality?"

"I am certain there has been a misunderstanding," Surplus said.

"Consider your fluoroimmunohistochemical systems. Consider your mitochondrial refresh rate."

The two apes, released from their chair-carrying chore, were running in panicked circles. One of them brushed against a lamp and sent it crashing to the floor.

It was exactly the sort of situation that Darger was best in. Thinking swiftly, he took two steps into the room and in an authoritative voice cried, "*If you please!*"

Silence. Every eye was upon him.

Smiling sternly, Darger said. "I will not ask for explanations. I think it is obvious to all of us what has happened. How Monsieur has come to misunderstand the import of the chapbook I cannot understand. But if, sir, you will be patient for the briefest moment, all will be made clear to you." He had the man! Monsieur was so perfectly confused (and anxious to be proved wrong, to boot) that he would accept anything Darger told him. Even the Dedicated Doctor was listening. Now he had but to invent some plausible story – for him a trifle – and the operation was on track again. "You see, there is – "

Behind him, the doors opened quietly. He put a hand over his eyes.

Mignonette d'Etranger entered the room, fully dressed, and carrying the chrome revolver. In her black silks, she was every inch the imperious widow. (Paradoxically, the fact that she obviously wore nothing beneath those silks only made her all the more imposing.) But she had thrown her veils back to reveal her face: cold, regal, and scornful.

"*You!*" She advanced wrathfully on her husband. "How dare you object to my taking a lover? How dare you!"

"You...you were..." The little man looked bewildered by her presence.

"I couldn't get what I need at home. It was only natural that I should look for it elsewhere. So it costs you a day of your life every time we make love! Aren't I worth it? So it costs you three days to tie me up and whip me! So what? Most men would *die* for the privilege."

She pressed the gun into his hands.

"If I mean so little to you," she cried histrionically, "then kill me!" She darted back and struck a melodramatic pose alongside Darger. "I will die beside the man I love!"

"Yes..." Belated comprehension dawned upon Monsieur's face,

followed closely by a cruel smile. "The man you love."

He pointed the pistol at Darger and pulled the trigger.

But in that same instant, Mignonette flung herself before her lover, as if to shelter his body with her own. In the confines of so small a room, the gun's report was world-shattering. She spun around, clutched her bosom, and collapsed in the bedroom doorway. Blood seeped onto the carpet from beneath her.

Monsieur held up the gun and stared at it with an expression of total disbelief.

It went off again.

He collapsed dead upon the carpet.

The police naturally suspected the worst. But a dispassionate exposition of events by the Dedicated Doctor, a creature compulsively incapable of lying, and an unobtrusive transfer of banknotes from Surplus allayed all suspicions. Monsieur d'Etranger's death was obviously an *accident d'amour*, and Darger and Surplus but innocent bystanders. With heartfelt expressions of condolence, the officers left.

When the morticians came to take away Monsieur's body, the Dedicated Doctor smiled. "What a horrible little man he was!" he exclaimed. "You cannot imagine what a relief it is to no longer give a damn about his health." He had signed death warrants for both Monsieur and his widow, though his examination of her had been cursory at best. He hadn't even touched the body.

Darger roused himself from his depressed state to ask, "Will you be returning for Madame d'Etranger's body?"

"No," the Dedicated Doctor said. "She is a cat, and therefore the disposition of her corpse is a matter for the department of sanitation."

Darger turned an ashen white. But Surplus deftly stepped beside him and seized the man's wrists in his own powerful paws. "Consider how tenuous our position is here," he murmured. Then the door closed, and they were alone again. "Anyway – what body?"

Darger whirled. Mignonette was gone.

"Between the money I had to slip to *les flics* in order to get them to leave as quickly as they did," Surplus told his morose companion, "and the legitimate claims of our creditors, we are only slightly better off than we were when we first arrived in Paris."

This news roused Darger from his funk. "You have paid off our creditors? That is extremely good to hear. Wherever did you get that sort of money?"

"*Ci*, *Ça*, and *l'Autre*. They wished to be bribed. So I let them buy shares in the salvage enterprise at a greatly reduced rate. You cannot imagine how grateful they were."

It was evening, and the two associates were taking a last slow stroll along the luminous banks of the Seine. They were scheduled to depart the city within the hour via river-barge, and their emotions were decidedly mixed. No man leaves Paris entirely happily.

They came to a stone bridge, and walked halfway across it. Below, they could see their barge awaiting them. Darger opened his Gladstone and took out the chrome pistol that had been so central in recent events. He placed it on the rail. "Talk," he said.

The gun said nothing.

He nudged it ever so slightly with one finger. "It would take but a flick of the wrist to send you to the bottom of the river. I don't know if you'd rust, but I am certain you cannot swim."

"All right, all right!" the pistol said. "How did you know?"

"Monsieur had possession of an extremely rare chapbook which gave away our scheme. He can only have gotten it from one of Mignonette's book scouts. Yet there was no way she could have known of its importance – unless she had somehow planted a spy in our midst. That first night, when she broke into our rooms, I heard voices. It is obvious now that she was talking with you."

"You are a more intelligent man than you appear."

"I'll take that for a compliment. Now tell me – what was this ridiculous charade all about?"

"How much do you know already?"

"The first bullet you fired lodged in the back wall of the bedroom. It did not come anywhere near Mignonette. The blood that leaked from under her body was bull's blood, released from a small leather bladder she left behind her. After the police departed, she unobtrusively slipped out the bedroom window. Doubtless she is a great distance away by now. I know all that occurred. What I do not understand is *why*."

"Very well. Monsieur was a vile old man. He did not deserve a beautiful creature like Mignonette."

"On this we are as one. Go on."

"But, as he had her made, he owned her. And as she was his property, he was free to do with her as he liked." Then, when Darger's face darkened, "You misapprehend me, sir! I do not speak of sexual or sadomasochistic practices but of chattel slavery. Monsieur was, as I am sure you have noted for yourself, a possessive man. He had left instructions that upon his death, his house was to be set afire, with Mignonette within it."

"Surely, this would not be legal!"

"Read the law," the gun said. "Mignonette determined to find her way free. She won me over to her cause, and together we hatched the plan you have seen played to fruition."

"Tell me one thing," Surplus said curiously. "You were programmed not to shoot your master. How then did you manage...?"

"I am many centuries old. Time enough to hack any amount of code."

"Ah," said Surplus, in a voice that indicated he was unwilling to admit unfamiliarity with the gun's terminologies.

"But why *me*?" Darger slammed a hand down on the stone rail. "Why did Madame d'Etranger act out her cruel drama with my assistance, rather than...than...with someone else's?"

"Because she is a cold-hearted bitch. Also, she found you attractive. For a whore such as she, that is justification enough for anything."

Darger flushed with anger. "How dare you speak so of a lady?"

"She abandoned me," the gun said bitterly. "I loved her, and she abandoned me. How else should I speak of her under such circumstances?"

"Under such circumstances, a gentleman would not speak of her at all," Surplus said mildly. "Nevertheless, you have, as required, explained everything. So we shall honor our implicit promise by leaving you here to be found by the next passer-by. A valuable weapon such as yourself will surely find another patron with ease. A good life to you, sir."

"Wait!"

Surplus quirked an eyebrow. "What is it?" Darger asked.

"Take me with you," the gun pleaded. "Do not leave me here to be picked up by some cutpurse or bourgeois lout. I am neither a criminal nor meant for a sedentary life. I am an adventurer, like yourselves! I can be of enormous aid to you, and an invaluable prop for your illicit schemes."

Darger saw how Surplus's ears perked up at this. Quickly, and in his coldest possible manner, he said, "We are not of the same social class, sir."

Taking his friend's arm, he turned away.

Below, at the landing-stage, their barge awaited, hung with loops of fairy-lights. They descended and boarded. The hawsers were cast off, the engine fed an extra handful of sugar to wake it to life, and they motored silently down-river, while behind them the pistol's frantic cries faded slowly in the warm Parisian night. It was not long before the City of Light was a luminous blur on the horizon, like the face of one's beloved seen through tears.

The Bordello in Faerie

How many miles to Babylon?
Three score miles and ten.
Can I get there by candle-light?
Yes, and back again.

IRONBECK WAS a weary old redbrick factory town located on the west bank of the Porpentine up in the northern marches along the border of Faerie. Ned Wilkins was an Ironbecker bred and born and, like everybody he knew, had graduated from school at age twelve and gone immediately to work the day after. He'd been a breaker boy at the colliery, a scrap sorter at the boiler works, a grease gunner in a machine shop, and a shit laborer more places than he cared to remember, and the one constant in his life was that if there was no other work for him to do, somebody would hand him a broom to keep him busy. He had a thick head, no imagination to speak of, and he could handle himself in a fight if the need arose. He considered himself one of the lads, and took it for granted that they accepted him on those same terms.

So it was a shock when, having come of an age when such knowledge suddenly became urgent, Ned discovered that no one would tell him the location of the bordello across the river.

The bordello was one of those things that nobody spoke openly of yet everyone made smutty slantwise reference to, like the men who hung out at the quarry and would suck the dick of any boy who let them or the clapped-out whore at the Bucket of Nails who'd do it for a beer. Ned had never actually laid eyes on the Bucket of Nails doxy and rather doubted she existed, but almost every night at sunset, once he knew to look, he could see the dim figures of men furtively slipping across the trestle railroad bridge to Faerie, where no honest business awaited.

"You've not got experience enough," Boyce told him, though Boyce had barely two years on him, and they'd shared the same sixth grade. Boyce was an apprentice steam fitter at the turbine factory where Ned was little more than a gofer. "Wait a bit, and when you've gotten your stick wet a few times...well, we'll talk about it."

"Bastard!" Ned cried, and punched Boyce so hard the cigarette flew out of his mouth. Which, given the size of Boyce, meant that it was inevitable Ned would be in no shape to go to work the next day. But there are things a man must do regardless of consequence. Just to keep his self-respect.

That spring, Ned took up with a girl named Rosalie who worked in the canteen at the wire-works. One astonishing night, she took him and a blanket to the woods out beyond the commons and taught him everything he'd been most desperate to know. For a season they lived together, coupling at every chance, and then, after two weeks in which nothing he did pleased her and everything he said provoked an argument, she moved out.

When he learned that Rosalie had gone directly from his flat to that of a mechanic's apprentice named Rusty Jones, Ned sharpened up his biggest knife and went hunting for him. But rumors flew faster than birds in Ironbeck, and when he finally located his rival's place, Rusty and four of his mates were waiting there. They took the knife away from him, blackened his eye, and spoke a few calm words of reason into his ear. All things told, they were decent to him. There were men who'd had their nuts crushed for less.

In the aftermath of which, Ned found himself thinking again of the bordello in Faerie. So, of a warm summer night, he waited in the woods by the tracks on the far side of the river. In the distance a signal light glowed red and green. Overhead, three moons shone. When finally Boyce came striding up the tracks, jauntily whistling "The Continental Soldier," Ned stepped out into the open and quietly said, "Yo."

Boyce stopped. "Yo," he said warily.

"I'm taking you up on your offer. Show me the way."

"How much money d'you have on you?"

"Enough." Ned had brought along his entire week's pay, knowing it was far too much but not wanting to risk the humiliation of being caught short.

"More than you need, in any case. Give me a bank note and I'll show you the way there and back again." It was extortion, and they both knew it. Knew, too, that the wisest thing was for Ned to pay without argument. Which he did.

Boyce grunted and turned away. Ned followed him down the gentle curve of the railroad tracks a quarter-mile or so and into a silvery stand of aspens. There, a trodden path took them down the verge and into the woods. "So what's the big secret about this place?" Ned asked, trying to hide his nervousness with conversation. "Why all the mystery?"

"Shut your hole. You'll know soon enough."

By twisty ways they went deep into the moonlit forest, across one creek on a red lacquered Chinese bridge and over another on a fallen log whose top had been trod clean of bark by travelers. A mossy road of timbers laid down in the mud took them though a sulfur-marsh where night-haunts beckoned and corpse-lights burned blue in the water. Up slope then they trudged into a dark grove of oaks where fireflies gently sifted upward through the leaves. Ned was far from certain he would remember the path in all its intricacies. He worried that perhaps Boyce had taken him by roundabout ways, so as to demand more money on the return trip. "How much farther is it?"

"We're here, asswipe. Look."

At Boyce's gesture, Ned lifted his gaze and saw a massive darkness beyond and among the oaks, the silhouette of a great house, impossible to make out in any detail and relieved only by the occasional glint of candles in its windows like so many distant stars.

"It's enormous."

"It's the World. That's what it's called. There's only one bordello to service all of Faerie and its entrances are everywhere and its name is the World. You take the left-hand path here. When you're done, return to this spot, and I'll guide you home."

"Aren't we going in the same way?" Ned asked, surprised.

"Every man enters by a different door. House rules. It's that kind of place." Boyce threw his cigarette down, ground it underfoot, and strode away.

Heart pounding, Ned let the path carry him to his entranceway.

The door was ordinary enough, but the frame it rested in was carved in graceful curves, like the lips of an enormous vulva. Wonderingly, Ned reached up his hand to touch the clitoris. Even by moonlight he could see it had been polished by many such casual rubs. The instant he touched it, the door flew open.

He went in.

The reception room was paneled in oak and lit by brass lanterns. Leather chairs were scattered here and there. It was posh, but surprisingly mundane. The only otherworldly touch to it was the imp who sat at the reception desk, his nose buried in an issue of *Mythology Today* while a barbed tail lashed back and forth behind him, as regular as a metronome.

The imp had a pince-nez at the tip of its nose, a sharp-toothed grimace beneath it, and three pairs of eyes above. All but the middle pair were shut. "A new one, eh?" The tail froze. He opened all six eyes wide and studied Ned for a long, silent moment. Then he closed the bottom four. "You'll do, I suppose."

Ned cleared his throat, unaccountably embarrassed. "I'd like – " he began.

"Oh, don't you worry about what you'd *like*. Gilbrig has a good one for you. Excellent for your first time, I assure you! Up the stairs and to the left. The green door. She'll be waiting there."

"I... uh, haven't been here before. How much will this be?"

The imp picked up his magazine again. "Take it up with the lady afterwards!"

Anxiously, Ned climbed the stairs, clutching the rail to keep from falling. It seemed a long way to the landing at the top and then, all too soon, he was there. He looked right and left. Though the hallway stretched on forever, there was only one door. It was green as a leaf in springtime. He pushed inside.

An elf-woman lounged naked upon the bed. She leaned up on an elbow, studying him thoughtfully. Her face was lovely but impassive, and her skin was palest blue. She had four breasts whose color gradually drained away at their tips, so that her nipples were white as mushrooms.

"Take off your clothes," she said at last, "and kiss my breasts, one by one."

But when he obeyed, the elf-woman snapped, "Not so fast! You treat them as if they were a quarryman's lunch! Linger. Fill your mouth with them. Suck on the nipples. Use your tongue." Ned altered his approach in accord with her directions. "Yes, that's better. And your hands as well. Yes. Mmm. Now, if you were to very delicately take one nipple between your teeth and gently pull... Ahhhhh."

Slowly, slowly, then, ran the chariot-horses of night. The elf-woman was as fragrant as a spice garden, redolent of wild thyme in the crook of her throat, of ginger and nutmeg beneath her breasts, of cinnamon further down. Her nipples tasted not of mushrooms but of honeydew. At times Ned felt his senses reeling from the intensity of sensations. Yet always he wanted more.

Though all the provinces of her flesh were duly visited, ever did the woman demand that he pay especial attention to her breasts. Nor was Ned loath to do so. Until at last, with him frantically working his yard back and forth between her lower breasts, which she pressed tight about him, and with his hands squeezing her upper breasts while pinching hard her nipples, he spasmed and spent. At which very instant she came as well, as though they two were ensorceled to achieve orgasm at the same time.

There was a basin of water on a stand by the bed. With preternatural grace, the elf dipped a washcloth in it, wrung it out, and cleansed her breasts of his seed. Supplely, she slid into a tight pair of trousers, pulled on high, red-leather boots, tucked in her silk blouse and, one-handed, tied up her hair with a ribbon. Over her blouse she strapped a sword harness so that the scabbard lay diagonal across her back with the blade's hilt peeking up over her left shoulder.

Ned fumbled for his trousers. "Um... How much do I...?"

Contemptuously, she tossed him a gold coin. He stared down at it in astonishment. When he looked up again, the elf-woman was gone.

———

Gilbrig snickered as Ned came down the stairs. "You see? That wasn't so difficult, after all! You are a true *sprutluder* now, eh? Come back next week and I'll have something special for you. Ohhh, yes. Something nice, something nasty, something like nothing you've ever had before." He stuck his fists in his armpits and, pumping his elbows like wings, threw back his head and crowed. "We'll make your rooster sing!"

Ned found Boyce waiting outside in the three-shadowed moonlight, as he had promised. The man threw down his cigarette and ground it underfoot. "I'm giving you good weight here," he said. "You should've been done an hour ago." Then, before Ned could speak, "Turn slowly in a circle. You feel how when you're facing toward the place, there's a little stiffening, a little rise down there? Eh? Well, that's how you get here. Follow your prick. After your first visit, it knows the way. Going home, you just take whichever path it's most reluctant to go down. It's as simple as that." He started down the path.

"Boyce, that woman *paid*—"

The apprentice steam fitter spun around, seized Ned by the collar, and shook him angrily. "All right! Now you know what the big secret is. Let's see if you have wit enough to keep your fat mouth shut about it, shithead."

The next day, at lunch break, Ned went to the bog and, standing inside one of the stalls with his back against the door, spat into his hand and, eyes closed, jerked off to the memory of the four-teated elf. The lingering scent of her, woman-smell and cinnamon commingled, rose up from his cock.

Ned was neither an introspective nor a reflective man. But the sudden reversal of expected roles last night had disturbed him. He had gone looking for whores, not to be one himself. In some way he couldn't logic out, it had tainted the experience. Now, however, in the warmth of the day, the memory of illicit flesh was sweet. He called forth specific memories of the little grunting noise she'd made when he entered her from behind and of how, when she'd leant over him to take his willy in her mouth, he'd stroked her moist cleft with his big toe. Always returning, of course, to those fabulous breasts, blue as a strangled man for most of their plumpness and white as corpse-flesh at their tips.

Other workers came and went as he stroked himself, so Ned was careful to maintain the strictest silence, even when he came. But it made him feel good to have such memories and a secret he need share with no one. Even the fact that the wooden stall was painted an industrial green, in crude harmony with the leaf-green door at the top of the bordello stairs, seemed auspicious. He walked back out onto the factory floor with renewed willingness to work and work hard.

The good mood this furtive act engendered lasted until, coming off shift, he remembered the gold he had been paid, stuck a hand in his pocket, and discovered that the fairy coin had overnight turned to a disk of soft dung.

"It's the new *bögyörö!*" Gilbrig whooped when Ned slouched in. "How's your *kurva'k fasza't* hanging? In good form and looking for some action? Locked, loaded, and ready to go, I bet."

"Fuck off."

"Your joan's upstairs, waiting for you. If she hasn't started already." The imp drew his middle finger under his nose, sniffing ostentatiously, as if it were a fine cigar. "Vintage *fitte*, nice-nice-nice! Ooh, baby, you've got a hot one tonight."

On first entering the room, however, Ned thought not. The woman therein was tall and homely, and was dressed in the dun, utilitarian garb of a cavalrywoman. "Strip down," she said brusquely, "and put these on." Drawing items one by one from a worn-looking pack, she dressed him in a silken under-sark, with over that linen, then leather, and finally chain mail. Yet from the waist down she left him naked. Critically, she looked him over. "You have the height. And as for the face – well, I can always close my eyes."

But when she put aside her gear and clothing, the body beneath them was as trim and strong and sweet as that of any girl he'd ever fantasized over in Ironbeck. Ned's shaft hardened at the sight of her.

"Not so fast. First I must anoint you." Now the cavalrywoman dabbed up three fingers' worth of ointment from one of several chased-silver boxes on the side table. Strong and calloused hands slathered it onto his tool with the same practiced sureness with which she would have curried her steed or oiled her sword.

Finally she knelt on the bed, legs apart, then leant down and placed the side of her face against the sheet, so that her rump stuck up in the air. "Take me as you would your stallion," she commanded.

For a moment Ned didn't understand her. Then, when he did, he flushed, and made such a fumble of his attempt at entry that she reached behind her and scornfully guided him into her lesser orifice. This was a liberty Rosalie had never granted Ned. He began slowly, marveling at the tightness of her nether place and the strangeness of finding himself performing such an act at all. But then the warrior reached a hand behind and slapped him on the haunch so hard that it stung, crying, "Faster, damn you — ride me for all you're worth!"

So he complied, grabbing her hips with both hands and thrusting into her as hard and fast as he could. In response, she ground her cheeks pink against the chain mail. "Give it your all!" the warrior cried. "For the Mark!"

Up hill and down they galloped. Now Ned knew for certain that there was a *geas* placed upon the room that he would not come before his client, for he lasted far longer than ever he had before, more than he would have thought humanly impossible, even. Despite all the bumping of bodies and squeezing of his prong, his physical energy did not lag, nor did he surrender to his own pleasure.

Until at last, of course, he did, she did, they did. He thought then to simply lie there and never move again. But the warrior had other ideas.

"Lie as if dead." She crossed his arms over his chest so that the tips of his forefingers touched his shoulders. "If you moan, if you move, if you try to put your arms about me, I'll kill you. Do you understand? My knife is here on the table, and I know how to use it. One way or another, you must be a corpse."

"Lady..."

"Shhhh. I'll give you something that will help." She drew a pinch of dust from one of the silver boxes, placed it on the back of her thumbnail, laid it under his nose as he was breathing in, and blew it into his nostril. A cold and wintry numbness spread through Ned's body. Sensation faded from his flesh. He tried to raise an arm and could not.

"Wait!" he tried to say, but no sound came from his mouth. But then, as if in obedience to some compensatory principle, his pecker tingled with heat and began to grow. Which told him that, whatever poison he had been given, at least he was not dying.

The elf-warrior straddled his body, seized him by the root, and then rose up and impaled herself upon him. "Ahhhh, sweet liege," she sighed, "at last you're mine."

She rode him like a trooper.

If there is lust after death, Ned discovered that night, if corpses couple in the grave or damned souls fuck in Hell, then it is a dark and wild mating indeed, compounded of ignorance and desire, abandon and despair. The warrior-woman's riding of him was tireless, and it went on until she'd worked herself into a frenzy. He, meanwhile, experiencing no sensations, but those of his cock, felt her madness overwhelm him, body and thoughts, so that he was nothing but urge, rage, and primal need. Until at last, crying, "Ah! My prince! I die for you!" the rider burst into tears and collapsed upon Ned's supine body.

Their gallop over, his joan rolled off him, sighed, and lay for a time motionless. Eventually, she blew another drug into his nostrils to undo the effects of the first and stripped him of the war-leader's costume. While sensation slowly returned to his body, Ned watched her pack away the gear and then dress herself. That pretty body disappeared beneath a cavalrywoman's practical garb. It was like watching the moon disappear behind clouds. A shirt obscured her breasts and then was tucked into her breeches, eclipsing the last sliver of belly and waist and plunging the world into darkness.

With a groan, Ned sat up. The warrior-woman finished cinching up her harness, then paused before donning her tabard. On it was embroidered a cockatrice silhouetted against the sun, surrounded by runes Ned assumed were of mystic import, though he could read not a one of them. "Do you recognize my livery? Do you ken what prince I have sworn allegiance to?"

"Lady, I do not," Ned replied. It was only the truth.

"That's good. I would not have wanted to have to... Well, never mind. Take this for your efforts." She upended her purse on the side-table. Gold coins bounced and went rolling across the hardwood floor.

"This is too much!" Ned cried. Had he been able to take it home with him untransformed, he would not have lacked the wit to keep such counsel to himself. But it was useless to him, and so he would not see it thrown away.

The warrior-lady's face was stern and stoic. "There is no place to spend it where I am going. I have betrayed my prince, my oath, and my company, and tomorrow we will all fall in battle together. Such is my weird. It is a sad and tangled tale and one that no bard shall ever sing." She took Ned's chin between thumb and forefinger and studied his face. Fleetingly, her harsh expression softened. "You've been a good whore. In another time and fate, perhaps we could have... Well, no matter."

She kissed him hard, hoisted her pack, and left.

Ned got dressed. Out of tidiness, he gathered up the gold and dumped the coins back in their bag. Out of frugality, he searched the room until he found a floor-board that might be pried up, and hid the bag beneath it. He had no specific reason to do so. But he reasoned that fairy gold might well stay constant in Faerie, and that if so it might prove useful someday. He had grown up in a household where nothing so utile even as rags or straw was ever thrown away.

Such were the experiences that brought Ned more and more frequently to the bordello beyond the world as he knew it. No man could visit that house every night and hold down a job as well. But he was young and strong and could manage two, three, sometimes even four visits in a week. He serviced fox spirits, fire women (here they were properly called salamanders), shape-shifters, a sphinx who scratched him raw and licked him rawer yet, women whose flesh was as cold as the grave though their passions were not, and nymphs with ivy growing in their hair and madness in their eyes. His work suffered, but he did not notice. Nor if he had would he have thought it important. Though he spent hours in Faerie and days in the mundane world, the latter weighed against the former as moonlight did to granite.

Diverse though his experiences were, some things were as unvarying as natural law: Gilbrig always leered at him on the way in and taunted him on the way out. He was always sent to the room with the green door. And not once did his joans treat him like a real man. Sometimes they looked on him with soft pity afterwards. Sometimes they favored him with avaricious smiles. But never did one smile at him in a kindly way. The doomed warrior who had paid him all her gold came as close as any did to regarding him fondly, but even she had not looked upon Ned himself but at a fantasy of what he might have been to her.

He could not have explained why this bothered him – he would not have treated a whore any better himself – but it did.

Deep in the sunless winter, when it was peril to attempt the railroad trestle and yet the river beneath the ice was so swift and treacherous that no sane man would try to cross the Porpentine afoot, Ned trudged that well-worn path to the World, and found Gilbrig anxiously awaiting him.

"Oh, why does it have to be a *lerppu* like you?" the imp fretted. "You're docile enough, granted, but... Sweet fucking Freya, why couldn't it have been somebody with a *brain?*" Gilbrig kept opening and closing his eyes, pair by pair, as if trying and failing to find a perspective from which he might like what he was seeing. "Listen up, *uskumru.* Tonight's client is important. You've never served anyone like her before, nor will you ever again. Understand? She might ask you to do something you don't want to. Do it! Or, by Lemminkainen's rosy anus, I'll rip off your balls and feed them to you."

"*Póg mo thón.*" Ned had picked up a few useful phrases in the fairy tongue. He repeated this one in English. "Kiss my ass."

Abruptly, Gilbrig changed tack. Climbing up on top of the desk so he could stand at eye level with Ned, he said, "Look, lad, I've always been good to you, eh? Given you a nice clean room and all the twat you could eat... I've said a few harsh things, maybe, but what are words? Air! Farts! Nothing!" He tugged worriedly at his goatee. "Give me this one thing in return. Treat this bitch as if she were Venus Coelestis herself, okay? You won't be that far wrong if you do."

"Why are you so worked up?" Ned demanded. "What's the big deal?"

"This one has power, boy. Power enough to burn down the World and everyone in it."

———

Warily, Ned climbed the stairs and entered the room.

The woman within was clad in a burka so that every least trace of her body was hidden. Veil and hood were all one piece, with a heavy mesh between. Not so much as a strand of hair showed. Her head turned toward him when he entered. "Lock the door," she said, "and make certain the window is securely shuttered. When that is done, you may strip yourself naked."

Item by item, he obeyed. Though he felt her gaze upon him constantly, she did not move at all. "Will you take off your clothing as well, Lady?"

"Douse the lights first."

One by one he blew out the lantern candles, until all was darkness. *What monster is this,* he wondered, *who dares not expose herself to the light?* For an instant he was filled with dread. Almost anything could lie hidden beneath that shapeless cloth. All he knew of this joan was her voice, dulcet and mild. She could be ugly as a toad, slimy as a frog, foul-smelling as a shift supervisor. She might well have tentacles, claws, unfortunate appetites... It was the appetites that worried him most.

There was a rustle of cloth, and then soft light blossomed into the room.

It came from the woman's body.

There was no describing that body, for it was Beauty incarnate. Had her breasts been a gram heavier or her hips a hair slimmer or had her stomach not swelled exactly so, she would have been merely ravishing. As it was, her loveliness was such that it hurt Ned's eyes simply to gaze upon her. Yet he could not look away. Her hair streamed down behind her, bright as comet tails. The burka lay at her feet like a spurned lover. A swath of black silk was wrapped around her head in a blindfold.

Involuntarily, Ned fell to his knees. "Lady," he whispered, "what *are* you?"

"I am perfection and power and gentle light," she replied. "I come from a distant land in the sky. Barefoot I trod the airy places and by forbidden ways descended to this house." Then, as if confessing to something shameful, "I am a star."

The goddess approached him on naked feet, until the fearful power of her body was but a single pace from his mouth. He inhaled. Her privities were hairless, and smelled of clean, distant lands, of winter air on midnight mountaintops, of the purity of the sky. "Worship me."

It was a delight to do so. The mere presence of the star-woman filled him with strength. Though he was still nothing before her greatness, briefly Ned became more than human. He lifted his voice and, in a clear high tenor he had not suspected he might possess, sang:

She walks in beauty, like the night...

Where the words and tune came from he did not know. Perhaps they'd been pulled down out of the sky. Bathed in the radiance of the star-lady, he felt the power of the music flow through and from him, as if he were one of the wizards who, at the dawn of time, had sung the universe into being.

And all that's best of dark and bright
Meet in her aspect and her eyes...

On he sang, until finally the song rose to a triumphant crescendo:

A mind at peace with all below,
A heart whose love is innocent!

The goddess took one small, sure step closer. Now her body was all but touching him. Naked, numinous, perfect, she said, "Stick your tongue in my cunt."

Hesitantly, Ned did, and from her throat escaped a small, shrill cry, like that of a night-bird flying low over a lake. She clutched his head, pushing it into her crotch for a minute or two, while he fervidly sought to please her, and then shoved him away.

Slowly as the evening star sinking below the horizon did she then recline onto the bed. Crooking a beckoning finger, she said, "Abuse me. Degrade me. Make me feel like filth."

"How shall I do that?" he asked fearfully. He did not think he could bring himself to use her harshly. He did not believe it possible.

"Be as kind and gentle and loving to me as you know how. That will suffice."

As she commanded, so did Ned pleasure her. It was an experience and an evening unlike anything he had ever known. He was as worshipfully respectful of the sky-woman as he could be. Never was any man more considerate of a woman nor so attentive to her desires. Yet she shuddered when he touched her, gasped with horror when he delicately kissed her shoulder, and cried out with humiliation when he entered her. Then, when he reflexively drew back, she grasped his shoulders and yanked her to him.

Her body was a delight beyond measure, yet possessing it gave him no real pleasure. He felt like a snail crawling across a marble statue of a goddess and leaving a trail of slime behind him. His every caress defiled her, his every kiss was a lecherous foulness. Had he broken into a cathedral and crapped on the high altar, he could have felt no more vile.

At last his client said, "Enough!" and he sprang away from her. She rose from the bed, went straight to her burka, and put it on. Darkness poured back into the room.

"Lady," Ned said humbly, "why do you wear a blindfold? And how, blindfolded, can you find your way about?"

"I cannot bear the sight of the Lower Realms," she replied. "Yet so repulsive are they to me that I can sense their every detail, even with my eyes shut and swaddled." She walked to the door, and with every step the sole of her foot briefly filled the room with light.

Ned followed her outside where, for the first time, he saw other clients of the bordello than his own, and other whores than he himself. Faces stared from all the windows. Elven warriors, courtiers, merchants, and craftswomen thronged the oak grove outside, stamping their feet in the snow and exhaling small puffs of white into the winter air. Of the women's varying heights, snail horns, hooves, extra limbs, high or low estates, he paid no mind. All his attention was on the star as she walked steadily up the path through the trees and then, by an unseen trail, into the sky.

The star's naked feet traced a dotted line high into the dark. There was a flare of light as she threw away the burka, to float forever in the interstellar aether. Briefly, the errant star wandered. Then she found her place and was still.

"She is one of the Pleiades," murmured somebody nearby (Ned looked down and saw Gilbrig by his knee), "and of high estate indeed."

Silently, then, all went home.

Ned came away from that night convinced that he would never look at another woman again so long as he lived, for they could not stand the comparison. But memories that are born in Faerie are frail and fickle things, quick to fade and quicker to lose their meaning. By early spring, Ned was eager to visit the bordello again.

"D'y'think you can pleasure two women?" Gilbrig jeered. "Well, hold on to your pizzle, boyo, because I'm giving you three! They're sailors, raftswomen from the upper reaches of the Porpentine, where it flows out of Ultima Thule. They've been weeks without a rogering, and their *vittujen* need a good workout."

"You're a tiresome little turd, Gilbrig," Ned wearily said from the stairway.

"At least I'm not a *kikkeli* like you."

The raftswomen were passing a bottle around when he entered. They were all of a racial subtype, superficially identical, blond and braided. One had already unbloused herself. They cheered when Ned entered the room. "It's the slut!" cried one. "Come here, slut, and let's see what you've got."

She thrust a hand down the front of his pants and seized his crank.

The semiclad elf pulled his head back by his hair and slapped his face with her breasts. "Do you like these, slut? Do you?"

Then he was wrenched away by the first elf or the third, he could not tell, who yanked his shirt out of his trousers and shouting, "Show us your chest, slut!" ripped it open. Buttons flew through the air.

The raftswomen howled with laughter. One of them shoved the bottle in his mouth, almost chipping a tooth. "Drink up, slut!" Ned tasted blood; she'd made him bite through his lip.

"Ow! Stop that, damn you! I don't like being treated like that!"

One of the raftswomen pinched his thigh, hard enough to bruise.

"Shut up, slut. *We'll* tell you what you like and what you don't." Another pinched his butt. "But you like this, now, don't you, slut?" The third slammed her elbow into his stomach and said, "But even if you don't, you'll put up with it." She smiled. "Because we want you to."

So began the most terrifying and humiliating night of Ned's life to date. He was stronger than any one of the elven women, weaker than any two, and helpless before all three. With slaps and pinches and the occasional hard punch, they bullied him through their pleasures, unheeding of his miseries. The bed was shoved aside and Ned forced to the floor where one squatted astride his yard, humping up and down, and a second impaled her orchid and anus upon his thumb and forefinger, while the third straddled his face and almost smothered him with her yoni. Every now and anon, they changed places. Always, they kissed and caressed each other in the empyrean above his contested body in a manner suggesting they greatly preferred each others' affections to his own.

When the three were done, they left a single silver coin on the dresser – though that were an ungenerous guerdon for even a lone woman – and lurched drunkenly down the stairs, singing a river-chanty and waving Ned's undershorts in the air like a flag.

Raging, Ned clattered down the stairs to confront Gilbrig. "You six-eyed little piece of shit! You set me up."

Gilbrig made an impudent face. "So?"

"So I don't cost you a copper, nor do I get anything out of this but an evening's entertainment. Which means I don't have to put up with being mistreated."

"You didn't mind the birch dryad, and the little games she liked to play with switches."

"That's not the same thing."

"Or the wench who stuck her tongue a good six inches up your – "

"*Not the same!*" Ned stuck his fist under the imp's nose. "If you do this to me again, I'm gone! I'm out of here!"

"Why wait? Go away now, little girl! If you can't take it, just get up on your high horse and fuck off into the sunset! But don't pretend you didn't like it. Your *mulkku* did, didn't you, little fella?" Gilbrig grabbed

Ned's crotch and squeezed, then laughed when Ned knocked his hand away. "Oh, yes, you did! You loved it! You loved it! You know you did!"

The next day, bruised and sore, Ned could barely hobble to work. His supervisor chewed him out three times that morning and sent him home at noon. "You've been drinking," the supervisor said, "Or worse. Whatever it is, if you don't stop soon, you're going to be out of a job."

To Ned's astonishment, he didn't much care. All he could think of was the bordello called the World, and what had happened to him there last night. He was certain that Gilbrig had said he'd enjoyed it only to offend him. But he wasn't at all sure the creature was entirely wrong.

Two days later, he was back in Faerie. "Green door, asshole," Gilbrig growled.

"Yeah, yeah," Ned replied. "And the same to you." Without paying much attention, he went into the room at the top of the stairs.

Something was wrong.

The room smelled of decay and the window had been smashed to flinders, along with half the furniture. The only light came from outside and, with but one moon above the horizon, it was faint indeed. "Hello?" Ned called uncertainly. "Is anybody here?"

Then there was a scraping noise, and a low, throaty, not entirely sane laugh. Something pulled itself out of the shadows into the half-light. It had curling horns, like a ram, an apish form, and two cold pinpricks of light for eyes.

"Who *are* you?" Ned cried.

"Have you forgotten me so soon, little Ned?" The creature was short, bandy-legged, big-butted, and had one dead hoof that dragged on the floor after it. Its clothes were all rags and mud and could not hide the fact that its teats were covered with fur. "I have many names. Some call me the Mother of Goats." A chill breeze from the window blew from her to him. The stench of her body was astonishing. There was stale piss in there for a foundation, strongly accented by fresher ordure and enhanced by grace notes of sweat, spent seed, carrion maggots, and other, less identifiable things as well.

"I... I don't know you!"

That dark shape bent over almost double, squinting. "I see," she said.

"You've wandered here from out of the past, have you? Gone through the wrong door and here you are?" That laugh again. "Well, can I do less than meet you halfway?"

She limped forward and with every step the stench lessened, the room brightened, and the repulsiveness of her aspect faded. Halfway to him, the limp was gone and her body was convincingly human. Her hair was long and greasy but it no longer covered her body. She still smelled gamy, but Ned had known girls who smelled worse after a double shift at the factory.

"You like me better now, don't you?" The goat-woman cocked her head and smiled flirtatiously. "I can see that you do."

Ned nodded wordlessly.

Smiling, she put aside her gown, which was rags no longer, to reveal a body as young and pleasant as any other woman's. Slowly, seductively, she lay back on the bed and spread her legs. To Ned's horror, a mouse squirmed its way out of her quaint. It ran down her leg and into the darkness.

With a cry of disgust, he stumbled back from her.

"A forfeit! A forfeit!" cried the Mother of Goats. "If you deny me what I came for, you must give me something of equal or greater value." Her broad yellow teeth gleamed. "Those are the house rules."

It was so. Though Ned had never heard such a thing spoken of before, he knew the truth of her words the instant they were spoken. Knew, too, that having come here penniless and without treasure of any kind, and lacking anything else the fey folk valued, he would be expected to cede something better. Such knowledge had been woven into the web and woof of the World at the time of its creation, and none who dwelled therein could avoid it.

He knew that the forfeit she wanted was his soul.

Yet all was not lost. For she would have to accept gold, if he were to offer it, and there was a bag of the stuff hidden under the floorboards of this very room.

The goat-woman's screams of rage still echoed in the air when Ned confronted Gilbrig.

Rather than shrinking from his wrath, however, the imp climbed up on the reception desk and thrust his face almost into Ned's. "The green door, the *green* one, you daft and fucking fool!" he shouted. "How hard is that to understand? How the fuck could you go through the black door? *Dati go fukne konj*, damn you! I'll spread your ass for the horse myself."

"She *knew* me." Ned could barely contain himself. "She said she came from my future!"

"Big fucking whoop. The black door leads forward. All that means is that you'll want her when the time comes. Maybe a decade, two at the outside. Quite possibly less."

"Never!"

"Sooner than you think, Missy. You're coming along nicely. You're not so far from felching Our Lady of Filth as you'd like to believe. We'll have you groveling at her feet, trout in hand, before you know it."

"Not without my cooperation, you won't! I told you I wouldn't put up with this kind of crap and I meant it. I'm done here, done for good, and you can just piss up a rope for all I care, because I'm never returning."

"Go, then! You'll be back! Once you get a taste for fairy flesh, you can never return to human meat. You're my stump-broke *cow!* When I tell you I want cream, you're going to haul out your hose and say, 'How many quarts?'"

With a roar, Ned grabbed Gilbrig by the neck. Maddened with rage, he choked and choked and choked the imp until the grotesque creature's face turned first red and then blue. When he stopped struggling, Ned convulsively released him.

Gilbrig's body fell to the floor, dead.

Horrified, Ned staggered back from the small corpse. All six of its eyes were blank and staring. He felt behind him for the door, seized the handle, and pulled it open. But when he turned to leave, Gilbrig laughed behind him.

"Oh, you don't get off as easy as *that*, Neddikins!" the dead imp cried. "You're one of my girls, now and forever. You'll return! If not this week, then next. If not then, the week after." The voice followed him as he fled down the dark and wind-swept path away from the World. "Three weeks! Three weeks, tops, and you're mine forever."

———

A week went by, then two. Every day Ned fought down the urge to cross over the river into Faerie. Every night it rose up again, stronger than before. Until eventually he was certain that sooner or later he must inevitably give in to it. But even then he resisted. Not yet, he thought. Not today. Just one more day.

Soon.

Not now.

The lads on the factory floor told each other that Ned was "elf-shot," that he'd gotten a taste for fairy snatch and it was only a matter of time before he disappeared across the river forever. It was an open secret that they'd formed a betting pool around the exact date that happened. He was passed up for a promotion to tool-maker's assistant, though he was apt with his hands, and he couldn't bring himself to care.

Such was his condition on the day of Barrington Turbine's annual picnic. It was held on the commons, with tables of food and wine and a small band for dancing on the green, on the theory that it was good for morale. Which it was, though only briefly, for it made the lives of the company's workers more pleasant for a day and no more.

Afterwards, he learned that the young women had been talking about him. "Elf-shot and fairy-whipped," said one, "and limp and useless to boot."

"He's a cold fish for certain," said a second. "Imagine kissing Ned. Ugh!"

But the third – Red Molly – said, "*I* can bring corpse-boy there back to life. Watch and see if I don't." And, seizing a half-emptied bottle of wine from a tub of melting ice, she walked firm of purpose toward Ned Wilkins.

All this he was to learn later. Now he happened to look up from the ground and saw a buxom red-haired woman walking straight toward him. Her breasts were lovely, though there were only two of them and they decently covered. Her skin glowed, though it did not shine of its own light. Her eyes were the green-or-gray color of the Northern oceans.

"Would you like a drink of wine?" she asked, a mischievous diabolus dimpling in her cheek.

But when Ned nodded and reached for the bottle, she held it away from him. Then, lifting her chin in a way that made her chest follow and her breasts rise to his attention, she put bottle to lips and hoisted it high, filling her mouth with wine. After which, she grabbed him by the back of his hair and yanked, forcing his head back and his mouth open.

Her mouth descended to his, and she squirted it full of wine. In astonishment, he swallowed and blinked, and realized that she was already walking away from him. "Wait!" he cried, and ran after her. "Would you... I mean, I'd... Could we dance?"

To his absolute confusion, all of Molly's girlfriends simultaneously broke into laughter.

Thus were Ned's eyes opened again to the beauty of human women. For a long season, he chased after Red Molly. And though he never came close to catching her, somehow in the course of trying, he took to seeing other women and discovered that, to differing degrees and with the occasional exception, they were all desirable and worthy of his respect as well.

Nor was that the only change in Ned's life. Not long after the company picnic, he took a deep breath and went up to his supervisor and said, "Mr. Murcheson? That opening for a machinist's mate – I want it."

Murcheson looked at him in surprise and said, "Do you think you're steady enough for the work?"

"Aye."

For a long still moment, the supervisor studied him shrewdly. "Then it's yours."

So Ned Wilkins got his promotion and, some years after that, became a machinist and then head of his entire division. By slow degrees he became known as a reliable man and the day came when only his oldest cronies remembered there had ever been a time he had slipped the traces and almost been lost to a certain place across the river. Meanwhile, he'd fallen in love with, wooed, and won his own dear Marion.

The borders of Faerie are not constant. They ebb and flow like the tides, though no man can chart them. As he grew older, Ned found that

The Last Geek

HE IS MET at the airport by an over-tall grad student with bad skin. The grad student is nervous. He's working toward a degree in Elvis Studies and is convinced that he is the worst possible choice for the job. He'll bungle it. He'll say all the wrong things. He won't be able to identify the man among the crush of travelers when he gets off the plane.

But the geek is unmistakable. A short, plump man with ginger hair, he has a sad, pink, ageless face. He could be thirty-seven. He could be seventy-three. He wears a sports jacket with no tie and matching white belt and shoes. Though the airport is thronged, he stands apart. He is in the crowd, but not of it.

"Sir!" The grad student jabs a graceless hand in his direction. He turns slowly, the way movie stars do, and unfolds the sweetest of smiles beneath the kindliest of wisdom-crinkled eyes. His speech is melodious. Somehow they are in the car. Somehow everything is all right.

There is a fruit basket waiting for the geek in his hotel room. Pristine in cellophane, it contains, in addition to the astonishing apples and oranges and pears, two small bottles of spring water, three foil-wrapped wedges of cheese, and a narrow box of gourmet crackers.

With the unthinking reflexes of the constant traveler, he snaps on the television set and immediately tunes it out. He hangs up his jacket in the bathroom and turns on the shower at its hottest setting so the room will fill up with steam and gentle out the wrinkles. Then he unpacks his bag, neatly filling the bureau drawers, shirt by shirt and shorts by shorts.

He takes off his shoes, but leaves his socks on.

Finally he removes the flask from its elastic pocket in the suitcase and carries it and an apple out onto the balcony. The night is warm and a strange city lies glittering at his feet. Behind him, the television laughs and screams, a familiar presence, the nomad's home and family.

There is a chair on the balcony. He sits in it, and puts his stockinged feet up on the rail. He unscrews the top of the flask. He takes a sip. Jack Daniel's.

He stares off into the night and thinks thoughts that are his and his alone.

He is eating a modest breakfast from the buffet in the lobby restaurant when the grad student reappears in the slipstream of a woman who pushes eagerly past the other diners. She is an academic, and dresses as one, but with a pashmina scarf thrown loosely over her shoulders and angular silver earrings to assert her individuality. She has a sharp and lively face. White teeth put a crisp bite into her smile when he rises to greet her. She glides into a chair at his table with the assurance of a woman who belongs there.

She is Professor Djuna Bloom and she is the head of the Department of Southern Culture at the university that has paid to bring him here. It's an honor to meet him at last and there are just a few details to go over about his appearance today so that everything goes smoothly. The words tumble out one after another, but so briskly and clearly enunciated that they do not seem rushed.

He nods at everything she says. "Foah the sun," he says when she comments on the Panama hat that rests on an empty chair alongside him. "As you can see, I have fair skin."

The department head is charmed.

Now she touches the back of his hand. She's actually *flirting* with him. The grad student (still there!) recalls first the legendarily easy way carnies have had with women and then old departmental gossip about Professor Bloom and a certain married faculty couple. To his intense embarrassment, he finds himself scowling and blushing.

———

After a tour of the campus, the geek is feted at a luncheon in the chancellor's mansion. The chancellor has a cook, but not a very good one. The food is dreadfully ordinary. Vegetables are boiled until they're limp, a roast cooked until it's brown. But the plates and silver are genuinely old, and the dining room is Victorian in the very best sense. It's a pleasure merely sitting in it.

"It must be wonderful," says Professor Martelli of Social Sciences, "to have a budget robust enough to fly in guest speakers." It is her long-standing opinion that Southern Culture is a subdivision of anthropology, and as such properly belongs within her department.

"I *think*, Rebecca," says Professor Bloom testily, "that you'll find..." Voices lift from every corner, objecting, pleading, calling for reconciliation. The chancellor half-rises from his chair.

A sudden chiming of spoon on crystal cuts through the voices and silences them. They turn to see their guest smiling gently at them.

"Watch this." He breathes upon the spoon, polishes it with his napkin, breathes upon it again. He places the bowl upon his nose, slides it downward, releases the handle.

As if by magic, the spoon hangs from the tip of his nose.

Delighted laughter fills the room. Even the chancellor laughs. Even Rebecca Martelli laughs.

He nods, removes the spoon from his nose, and returns to his food.

After the meal, the geek goes back to his hotel for a nap. Then the long-suffering grad student ferries him back to campus for an informal chat with the Senior Honors Seminar for the department's most promising undergrads.

"It's a dying profession," he tells them. "I mean that quite literally. I've lost so many dear friends to death. Now I'm the last practitioner of my...peculiar profession," he pauses while they chuckle, "and when I'm gone, it won't be revived, any more than you're ever going to see Minoan bull-leapers again. I am a revenant of a vanished way of life."

Because this is a closed seminar, he is free to tell them things that will not be touched on in his public presentation tonight. He talks about the kootch dancers and what they did with boiled eggs. He discusses the folk cures for syphilis that were still being practiced in his youth, and their appalling effects. Then he tells a story about the tattooed lady and what she charged amorous suitors twenty dollars to see that is so raw it makes Dr. Petri, the seminar leader, laugh like a horse.

Wiping tears from his eyes, Dr. Petri exclaims that this, *this* is why he went into teaching in the first place!

There is a light supper at a local restaurant alone with Professor Bloom, who insists he call her Djuna. Afterwards, she leads him across campus to Vanderbilt Hall, where the department holds a sherry reception. There are crackers and a wheel of blue cheese and they drink out of tiny little glasses from what the undergraduates jokingly call the Hereditary Bottle because no one can remember when it was first opened and it isn't near empty yet.

The geek stands holding a glass, with his other hand in his pocket, perfectly at ease. The purpose of the party is to allow the students to interact with him informally. Most can't. The teachers cluster about him so tightly that only the most aggressive students are able to worm their way into that tight knot of conversation and score an acknowledged remark off of him. Even the shyest undergrad, however, even Debbie Harcourt, who wears thick glasses and ugly dresses and walks about in a perpetual cringe, can feel the calm aura of authority that radiates from him. It's simple charisma. Some people have it. The rest flock about those lucky few.

The presentation is an enormous success. Every seat in the auditorium is filled and in defiance of all fire regulations there are people sitting in the aisles and standing, arms folded, against the back wall. When the geek appears, his soft voice is picked up by the microphones and permeates the room.

"Good evening," he says. "How y'all doing?"

They applaud warmly.

He begins with a little autobiography, talking about his impoverished rural childhood and how he ran away to join first a forty-miler, then a full-fledged tent show. When he explains how some of the games of chance are rigged so that nobody can win, mouths open into astonished circles throughout the audience. He is too much the gentleman to use the term "sucker," but many of those present realize that that's exactly what they've been.

He talks about traveling around the Old South by rail. His stories evoke a kinder, gentler era, a time without haste and worry, one filled with simpler pleasures and a hunger for wonder that a carnival could perfectly fulfill.

But then he turns to the question of racial prejudice. "Oh, it was awful," he says. "You have no idea." He tells of the time he witnessed a lynching. The audience listens in a silence so profound that when somebody coughs, half of them *jump*. It's a harrowing story. It makes their hair stand on end.

"And they brought their children along to see," he concludes. "Their children!" He shakes his head sadly. "For all the very real problems we have today, it's a miracle that things aren't worse."

The hours fly by. He finishes up with an exploration of the deeper significance of his profession. He quotes Derrida. He quotes Barzun. He quotes Rousseau. The audience is in his hands.

Finally, the Dean of Admissions comes out from backstage carrying a live chicken. Grinning, the dean holds it out to the geek, who solemnly accepts it. He strokes the bird's feathers, calming it, hypnotizing it. He holds the creature up before his eyes.

Then he bites off its head.

The audience roars. Their applause swells as he walks offstage with a modest little wave. The students are on their feet, clapping and stamping as if they were at a basketball game. The sound is thunderous. After only the slightest of pauses, the chancellor, deans, and dignitaries seated in the front row also stand, making the ovation universal.

Backstage, Djuna hands him an envelope with his honorarium check, which he places in an inside pocket of his jacket. Impetuously, she darts forward and plants a chaste peck on his cheek. The grad student, tears in eyes, seizes his hand and pumps it up and down.

Then it's back to his hotel room, alone. In the morning, he'll catch a plane for his next appearance. He is the last of his breed, as American as John Wayne or Buzz Aldrin, a solitary man perhaps, as all great men are, a living cultural treasure and an acknowledged national icon. But when the applause dies down, there's nothing but the night, the road ahead and one more gig. He's alone again with silence and his own thoughts.

Girls and Boys, Come Out to Play

ON A HILLTOP IN ARCADIA, Darger sat talking with a satyr.

"Oh, the *sex* is good," the satyr said. "Nobody could say it wasn't. But is it the be-all and end-all of life? I don't see that." The satyr's name was Demetrios Papatragos, and evenings he played the saxophone in a local jazz club.

"You're a bit of a philosopher," Darger observed.

"Oh, well, in a home-grown front porch sense, I suppose I am." The satyr adjusted the small leather apron that was his only item of clothing. "But enough about me. What brings *you* here? We don't get that many travelers these days. Other than the African scientists, of course."

"Of course. What *are* the Africans here for, anyway?"

"They are building gods."

"Gods! Surely not! Whatever for?"

"Who can fathom the ways of scientists? All the way from Greater Zimbabwe they came across the wine-dark Mediterranean and into these romance-haunted hills, and for what? To lock themselves up within the ruins of the Monastery of St. Vasilios, where they labor as diligently and joylessly as if they were indeed monks. They never come out, save to buy food and wine or to take the occasional blood sample or skin scraping. Once, one of them offered a nymph money to have sex with him, if you can believe such a thing."

"Scandalous!" Nymphs, though they were female satyrs, had neither hoofs nor horns. They were, however, not cross-fertile with humans. It was the only way, other than a small tail at the base of their spines (and *that* was normally covered by their dresses), to determine their race.

Needless to say, they were as wildly popular with human men as their male counterparts were with women. "Sex is either freely given or it is nothing."

"You're a bit of a philosopher yourself," Papatragos said. "Say — a few of our young ladies might be in heat. You want me to ask around?"

"My good friend Surplus, perhaps, would avail himself of their kind offers. But not I. Much though I'd enjoy the act, I'd only feel guilty afterwards. It is one of the drawbacks of having a depressive turn of mind."

So Darger made his farewells, picked up his walking stick, and sauntered back to town. The conversation had given him much to think about.

"What word of the Evangelos bronzes?" Surplus asked. He was sitting at a table out back of their inn, nursing a small glass of retsina and admiring the sunset. The inn stood at the outskirts of town at the verge of a forest, where pine, fir, and chestnut gave way to orchards, olive trees, cultivated fields, and pastures for sheep and goats. The view from its garden could scarce be improved upon.

"None whatsoever. The locals are happy to recommend the ruins of this amphitheater or that nuclear power plant, but any mention of bronze lions or a metal man causes them only to look blank and shake their heads in confusion. I begin to suspect that scholar in Athens sold us a bill of goods."

"The biters bit! Well, 'tis an occupational hazard in our line of business."

"Sadly true. Still, if the bronzes will not serve us in one manner, they shall in another. Does it not strike you as odd that two such avid antiquarians as ourselves have yet to see the ruins of St. Vasilios? I propose that tomorrow we pay a courtesy visit upon the scientists there."

Surplus grinned like a hound — which he was not, quite. He shook out his lace cuffs and, seizing his silver-knobbed cane, stood. "I look forward to making their acquaintance."

"The locals say that they are building gods."

"Are they really? Well, there's a market for everything, I suppose."

Their plans were to take a strange turn, however. For that evening

Dionysus danced through the town.

Darger was writing a melancholy letter home when the first shouts sounded outside his room. He heard cries of "Pan! Great Pan!" and wild skirls of music. Going to the window, he saw an astonishing sight: The townsfolk were pouring into the street, shedding their clothes, dancing naked in the moonlight for all to see. At their head was a tall, dark figure who pranced and leaped, all the while playing the pipes.

He got only a glimpse, but its effect was riveting. He *felt* the god's passage as a physical thing. Stiffening, he gripped the windowsill with both hands, and tried to control the wildness that made his heart pound and his body quiver.

But then two young women, one a nymph and the other Theodosia, the innkeeper's daughter, burst into his room and began kissing his face and urging him toward the bed.

Under normal circumstances, he would have sent them packing – he hardly knew the ladies. But the innkeeper's daughter and her goat-girl companion were both laughing and blushing so charmingly and were furthermore so eager to grapple that it seemed a pity to disappoint them. Then, too, the night was rapidly filling with the sighs and groans of human passion – no adult, apparently, was immune to the god's influence – and it seemed to Darger perverse that he alone in all the world should refuse to give in to pleasure.

So, protesting insincerely, he allowed the women to crowd him back onto the bed, to remove his clothing, and to have their wicked way with him. Nor was he backwards with them. Having once set his mind to a task, he labored at it with a will.

In a distant corner of his mind, he heard Surplus in the room down the hall raise his voice in an ecstatic howl.

Darger slept late the next morning. When he went down to breakfast, Theodosia was all blushes and shy smiles. She brought him a platter piled high with food, gave him a fleet peck on the cheek, and then fled happily back into the kitchen.

Women never ceased to amaze Darger. One might make free of their bodies in the most intimate manner possible, handling them not only lustfully but self-indulgently, and denying oneself not a single pleasure...yet it only made them like you the better afterwards. Darger was a staunch atheist. He did not believe in the existence of a benevolent and loving God who manipulated the world in order to maximize the happiness of His creations. Still, on a morning like this, he had to admit that all the evidence was against him.

Through an open doorway, he saw the landlord make a playful grab at his fat wife's rump. She pushed him away and, with a giggle, fled into the interior of the inn. The landlord followed.

Darger scowled. He gathered his hat and walking stick, and went outside. Surplus was waiting in the garden. "Your thoughts trend the same way as mine?" Darger asked.

"Where else could they go?" Surplus asked grimly. "We must have a word with the Africans."

The monastery was less than a mile distant, but the stroll up and down dusty country roads gave them both time enough to recover their *savoir-faire*. St. Vasilios, when they came to it, was dominated by a translucent green bubble-roof, fresh-grown to render the ruins habitable. The grounds were surrounded by an ancient stone wall. A wooden gate, latched but not locked, filled the lower half of a stone arch. Above it was a bell.

They rang.

Several orange-robed men were in the yard, unloading crated laboratory equipment from a wagon. They had the appearance and the formidable height of that handsomest of the world's peoples, the Masai. But whether they were of Masai descent or had merely incorporated Masai features into their genes, Darger could not say. The stocky, sweating wagoner looked like a gnome beside them. He cursed and tugged at his horses' harness to keep the skittish beasts from bolting.

At the sound of the bell, one of the scientists separated himself from the others and strode briskly to the gate. "Yes?" he said in a dubious tone.

"We wish to speak with the god Pan." Darger said. "We are from the government."

"You do not look Greek."

"Not the local government, sir. The *British* government." Darger smiled into the man's baffled expression. "May we come in?"

They were not brought to see Dionysus immediately, of course, but to the Chief Researcher. The scientist-monk led them to an office that was almost Spartan in its appointments: a chair, a desk, a lamp, and nothing more. Behind the desk sat a girl who looked to be at most ten years old, reading a report by the lamp's gentle biofluorescence. She was a scrawny thing with a large and tightly cornrowed head. "Tell her you love her," she said curtly.

"I beg your pardon?" Surplus said.

"Tell her that, and then kiss her. That'll work better than any aphrodisiac I could give you. I presume that's what you came to this den of scientists for — that or poison. In which case, I recommend a stout cudgel at midnight and dumping the body in a marsh before daybreak. Poisons are notoriously uncertain. In either case, there is no need to involve my people in your personal affairs."

Taken aback, Darger said, "Ah, actually, we are here on official business."

The girl raised her head.

Her eyes were as dark and motionless as a snake's. They were not the eyes of a child but more like those of the legendary artificial intellects of the Utopian era — cold, timeless, calculating. A shudder ran through Darger's body. Her gaze was electrifying. Almost, it was terrifying.

Recovering himself, Darger said, "I am Inspector Darger, and this is my colleague, Sir Blackthorpe Ravenscairn de Plus Precieux. By birth an American, it goes without saying."

She did not blink. "What brings two representatives of Her Majesty's government here?"

"We have been despatched to search out and recover the Evangelos bronzes. Doubtless you know of them."

"Vaguely. They were liberated from London, were they not?"

"Looted, rather! Wrenched from Britain's loving arms by that dastard Konstantin Evangelos in an age when she was weak and Greece powerful, and upon the shoddiest of excuses — something about some ancient marbles that had supposedly...well, that hardly matters."

"Our mission is to find and recover them," Surplus elucidated.

"They must be valuable."

"Were *you* to discover them, they would be worth a king's ransom, and it would be my proud privilege to write you a promissory note for the full amount. However – " Darger coughed into his hand. "We, of course, are civil servants. The thanks of a grateful nation will be our reward."

"I see." Abruptly changing the subject, the Chief Researcher said, "Your friend – is he a chimeric mixture of human and animal genes, like the satyrs? Or is he a genetically modified dog? I ask only out of professional curiosity."

"His friend is capable of answering your questions for himself," Surplus said coldly. "There is no need to speak of him as if he were not present. I mention this only as a point of common courtesy. I realize that you are young, but – "

"I am older than you think, sirrah!" the girl-woman snapped. "There are disadvantages to having a childish body, but it heals quickly, and my brain cells – in stark contrast to your own, gentlemen – continually replenish themselves. A useful quality in a researcher." Her voice was utterly without warmth, but compelling nonetheless. She radiated a dark aura of authority. "Why do you wish to meet our Pan?"

"You have said it yourself – out of professional curiosity. We are government agents, and therefore interested in any new products Her Majesty might be pleased to consider."

The Chief Researcher stood. "I am not at all convinced that the Scientifically Rational Government of Greater Zimbabwe will want to export this technology after it has been tested and perfected. However, odder things have happened. So I will humor you. You must wear these patches, as do we." The Chief Researcher took two plastic bandages from a nearby box and showed how they should be applied. "Otherwise, you would be susceptible to the god's influence."

Darger noted how, when the chemicals from the drug-patch hit his bloodstream, the Chief Researcher's bleak charisma distinctly faded. These patches were, he decided, useful things indeed.

The Chief Researcher opened the office door, and cried, "Bast!"

The scientist who had led them in stood waiting outside. But it was not he who was summoned. Rather, there came the soft sound of heavy paws on stone, and a black panther stalked into the office. It glanced at Darger and Surplus with cool intelligence, then turned to the Chief Researcher. "Sssssoooooo...?"

"Kneel!" The Chief Researcher climbed onto the beast's back, commenting offhandedly, "These tiny legs make walking long distances tiresome." To the waiting scientist she said, "Light the way for us."

Taking a thurible from a nearby hook, the scientist led them down a labyrinthine series of halls and stairways, proceeding ever deeper into the earth. He swung the thurible at the end of its chain as he went, and the chemical triggers it released into the air activated the moss growing on the stone walls and ceiling so that they glowed brightly before them, and gently faded behind them.

It was like a ceremony from some forgotten religion, Darger reflected. First came the thurifer, swinging his censer with a pleasant near-regular clanking, then the dwarfish lady on her great cat, followed by the two congregants, one fully human and the other possessed of the head and other tokens of the noble dog. He could easily picture the scene painted upon an interior wall of an ancient pyramid. The fact that they were going to converse with a god only made the conceit that much more apt.

At last the passage opened into their destination.

It was a scene out of Piranesi. The laboratory had been retrofitted into the deepest basement of the monastery. The floors and roofs above had fallen in long ago, leaving shattered walls, topless pillars, and fragmentary buttresses. Sickly green light filtered through the translucent dome overhead, impeded by the many tendrils or roots that descended from above to anchor the dome by wrapping themselves about toppled stones or columnar stumps. There was a complexity of structure to the growths that made Darger feel as though he were standing within a monstrous jellyfish, or else one of those man-created beasts which, ages ago (or so legend had it), the Utopians had launched into the void between the stars in the hope that, eons hence, they might make contact with alien civilizations.

Scientists moved purposely through the gloom, feeding mice to their organic alembics and sprinkling nutrients into pulsing bioreactors. Everywhere, ungainly tangles of booms and cranes rose up from the floor or stuck out from high perches on the walls. Two limbs from the nearest dipped delicately downward, as if in curiosity. They moved in a strangely fluid manner.

"Oh, dear God!" Surplus cried.

Darger gaped and, all in an instant, the groping booms and cranes revealed themselves as tentacles. The round blobs they had taken at first for bases became living flesh. Eyes as large as dinner plates clicked open and focused on the two adventurers.

His senses reeled. Squids! And by his quick estimation, there were at a minimum several score of the creatures!

The Chief Researcher slid off her feline mount, and waved the inquiring tentacles away. "Remove Experiment One from its crypt," she commanded, and the creature flowed across the wall to do her bidding. It held itself upon the vertical surface by its suckered tentacles, Darger noted, but scuttled along the stone on short sharp legs like those of a hermit crab's. He understood now why the Chief Researcher was so interested in chimeras.

In very little time, two squids came skittering across the floor, a stone coffin in their conjoined tentacles. Gracefully, they laid it down. In unison, they raised their tentacles and lowered them in a grotesque imitation of a bow. Their beaks clacked repeatedly.

"They are intelligent creatures," the Chief Researcher commented. "But no great conversationalists."

To help regain his equilibrium, Darger fumbled out his pipe from a jacket pocket, and his tobacco pouch and a striking-box as well. But at the sight of this latter device, the squids squealed in alarm. Tentacles thrashing, they retreated several yards.

The Chief Researcher rounded on Darger. "*Put that thing away!*" Then, in a calmer tone, "We tolerate no open flames. The dome is a glycerol-based organism. It could go up at a spark."

Darger complied. But, true though the observation about the dome might be, he knew a lie when he heard one. So the creatures feared fire! That might be worth remembering.

"You wanted to meet Dionysus." The Chief Researcher laid a hand on the coffin. "He is here. Subordinate Researcher Mbutu, open it up."

Surplus raised his eyebrows, but said nothing.

The scientist pried open the coffin lid. For an instant nothing was visible within but darkness. Then a thousand black beetles poured from the coffin (both Darger and Surplus shuddered at the uncanniness of it) and fled into the shadows, revealing a naked man who sat up, blinking, as if just awakened.

"Behold the god."

Dionysus was an enormous man, easily seven feet tall when he stood and proportionately built, though he projected no sense of power at all. His head was either bald or shaven but in either case perfectly hairless. The scientist handed him a simple brown robe, and when he tied it up with a length of rope, he looked as if he were indeed a monk.

The panther, Bast, sat licking one enormous paw, ignoring the god entirely.

When Darger introduced himself and Surplus, Dionysus smiled weakly and reached out a trembling hand to shake. "It is very pleasant to meet folks from England," he said. "I have so few visitors." His brow was damp with sweat and his skin a pallid grey.

"This man is sick!" Darger said.

"It is but weariness from the other night. He needs more time with the physician scarabs to replenish his physical systems," the Chief Researcher said impatiently. "Ask your questions."

Surplus placed a paw on the god's shoulder. "You look unhappy, my friend."

"I—"

"Not to *him*," the dwarfish woman snapped, "to *me!* He is a proprietary creation and thus not qualified to comment upon himself."

"Very well," Darger said. "To begin, madam — why? You have made a god, I presume by so manipulating his endocrine system that he produces massive amounts of targeted pheromones on demand. But what is the point?"

"If you were in town last night, you must know what the point is. Dionysus will be used by the Scientifically Rational Government to provide its people with festivals in times of peace and prosperity as a reward for their good citizenship, and in times of unrest as a pacifying influence. He may also be useful in quelling riots. We shall see."

"I note that you referred to this man as Experiment One. May I presume you are building more gods?"

"Our work progresses well. More than that I cannot say."

"Perhaps you are also building an Athena, goddess of wisdom?"

"Wisdom, as you surely know, being a matter of pure reason, cannot be produced by the application of pheromones."

"No? Then a Ceres, goddess of the harvest? Or a Hephaestus, god of the forge? Possibly a Hestia, goddess of the hearth?"

The girl-woman shrugged. "By the tone of your questions, you know the answers already. Pheromones cannot compel skills, virtues, or abstractions – only emotions."

"Then reassure me, madam, that you are not building a Nemesis, goddess of revenge? Nor an Eris, goddess of discord. Nor an Ares, god of war. Nor a Thanatos, god of death. For if you were, the only reason I can imagine for your presence here would be that you did not care to test them out upon your own population."

The Chief Researcher did not smile. "You are quick on the uptake for a European."

"Young societies are prone to presume that simply because a culture is old, it must therefore be decadent. Yet it is not we who are running experiments upon innocent people without their knowledge or consent."

"I do not think of Europeans as people. Which I find takes care of any ethical dilemmas."

Darger's hand whitened on the knob of his cane. "Then I fear, madam, that our interview is over."

On the way out, Surplus accidentally knocked over a beaker. In the attendant confusion, Darger was able to surreptitiously slip a box of the anti-pheromonal patches under his coat. There was no obvious immediate use for the things. But from long experience, they both knew that such precautions often prove useful.

The journey back to town was slower and more thoughtful than the journey out had been. Surplus broke the silence at last by saying, "The Chief Researcher did not rise to the bait."

"Indeed. And I could not have been any more obvious. I as good as told her that we knew where the bronzes were, and were amenable to being bribed."

"It makes one wonder," Surplus said, "if our chosen profession is not, essentially, sexual in nature."

"How so?"

"The parallels between cozening and seduction are obvious. One presents oneself as attractively as possible and then seeds the situation with small deceits, strategic retreats, and warm confidences. The desired outcome is never spoken of directly until it has been achieved, though all parties involved are painfully aware of it. Both activities are woven of silences, whispers, and meaningful looks. And – most significantly – the Chief Researcher, artificially maintained in an eternal prepubescence, appears to be immune to both."

"I think – "

Abruptly, a nymph stepped out into the road before them and stood, hands on hips, blocking their way.

Darger, quick-thinking as ever, swept off his hat and bowed deeply. "My *dear* miss! You must think me a dreadful person, but in all the excitement last night, I failed to discover your name. If you would be so merciful as to bestow upon me that knowledge and your forgiveness… and a smile…I would be the happiest man on earth."

A smile tugged at one corner of the nymph's mouth, but she scowled it down. "Call me Anya. But I'm not here to talk about myself, but about Theodosia. I'm used to the ways of men, but she is not. You were her first."

"You mean she was a…?" Darger asked, shocked.

"With my brothers and cousins and uncles around? Not likely! There's not a girl in Arcadia who keeps her hymen a day longer than she desires it. But you were her first *human* male. That's special to a lass."

"I feel honored, of course. But what is it specifically that you are asking me?"

"Just – " her finger tapped his chest – "*watch it!* Theodosia is a good friend of mine. I'll not have her hurt." And, so saying, she flounced back into the forest and was gone.

"Well!" Surplus said. "Further proof, if any were needed, that women remain beyond the comprehension of men."

"Interestingly enough, I had exactly this conversation with a woman friend of mine some years ago," Darger said, staring off into the green shadows, "and she assured me that women find men equally baffling. It may be that the problem lies not in gender but in human nature itself."

"But surely –" Surplus began.

So discoursing, they wended their way home.

A few days later, Darger and Surplus were making their preparations to leave – and arguing over whether to head straight for Moscow or to make a side-trip to Prague – when Eris, the goddess of discord, came stalking through the center of town, leaving fights and arguments in her wake.

Darger was lying fully clothed atop his bed, savoring the smell of flowers, when he heard the first angry noises. Theodosia had filled the room with vases of hyacinths as an apology because she and Anya had to drive to a nearby duck farm to pick up several new eider-down mattresses for the inn, and as a promise that they would not be over-late coming to him. He jumped up and saw the spreading violence from the window. Making a hasty grab for the box of patches they had purloined from the monastery, he slapped one on his neck.

He was going to bring a patch to Surplus's room, when the door flew open, and that same worthy rushed in, seized him, and slammed him into wall.

"You false friend!" Surplus growled. "You smiling, scheming... anthropocentrist!"

Darger could not respond. His friend's paws were about his neck, choking him. Surplus was in a frenzy, due possibly to his superior olfactory senses, and there was no hope of talking sense into him.

To Darger's lasting regret, his childhood had not been one of privilege and gentility, but spent in the rough-and-tumble slums of Mayfair. There, perforce, he had learned to defend himself with his fists. Now, for a silver lining, he found those deplorable skills useful.

Quickly, he brought up his forearms, crossed at the wrists, between Surplus's arms. Then, all in one motion, he thrust his arms outward, to force his friend's paws from his throat. Simultaneously, he brought up one knee between Surplus's legs as hard as he could.

Surplus gasped, and reflexively clutched his wounded part.

A shove sent Surplus to the floor. Darger pinned him.

Now, however, a new problem arose. Where to put the patch. Surplus was covered with fur, head to foot. Darger thought back to their first receiving the patches, twisted around one arm, and found a small bald spot just beneath the paw, on his wrist.

A motion, and it was done.

"They're worse than football hooligans," Surplus commented. Somebody had dumped a wagonload of hay in the town square and set it ablaze. By its unsteady light could be seen small knots of townsfolk wandering the streets, looking for trouble and, often enough, finding it. Darger and Surplus had doused their own room's lights, so they could observe without drawing attention to themselves.

"Not so, dear friend, for such ruffians go to the matches *intending* trouble, while these poor souls..." His words were cut off by the rattle of a wagon on the street below.

It was Theodosia and Anya, returned from their chore. But before Darger could cry out to them, several men rushed toward them with threatening shouts and upraised fists. Alarmed, Theodosia gestured menacingly with her whip for them to keep back. But one of their number rushed forward, grabbed the whip, and yanked her off the wagon.

"Theodosia!" Darger cried in horror.

Surplus leaped to the windowsill and gallantly launched himself into space, toward the wagonload of mattresses. Darger, who had a touch of acrophobia and had once broken a leg performing a similar stunt, pounded down the stairs.

There were only five thugs in the attacking group, which explained why they were so perturbed when Darger burst from the inn, shouting and wielding his walking stick as if it were a cudgel and Surplus suddenly popped up from within the wagon, teeth bared and fur all a-hackle. Then Anya regained the whip and laid about her, left and right, with a good will.

The rioters scattered like pigeons.

When they were gone, Anya turned on Darger. "You *knew* something like this was going to happen!" she cried. "Why didn't you warn anybody?"

"I did! Repeatedly! You laughed in my face!"

"There is a time for lovers' spats," Surplus said firmly, "and this is not it. This young lady is unconscious; help me lift her into the wagon. We must get her out of town immediately."

The nearest place of haven, Anya decided, was her father's croft, just outside town. Not ten minutes later, they were unloading Theodosia from the wagon, using one of the feather mattresses as a stretcher. A plump nymph, Anya's mother, met them at the door.

"She will be fine," the mother said. "I know these things, I used to be a nurse." She frowned. "Provided she doesn't have a concussion." She looked at Darger shrewdly. "Has this anything to do with the fire?"

But when Darger started to explain, Surplus tugged at his sleeve. "Look outside," he said. "The locals have formed a fire brigade."

Indeed, there were figures coming down the road, hurrying toward town. Darger ran out and placed himself in front of the first, a pimply-faced young satyr lugging a leather bucketful of water. "Stop!" he cried. "Go no further!"

The satyr paused, confused. "But the fires..."

"Worse than fires await you in town," Darger said. "Anyway, it's only a hay-rick."

A second bucket-carrying satyr pulled to a stop. It was Papatragos. "Darger!" he cried. "What are you doing here at my croft? Is Anya with you?"

For an instant, Darger was nonplused. "Anya is your daughter?"

"Aye." Papatragos grinned. "I gather that makes me practically your father-in-law."

By now all the satyrs who had been near enough to see the flames and had come with buckets to fight them – some twenty in all – were clustered about the two men. Hurriedly, Surplus told all that they knew of Pan, Eris and the troubles in town.

"Nor is this matter finished," Darger said. "The Chief Researcher said something about using Dionysus to stop riots. Since he has not appeared to do so tonight, that means they will have to create another set of riots to test that ability as well. More trouble is imminent."

"That is no concern of mine," said one stodgy-looking crofter.

"It *will* be ours," Darger declared, with his usual highhanded employment of the first person plural pronoun. "As soon as the agent of the riots has left town, she will surely show up here next. Did not Dionysus dance in the fields after he danced in the streets? Then Eris is on her way here to set brother against brother, and father against son."

Angry mutters passed among the satyrs. Papatragos held up his hands for silence. "Tragopropos!" he said to the pimplyfaced satyr. "Run and gather together every adult satyr you can. Tell them to seize whatever weapons they can and advance upon the monastery."

"What of the townsfolk?"

"Somebody else will be sent for them. Why are you still standing here?"

"I'm gone!"

"The fire in town has gone out," Papatragos continued. "Which means that Eris is done her work and has left. She will be coming up this very road in not too long."

"Fortunately," Darger said, "I have a plan."

Darger and Surplus stood exposed in the moonlight at the very center of the road, while the satyrs hid in the bushes at its verge. They did not have long to wait.

A shadow moved toward them, grew, solidified, and became a goddess.

Eris stalked up the road, eyes wild and hair in disarray. Her clothes had been ripped to shreds; only a few rags hung from waist and ankles, and they hid nothing of her body at all. She made odd chirping and shrieking noises as she came, with sudden small hops to the side and leaps into the air. Darger had known all manner of madmen in his time. This went far beyond anything he had ever seen for sheer chaotic irrationality.

Spying them, Eris threw back her head and trilled like a bird. Then she came running and dancing toward the two friends, spinning about and beating her arms against her sides. Had she lacked the strength of the frenzied, she would still have been terrifying, for it was clear that she was capable of absolutely anything. As it was, she was enough to make a brave man cringe.

"*Now!*"

At Darger's command, every satyr stepped forward onto the road and threw his bucket of water at the goddess. Briefly, she was inundated. All her sweat – and, hopefully, her pheromones as well – was washed clear of her body.

As one, the satyrs dropped their buckets. Ten of them rushed forward with drug patches and slapped them onto her body. Put off her balance by the sudden onslaught, Eris fell to the ground.

"Now stand clear!" Darger cried.

The satyrs danced back. One who had hesitated just a bit in finding a space for his patch stayed just a little too long and was caught by her lingering pheromones. He drew back his foot to kick the prone goddess. But Papatragos darted forward to drag him out of her aura before he could do so.

"Behave yourself," he said.

Eris convulsed in the dirt, flipped over on her stomach, and vomited. Slowly, then, she stood. She looked around her dimly, wonderingly. Her eyes cleared, and an expression of horror and remorse came over her face.

"Oh, sweet science, what have I done?" she said. Then she wailed, "What has happened to my *clothes?*"

She tried to cover herself with her hands.

One of the young satyrs snickered, but Papatragos quelled him with a look. Surplus, meanwhile, handed the goddess his jacket. "Pray, madam, don this," he said courteously and, to the others, "Didn't one of you bring a blanket for the victims of the fire? Toss that to the lady – it'll make a fine skirt."

Somebody started forward with a blanket, then hesitated. "Is it safe?"

"The patches we gave you will protect against her influence," Darger assured him.

"Unfortunately, those were the last," Surplus said sadly. He turned the box upside down and shook it.

"The lady Eris will be enormously tired for at least a day. Have you a guest room?" Darger asked Papatragos. "Can she use it?"

"I suppose so. The place already looks like an infirmary."

At which reminder, Darger hurried inside to see how Theodosia was doing.

But when he got there, Theodosia was gone, and Anya and her mother as well. At first, Darger suspected foul play. But a quick search of the premises showed no signs of disorder. Indeed, the mattress had been removed (presumably to the wagon, which was also gone) and all the dislocations attendant upon it having been brought into the farmhouse had been tidied away. Clearly, the women had gone off somewhere, for purposes of their own. Which thought made Darger very uneasy indeed.

Meanwhile, the voices of gathering men and satyrs could be heard outside. Surplus stuck his head through the door and cleared his throat. "Your mob awaits."

The stream of satyrs and men, armed with flails, pruning-hooks, pitchforks and torches, flowed up the mountain roads toward the Monastery of St. Vasilios. Where roads met, more crofters and townsfolk poured out of the darkness, streams merging and the whole surging onward with renewed force.

Darger began to worry about what would happen when the vigilantes reached their destination. Tugging at Surplus's sleeve, he drew his friend aside. "The scientists can escape easily enough," he said. "All they need do is flee into the woods. But I worry about Dionysus, locked in his crypt. This expedition is quite capable of torching the building."

"If I cut across the fields, I could arrive at the monastery before the vigilantes do, though not long before. It would be no great feat to slip over a back wall, force a door, and free the man."

Darger felt himself moved. "That is inutterably good of you, my friend."

"Poof!" Surplus said haughtily. "It is a nothing."

And he was gone.

By Darger's estimate, the vigilantes were a hundred strong by the time they reached the Monastery of St. Vasilios. The moon rode high among scattered shreds of cloud, and shone so bright that they did not need torches to see by, but only for their psychological effect. They raised a cry when they saw the ruins, and began running toward them.

Then they stopped.

The field before the monastery was alive with squids.

The creatures had been loathsome enough in the context of the laboratory. Here, under a cloud-torn sky, arrayed in regular ranks like an army, they were grotesque and terrifying. Tentacles lashing, the cephalopods advanced, and as they did so it could be seen that they held swords and pikes and other weapons, hastily forged but obviously suitable for murderous work.

Remembering, however, how they feared fire, Darger snatched up a torch and thrust it at the nearest rank of attackers. Chittering and clacking, they drew away from him. "Torches to the fore!" he cried. "All others follow in their wake!"

So they advanced, the squid-army retreating, until they were almost to St. Vasilios itself.

But an imp-like creature waited for them atop the monastery wall. It was a small black lump of a being, yet its brisk movements and rapid walk conveyed an enormous sense of vitality. There was a *presence* to this thing. It could not be ignored.

It was, Darger saw, the Chief Researcher.

One by one, the satyrs and men stumbled to a halt. They milled about, uneasy and uncertain, under the force of her scornful glare.

"You've come at least, have you?" The Chief Researcher strutted back and forth on the wall, as active and intimidating as a basilisk. A dark miasma seemed to radiate from her, settling upon the crowd and sapping its will. Filling them all with doubts and dark imaginings. "Doubtless you think you came of your own free will, driven by anger and self-righteousness. But you're here by my invitation. I sent you first Dionysus and then Eris to lure you to my doorstep, so that I might test the third deity of my great trilogy."

Standing at the front of the mob, Darger cried, "You cannot bluff us!"

"You think I'm bluffing?" The Chief Researcher flung out an arm toward the looming ruins behind her. "Behold my masterpiece – a god who is neither anthropomorphic nor limited to a single species, a god for humans and squids alike, a chimera stitched together from the genes of a hundred sires..." Her laughter was not in the least bit sane. "*I give you Thanatos—the god of death!*"

The dome of the monastery rippled and stirred. Enormous flaps of translucent flesh, like great wings, unfolded to either side, and the forward edge heaved up to reveal a lightless space from which slowly unreeled long, barb-covered tentacles.

Worse than any merely visual horror, however, was the overwhelming sense of futility and despair that now filled the world. All felt its immensely dispiriting effect. Darger, whose inclination was naturally toward the melancholic, found himself thinking of annihilation. Nor was this entirely unattractive. His thoughts turned to the Isle of the Dead, outside Venice, where the graves were twined with nightshade and wolfsbane, and yew-trees dropped their berries on the silent earth. He yearned to drink of Lethe's ruby cup, while beetles crawled about his feet, and death-moths fluttered about his head. To slip into the voluptuously accommodating bed of the soil, and there consort with the myriad who had gone before.

All around him, people were putting down their makeshift agricultural weapons. One let fall a torch. Even the squids dropped their swords and huddled in despair.

Something deep within Darger struggled to awaken. This was not, he knew, natural. The Chief Researcher's god was imposing despair upon them all against their better judgments. But, like rain from a weeping cloud, sorrow poured down over him, and he was helpless before it. All beauty must someday die, after all, and should he who was a lover of beauty survive? Perish the thought!

Beside him, a satyr slid to the ground and wept.

Alas, he simply did not care.

Surplus, meanwhile, was in his element. Running headlong through the night, with the moon bouncing in the sky above, he felt his every sense to be fully engaged, fully alive. Through spinneys and over fields he ran, savoring every smell, alert to the slightest sound.

By roundabout ways he came at last to the monastery. The ground at its rear was untended and covered with scrub forest. All to the good. Nobody would see him here. He could find a back entrance or a window that might be forced and...

At that very instant, he felt a warm puff of breath on the back of his neck. His hackles rose. Only one creature could have come up behind him so silently as to avoid detection.

"Nobody's here," Bast said.

Surplus spun about, prepared to defend himself to the death. But the great cat merely sat down and began tending to the claws of one enormous paw, biting and tugging at them with fastidious care.

"Excuse me?"

"Our work now being effectively over, we shall soon return to Greater Zimbabwe. So, in the spirit of tying up all loose ends, the monks have been sent to seize the Evangelos bronzes as a gift for the Scientifically Chosen Council of Rational Governance back home. The Chief Researcher, meanwhile, is out front, preparing to deal with insurgent local rabble."

Surplus rubbed his chin thoughtfully with the knob of his cane. "Hum. Well...in any case, that is not why I am here. I have come for Dionysus."

"The crypt is empty," Bast said. "Shortly after the monks and the Chief Researcher left, an army of nymphs came and wrested the god from his tomb. If you look, you can see where they broke a door in."

"Do you know where they have taken him?" Surplus asked.

"Yes."

"Then, will you lead me there?"

"Why should I?"

Surplus started to reply, then bit his words short. Argument would not suffice with this creature — he was a cat, and cats did not respond to reason. Best, then, to appeal to his innate nature. "Because it would be a pointless and spiteful act of mischief."

Bast grinned. "They have taken him to their temple. It isn't far — a mile, perhaps less."

He turned away. Darger followed.

The temple was little more than a glen surrounded by evenly spaced, slim white trees, like so many marble pillars. A small and simple altar stood to one end. But the entrance was flanked by two enormous pairs of metal lions, and off to one side stood the heroic bronze of a lordly man, three times the height of a mere mortal.

They arrived at the tail end of a small war.

The monks had arrived first and begun to set up blocks and tackle, in order to lower the bronze man to the ground. Barely had they begun their enterprise, however, when an army of nymphs arrived, with Dionysus cradled in a wagonload of feather mattresses. Their initial outrage at what they saw could only be imagined by its aftermath: Orange-robed monks fled wildly through the woods, pursued by packs of raging nymphs. Here and there, one had fallen, and the women performed abominable deeds upon their bodies.

Surplus looked resolutely away. He could feel the violent emotion possessing the women right through the soothing chemical voice of the patches he still wore, a passion that went far beyond sex into realms of fear and terror. He could not help remembering that the word "panic" was originally derived from the name Pan.

He strolled up to the wagon, and said, "Good evening, sir. I came to make sure you are well."

Dionysus looked up and smiled wanly. "I am, and I thank you for your concern." A monk's scream split the night. "However, if my ladies catch sight of you, I fear you will suffer even as many of my former associates do now. I'll do my best to calm them, but meanwhile, I suggest that you – " He looked suddenly alarmed. "Run!"

Lethargy filled Darger. His arms were leaden and his feet were unable to move. It seemed too much effort even to breathe. A listless glance around him showed that all his brave mob were incapacitated, some crouched and others weeping, in various attitudes of despair. Even the chimeric squid had collapsed into moist and listless blobs on the grass. He saw one taken up by Thanatos's tentacles, held high above the monastery, and then dropped into an unsuspected maw therein.

It did not matter. Nothing did.

Luckily, however, such sensations were nothing new to Darger. He was a depressive by humor, well familiar with the black weight of futility, like a hound sitting upon his heart. How many nights had he lain sleepless and waiting for a dawn he knew would never arrive? How many mornings had he forced himself out of bed, though he could see no point to the effort? More than he could count.

There was still a torch in his hand. Slowly, Darger made his shuffling way through the unresisting forms of his supporters. He lacked the energy to climb the wall, so he walked around it until he came to the gate, reached in to unlatch it, and then walked through.

He trudged up to the monastery.

So far, he had gone unnoticed because the men and satyrs wandered aimlessly about in their despair, and his movement had been cloaked by theirs. Within the monastery grounds, however, he was alone. The bright line traced by his torch attracted the Chief Researcher's eye.

"You!" she cried. "British government man! Put that torch down." She jumped down from the wall and trotted toward him. "It's hopeless, you know. You've already lost. You're as good as dead."

She was at his side now, and reaching for the torch. He raised it up, out of her reach.

"You don't think this is going to work, do you?" She punched and kicked him, but they were the blows of a child, and easy to ignore. "You don't honestly think there's any hope for you?"

He sighed. "No."

Then he threw the torch.

Whomp! The dome went up in flames. Light and heat filled the courtyard. Shielding his eyes, Darger looked away, to see satyrs and men staggering to their feet, and squids fluidly slipping downslope toward the river. Into the water they went and downstream, swimming with the current toward the distant Aegean.

Thanatos screamed. It was a horrid, indescribable sound, like fingernails on slate impossibly magnified, like agony made physical. Enormous tentacles slammed at the ground in agony, snatching up whatever they encountered and flinging it into the night sky.

A little aghast at what he had unleashed, Darger saw one of the tentacles seize the Chief Researcher and haul her high into the air, before catching fire itself and raining down black soot, both chimeric and human, on the upturned faces below.

———

Afterwards, staring at the burning monastery from a distance, Darger murmured, "I have the most horrid sensation of *déjà vu*. Must all our adventures end the same way?"

"For the sake of those cities we have yet to visit, I sincerely hope not," Surplus replied.

There was a sudden surge of flesh and the great cat Bast took a seat alongside them. "She was the last of her kind," he remarked.

"Eh?" Darger said.

"No living creature remembers her name, but the Chief Researcher was born – or perhaps created – in the waning days of Utopia. I always suspected that her ultimate end was to recreate that lost and bygone world." Bast yawned vastly, his pink tongue curling into a question mark which then disappeared as his great black jaws snapped shut. "Well, no matter. With her gone, it's back to Greater Zimbabwe for the rest of us. I'll be glad to see the old place again. The food here is good, but the hunting is wretched."

With a leap, he disappeared into the night.

But now Papatragos strode up and clapped them both on the shoulders. "That was well done, lads. Very well done, indeed."

"You lied to me, Papatragos," Darger said sternly. "The Evangelos bronzes were yours all along."

Papatragos pulled an innocent face. "Why, whatever do you mean?"

"I've seen the lions *and* the bronze man," Surplus said. "It is unquestionably the statue of Lord Nelson himself, stolen from Trafalgar Square in ancient times by the rapacious Grecian Empire. How can you possibly justify keeping it?"

Now Papatragos looked properly abashed. "Well, we're sort of attached to the old thing. We walk past it every time we go to worship. It's not really a part of our religion, but it's been here so long, it almost feels as if it should be, you see."

"Exactly what *is* your religion?" Surplus asked curiously.

"We're Jewish," Papatragos said. "All satyrs are."

"Jewish?!"

"Well, not exactly *Orthodox* Jews." He shuffled his feet. "We couldn't be, not with these cloven hooves. But we have our rabbis and our shuls. We manage."

It was then that Dionysus began to play his panpipes and the crowd of nymphs and women from the temple flowed onto the former battle-ground. Surplus's ears pricked up. "Well, it seems the night will not be a total waste of time, after all," Papatragos said brightly. "Will you be staying?"

"No," Darger said, "I believe I will return to our inn to contemplate mortality and the fate of gods."

Yet Darger was no more than halfway back to town when he came upon a wagon piled high with feather mattresses, pulled over to the side of the road. The horses had been unharnessed so they could graze, and sweet sighs and giggles came from the top of the mattresses.

Darger stopped, appalled. He knew those sounds well, and recognized too the pink knee that stuck out here, the tawny shoulders draped with long black hair that arched up there. It was Theodosia and Anya. Together. Alone.

In an instant's blinding insight, he understood all. It was an old and familiar situation: Two women who loved each other but were too young to embrace the fact in all its implications, and so brought a third, male, partner into their dalliances. It hardly mattered who. Unless, of course, you were the unimportant male himself. In which case, it was a damnable insult.

"Who's there?" The two women pulled apart and struggled up out of the mattresses. Their heads appeared over the top of the wagon. Hair black and blond, eyes brown and green, one mouth sweet and the other sassily sticking out a little pink triangle of tongue. Both were, implicitly, laughing at him.

"Never mind about me," Darger said stiffly. "I see the way the wind blows. Continue, I pray you. I retain the fondest memories of you both, and I wish you nothing but well."

The women stared at him with frank astonishment. Then Theodosia whispered in Anya's ear, and Anya smiled and nodded. "Well?" Theodosia said to Darger. "Are you joining us or not?"

Darger wanted to spurn their offer, if for no other reason than his dignity's sake. But, being merely human – and male to boot – he complied.

So for a space of time Darger and Surplus stayed in Arcadia and were content. Being the sort of men they were, however, mere contentment could never satisfy them for long, and so one day they loaded their bags into a rented pony-cart and departed. For once, though, they left behind people who genuinely regretted seeing them leave.

Some distance down the road, as they passed by the ruins of the Monastery of St. Vasilios, the pony grew restive and they heard the music of pipes.

There, sitting atop the wall, waiting for them, was Dionysus. He was wearing a peasant's blouse and trousers, but even so, he looked every inch a god. He casually set down his panpipes. "Bach," he said. "The old tunes are best, don't you agree?"

"I prefer Vivaldi," Darger said. "But for a German, Bach wasn't bad."

"So. You're leaving, are you?"

"Perhaps we'll be back, someday," Surplus said.

"I hope you're not thinking of returning for the bronzes?"

It was as if a cloud had passed before the sun. A dark shiver ran through the air. Dionysus was, Darger realized, preparing to assume his aspects of godhead should that prove necessary.

"If we were," he said, "would this be a problem?"

"Aye. I have no objection to your bronze man and his lions going home. Though the morality of their staying or returning is more properly a matter for the local rabbis to establish. Unfortunately, there would be curiosity as to their provenance and from whence they had come. This land would be the talk of the world. But I would keep our friends as obscure as possible for as long as may be. And you?"

Surplus sighed. "It is hard to put this into words. It would be a violation of our professional ethics *not* to return for the bronzes. And yet..."

"And yet," Darger said, "I find myself reluctant to reintroduce this timeless land to the modern world. These are gentle folk, their destruction of St. Vasilios notwithstanding, and I fear for them all. History has never been kind to gentle folk."

"I agree with you entirely. Which is why I have decided to stay and to protect them."

"Thank you. I have grown strangely fond of them all."

"I as well," Surplus said.

Dionysus leaned forward. "That is good to hear. It softens the hurt of what I must say to you. Which is: *Do not return.* I know what sort of men you are. A week from now, or a month, or a year, you will think again of the value of the bronzes. They are in and of themselves worth a fortune. Returned to England, the prestige they would confer upon their finders is beyond price. Perhaps you have been guilty of criminal activities; for this discovery, much would be forgiven. Such thoughts will occur to you. Think, also this: That these folk are protected not by me alone, but by the madness I can bring upon them. I want you to leave this land and never come back."

"What — never return to Arcadia?" Surplus said.

"You do not know what you ask, sir!" Darger cried.

"Let this be an Arcadia of the heart to you. All places abandoned and returned to must necessarily disappoint. Distance will keep its memory evergreen in your hearts." Now Dionysus reached out and embraced them both, drawing them to his bosom. In a murmurous voice, he said, "You need a new desire. Let me tell you of a place I glimpsed en route to Greece, back when I was merely human. It has many names, Istanbul and Constantinople not the least among them, but currently it is called Byzantium."

Then for a time he spoke of that most cosmopolitan of cities, of its mosques and minarets and holographic pleasure-gardens, of its temples and palaces and baths, where all the many races of the world met and shared their lore. He spoke of regal women as alluring as dreams, and of philosophers so subtle in their equivocations that no three could agree what day of the week it was. He spoke too of treasures: gold chalices, chess sets carved of porphyry and jade, silver-stemmed cups of narwhale-ivory delicately carved with unicorns and maidens, swords whose hilts were flecked with gems and whose blades no force could shatter, tuns of wine whose intoxicating effects had been handcrafted by the finest storytellers in the East, vast libraries whose every book was the last surviving copy of its text. There was always music in the air of Byzantium, and the delicate foods of a hundred cultures, and of a summer's night, lovers gathered on the star-gazing platforms to practice the amatory arts in the velvety perfumed darkness. For the Festival of the Red and White Roses, streams and rivers were rerouted to run through the city streets, and a province's worth of flowers were plucked and their petals cast into the flowing waters. For the Festival of the Honey of Eden...

Some time later, Darger shook himself from his reverie, and discovered that Surplus was staring blindly into the distance, while their little pony stamped his feet and shook his harness, anxious to be off. He gripped his friend's shoulder. "Ho! Sleepy-head! You've wandered off into the Empyrean, when you're needed here on Earth."

Surplus shook himself. "I dreamed...what did I dream? It's lost now, and yet it seemed vitally important at the time, as if it were something I should remember, and even cherish." He yawned greatly. "Well, no matter! Our stay in the countryside has been pleasant, but unproductive. The Evangelos bronzes remain lost, and our purses are perilously close to empty. Where shall we go now, to replenish them?"

"East," Darger said decisively. "East, to the Bosporus. I have heard – somewhere – great things of that city called...called..."

"Byzantium!" Surplus said. "I too have heard wondrous tales – somehow – of its wealth and beauty. Two such men as ourselves should do marvelous well there."

"Then we are agreed." Darger shook the harness, and the pony set out at a trot. They both whooped and laughed, and if there was a small hurt in their hearts they did not know what it was or what they should do about it, and so it was ignored.

Surplus waved his tricorn hat in the air. "Byzantium awaits!"

A Great Day for Brontosaurs

"you're going to love this guy," the Project Director said.

"I doubt it," the Financial Officer said. "Quite frankly, I have my doubts about the entire project. I really can't see dedicating that much capital to a...well, pardon me for saying this, but a fantasy, really. Where's the profit? What's the point? I'm afraid you've chosen the wrong one to pass on this."

"But that's exactly why I *did* choose you," the Project Director said. "If I can get your approval, the others will be easy."

"You're a visionary," the Financial Officer said. No one could have mistaken this for a compliment. "Shall we get on with it?"

The Project Director touched a device on the table beside him, and said, "Mr. Adams? Would you come in now?"

The door opened. Adams was a lanky man in his late twenties, all wrists, elbows, and throat. He had high cheekbones, and a bright and glittering eye. He grinned as he came in, as if he couldn't wait to explain himself.

Introductions were made. He took a seat. Then the Project Director said, "Well, we're finally gearing up to decide whether to fund the project or not."

"Good!" the young man said too loudly. He blushed. "Excuse me, I get a little overexcited on this subject."

"No, no, enthusiasm is a good thing in a researcher." The Project Director smiled encouragingly.

The Financial Officer cleared his throat. "So, I gather you're talking about cloning dinosaurs," he said in a dubious tone.

"No, sir. You're thinking of *Jurassic Park*. Wonderful movie. I saw a video of it when I was a kid, and I knew right then and there that I wanted to study dinosaurs when I grew up. But, alas, no, that's all hogwash. Even then they knew, really, that it couldn't be done."

The Financial Officer looked baffled. "Why not?"

"Okay, let's crunch a few numbers. The human genome contains about three billion base pairs..."

"Base pairs?"

"Base pairs are – " The young man paused. "Can I wildly oversimplify?"

"Please do," the Financial Officer said dryly.

"If the genome is the complete description of a living creature, then the base pairs are the alphabet in which that description is written. It's a four-letter alphabet consisting of the letters G, A, T, and C, for Guanine, Adenine – "

The Financial Officer said, "Yes, I think we understand that part sufficiently now."

Adams laughed. "I told you I was an enthusiast! Anyway, humans have over three billion base pairs. The fruit fly has one hundred eighty million. The *E. coli* bacterium has four point six million. And there's a lizard that has one hundred eleven billion base pairs. So there's a great deal of variation here."

"How many would a dinosaur have?" the Financial Officer asked.

"Good question! Nobody knows, not really. But a good bet would be that it comes out somewhere in the range of a house finch. Say, two billion base pairs. Now most of that is going to be junk DNA – nonsense sequences that code for impossible protein substances, incomplete duplicates, and so on. Even so, we're talking about a lot of very complex code. Now ask me what the longest string of fossil dino DNA we've recovered so far is."

"How much?"

"Three hundred base pairs! And those were from mitochondrial DNA. The problem is that DNA is fragile stuff. And tiny. Most of the fossils we've ever found have been of the hard parts of animals. Bones, teeth, shells. Soft tissue is only preserved under extremely rare conditions. In fossils as old as the Mesozoic, it's not the tissue itself that's preserved, but an imprint of it. So the whole fossil cloning thing is just a pipe dream. It's simply not going to happen."

"Thank you," the Project Director said. "I think that sums up the difficulties."

"But even supposing we *could* somehow patch together a complete set of genes for a dino-zygote, we *still* couldn't build one. Because we don't have a dinosaur egg."

"What would we need an egg for?" the Financial Officer asked. "I thought we were talking about cloning."

"We need an egg because it's a complex mechanism that not only nurtures the zygote, but tells it which genes to express and which to repress, and in what order. Having a zygote without an egg is like having all the parts for a supercomputer, and no instructions on how to put them together."

"So...if it can't be done," the Financial Officer said. "I don't understand why we're even having this meeting."

The Project Director chuckled. "Our Mr. Adams is a scientist, I fear, not a salesman."

"Oh, but it's only *cloning* that's impossible," Adams said intensely. "We can still have dinosaurs! "We can *back-engineer* them. We can build a dinosaur out of existing material. We start with a bird..."

"A bird! Birds aren't dinosaurs."

"Cladistically speaking, they are. Birds are directly descended from coelurosaurs, which means that they *are* dinosaurs, in the same sense that you and I, having backbones and thus being descended from the first primitive creatures with notochords, are chordates, *and* vertebrates, *and* mammals, *and* anthropoids, *and* human beings all at one and the same time. A bird is simply a dinosaur that's evolved into something more elaborate. It's a refinement, not something new.

"Most of the old instructions are still there, waiting to be turned on again. Tweak one simple gene sequence, and birds sprout teeth again! Tweak another and their wings have claws. Those traits that have been lost entirely can be borrowed from the genes of other creatures – crocodiles and salamanders and whatnot. It's simply a matter of picking and choosing. After all, we know the outcome we want."

"We can do this," the Project Director said. "We have the tools."

The Financial Officer shook his head in wonderment.

"Now we've got the genes, and we insert them into a specially prepared ostrich ovum, and let it grow into a full-sized egg within the mother."

"An ostrich egg? Would that be large enough?"

"Very few dinosaur eggs were much larger. Apatosaurs were so tiny at birth that nobody's been able to figure out how the mothers avoided stepping on them."

"You'd be starting out with apatosaurs, then?"

"No, we'll start out easy, with gallimimuses and troodons – beasts not too far distant, genetically speaking, from living birds. Then we'll expand outward, to allosaurs and plateosaurs, stegosaurs and apatosaurs."

"Marketing has decided to go with 'brontosaurs' rather than 'apatosaurs,'" the Project Director said. "It's got a more commercial ring to it."

"But it's not –"

" – in accord with the rules of scientific nomenclature. Yes, yes. Tell me, which would you rather have – a living, breathing *Brontosaurus*, or plans for an *Apatosaurus* that never got funded?"

The young man flushed, but said nothing.

"Now, as I understand it," the Financial Officer said, "you'll be wanting to establish breeding populations. Won't that be a little tricky? The environment has changed a great deal from Mesozoic times. Will the herbivores even be able to eat contemporary plants?"

"Oh, we can work up some chow for them. As for the environment... well, there'd be a certain amount of trickery involved there, I'm afraid. We don't have any continental expanses of land at hand to turn over to them. But we've done wonders with zoos. We could create an environment good enough to fool the dinosaurs themselves. Good enough to make them happy." Eyes gleaming, the young man said, "Give me the funding, and within the year I'll show you something indistinguishable from a living dinosaur."

"Would it actually be a dinosaur, though?"

"Would it *be* a dinosaur? No. Would it act and behave and think like one? Pretty damn close."

"Well!" The Project Director slapped his hands together. "I told you our young fellow would give you a good show."

The Financial Officer looked thoughtful. "I've only got one more question," he said. "Why?"

"Why, sir?"

"Yes, why? Why even bother? Dinosaurs have been dead for...for millions of years. They had their shot. Why bring them back?"

"Because dinosaurs are wonderful animals! Of *course* we want them back. What is so beautiful and useless as a dinosaur? Who *wouldn't* want to have them around?"

The Financial Officer turned toward the Project Director and nodded. The Project Director stood. "Thank you, Mr. Adams."

"Thank you, sir! For giving me this chance, I mean. To explain what I want to do."

Almost stumbling over himself in his eagerness to make a good impression, the young man left the room.

When the door closed, the Project Director and the Financial Officer looked at one another. Their human shapes wavered and collapsed, revealing their true forms.

The Project Director stretched, shaking out his feathers. "Well?"

"He's wonderful!" the Financial Officer said. "He's everything you said he would be."

"I told you so. Humans are such delightful creatures! So inquisitive, so inventive. I think everyone will agree that they're an ornament to the world."

"Well, you've certainly sold *me*."

"You're satisfied, then?"

"Yes."

"You're prepared to support me for Phase Two? The creation of an environment, and establishment of a permanent breeding population?"

"If the female makes as good an impression, then yes. I'd have to say I am."

"Excellent! Let's interview her right now."

The Project Director shimmered back into human form. He touched the device on the table. "You can come in now, Eve."

Dirty Little War

THE DAIQUIRIS were made with crushed ice and poured into cut-glass tumblers from a pitcher that sat on a towel on the hunt cabinet. The men wore jackets without ties and the women wore cocktail dresses. Herb Alpert's latest album was on the hi-fi, turned down low so it wouldn't disrupt conversation. The hostess had timed the roast so they could linger over their drinks.

Nobody acknowledged the patrol, smaller than mice, that was fearfully making its way across the room.

"Did you hear?" the hostess said eagerly. "Did you hear what Diana Vreeland said? She wants women to wear belts like rings. Four, five, six at a time – the woman's perfectly mad!"

"But who could *wear* them?" Annie Halpern asked. "I'm not exactly Twiggy, you know."

"And thank God for that," her husband threw in.

She patted his cheek. "Isn't he sweet? He always knows the right thing to say."

"Then he's the only man in the world who does," Andy Wexler said belligerently. His wife reached swiftly for his drink, but he held it out of her reach. "None of that, now. I'm wise to your little tricks."

Cindy Wexler laughed with embarrassment. "Why, dear, I don't know what you're talking about."

"I'm sure you don't."

The mission was completely fucked. It had been fucked from its inception, and probably for a long time before that. You didn't get this bollixed up without lots and lots of planning. There'd been seventeen men in the platoon when they'd started out but only eight had made it this far, and yet they were still supposed to go on. The Lieutenant didn't even understand what the point of this operation was supposed to be. The orders made fuck-all sense, as far as he was concerned.

Fuck it. That's all you could say. Just fuck it.

Out on the deck, several of the men were smoking cigarettes and holding forth on greens fees and the economy. "Freezing prices!" one of them said. "It doesn't do any good – it's just political grandstanding. You'll notice that the price of a membership at the club has just doubled and yet, oddly enough, nobody's been arrested for it."

"This isn't Russia," the host agreed. "That's for sure."

"I just don't know what's happening to this country," Lionel Wallace said. "Riots and draft-dodgers and bra-burners and I-don't-know-what."

The host stubbed out his cigarette in an overflowing glass ashtray perched precariously atop the railing. "I blame Nixon."

His wife materialized at his side and scooped up the ashtray. "We won't mention that name tonight," she said firmly. "Let me empty this for you."

Lionel batted irritably at a hornet, and gazed out over the yard. The Japanese maples were beginning to turn. "You're going to have to drain your pool soon," he commented.

"Don't I know it."

It was Joe Martinez who bought it first. He'd been walking point, and he'd tripped the mine, and then he was dead, and Red Walker was lying on the ground beside him clutching his stomach and howling, and then Howie Simms was shot right in the head.

It happened as fast as that.

They'd returned fire, of course, even though they were in deep bush and couldn't even figure out where the enemy *was*. They'd just blasted the hell out of everything, and called for air support, and then air support came and blasted the hell out of everything too.

When the jungle was quiet again, the dead were coptered out in body bags. Red was among them. Also Jimmy O'Brien, their medic, who'd tried to crawl over to Red and drag him back to cover, even though that was exactly what the snipers waited for you to do.

Then, because they had a mission to fulfill and it didn't matter to anyone back at HQ whether it made any sense or not, the platoon proceeded on its way.

The Falkners arrived, and a tension, light and bracing as the first touch of autumn, raced through the women. The Falkners' marriage was like a loose tooth, hanging by a thread, that might go at any instant. Genevieve had responded with peroxide and tennis lessons. She and Daniel fled each other the moment they entered the room. It pained the hostess to see how little care they took to hide their antipathy.

"Seat?" Andy Wexler said, popping out of a leather armchair. Genevieve smiled widely, graciously accepted, and sat down carefully. She *had* to sit down carefully, in a dress as short as that.

Cindy Wexler turned her back and marched out onto the deck. "This is so bad of me," she said brightly. "But I would *kill* for a cigarette."

Lionel gave her one of his, then lit it for her. When he bowed his head over the match, the sun caught on his fine, thinning hair and on the pink scalp underneath.

It was a nightmare. It was like being run down a gauntlet. They couldn't run the one way because the river was there, and the land got boggy. To the other side, the land rose and there weren't any trails. There was mortar fire behind them. Were those fuckers sadists, or just incompetent? The Lieutenant couldn't tell. But so long as they kept moving ahead, changing position, the vc couldn't seem to get any kind of accurate fire on them. So they ran, straight down the trail.

The Lieutenant flashed back to the gauntlet he'd had to run down, blindfolded and in his briefs, when he pledged a fraternity in college. That was before he'd flunked out. He'd been shoved through a doorway, blind, and forced to run between two howling lines of fists and sticks.

He wished they'd try that on him now.

Suddenly, the vc had their range, and the mortar fire swept over the rear of the line, like a rainstorm.

Then, mysteriously, it stopped.

They burst into a village. Right through some fields and into a village. It was so unexpected that for a second they could only stand and gawk. It was like suddenly finding yourself in Disneyland. Then the Lieutenant fired his rifle into the air, and they were all running again and shouting at the top of their lungs. Villagers came boiling out of the huts, and scattered like pigeons. He figured it would distract Charlie. Maybe they'd be lost in the confusion.

When the barrage started again, it fell upon the soldiers and the villagers with terrifying impartiality.

"I'll have you know, my dear, that we saw Woody Allen in New York, back when he was a stand-up..." The hostess heard Dorothea Dunletz make a high-pitched kind of an *eep* noise. "Excuse me."

She hurried over to see what was wrong. To her horror, she discovered that Dorothea had stepped on one of the soldiers.

"Don't give it a thought, dear," she said soothingly. "These things happen. I'll take care of it. No, really, you wouldn't know where anything is."

She got the sports section of yesterday's *Times-Dispatch* and some paper towels. Then, crouching and averting her eyes, she managed to brush the little body onto the newspaper with a few anxious jabs of the bunched-up towels. Hurrying into the kitchen, she hastily dumped the body into the trash can in the cabinet under the sink.

Then she returned with seltzer and more towels, to scrub the stain out of the carpet.

At last, with relief and a certain sense of accomplishment, she was able to rejoin the party.

The Lieutenant wasn't sure when he'd started seeing the hallucinations. But there they were: People eighty, a hundred, a thousand feet high, with legs like sequoia trees, dwindling away from you, and faces so distant you couldn't make out their expressions when they thought you weren't looking and glanced downward. It must've been the bennies he was popping to keep going. Sometimes he was in the bush and other times in a room so vast it seemed they would never cross it. At its end was the wall that, for no reason he could understand, they were supposed, at any cost, to reach.

Not that he believed they were any of them going to make it that far. There were only Sammy and Larry and Crazy Bill and himself left out of all who had started the mission. It seemed impossible that so many had died. It seemed impossible that so few could survive.

The roast was ready.

The hostess stuck a fork in it to make sure, then called her husband into the kitchen and told him it was time to start bringing the men inside. "And stop talking about McNamara!" she whispered fiercely. "We're not mentioning *that* name either."

"You're the boss, dear." Her husband patted her on the fanny, smiling that tolerant smile she found so infuriating, and turned away.

In the living room, Andy was still hanging over Genevieve's chair, and Genevieve in her turn was laughing far too loudly at his jokes. The only saving grace that the hostess could see was that it was keeping Andy away from the daiquiris. Twice he'd asked her to bring him another, and twice she'd gotten conveniently waylaid by other obligations.

"Everybody — everybody, it's time to sit down. Everyone? Dinner is served. Sweetheart, would you carve? You're so good at it."

As the guests came drifting into the dining room in twos and threes, she guided them to their chairs. She was careful to place the Falkners and the Wexlers as far apart as possible.

Sammy died.

Larry died.

Crazy Bill lasted a little longer than the others, but he died too.

The Lieutenant felt like he'd somehow outlived the end of the world. Everyone he cared about — everyone he *loved* was dead. He had family back home, and he supposed that in a sense he loved them too. But it wasn't that kind of intense feeling you had here for the guys you relied on to keep you alive. It didn't grab you in the gut and make you ready to lay down your life for somebody.

The guilt he felt was a living thing. These men had relied on him to keep them alive, and he'd failed them, failed them utterly.

It almost made him grateful that he'd been shot as well.

The host rapped a water glass with a fork to get everybody's attention. He cleared his throat. "I'd like to propose a toast." He raised his wine glass and said, "To good friends – " There was a rumble of approval. " – both present and far away. And, if I might add a personal note, to family as well. Some of whom are close at hand, and others of whom are far away. Some of whom are – "

His wife caught his eye, and he coughed again. "All of whom are missed."

He sat down.

The Lieutenant hurt like a sonofabitch. He'd dropped his pack and his rifle, and was just running now, stumbling really, through the bush. Leaves and branches whipped against him. They hurt pretty bad, but not as bad as this fucking wound in his side. It hurt like fuck. He was afraid even to look at it.

He smashed full-tilt into something hard.

Dazed, he staggered back a step or two. Then he pulled himself together. The jungle was entirely gone now. There was nothing in front of him but featureless, colorless nothingness.

He reached out a wondering hand. It touched plaster, smooth and cool.

Somehow, he'd reached the wall.

For a second, he couldn't find his pencil. He slapped at his clothing in a panic, and on the third attempt found it, right where it should be, in his shirt pocket. It was a little stub of a thing, but functional.

Carefully, ignoring the pain, he wrote the names of all the men in his platoon on the wall. Joseph Martinez. Johnny Walker. Howard Simms. James O'Brien. Paul S. Holloway III. Pedro Swenson. Francis Parks. Ulysses S. Brown. Garry Liones. Robert Starbuck. Kent Johnstone. Barry Moyer. Kenneth Fletcher. Samuel Brown. Larry E. Lee. William Daugherty. Last of all, he wrote his own name.

"We were here, damn it," he muttered. "*We were here!*"

But then all the strength left him, and he slid to the carpet. Away in the distance, he could hear the doorbell chime. It had nothing to do with him anymore. He was busy at the business of dying.

Death was a smooth and featureless black wall. It stretched to infinity in all directions. He felt himself moving toward it. It was so close now, he could almost touch it. On this side were warmth and light, trees and grass and bumblebees, filing cabinets, the Miss America pageant, rebuilt carburetors, Saturday morning cartoons...everything he had ever known or thought or experienced. And on the other? He had no way of knowing. He was going to find out.

In the dinner party far above, the doorbell rang, and somebody got up and went to the door. A courier stood there, envelope in hand. He said the hostess's name, with a little rise in his voice at the end, like a question mark. The soldier looked up, vaguely curious. Then the wall was upon him. For an instant it filled the universe. He took a last gasping breath. Then he passed through.

He didn't hear his mother scream when she read the telegram.

A Small Room in Koboldtown

THAT WINTER, Will le Fey held down a job working for a haint politician named Salem Toussaint. Chiefly, his function was to run errands while looking conspicuously solid. He fetched tax forms for the alderman's constituents, delivered stacks of documents to trollish functionaries, fixed L&I violations, presented boxes of candied John-the-Conqueror root to retiring secretaries, absent-mindedly dropped slim envelopes containing twenty-dollar bills on desks. When somebody important died, he brought a white goat to the back door of the Fane of Darkness to be sacrificed to the Nameless One. When somebody else's son was drafted or went to prison, he hammered a nail in the nkisi nkonde that Toussaint kept in the office to ensure his safe return. He canvassed voters in haint neighborhoods like Ginny Gall, Beluthahatchie, and Diddy-Wah-Diddy, where the bars were smoky, the music was good, and it was dangerous to smile at the whores. He negotiated the labyrinthine bureaucracies of City Hall. Not everything he did was strictly legal, but none of it was actually criminal. Salem Toussaint didn't trust him enough for that.

One evening, Will was stuffing envelopes with Ghostface while Jimi Begood went over a list of ward-heelers with the alderman, checking those who could be trusted to turn out the troops in the upcoming election and crossing out those who had a history of pocketing the walking-around money and standing idle on election day or, worse, steering the vote the wrong way because they were double-dipping from the opposition. The door between Toussaint's office and the anteroom was open a crack and Will could eavesdrop on their conversation.

"Grandfather Domovoy was turned to stone last August," Jimi

Begood said, "so we're going to have to find somebody new to bring out the Slovaks. There's a vila named—"

Ghostface snapped a rubber band around a bundle of envelopes and lofted them into the mail cart on the far side of the room. "Three points!" he said. Then, "You want to know what burns my ass?"

"No," Will said.

"What burns my ass is how you and me are doing the exact same job, but you're headed straight for the top while I'm going to be stuck here licking envelopes forever. And you know why? Because you're solid."

"That's just racist bullshit," Will said. "Toussaint is never going to promote me any higher than I am now. Haints like seeing a fey truckle to the Big Guy, but they'd never accept me as one of his advisors. You know that as well as I do."

"Yeah, but you're not going to be here forever, are you? In a couple of years, you'll be holding down an office in the Mayoralty. Wouldn't surprise me one bit if you made it all the way to the Palace of Leaves."

"Either you're just busting my chops, or else you're a fool. Because if you meant it, you'd be a fool to be ragging on me about it. If Toussaint were in your position, he'd make sure I was his friend, and wherever I wound up he'd have an ally. You could learn from his example."

Ghostface lowered his voice to a near-whisper. "Toussaint is old school. I've got nothing to learn from a glad-handing, pompous, shucking-and-jiving—"

The office door slammed open. They both looked up.

Salem Toussaint stood in the doorway, eyes rolled up in his head so far that only the whites showed. He held up a hand and in a hollow voice said, "One of my constituents is in trouble."

The alderman was spooky in that way. He had trodden the streets of Babel for so many decades that its molecules had insinuated themselves into his body through a million feather-light touches on its bricks and railings, its bars and brothel doors, its accountants' offices and parking garages, and his own molecules in turn been absorbed by the city, so that there was no longer any absolute distinction between the two. He could read Babel's moods and thoughts and sometimes—as now—it spoke to him directly.

Toussaint grabbed his homburg and threw his greatcoat over his arm. "Jimi, stay here and arrange for a lawyer. We can finish that list later. Ghostface, Will—you boys come with me."

The alderman plunged through the door. Ghostface followed.

Will hurried after them, opening the door and closing it behind him, then running to make up for lost time.

Ghostface doubled as Toussaint's chauffeur. In the limo, he said, "Where to, Boss?"

"Koboldtown. A haint's been arrested for murder and we got to get him off."

"You think he was framed?" Will asked.

"What the fuck difference does it make? He's a voter."

Koboldtown was a transitional neighborhood with all the attendant tensions. There were lots of haints on the streets, but the apartment building the police cars were clustered about had sprigs of fennel over the doorway to keep them out. Salem Toussaint's limousine pulled up just in time for them to see a defiant haint being hauled away in rowan-wood handcuffs. The beads at the ends of his duppy-braids clicked angrily as he swung his head around. "I ain't done nothin'!" he shouted. "This is all bullshit, motherfucker! I'mna come back an' kill you all!" His eyes glowed hellishly and an eerie blue nimbus surrounded his head; clear indicators that he'd been shooting up crystal goon. Will was surprised he was even able to stand.

The limo came to a stop and Will hopped out to open Salem Toussaint's door. Toussaint climbed ponderously out and stopped the guards with an imperious gesture. Then he spoke briefly with their captive. "Go quietly, son. I'll see you get a good lawyer, the best money can buy." Will flipped open his cell, punched a number, and began speaking into it in an earnest murmur. It was all theater—he'd dialed the weather and Jimi Begood had doubtless already engaged a defender —but, combined with Toussaint's presence, it calmed the haint down. He listened carefully as the alderman concluded, "Just don't get yourself killed, that's the important thing. Understand?"

The haint nodded.

In the lobby, two officers were talking with the doorman. All three stiffened at the sight of haints walking in the door, relaxed when they saw Will restoring the twigs of fennel, and smiled with relief as they recognized Toussaint. It all happened in a flicker, but Will saw it. And if he noticed, how could his companions not? Nevertheless, the alderman glided in, shaking hands and passing out cigars which the police acknowledged gratefully and stowed away in the inside pockets of their coats. "What's the crime?" he asked.

"Murder," said one of the cops.

Toussaint whistled once, low and long, as if he hadn't already known. "Which floor?"

"Second."

They waited for the elevator, though the stairs were handy and it would have been faster to walk. Salem Toussaint would no more have climbed those stairs than he would have driven his own car. He made sure you understood what a big mahoff he was before he slapped you on the back and gave your nice horse a sugar cube. As the doors opened, Toussaint turned to Ghostface and remarked, "You're looking mighty grim. Something the matter?"

Ghostface shook his head stiffly. He stared, unblinking, straight ahead of himself all the way to their destination.

There were two detectives in the frigid apartment, both Tylwyth Teg, golden-skinned and leaf-eared, in trench coats that looked like they had been sent out to be professionally rumpled. They turned, annoyed, when the cop standing guard at the door let the three of them in, then looked resigned as they recognized the alderman.

"Shulpae! Xisuthros!" Toussaint slapped backs and shook hands as if he were working the room at a campaign fund-raiser. "You're looking good, the both of you."

"Welcome to our humble crime scene, Salem," Detective Xisuthros said. He swept a hand to take in the room: One window, half open, with cold winter air still flowing in through it. Its sill and the wall beneath, black with blood. The burglar bars looked intact. A single dresser, a bed, a chair that had been smashed to flinders. A dribble of blood that led from the window to a tiny bathroom with the door thrown wide. "I should have known you'd show up."

A boggart sprawled lifeless on the bathroom floor. Its chest had been ripped open. There was a gaping hole where the heart should have been.

"Who's the stiff?" Toussaint asked.

"Name's Bobby Buggane. Just another lowlife."

"I see you hauled off an innocent haint."

"Now, Salem, don't be like that. It's an open and shut case. The door was locked and bolted from the inside. Burglar bars on the window and a sprig of fennel over it. The only one who could have gotten in was the spook. He works as a janitor here. We found him sleeping it off on a cot in the basement."

"Haint." Salem Toussaint's eyes were hard. "Please."

After the briefest of pauses, the detective said, "Haint."

"Give me the story."

"About an hour ago, there was a fight. Bodies slamming against the wall, furniture smashing. Everybody on the hall complained. By the time the concierge got here, it was all over. She called us. We broke in."

"Why didn't the concierge have a key?"

"She did. Buggane put in a deadbolt. You can imagine what the old bat had to say about that."

"Why wasn't there a haint-ward on the door?"

"Didn't need one. Doorman in the lobby. Only one haint in the building."

Will squinted at the wall above the door. "There's a kind of pale patch up there, like there used to be a ward and somebody took it down."

Detective Shulpae, the quiet one, turned to stare at him. "So?"

"So what kind of guy installs a deadbolt but takes down the ward? That doesn't make sense."

"The kind who likes to invite his haint buddy over for a shooting party every now and then." Detective Xisuthros pointed toward the dresser with his chin. A set of used works lay atop it. "The concierge says they were so thick that some of the neighbors thought they were fags." He turned back to Toussaint. "Alderman, if you want to question our work here, fine, go ahead. I'm just saying. There's not a lot of hope for the boy."

"Will's right!" Ghostface said. He went to the window. "And another thing. Look at all the blood on the sill. This is where it happened. So how the hell did he get all the way into the bathroom? Somebody ripped his heart out, so he decided to wash his hands?"

Now both detectives were staring at him, hard. "You don't know much about boggarts," Xisuthros said. "They're tough. They can live for five minutes with their heads ripped off. A heart's nothing. And, yeah, that's exactly what he did—wash his hands. Old habits go last. One of the first things we did was turn off the water. Otherwise, I thought the concierge was going to have a seizure."

Ghostface looked around wildly. "What happened to the heart? Why isn't it here? I suppose you think the haint *ate* it, huh? I suppose you think we're all cannibals."

In a disgusted tone, Detective Xisuthros said, "Get Sherlock Holmes Junior the fuck out of here."

Salem Toussaint took Ghostface by the elbow, led him to the door. "Why don't you wait outside?"

Ghostface turned grey. But he stamped angrily out of the room and down the hall. Will followed. He didn't have to be told that this was part of his job.

Outside, Ghostface went straight to the alley below Buggane's window. There were no chalk marks or crime scene tape, so the police obviously hadn't found any evidence there. Nor was there a heart lying on the pavement. A dog or a night-gaunt could have run off with it, of course. But there was no blood either, except for a stain under the window and maybe a stray drop or two that couldn't be seen in the dark.

"So what happened to the heart?" Ghostface paced back and forth, unable to keep still. "It didn't just fly away."

"I don't know," Will said.

"You be Buggane." Ghostface slapped a hand against the brick wall. "Here's the window. You stand here looking out it. Now. I come up behind you. How do I rip your heart out in a way that leaves all that blood on the windowsill? From behind you, I can't get at your heart. If you turn around to face me, the blood doesn't splash on the sill. Now, those ignorant peckerwood detectives probably think I could shove my hands through Buggane's back and *push* his heart out. But it doesn't work like that. Two things can't occupy the same space at the same time. If I make my hands solid while I'm inside your chest, I'm going to fuck them up seriously. So I didn't come at you from behind."

"Okay."

"But if you turn around so I can come at you from the front, the blood's not going to spray over the sill, is it? So I've got to be between you and the window. I don't know if you noticed, but Ice didn't have any blood on him. None. Zip. Nada. Maybe you think I could rip somebody's heart out and then make myself insubstantial fast enough that the blood would spray through me. I don't think so. But even if I could, the blood's going to spatter all over the floor too. Which it didn't. So you tell me—how could I rip your heart out and leave the blood all over the sill like that?"

"You couldn't."

"Thank you. *Thank* you. That's right. You couldn't."

"So?" Will said.

"So there's something fishy going on, that's all. Something suspicious. Something wrong."

"Like what?"

"I don't know." Abruptly, Ghostface's hands fell to his sides. Just like that, all the life went out of him. He slumped despondently. "I just don't know."

"Ghostface," Will said, "why does all this matter? You called this guy Ice. What's he to you?"

The haint's face was as pale as ash, as stiff as bone. In a stricken voice, he said, "He's my brother."

They went to a diner across the street and ordered coffee. Ghostface stared down into his cup without drinking. "Ice always was a hard case. He liked the streets too much, he liked the drugs, he liked the thug life. That's why he never made anything of himself." Ghostface picked up a spoon, looked at it, set it down. "I dunno. Maybe he did it. Maybe he did."

"You know he didn't. You proved he couldn't have."

"Yeah, but that's not going to convince a judge, now is it?"

Will had to admit it would not. "You guys keep in touch?"

"Not really. I saw him a few months ago. He was all hopped up and talking trash about how he'd finally made a big score. He was going to be smoking hundred-dollar cigars and bedding thousand-dollar whores. Maybe he stole something. I told him to get the hell out, I didn't want to know anything about his criminal activities. My own brother. The last time I saw him, I told him to go to hell."

They were silent for a bit. "Nobody said anything about finding anything valuable," Will observed.

"Sometimes the cops will pocket that kind of stuff."

"That's true." Will dipped a finger in his coffee and drew the Sigil of Inspiration on the linoleum counter. Nothing came to him. He sighed. "What would the Big Guy do in this situation?"

"Him?" Ghostface said bitterly. "Probably hand out cigars."

"Hey." Will sat up straight. "That's not a half bad idea. It's pretty cold out there." He counted cops through the window. Then he called the waitress over. "Give me four large coffees, cream and sugar on the side."

Leaving Ghostface hunched over the counter, Will carried the cardboard tray out to where the police stood stamping their feet to keep warm. They accepted the gift with small nods. All four had dark skin, short horns, and the kind of attitude that came from knowing they'd never, ever make detective. The oldest of the lot said, "Working for the spook, are you?"

"Oh, Salem's okay."

The cop grinned on one side of his oak-brown face. "You're what the micks would call his Hound of Hoolan. You know what that is?"

"No, sir."

"It means that if he says he wants to drive, you bend over and bark."

The cops all laughed. Then three of them wandered away, leaving only the rookie. Will took out a pack of Marlboros, offered one, took one for himself, then lit both. They smoked them down to the end without saying much. Will flicked his butt away. The rookie pinched the coal off of his and ate it.

Finally Will said, "This Buggane guy – you know him?"

"Everybody knew him. A real bad character. In jail as often as not. His girlfriend's cute, though. Used to come to the station to bail him out. Skinny little thing, no tits to speak of. The big lugs always like 'em petite, you ever noticed?"

"Some of the neighbors thought he was queer."

"They sure wouldn't of said that to his face. Buggane was a bruiser. Used to fight some, under the name of Dullahan the Deathless."

"No kidding," Will said. "His gym anywhere around here?"

"Down the street and over a couple of blocks. Place called the Sucker Punch. You can't miss it."

Ghostface was still in the diner, so Will left a note on the dash of the limo. A few minutes later, he was at the Sucker Punch A.C. If there was one thing Will had learned working for Toussaint, it was how to walk through any front door in the world and act as if he had a perfect right to be there. He went in.

The gym was dark and smelled serious. Punching bags hung from the gloom. Somebody grunted in a slow and regular fashion, like a mechanical pig, from the free-weight area. There was a single regulation ring in the center of the room. A trollweight bounced up and down on his toes, shadow-boxing.

"Go home, little boy," an ogre in a pug hat said. "There ain't nothing here for you."

"Oh, it's not about that, sir," Will said quickly. By *that* meaning whatever the ogre thought it meant. The alderman had schooled him never to meet aggression head-on.

"No? You don't wanna build yourself up, get the girl, and beat the crap out of whoever's pushing you around?" The ogre squeezed Will's biceps. "You could use it. Only not here. This is a serious club for serious fighters only."

"No, sir, I'm with Alderman Toussaint." By the ogre's expression, Will could see that he recognized the name and was not impressed.

"I was hoping you could tell me something about Bobby Buggane."

"The bum. What's he done now?"

"He was murdered."

"Well, I ain't surprised. Buggane was no damn good. Coulda worked his way up to the middle of the card, but he wasn't willing to put in the effort. Always jerking off somewhere with his spook buddy when he shoulda been working out."

"Somebody said they got into doing crimes together." It was a shot in the dark, but Will figured the odds were good

"Yeah, well, like I said, I wouldn't be surprised. There's a lot of crap a gorilla like Buggane can pull off if he's got a haint accomplice. You go into a jewelry store and pinch the ward when the guy ain't lookin' and replace it with a sprig of plastic fennel. Looks just like the real thing. Then that night the spook slips in and shuts off the alarm. If you're like Buggane, and can rip a safe door off its hinges, you can walk off with a bundle. Somebody pulled something like that at a warehouse down in the Village about six months ago. Got away with a fortune in slabs of raw jade. I remember it because Buggane quit the gym right after that, and I always wondered."

"Raw jade's got to be hard to sell, though," Will said. "I mean, in bulk."

"Not if you got connections. Even if you don't, something big like that could be moved through your regular fence, provided you waited until things had cooled down some. Not that I'd know personally. But you hear things."

"Huh," Will said. "This girlfriend of his – you remember her name?"

"Naw. Daiera, Damia, something like that. Maybe Danae. Only reason I recollect at all is that I asked Buggane once was she a pixie or a russalka or what and he said she was a diener. Deianira the Diener, that was it. That's a new one on me. I thought I knew all the ethnics, but I ain't never heard of a diener before. Listen, kid, I really have got work to do."

"I'll be out of your way, then," Will said. "Thanks for your help." He took one last look around the gym. "I guess Buggane should have stayed in the ring."

"Oh, he wasn't a ring boxer," the ogre said. "He was a pit boxer."

"What's the difference?"

"Pit boxing's strictly death-match. Two fighters climb down, only one climbs out. Buggane had a three-and-two record when he quit."

"How the fuck," Will said, "can somebody have a three-and-two record when he's fighting to the death?"

The ogre grinned. Then he explained.

Less than an hour later, Will, Salem Toussaint, and Ghostface stood waiting in the shadows outside the city morgue. "Okay," Ghostface said. "I thought I knew all the racial types from Litvak night-hags to Thai shit demons, but you say this girl is a *what?*"

"A diener. It's not a type, it's a job. A diener is a morgue attendant who's responsible for moving and cleaning the body. She also assists the coroner in the autopsy. I made a few calls and Deianira's on night duty this week. Though I'm guessing she might take off a little early tonight."

"Why's that?"

"This is where Bobby Buggane's body wound up."

"I think, boy," Toussaint said firmly, "you'd best tell us the whole story."

"All right," Will said. "Here's how I put it together. Buggane and Ice steal a truckload of jewelry-grade jade together and agree to wait six months before trying to fence it. Buggane keeps possession – I'm guessing it's stashed with his girlfriend, but that's not really important – and everyone has half a year to reflect on how much bigger Buggane's share will be if he stiffs Ice. Maybe Ice starts worrying about it out loud. So Buggane goes down to the basement to talk it over with his good buddy. They have a couple of drinks, maybe they smoke a little crack. Then he breaks out the crystal goon. By this time, your brother's lost whatever good judgment he had in the first place, and says sure."

Ghostface nodded glumly.

"Ice shoots up first, then Buggane. Only he shoots up pure water. That's easy to pull – what druggie's going to suspect another druggie of shortchanging *himself?* Then, when Ice nods off, Buggane goes back to his room, takes down the ward, and flushes it down the toilet.

That way, when he's found dead, suspicion's naturally going to fall on the only individual in the building able to walk through a locked door. One who he's made certain will be easy to find when the police come calling."

"So who kills Buggane?"

"It's a set-up job. Buggane opens the window halfway and checks to make sure his girlfriend is waiting in the alley. Everything's ready. Now he stages a fight. He screams, roars, pounds the wall, smashes a chair. Then, when the neighbors are all yelling at him to shut up, he goes to the window, takes a deep breath, and rips open his rib cage with his bare hands."

"Can he *do* that?"

"Boggarts are strong, remember. Plus, if you checked out the syringe on his dresser, I wouldn't be surprised to find traces not of goon but of morphine. Either way, with or without painkiller, he tears out his own heart. Then he drops it out the window. Deianira catches it in a basket or a sheet, so there's no blood on the ground. Nothing that will direct the investigators' attention outside.

"She leaves with his heart.

"Now Buggane's still got a couple of minutes before he collapses. He's smart enough not to close the window – there'd be blood on the outside part of the sill and that would draw attention outward again. But his hands are slick with blood and he doesn't want the detectives to realize he did the deed himself, so he goes to the bathroom sink and washes them. By this time, the concierge is hammering on the door.

"He dies. Everything is going exactly according to plan."

"Hell of a plan," Toussaint murmured.

"Yeah. You know the middle part. The cops come, they see, they believe. If it wasn't for Ghostface kicking up a fuss, we'd never have found all this other stuff."

"Me? I didn't do anything."

"Well, it looked hinky to me, but I wasn't going to meddle in police business until I learned it mattered to you."

"You left out the best part," Toussaint said. "How Buggane manages to turn killing himself to his own advantage."

"Yeah, that had me baffled too. But when a boxer picks up a nickname like 'the Deathless,' you have to wonder why. Then the ogre at the gym told me that Buggane had a three-two record pit boxing. That's to the death, you know. It turns out Buggane's got a glass heart. Big lump of crystal the size of your fist. No matter how badly he's injured, the heart can repair him. Even if he's clinically dead."

"So his girlfriend waits for his body to show up and sticks the heart back in?" Ghostface said. "No, that's just crazy. That wouldn't really work, would it?"

"Shhh," Will said. "I think we're about to find out. Look."

A little door opened in the side of the morgue. Two figures came out. The smaller one was helping the larger to stand.

For the first time all evening, Toussaint smiled. Gold teeth gleamed. Then he put a police whistle to his mouth.

After Buggane and his girlfriend had been arrested, Ghostface gave Will a short, fierce hug and then ran off to arrange his brother's release. Will and the alderman strolled back to the limousine, parked two blocks away. As they walked, Will worried how he was going to explain to his boss that he couldn't chauffeur because he didn't have a license.

"You done good, boy," Salem Toussaint said. "I'm proud of you."

Something in his voice, or perhaps the amused way he glanced down at Will out of the corner of his eye said more than mere words could have.

"You *knew*," Will said. "You knew all the time."

Toussaint chuckled. "Perhaps I did. But I had the advantage of knowing what the city knows. It was still mighty clever of you to figure it out all on your own."

"But why should I have had to? Why didn't you just tell the detectives what you knew?"

"Let me answer that question with one of my own: Why did you tell Ghostface he was the one who uncovered the crime?"

They'd reached the limo now. It flickered its lights, glad to see them. But they didn't climb in just yet. "Because I've got to live with the guy. I don't want him thinking I think I'm superior to him."

"Exactly so! The police liked hearing the story from a solid boy better than they would from me. I'm not quite a buffoon in their eyes, but

I'm something close to it. My power has to be respected, and my office too. It would make folks nervous if they had to take me seriously as well."

"Alderman, I..."

"Hush up, boy. I know everything you're about to say." The alderman opened a door for Will. "Climb in the back. I'll drive."

Urdumheim

EVERY MORNING King Nimrod walked to the mountain, climbed its steep sides to the very top, and sang it higher. At noon ravens brought him bread and cheese. At dinner time they brought him manna. At sunset he came down. He had called the granite up from under the ground shortly after Utnapishtim the Navigator landed the boats there. First Inanna had called upon her powers to put the rains to sleep. Then Shaleb the Scribe had picked up a stick and scratched a straight line in the mud, indicating simply: *We are here.* Thus did history begin.

But before history existed, before time began, King Nimrod led the People out of Urdumheim. Across the stunned and empty spaces of the world they fled, through the plains and over the silent snowy mountains, not knowing if these places had existed before then or if their need and desire had pulled them into being. The land was as large as the sky in those days, and as unpopulated. But in no place could they linger, for always their enemies were close on their heels, eager to return them to slavery.

So came they at last to the limitless salt marshes that lay between the land and the distant sea. It was a time of great floods, when the waters poured endlessly from the heavens and the grass-choked streams were become mighty rivers and there was no dry ground anywhere to be seen. They built shallow-drafted reed boats then, well-pitched beneath, and set across the waters, where no demon could follow. Skimming swiftly over the drowned lands, they drove into the white rains, seeking refuge. Until at last they came upon what was then an island barely distinguishable from the waters. Here they settled, and here they prospered.

They were giants, that first generation, and half the things in the world were made by them first. Utnapishtim invented boats and navigation. Shaleb invented writing and record-keeping. Inanna invented weaving and the arts of lovemaking. Nimrod himself was responsible for bridges, houses, coins, and stoneworking, as well as cultivation and animal husbandry and many other things as well. But greatest of all his inventions was language. The People could not speak before he taught them how.

I was a boy when the winged lion came. That morning, Ninsun had set me to work pitting cherries. It was a tedious, fiddling chore, and because Ninsun had gathered four bushels, it lasted for hours, but there was no way out of it. So as I labored, I asked her questions about the way things used to be and why things were as they are now. Of all the First, she was the least closed-mouthed. Which is not to say she was at all talkative.

"Why is there work?" I asked.

"Because we are lucky."

It didn't seem lucky to me to have to work, and I said so.

"Work makes sense. You labor, you grow tired. You make something, you're better off than you were before. Imagine the world if it weren't that way."

"What was the world like before the People came here?"

"There are no words to describe it."

"Why not?"

"Because there was no language. Nimrod invented language as a way for us to escape from Urdumheim."

"What was Urdumheim like?"

"King Nimrod gave it that name afterwards so we could talk about it. When we lived there, it wasn't called anything."

"But what was it *like?*"

She looked at me without answering. Then abruptly she opened her mouth in a great O. The interior of her mouth was blacker than soot, blacker than midnight, black beyond imagining. That horrible hole in reality opened wider and wider, growing until it was larger than her face, larger than the room, until it threatened to swallow me up and along with me the entire village and King Nimrod's mountain and all the universe beyond. There were flames within the darkness, though they shed no light, and cold mud underfoot. My stomach lurched and I was overcome by a pervasive sense of wrongness. It seemed to me that I had no name and that it was thus impossible to distinguish between myself and everything else, and that therefore I could by definition never, ever escape from this dreadful and malodorous place.

Ninsun closed her mouth. "It was like that." The clay pot where we dumped the discarded pits was full, so she tossed them out the window. "This is almost done. When we're finished here, you can run along and play."

I don't think that Ninsun was my mother, but who can tell? We had not invented parentage at that time. No one had ever died, and thus no one had foreseen the need to record the passing of generations. Children were simply raised in common, their needs seen to by whoever was closest.

Nor was I the child Ninsun thought me. True, when she released me at last, I did indeed react exactly as a child would in the same circumstances. Which is to say, I was out the door in an instant and hurtling across the fields so fast that a shout to come back would never have reached my ears. My reasons, however, were not those of a boy but of a man, albeit a young one still.

I plunged into the woods and cool green shadows flowed over my body. Only when I could no longer hear the homely village noises of Whitemarsh, the clang of metal in the smithy and the snore of wood at the sawyer's, did I slow to a walk.

Whitemarsh was one of seven villages on an archipelago of low hills that rose gently from the reeds. On Great Island were Landfall, Providence, and First Haven. Further out on islands of their own were Whitemarsh, Fishweir, Oak Hill, and Market. Other, smaller communities there were, some consisting of as few as three or two houses, in such profusion that no man knew them all. But the chief and more populous islands were connected by marsh-roads of poured sand paved with squared-off logs.

By secret ways known only to children (though I was no longer a child, I had been one not long before), I passed through the marshes to a certain hidden place I knew. It was a small meadow clearing just above the banks of one of the numberless crystal-clear creeks that wandered mazily through the reeds. In midday the meadow lay half in sun and half in shade, so that it was a place of comfort whatever the temperature might be. There I threw myself down on the grass to await Silili.

Time passed with agonizing slowness. I worried that Silili had come early and, not finding me there, thought me faithless and left. I worried that she had been sent to Fishweir to make baskets for a season. A thousand horrid possibilities haunted my imagination. But then, at last, she stepped into the clearing.

I rose at the sight of her, and she knelt down beside me. We clasped hands fervently. Her eyes shone. When I looked into those eyes, I felt the way the People must have when the first dawn filled the sky with colors and Aruru sent her voice upward to meet them and so sang the first song. The joy I felt then was almost unbearable; it filled me to bursting.

We lay together, as we had every day for almost a month, kissing and fondling each other. Silili's skin was the color of aged ivory and her nipples were pale apricot. Her pubic hair was light and downy, a golden mist over her mons. It offered no more resistance than a cloud when I ran my fingers through it. She stroked my thighs, my chest, the side of my face. Then, blushing and yet not once taking her eyes from mine, she said, "Gil...I'm ready now."

"Are you sure?" It is a measure of how deeply I loved Silili that I asked at all instead of simply taking her at her word. And a measure of how much I wanted her that when I asked I did not stop stroking her gently with one finger, over and over, along the cleft between her legs, fearful that if I removed my hand her desire for me would go with it. "I can wait, if you want."

"No," she said, "now."

We did then as lovers always do.

Afterwards, we lay together talking quietly, sometimes laughing. Inevitably, our conversation turned to what we would be wearing when next we saw each other.

Children, of course, go everywhere naked. But after this, Silili and I would need to wear clothing in public. Tonight she would go to Inanna and beg enough cloth to make a dress, and thus claim for herself the modesty of a grown woman. Like any male my age, I had already made a shirt and trousers and hidden them away against this very day.

Silili brushed her hands down the front of her body, imagining the dress. "What color should it be?" she asked.

"Green, like the forest. Reddish-orange, like the flames of the sun."

"Which I am to be, then – forest or sun? You are as inconstant as the sky, Gil."

"Blue," I said, "like the sky. White, like the moon and the clouds. Red and yellow and blue like the stars. Orange and purple like the sunset or the mountains at dawn." For she was all things to me and, since in my present frame of mind all things were good, all things in turn put me in mind of her.

She made an exasperated noise, but I could tell she was pleased.

It was at that instant that I heard a soft, heavy *thump* on the ground behind me. Lazily, I turned my head to see what it was.

I froze.

An enormous winged lion stood on the bank of the stream opposite us. Its fur and feathers were red as blood. Its eyes were black from rim to rim.

Silili, who in all her life had never feared anything, sat up beside me and smiled at the thing. "Hello," she said. "What are you?"

"Hello," the great beast replied. "What are you? Hello. Hellohellohello." Lifting its front paws in the air, it began to prance about on its hind legs in the drollest manner imaginable. "What are you are what. You are what you are what you are. Hello? Hellello. Lo-l o-lo-lo-lo! Hell you are lo you are. What what what!"

Silili threw back her head and laughed peals of silvery laughter. I laughed as well, but uneasily. The creature's teeth were enormous, and it did not seem to me that the cast of its face was at all kindly. "A lion?" Silili asked. "A bird?"

"A bird a bird a bird! A lion a lion a bird!" the beast sang. "You are a lion you are hello what are a bird hello you are a what a what hello. Bird-lion bird-lion lion lion *bird!*" Then he bounded up into the air, snapped out his mighty wings, and, flapping heavily, flew up and off into the sky, leaving nothing behind him but a foul stench, like rotting garbage.

We both laughed and applauded. How could we not?

But when later I returned to Whitemarsh, and my sister came running out from the village to meet me, I raised my hand in greeting and I could not remember what word I normally used in such circumstances. I wracked my brain for it time and again, to no avail. It was completely gone. And when I tried to describe the beast I had seen, I could remember the words for neither "bird" nor "lion."

Still, that strange incident did not stay long in our minds, for that was the summer when Delondra invented dancing. This was an enormous event among our generation not only for its own sake but because this was the first major creation by anyone who was not of the First. As adults we had to spend our days in labor of various sorts, of course, but we met every evening on the greensward to dance until weariness or romance led us away.

Music had been invented by Enlil years before and we had three instruments then: the box lute, the tabor, and the reed pipe. When the evening darkened, we lit pine-tar torches and set them in a circle about the periphery of the dancing ground and so continued until the stars were high in the sky. Then by ones and twos we drifted homeward, some to make love, others to their lonely beds, and still others to weep and rage, for our hearts were young and active and no way had yet been invented to keep them from being broken.

Which is what we at first thought had happened when Mylitta, who had hours before wandered off into the woods with Irra, returned in tears. (This was late in the summer, when we had been dancing for months.) Mylitta and Irra were lovers, a station or distinction we of the second generation had created on our own. None of the First had lovers, but rather coupled with whoever caught their fancy; but we, being younger and, we thought, wiser, preferred our own arrangements. Even though they did not always bring us joy.

As, we thought, now. Everybody assumed the worst of Irra, of course. But when Mylitta's friends gathered around to comfort her, it turned out that she had been frightened by some creature she had seen.

"What was it like?" Silili asked.

"White," Mylitta said, "like the moon. It came up from the ground like...something long and slithery that moves its head like this." She moved her hand from side to side in a sinuous, undulating motion.

"A snake?" somebody said.

Mylitta looked puzzled, as if the word meant nothing to her. She shook her head, as if dismissing nonsense and, still upset, said, "Its mouth was horrible, with teeth set in circles. And it...and it...*talked!*"

Now the forgotten lion came to my mind again and, apprehensively, I asked, "Did it say anything? Tell us what it said."

But to this Mylitta could only shake her head.

"Where is Irra?" Silili asked.

"He stayed behind to talk some more."

There was then such a hubbub of talk and argument as only the young can have. In quick order we put together a party to go after our friend and bring him back to us safe. Snatching up knives and staves – knives had been invented long ago, and even then staves had been employed as weapons – we started towards the woods.

Then Irra himself came sauntering out of the darkness, hands behind his back, grinning widely. Mylitta ran to his side and kissed him, but he pushed her playfully away. Then he made a gesture that took in all of us, with our knives and staves and grim expressions, and raised one eyebrow.

"We were going to look for you."

"Mylitta said there was a..." With Irra's eyes boring into mine, I could not think of the word for snake. "One of those long, slithery things. Only large. And white."

"Why won't you talk?" Mylitta cried. "Why don't you say anything?"

Irra grinned wider and wider. And now a peculiar thing happened. His face began to glow brighter and brighter, until it shone like the moon.

He held out his hand, fingers spread. Then he squeezed it into a fist. When he opened it again, the fingers had merged into one another, forming a smooth brown flipper. "The...whatever...showed me how to do this."

Nobody knew what to make of his stunt. But then Mylitta started crying again, and by the time we had her soothed down, Irra was gone and it was too late for dancing anyway. So we all went home.

After that evening, strange creatures appeared in more and more profusion at the edges of our settlements. They were never the same twice. There was a thing like an elephant but with impossibly long legs, like a spider's. There was a swarm of scorpions with human faces that were somehow all a single organism. There was a ball of serpents. There was a bird of flame. They arrived suddenly, spoke enigmatically, and then they left.

Every time somebody talked to one of these monsters, words vanished from his or her vocabulary.

Why didn't we go to our elders? The First had powers that dwarfed anything we could do on our own. But we didn't realize initially that this was anything to do with *them*. It seemed of a piece with the messy emotional stuff of our young lives. Particularly since, for the longest time, Irra was at the center of it.

We did not have a name for it then, but Irra had become a wizard. He had a wizard's power and a wizard's weirdness. He would pop up without warning – striding out of a thicket, jumping down from a rooftop – to perform some never-before-seen action, and then leave. Once he walked right past Mylitta and into her house and before her astonished eyes urinated on the pallet where she slept! Another time, he rode across the fields on a horse of snow, only half-visible in the white mist which steamed off its back, and when the children came running madly out to see, shouting, "Irra! Irra!" and "Give us a ride!" he pelted them with snowballs made from the living substance of his steed, and galloped off, jeering.

These were troubling occurrences, but they did not seem serious enough to warrant bothering the First. Not until I lost Silili.

I was working in the marshes that day, cutting salt hay for winter fodder. It was hot work, and I was sweating so hard that I took off my tunic and labored in my trousers alone. But Silili had promised to bring a lunch to me and I wanted her to see how hard I could work. I bent, I cut, I straightened, and as I turned to drop an armful of hay I saw her standing at the edge of the trees, staring at me. Just the sight of her took my breath away.

I must have looked pleasing to her as well for, without saying a word, she came to me, took my hand, and led me to that same meadow where we first made love. Wordlessly, then, we repeated our original vows.

Afterwards, we lay neither speaking nor touching each other. Just savoring our closeness. I remember that I was lying on my stomach, staring at a big, goggle-eyed bullfrog that sat pompously in the shallows of the stream, his great grin out of the water, his pulsing throat within, when suddenly the ground shook under us and a grinding noise filled the air.

We danced to our feet as something like an enormous metal beetle with a kind of grinder or drill in place of a head erupted from the ground, spattering dirt in all directions. The gleaming round body was armored with polished iron plates. A crude mouth opened at the end of an upheld leg and said, "Who." Then, "Are." And finally, "You?"

"Go away," I said sulkily.

"Goooooooo," it moaned. "Waaaaaaaaaay. Aaaaaaaaa."

"No!" I pelted the thing with clods of dirt, but it did not go away. I snatched up a stick and broke it across the beetle's back, to no visible effect. "Nobody wants you here."

"Noooooobody." Its voice was rough and metallic, like nothing I had ever heard before. It reared up on its four hind legs, waving its front pair in the air. "Waaaaaaants." I smashed a stone against one of those hind legs, snapping it off at the joint. Untroubled, it snatched up Silili with its forelegs. "Yooooooouuuuu!"

Then the monstrosity disappeared into the forest.

It had all happened too quickly. For the merest instant I was still, stunned, unable to move. And in that instant, faster than quicksilver, the beetle sped through the trees so nimbly that it was gone before I could react. Leaving behind it nothing but Silili's rapidly dwindling scream.

"Silili!" I cried after her. "Come back! *Silili!*"

Which is how, fool that I was, I lost her name.

Afterwards, however, I discovered that the limb I had torn from the beetle was that same one which held the creature's mouth. "Where is she?" I demanded. "Where has she been taken to?"

"Ur," it said. "Dum." A long silence. "Heim."

I ran back to Whitemarsh. There was an enormous copper disk, as tall as I was, leaning against the side of the redsmith's forge. I seized a hammer and began slamming on it to raise a great din and bring out everyone within earshot. They say that this was the first alarm that was ever sounded, but what did I care for that?

All the village came running up. Several of the First – Ninsun, Humbaba, two or three others – were among them.

I flung down the hammer.

"Girl!" I cried. Then, shaking my head, "Not girl – woman!" I had questioned the beetle-limb most of the way back to Whitemarsh before concluding that I would learn nothing useful from it and throwing it away in disgust. The interrogation had been a mistake, however, for it half-drained me of language. Now, because I had lost the word *lover*, I slapped my chest. "Mine." And, howling, "Gone, gone, gone!"

A gabble of voices, questions, outraged cries rose up from the crowd. But Ninsun *slammed* her hands together and silenced them all with a glare. Then she folded herself down and patted the ground beside her.

"Sit," she said to me. "Tell."

It took time and labor, but I eventually made myself understood.

"When did this begin?" Ninsun asked and, when everybody began talking at once, "You first," she said, pointing. "Then you. Then you." The story that she eventually stitched together was clumsily told, but the old woman nodded and clucked and probed until it had all been brought to light. At last she sighed and said, "The Igigi have come, then."

"What are the Igigi?" Mylitta asked. My body had caught up with the horror of Silili's loss by then. I was heavy with grief and speechless with despair.

"'Igigi' is just a name we gave to them so we could talk about them."

"Yes, but what *are* they?" Mylitta insisted.

"There are not the words to describe the Igigi."

A frustrated growl rose up from the assembled young. I noticed the First scowling at each other when this happened.

"It is the Igigi," Ninsun said, "who ruled over us in Urdumheim. Surely I have told you about them before?"

Some of us nodded. Others shook their heads.

"The Igigi are logophages." Ninsun regarded us keenly from under those bushy eyebrows of hers. "Nimrod put much of his power into words, and they make us strong. The Igigi feed upon words in order to deny us that strength. Thus they gain power over us."

"Girl-woman-mine," I reminded her. I flung an arm out toward the forest and then drew it back to me. "Woman-to-me. Woman-to-me!"

"Enmul," Ninsun said. A boy who was known to all for his speed and endurance stepped forward. "Run to the top of Ararat. Bring Nimrod here."

King Nimrod came down from the mountain like a storm cloud in his fury. His hair and robes lashed about him, as if in a mighty wind, and sparks shot out from his beard. "You should have told me this long ago," he said to me, glowering, when Ninsun had told him all. "Fool! What did you think language is *for?*"

Humbly kneeling before him, I said, "Girl-woman-mine." Then I slammed my heart three times to show that I hurt. "Lost-fetch-again!"

With a roar, the king knocked me flat with his enormous fist. When I stood up, he struck me down again. When I stretched out a hand in supplication he kicked me. Finally, when I could not move, Ninsun snapped an order and I was lifted up by the arms and carried away. Radjni and Mammetum laid me down in the shade of a tree, cleaning my wounds and applying mint leaves and mustards to my bruises.

Miserably, I watched as King Nimrod sent runners to every village and outlying house, to gather the People together. Already the First were gathering (they did not need to be sent for), and it was not long before there was such an assembly as had never gathered before nor has since, nor ever will again: all the People in the world.

King Nimrod then spoke: "Oh ye of little faith! I sang high the mountain so that it might be a fortress and protection for the People in times of peril. When I was done, Ararat was to tower so high it would touch the sky, where no demon would dare go. Then would we have made our homes there and been safe forever.

"Alas, our enemies have arrived before my work was done. The slopes of Ararat will slow but not stop them. So before their armies converge upon us, we must prepare to defend ourselves."

All this I narrate as things I have heard and know to be true. Yet, even though I was there, Nimrod's speech was incomprehensible to me. This is what I actually heard:

<pre>
                                        faith!
mountain   fortress   protection
                              Ararat   tower
                    demon
                        safe forever.

        Alas   enemies
        Ararat   armies converge
</pre>

After a hurried consultation among the First, Shaleb the Scribe began sketching plans for a defense. With a gesture, he stripped the land before him of vegetation. Enkidu handed him a staff and he drew a circle: "Ararat," he said. Along its flanks, he drew three nested semicircles: "Curtain wall. Barbican. Palisades." Squiggly lines made a river. He drew a line across it: "Dam." Other lines represented streams. He reshaped them: "Channels."

So it began. At King Nimrod's orders, we cut down trees and built palisades. We dug trenches, redirected streams, created lakes. Foodstuffs were brought in and locked away in warehouses we built for that purpose. Weapons were forged. All this was done under direction of the First. Those of the second generation who'd had the least exposure to the Igigi were made overseers and supervisors, in proportion to their ability to understand directions. Those who could follow only the simplest orders were made runners and carriers. Down at the very bottom of the social order were those such as I who could not be trusted to comprehend the plainest commands and so were used as brute labor, hauling logs or lugging stones, driven to obedience by kicks, cuffs, and curses.

I will not dwell upon my misery, for all that it was compounded by being so richly deserved. Suffice it to say, I suffered.

Then one day a pillar of smoke appeared on the horizon. We put down our shovels and axes – those who were trusted with tools – and as we did so a second pillar arose, and then a third, and a fourth, and a hundredth, until we could no longer count them all. Dark they rose up and wide they spread, until they merged and turned the sky black.

Inanna, who was best-liked of all the First, passed through the camp, handing out strips of cotton cloth. So quick was she that her feet never once touched the earth, and to each one she met she said, "The Igigi are burning the forests. When the smoke comes, fold this cloth like so, dip it in the water, and hold it to your face. This will make breathing easier." When she saw that I did not understand her instructions, she took me by the hand and comprehension flowed through me like a stream of crystal-clear water.

All in an instant, I understood the magnitude of her sacrifice. For the trickle of power that had flowed out of her was gone forever. She would never have it again.

Shocked, I bowed low before her.

My face must have revealed my every thought, for Inanna smiled. "I thank you for your sympathy," she said. "But your gratitude comes too soon. I cannot stay here, holding your hand, and without my touch you will revert to what you were before. But be patient. Be brave. Work hard. And when all is done, there will be a time of healing."

Then she was gone, and with her the temporary gift of understanding.

That night, for the first time, I wept for myself as well as for Silili.

In the morning, walls of flame converged upon us, destroying forests and reed marshes alike. But Inanna's charm was strong, and Shaleb had so cunningly redirected the waters that the flames could not reach us. Even so, the sun did not shine that day, and when night came, we could see the campfires of the Igigi, ring upon ring of them through the murky distance. Their numbers were legion. My heart grew cold at the sight.

For an instant I felt a bleak and total despair. And in that instant, I leapt up from where I had been lying, exhausted, and seized a rope, looped it around a nearby log, and turned to the nearest supervisor. It was Damuzi, who had never been particularly fond of me.

I snorted, as if I were an ox. Then I tugged at the rope. I looked around me, from one quarter of the camp to another. Then I snorted again.

Damuzi looked astonished. Then he laughed. He pointed to a far section of our defenses where the palisades were incomplete. His finger moved from palisades to logs, back and forth repeatedly, until I nodded my comprehension: As many logs as I could manage. Mylitta, who, through her frequent exposure to Irra, had become a man-beast like myself, had been watching us intently. Now she leaped up and looped a length of rope around the far side of my log. She looked at me and snorted.

Together we pulled.

The next day, the Igigi had advanced so close that they could be seen, like swarming insects, on the far side of the lake we had created as our first line of defense. Those who could – those with wings or the ability to swim – attacked us directly. A monstrous feathered serpent came twisting through the water and smashed into the lakefront wall with such force that logs splintered and buckled. Meanwhile, creatures that were something like bears and something like squids descended from the sky and tried to seize People in their tentacles.

Though we cast them back, they kept returning. Pain meant nothing to the Igigi and so varied were their forms that it was difficult to find a way to cripple them all. Even King Nimrod was hard pressed to counter them.

It was then that Humbaba came lumbering forward. "Great hunter, draw your bow!" he cried. And when Nimrod had done as he directed: "Point it toward the nearest of the foe. Let loose thy arrow. Speed it toward the abomination's body!"

The arrow sped. When it struck the feathered serpent, the demon threw back its head and howled. Then it fell and did not rise again.

"What wonder is this?" somebody asked.

"It is my greatest gift, for once given it cannot be taken back," Humbaba said. "I call it *death*."

At his direction, we set upon the invaders with sticks and knives and rocks. They fell before our onslaught and, briefly, all was satisfactory. But in the aftermath, there lay one body on the ground which was not that of an Igigi. It belonged to Shullat, who was gentle and fond of animals and of whom nobody ever had a bad word to say.

Shullat's death saddened us all greatly, for she was the first of the People ever to die.

That same day, shortly after sundown, Atraharsis passed through the camp distributing spears and knives as long as a tall man's arm. These latter were unknown to us before this, and he had to demonstrate their use over and over again, the sweat on his face glistening by the light of our campfires.

He did not offer any to the oxen, of course, for we were no longer People. But I watched carefully and when I thought I understood how the knives were to be used, stood before him and made a coughing sound to get his attention. Then I pointed to the long-knife, made a slashing motion, and said, "Swssh."

Atraharsis stared in astonishment. I gestured in the direction of the Igigi hordes. Then I turned my back on them and, waving my arms in a whimsical fashion, cried, "Uloolaloolaloo!" in as close as I could manage to the demons' nonsense-speech.

Those standing nearby laughed.

I pretended I held a long-knife and spun around. I jabbed. "Swssh!" I became an Igigi again, clutched my stomach, and made "Glugluglug" noises to indicate blood flowing out. Finally, I became myself and, face furious with hatred, hacked and slashed at my imagined foe. "Swssh! Swssh! Swssh!"

Then I pointed to the bundle of long-knives in Atraharsis's arms. "Swssh." I held out my hand.

Atraharsis's face darkened.

He aimed a kick at me.

I danced back and nearly fell into the campfire. He advanced upon me, speaking angrily. Out of all he said, I caught only the words "traitor" and "Igigi." But it enraged those listening and they rained blows upon me.

All in a panic, I broke free of the throng and tried to escape their wrath. Jeers and clods of mud flew after me. The children pursued me with sticks.

I was harried across the camp all the way to the outermost palisade. There I slipped through the half-rebuilt gap in the wall created when the feathered serpent had smashed into it. I ran up the new lakefront until it opened out into marshland again, and there I lost my pursuers. For a time I wandered, lost and miserable, among the reeds and island copses, with nowhere to go and no place I could stay. Then a pack of seven-tailed wolves that glowed a gentle blue in the moonlight surrounded me and took me captive.

I became a prisoner of the Igigi.

Now began for me the darkest part of that dark era. Every day I was driven along with the other captives to the lakeside across from the First Haven fortifications. The first time, we were lashed with whips that stung like scorpions while we tried desperately to intuit what we were meant to do. Finally, randomly, one of our number began scooping up mud with his hands and the whips moved away from him. We others joined him with hands and flat stones and scraps of wood and soon it became apparent that we were digging a trench to drain the lake.

How often I looked up from my work to stare longingly across that lake! The Igigi continued to attack the People by ones and threes. Sometimes they returned with captives, but more commonly they were slain. Yet they seemed not to learn from this, for they neither lessened nor increased their attacks, nor did they alter their tactics.

Nighttimes, we were herded into a walled enclosure (we had built it ourselves, of course) where we were fed from a trough and slept huddled together like animals. If I'd thought I was an ox before, I was doubly so now, for my fellows were no longer recognizable as People. They had given up all hope of rescue, and when I tried to re-create my crude system of snorts and signs with them, they did not respond. They crapped and coupled in the open as the urge took them and pissed right where they stood. Their eyes, when they looked upon me at all, were dull and lifeless.

They had despaired.

Almost, I despaired as well. But the Igigi had taken Silili from me and that meant that she was out there, somewhere, in their vast encampment. So my thoughts were foremost and forever upon her and even when I was most exhausted I never ceased from looking for her. Hopeless though my cause might be, it maintained me when nothing else could.

Then, one evening, Irra came to the slave pens. He was dressed in spotless white blouse and trousers. There was a coiled leather strap in his hand and a knowing smile on his face.

Reflexively, I tried to cry out his name – but of course that had disappeared from my mind long ago – and managed only a kind of barking sound.

Unhurriedly, Irra tied the strap about my neck. Then, holding one end in a negligent hand, he turned and walked away.

Perforce, I followed.

We walked not toward the dam but through the Igigi encampment. What a foulness they had made of the clean, stream-fed lands! The trees were uprooted and the marsh grasses burnt to stubble and ashes. Craters had been blasted in the earth. The ground was trampled into mud. This did not bother Irra, for he walked a hand's-breadth above it, but there were places where I sank to the knees in cold muck and was half-choked by his impatient tugging on the leash before I could struggle free. Dimly, then, I began to realize that Urdumheim was not a place but a condition...and that, struggle though I might, I was helplessly mired within it.

Eventually we came to a halt in a place that was neither better nor worse than any other in that horrid and despoiled landscape. Here, Irra pulled a small but obviously sharp knife from his pocket. He held up his little finger before my face and made a long and angry speech, not a word of which I understood.

Then he cut off the tip of his finger.

Blood spurted.

Irra thrust the finger-stub at me, and I backed away uncomprehendingly. With a noise of disgust, he pried open my mouth and shoved the gobbet of flesh in. I gagged, but he forced me to swallow.

"Can you understand me now?" he asked.

I could!

"This will only work between the two of us," Irra said sternly. "Do not think you can return to the People now, for you cannot. To them, you will remain as dumb as a stone and their speech shall be to you as the twittering of birds."

"I understand." I almost didn't care, so great was my relief to be able to speak again. I felt as if a part of my mind had been restored to me. I could think clearly for the first time since my capture.

"Then follow me."

Deep in the Igigi encampment, we came upon a tremendous fish. It was larger by far than any whale. A silvery film covered the vast, listless eye that stared blindly at the sky from its rotting side. Flies swarmed all about it and the smell was so terrible I almost vomited. Irra had to half-choke me to keep me going. The stench grew worse the closer we got, until we reached the pink gill slit and so passed within.

The interior was opulent beyond imagining. Polished stone floors supported pillars of agate and turquoise and jade, which rose to a vaulted ceiling so high that shadows nested in it. Flambeaux lined the fishbone-ribbed walls and wavering lines of white candles floated high in the air above. Beneath them clay-fleshed homunculi stumped and winged eyeballs flew and giant snails slid, all passing to and fro without any visible purpose amid splendors that dwarfed everything the People had. Such was the power of the Igigi. Yet they had forced their captives to slave in the mud to build what they could have made with a thought!

To the far end of the great room, a sweep of serpentine steps rose to a dais atop which were what at first appeared to be two mounds of garbage, but on approach revealed themselves as crudely built thrones.

We stopped at the foot of the dais, and the figures seated upon the thrones arose.

"Kneel!" Irra whispered urgently. He did not name the two, but by the awe and disgust I felt within me, I knew them for who they were.

The King and Queen of the Igigi advanced to the top of the steps and stared down on us.

The Queen's face was perfection itself, as sweet and beautiful as the dawn of the very first day. She wore a billowing robe of soft scarlet feathers which opened here and there to reveal a body that would have been as ravishing as her face were it not for her breasts, which reached down to the ground and dragged on the floor behind her.

The King was entirely naked, but his legs were jointed wrong, forcing him to walk backwards, buttocks-first. He had no head, but when he came to a stop and turned, I saw that his features were on his chest and abdomen, so that when he opened his mouth to speak, his stomach gaped wide and his penis waggled on his chin like a goatee.

The hall hushed in anticipation of his words.

"Brekekekek koax koax!" he cried. "Tarball honeycrat kadaa muil. Thrippsy pillivinx. Jolifanto bambla o falli bambla. Aeroflux electroluxe. Flosky! Beebul trimble flosky! Grossiga m'pfa habla horem. Archer Daniel Midlands codfeather squinks. Spectrophotometer. AK-47. Rauserauserauserause. Zero commercials *next!*"

The Queen threw back her head and laughed like a hyena.

"They demand to know," Irra said, "what new thing this is that the First have done. We send out our best warriors and they do not return. Why?"

I said nothing.

"Why?" Irra repeated angrily. But still I did not respond.

The Queen looked at the King and yipped sharply twice.

"I don't think we need to be subliminal," the King said. "I think we agree, the past is over. I'm looking forward to a good night's sleep on the soil of a friend. And, you know, it'll take time to restore chaos and order – order out of chaos. But we will. I understand reality. If you're asking me...would I understand reality, I do. There will be serious consequences, and if there isn't serious consequences, it creates adverse consequences. Our enemies never stop thinking about new ways to harm our country and our people, and neither do we. Does that make any sense to you? It's kind of muddled. I understand small business growth. I was one. They misunderestimated me. My answer is bring 'em on."

"He says that if you do not speak voluntarily, you will be made to speak."

I crossed my arms.

The King shrugged. Almost casually, he said, "Pain."

"Paain," the Queen repeated. "Paaaaaiiiinnnn," she moaned. She made it sound as if it were a good and desirable thing. Then she nodded in my direction.

Pain fell on me.

How to describe what I felt then? Perhaps once, when you were chopping wood, your axe took an unlucky bounce off a knot and the blade sank itself in your leg, so that you fell down screaming and all the world disappeared save your agony alone. Maybe your clothes caught fire and when your friends slapped out the flames, the burning went on and on because your flesh was blackened and blistered. You could not reason then. You howled. You could not think of anything except the pain. That was how it was for me. I folded into myself, weeping.

"Kraw," said the King. "Craaaaaawwwawaw. Craw-aw-wul. Crawl."

Irra looked at me. "Crawl!" he said.

And, pity help me, I did. I crawled, I groveled, I wailed, I pleaded, and when at last my tormentors granted me permission to speak, I told them everything I knew. "It is called death," I said. "Humbaba invented it." And I explained its nature as best I could, including the fact that the People were subject to it as well as the Igigi. It would have been better, far better, had I said nothing. But the pain unmanned me, and I babbled on and on until Irra finally said, "Enough."

Thus it was that I became a traitor.

The next day the war began in earnest. Where before the Igigi had attacked in ones and threes, now they came in phalanxes. Where before they had taken captives, now they sought only to kill. Such were the fruits of my treachery.

The People fought like heroes, every one. They *were* heroes – the first and the best that ever were. They fought as no one had ever fought before or ever will again. Glory shone about their brows. Lightnings shot out of their eyes.

They lost.

Do I need to tell you about the fighting? It was as ugly and confusing then as it is today. There were shouts of anger and screams of pain. Blood gushed. Bodies fell. I saw it all from across the lake where – pointlessly, needlessly – we animals labored to widen the drainage canal. This despite the fact that the lake was half-empty already and its mud flats no hindrance to the attacking Igigi at all. But if we stopped we were whipped, and so we toiled on.

The palisades fell. Then the inner walls behind them.

The People retreated up the mountain. Halfway to the summit they had built a final redoubt and this they held against all the Igigi could throw against them. The sides of Ararat were steep and the way up it narrow, and thus the demons could only attack in small numbers. Always, Nimrod stalked the heights, his great bow in hand, so that they dared not approach by air.

At night, as I was herded back to the slave pens, I could see the lower slopes of Ararat ablaze with fires too numerous to count. These were not campfires such as armies build against the cold and to cook their food, for the Igigi needed neither warmth nor sustenance. They were built for no good reason at all, as acts of vandalism. The closer ones flickered as the bodies of the Igigi passed before them, for their numbers were legion.

One evening as the gates to the slave compound slammed shut behind me and I sank to the ground, too tired to struggle through the other animals and fight for food at the trough, it struck me that I was going to die soon and that under the circumstances this might well be no bad thing. As I was thinking these dark thoughts, the gates opened again and in rode Irra on a beast that stumbled and struggled to bear up under his weight. He leapt down from his mount and the beast straightened. It was a woman. She was naked as a child, but leather straps had been lashed about her so that her arms were bound tight to her sides. A saddle was strapped to her back, and there was a bit in her mouth.

For a second I thought it was Silili and my heart leapt up with anger and joy. I rose to my feet. Then I recognized her and my heart fell again.

"Mylitta," I said sadly. "You were captured too."

"She cannot understand you," Irra said. "Have you forgotten?"

I had. Now, however, I moved one foot like an ox pawing the ground: Hello.

Mylitta did not respond. Her eyes were dull and lifeless, and so I knew that she had, like so many other captives, given up all hope and sunk down into a less-than-animal state. Either she had been captured in an Igigi raid or—more likely, it seemed to me—she had slipped away to look for her lover. And, finding him, been treated thus.

I do not think I have ever hated another human being as in that instant I hated Irra.

"Stop staring at the beast!" Irra commanded. "Nimrod broods upon the mountaintop. Our King and Queen believe he contemplates some sorcery so mighty that even he fears its consequences. They feel his growing resolve upon the night winds. So he must be stopped. It is their command that you kill him."

"Me?" I struggled against the urge to sink back to the ground. "I can barely stand. I'd laugh if I had the strength for it."

"You shall have all the strength you need." Irra drew a peeled willow wand from his tunic and with it struck me between the shoulder blades. I grunted and bent over double as enormous wings of bone and leather erupted from my back. When I straightened, I saw that Irra had given himself bat-wings as well.

"Follow!" he cried, and leapt into the air.

Involuntarily, I surged after him. Below me, poor Mylitta dwindled into an unmoving speck and was lost among the other captive slaves. That was the last that ever I saw her.

We flew.

Under other circumstances, it would have been a glorious experience. Flying was easier than swimming. My muscles worked surely and strongly, and the wind felt silky-smooth under my wings. But the lands we flew over were ugly and defiled. Pits and trenches had been gouged into it for no purpose whatsoever. A constellation of trash-fires that had once been our crofts smoldered under us. The very clouds overhead were lit a sullen orange by them.

"Look upon your work," I said bitterly.

Irra swooped downward, drawing me involuntarily after him, so that we skimmed low over the mud-flats of the half-drained lake. They were littered with corpses. "Behold *yours*," he said. "And tell me—whose creation is the more monstrous?"

To this I had no response.

We flew in a wide circle around Ararat, in order to approach the redoubt from its less defended side. For hours we flew. From my lofty vantage I could see the multitudes of invaders infesting and defiling the land below. Their numbers took my breath away. It is scant exaggeration to declare that there was a nation of monsters for each one of the People. I did not see how we could possibly prevail. But at last, in the long grey hour of false dawn, we alit on the steep and disputed mountainside between the People's final fortress and the Igigi encampments. There, at a touch of Irra's wand, my wings folded themselves back into my body. Without dismissing his own wings, he proceeded to take a long and leisurely leak against a nearby boulder.

Finally, I spoke. "Mylitta *loved* you! How could you treat her so?"

Irra smiled over his shoulder. "You want reasons. But there are none. Even this stone is wiser than you are." He turned, still pissing. I had to jump backwards, almost spraining an ankle, to avoid being sprayed. "You see? The stone knows that the world is what it is, and so it endures what it must. You hope for better, and so you suffer."

Done, he tucked himself in and said, "Wait here." Then he threw himself into the air again, soaring higher and higher until he was no larger than a flea. Up he went and down he came. Yet as he drew closer he dwindled in size, so that he grew no larger to the eye. When he reached his starting place, he was as small as a midge. Three times he buzzed around my head.

Then he flew into my ear.

With a dreadful itching sensation that made me claw desperately at my head, Irra burrowed deep into my brain. Coming at last to rest, he said, "Climb upward. When you reach the redoubt, its defenders will recognize you and let you in. If your actions displease me, I will treat you *thus*."

I screamed as every bone in my body shattered and blood exploded from all my orifices.

Then, as quickly as it had come, the pain was gone. I was still standing, and unhurt. Everything but the pain had been an illusion. "That was but a warning," Irra said. "If you disobey or displease me in the least way, I will visit such torments upon you that you will remember the Igigi Queen's ministrations with fond nostalgia. Do you understand?"

Abjectly, I nodded my head.

"Then go!"

Like a mouse, I crept up the mountain's flank, using its trees and bushes for cover when I could and furtively clinging to the bare rock when I could not. Once, I caught a glimpse of Nimrod's gigantic figure as he stood at the topmost peak, back to me, contemplating the war below. His power was a palpable thing, and in that instant I felt sure that Irra's cause was hopeless for his merest glance, were it to fall upon me, would have burnt me to ashes. Simultaneously, I experienced an involuntary lifting of my spirits, for the upper slopes of Ararat were untouched by the Igigi and the scent of the pines was clean and invigorating. I began to hope and, hoping, began to scheme.

The redoubt, when we reached it, was less a thing than a congeries of defenses – here a wall, there a scarp at the top of which defenders stood with piles of stones. If the mountain had been taller and steeper, the People could have held it forever. But I had seen the Igigi's swarming millions and knew that inevitably Ararat must fall. Nevertheless, when I came strolling up King Nimrod's path, whistling and swinging my arms as Irra had directed me to do, I was waved on upward by the guards after the most cursory of examinations.

I was home again.

Despite everything, it felt wonderful.

The People were everywhere working urgently. Shelters were being built and defenses strengthened. Sparks flew upward from the smithies and baskets of apples and cattail roots were hustled away into newly dug caves. Most astonishing of all, the oxen were People once more! I saw them carrying long-knives and spears and huddled over plans for the defenses, arguing in grunts and snorts. They were clapped on the shoulder in passing by others who clearly could not understand them, and there were even those – I noticed them, though Irra did not seem to – who could speak both tongues. One tall woman strode by with a war-trident over her shoulder, singing words that sounded like nothing I had ever heard before. Clearly, the oxen-speech had evolved.

I was but newly arrived when my old friend Namtar rushed up and, dropping an armful of long-knives on the ground, hugged me.

I pawed the ground with one foot: Hello.

Namtar made a cage of one hand and whistled frantically like a captive bird. Then, opening the hand, he trilled like that same bird escaping. Finally, he said, "Eh?" Meaning: How had I escaped?

I slammed one fist into the other. Holding my hands out as if throttling a monster's neck, I twisted them. "Snap!" I lied: I fought my way free.

Namtar grinned appreciatively. Then he made a noise – "Shhhweeoo, shhhweeoo!" – like the hurrying wind and pointing first to me and then to the swords, made a carrying gesture. He lifted his voice in a sweet, clear note, which could only refer to she who had invented song: He had to hurry. Would I bring these things to Aruru?

I snorted assent, and he was gone.

"That was well done," Irra said from within my ear. "Walk briskly. Wait until nobody is watching. Then get rid of this junk."

I dumped the long-knives on a dung heap, and threw an armload of hay over them so that no one would know. Soon after, somebody called me to her and gave me another chore. So went my day. I worked my way up the slope, smiling cheerfully (for Irra punished me if I was anything less than upbeat), accepting whatever work was given me and then abandoning it when I could and performing it with apparent enthusiasm when I could not. Three steps forward, two steps back. By degrees, I pushed toward Ararat's summit.

At midday I ate a meager lunch of two taro-cakes and an apple while sitting at the top of a short cliff. It was not far to its bottom, I reflected, only five body-lengths or so, yet the fall would certainly be enough to kill me.

Though he could not read them, Irra was able to intuit my thoughts. "Cast yourself off," he suggested mockingly. "If you die, so will I, and Their Anarchic Majesties' plans will come to nothing."

I shivered involuntarily at the awfulness of his suggestion. For, wretched as I was, I did not wish to die. Nobody truly knows what death is, and so we fear it above all things. Moreover, my dread was all the greater for the idea of death being so new to me.

And yet – was it an altogether ignoble idea?

Irra, I reasoned, taunted me because he thought that I would not – that I *could* not – kill myself, and surely this was an understandable thing to assume since nobody had ever done so before. But after all I had seen and experienced, nothing seemed impossible to me anymore. I went to the very brink of the precipice and looked down. I thought of the People and how much I loved them. I thought of Nimrod, their bulwark and strength. I thought of my joyless existence. But mostly I thought of Silili, lost to me forever. Then I did the bravest thing I had ever done in all my life.

Light and giddy with relief and fear, I stepped off.

Or, rather, I tried to.

My feet would not obey me. Will it though I might, I could not take that one crucial step forward. Deep within my ear, Irra laughed and laughed. "You see? I can control your actions. Never forget that."

All this time I had been thinking, and the more I thought, the less plausible it seemed that when I finally stood face to face with King Nimrod, I would defeat him in combat. A hundred such as I could not have done so. It did not matter what magics and powers Irra might have. The very idea was absurd.

Now I was angry enough to say so.

Irra was unmoved. "Humbaba invented death," he said complacently. "Between them, the Igigi and the People invented war. Great works come in threes. You and I, Gil, will create a third and final novelty, and in some ways it will be the greatest of all, for where the others are universal and impersonal, this will be singular and intimate."

"Will we?"

"Oh, yes, I call it *murder*."

Irra explained his intent. I was unimpressed. "How does this differ from simply killing somebody?"

"By its treachery. You will approach Nimrod with smiles and salaams. You will oil and braid his hair for him, all the while praising his wisdom and his strength. Then, with his back turned and he unsuspicious, you will pick up a rock and smash it down upon his head with all your might."

The picture he drew sickened me for I could imagine it all too well: The weight of the rock in my hands. The unsuspecting king. The sound of that great skull splitting. And afterwards, his blood on my hands. I would give anything not to have this crime on my hands. But Irra had already taught me that pain could render me helpless before it. I sobbed wordlessly.

"Come. We have mighty deeds to accomplish."

Irra walked me away from the cliff.

The sun was sinking in the west by the time I found myself standing outside a line of new-dug storage caves near the top of the redoubt. Only a steep and stony path separated me from the summit of Ararat, where King Nimrod stood thinking his dark thoughts alone. I put down the basket of bread I had carried hither. From one of the caves I retrieved a jug of oil.

Nobody was looking. I carried the oil and a loaf of bread upward.

Though Nimrod was king and mage, the crest of Ararat was stony and bare. No advisors waited upon him, nor was there any furniture of any sort. He sat brooding upon a rock outcrop, his bow and quiver at his feet. A goatskin of water rested in his shadow, along with a shallow clay bowl for him to drink from. And that was all.

"I remember you, little one," the king rumbled, glancing down at me. "Whatever became of your lover, your woman-to-me?"

Irra whispered: "He wills comprehension upon you. You may reply."

I made a bird of my hands and flew it off into the sky. "Chree!" I said, in imitation of its cry. Gone.

King Nimrod looked sad at that. He reached out one tremendous

290 | *Michael Swanwick*

hand, closed it lightly on my shoulder, and squeezed gently. I thought he would say something consoling, then, and the very thought of him doing so when I had come to kill him nauseated me. But he said only, "Why are you here?"

I proffered the bread.

King Nimrod accepted it. The loaf was large enough to feed three ordinary men, but it looked small in his hand. He began to eat, staring moodily into the distance. Though the invaders had destroyed the trees and rushes, they could not make the waters go away, and so the setting sun filled the land with reflected oranges and reds, rendering it briefly beautiful again.

After a long silence Nimrod spoke to me as one might to a beloved dog – affectionately, but expecting neither comprehension nor response. He was speaking to himself, really, sorting out his thoughts and feelings. "Behold the world," he said. "For a time it was our garden. No more. When Humbaba introduced death, I thought it an evil that might be endured and later undone. For though I cannot negate its effects and those who have died will never return to us, yet I have power to put an end to death. It would drain me completely to do so. But afterwards, nobody would ever die again.

"Alas, the world is become a wasteland and there is no way back into the garden. Our choice now is enslavement or death. There is no third way."

I thought that Irra would make his play then, while Nimrod was distracted. But he was cannier than that. Perhaps he noticed some lingering trace of vigilance in the king. Perhaps, knowing that he would have but one opportunity, he was taking no chances. In any event, he waited.

"Ah, child! I am contemplating a great and terrible crime. Would you forgive me for it, if you understood its cost? For henceforth, every man and woman must grow old and die. Is slavery truly worse than that? Yet so great is my hatred for the Igigi that I would rather you and I and everyone else die and turn to dust than that we should submit to them again."

I could not bear to look at the king, knowing what I was about to do.

So I stared down at the ground instead. There was the slightest motion in the gloom as a small and torpid animal shifted itself slightly.

It was a toad.

In that instant, a plan flashed into my mind. Casually, so as not to alert Irra, I squatted and picked up a stone. Then I cleared my throat: Watch.

King Nimrod glanced incuriously at me.

Forgive me, little brother, I thought, and I smashed the toad with the stone.

Beaming, I said, "Squirp!" In imitation of the sound it made.

Nimrod's face was a wall of granite. "Never do that again," he said. And, when I flung out an arm indicating all the lands below, infested with demons and suffering and death, "Yes, the world is full of cruelty. Let us not add to it."

He turned away.

Irra was furious. But in Nimrod's presence, he dared not punish me. "This is no time for playing games!" he cried. "After we have done our great deed, I promise you that there will be suffering enough for everyone and that if you want to be among the tormentors, that honor will be yours. But for now, you must think of nothing but our goal and how to reach it. Pick up the oil."

I did.

Standing before the king, I held up the jug in one hand and a comb which I had stolen earlier in the day in the other. I gestured toward his beard. Nimrod nodded abstractedly, so I poured oil into my hands and then, rubbing them together, applied it. I had to stand on tiptoe to do so. When his beard was fragrant and glossy, I began combing it out. Finally, I braided it in many strands, as befit a ruler of his dignity.

I had just finished when, with sudden resolution, King Nimrod stood. "I fear you will curse me every day of your short life for what I am about to do, little one," he said. His words were an almost physical force. I did not need Irra to tell me that he was willing comprehension upon me. "Yet I see no alternative. So it shall be done. This will take all my power and concentration, so I must ask that you not disturb me before it is finished."

At Irra's direction, I tugged my hair and made braiding gestures. "Eh?"

Nimrod laughed gently, as one might at the antics of a child. "If it makes you happy."

Closing his eyes, King Nimrod stretched out his arms to either side, palms upward. His fingers flexed, as if grasping for something in the air, and then clenched as if grasping that intangible thing. A low sound escaped from somewhere deep within his chest. It might have been the mountain talking. A shudder passed through his body, and then Nimrod stood as motionless as the moon before Humbaba had set it in the sky. His face was grim as granite.

After a few minutes, drops of blood appeared on his forehead.

"Go!" Irra whispered urgently.

I picked up a large rock and climbed to the top of the low crag behind the king. There, I set the rock down and, standing beside it, began to oil and comb his hair.

Thunder rolled in the distance, then fell silent. But there was an uneasiness to the silence. It was like unto a distant sound too vast and low to be heard which nevertheless can be felt in the pit of one's stomach and in the back of one's skull. Time passed. The sun touched the horizon and a thin line of liquid gold spread to either side faster than quicksilver.

"What is he doing?" Irra fretted. "What is he *doing?*"

I shrugged, and continued my work.

Never had the sun moved below the edge of the world so quickly. All the land beneath it was an oily darkness, as if something were moving there unseen. Perhaps, I thought, Nimrod was calling great armies of beasts to eat the Igigi. Perhaps he was turning the marshes to tar, to envelop and swallow up our enemies. If such was his contemplated crime – the death of billions – I did not care. Let it happen! Yet the tension in the air intensified as if somewhere too far away to be heard, a giant were silently screaming.

Nimrod was a statue. The blood from his brow ran down his face and pooled at his feet.

Then the horizon *bulged*.

Deep in the fastness of my mind, Irra cried in a tone of mingled hor-ror and awe, "He is calling in the ocean! He is commanding it to come to Ararat."

I passed the comb through King Nimrod's hair over and over again, smoothing out the tangles. "So?"

"It will roll over the armies below. It will kill the King and Queen and all their servants!"

"Good. Then there will be a cleansing."

"There is still time!" I hopped down from the rock on which I stood, dropping the comb. I bent down to seize the rock in both hands. With a mighty effort, I raised it up to my chest. None of this had been my doing. Indeed, I tried desperately to resist it. But Irra had seized con-trol of my body.

If Irra could control my body now, that meant he could always have done so. There had been no need for him to drive me with threats and pain. He had only done so in order to make me complicit in his guilt and thus increase my suffering, so that he might enjoy my revulsion and shame,

King Nimrod towered above me. With a jerk, Irra raised the stone up above my head. I gasped in pain.

That was the extraordinary thing. I had gasped in pain. Irra had not made me gasp. I had simply done so. Which meant that he controlled only those parts of my body he set his thoughts to controlling. All else was still mine.

I licked my lips to test my theory. And it worked. My mouth remained my own.

"*Squirp!*" I cried as loudly as I could.

Had Nimrod turned to see why I had made such an extraordinary noise, he would have died then and there, for already the stone was descending upon his head. But I had taught him the meaning of my new word, and so he instantly apprehended my warning. Using only a small fraction of his power, the mighty wizard caused tree branches to sprout from his head and shoulders and back. They burst through his skin and clothing. With dazzling swiftness, they divided and multi-plied, the end of each branch and twig putting out a long, sharp thorn.

My stone crashed down into the tangled thorn-tree, snapping limbs but coming nowhere near King Nimrod's body, motionless at its center. Twisted black branches grew around me in a cage. The thorns grasped me tightly and I was flung high into the air.

A despairing wail escaped my lips. I did not know if it came from myself or from Irra.

Then, with a roar like the end of the world, I fell into darkness.

When I came to, it was morning and Irra's body lay on the ground beside me. I sat up and touched his throat. It was stone cold. Irra was dead.

Sore and aching though I was, I could not help but feel glad.

The sunlight was brighter than I remembered ever seeing it, and the air smelled of salt. I stared down the slopes of Ararat and for the first time in my life I saw the ocean. It sparkled and danced. White gulls flew above it with shrill cries. To one side, fierce waves crashed against the mountainside with a thunder and boom that said they had come to stay. First Haven was a seaport now and its inhabitants would henceforth be fishermen and sailors as well as hunters and crofters.

The Igigi were nowhere to be seen.

King Nimrod sat hunched nearby, his head resting in his hands. But when I tried to hail him, nothing came from my mouth but a wordless cry. So by this token I knew that our first language – the one that Nimrod had invented to deliver us from Urdumheim – was gone forever, drowned with our demonic foes.

At the sound of my voice, Nimrod stood. To my surprise, when he saw me he grinned broadly. He pawed the ground with one foot, as might an ox. Meaning: Hello. Then he rubbed his hands together and snorted: Let's get to work.

Uncomprehendingly, I watched as Nimrod stooped to pick up a stone from the ground. He held it out toward me. "*Harri*," he said. "*Harri*."

Then, like the sun coming out from the clouds, I understood. He was creating a new language – not a makeshift thing like my oxen-speech, but something solid and enduring.

"*Harri*," I said.

The king clapped me approvingly on the shoulder.

Then he went down the mountain to teach the People language for a second time.

Thus began the Great Work. For shortly thereafter, Nimrod set us to work building upon the base of Ararat a tower so tall that it would reach to the sky, and so large that a hundred generations would not suffice to complete it. Indeed, our monarch explained, it was entirely possible that the tower never *would* reach completion. But this did not matter. For within the tower a thousand languages would bloom and those languages, through exposure to each other, would be in constant flux and variation, every profession creating its specialized argot and every new generation its own slang. Like the tower itself, each language would be a work forever in progress and never completed. So that if the Igigi returned, they could never again prevail over us, though they stuffed their stomachs so full of language that they burst. In token of which, we named the tower Babel – "Mountain of Words."

Thus ends my story.

Except for one last thing.

One day, when I was working in the fields, Silili returned from the forest. She was scratched and bruised and filthy from living like an animal, and half-starved because unlike those who are born animals, she was not good at it. One of her fingers was crooked, for it had broken and not set well. She was naked.

I froze motionless.

Silili shivered with fear. She took a step into the field, and then retreated back to the shadow of the trees. Whether she remembered me at all, I could not say. But she was as wild and shy as any creature of the woods, and I knew that a sudden movement on my part would drive her away and I might never see her again. So slowly, very slowly, I crouched down and groped with a blind hand for the wicker basket in which I had brought my midday meal.

I opened its lid and reached within. Then I stood.

I held out a yam to her. "*Janari*," I said. This was our new word for food.

Timidly, she approached. Three times, she almost bolted and ran. But at last she snatched the yam from me and ravenously began eating it.

"*Janari*," I repeated insistently. "*Janari!*" And finally, "*Janari*," she replied.

It was a beginning.

All this happened long ago, when I was young and there was only one language and People did not die. All things were new in those days and the world was not at all like what it is today.